AT THE AGE OF SIX, SHE HAD NO IDEA THAT SHE WAS THE REINCARNATION OF HECATE, GODDESS OF HELL

She remembered nothing of ruling, of killing, of the flames of Hades. She knew nothing of the vast powers at her command. Not yet.

Then, one sleepy afternoon, a neighbor's dog chased her cat. The child's reaction was automatic. Snapping her fingers twice, she pointed to the dog.

Instantly it was engulfed in a ring of intense orange flame. Its frantic yelps of pain turned to whines as it was abruptly flipped in a circle, as though roasting on an unseen spit.

The child stood watching, surprised and pleased. As soon as the dog's body had finished twitching, she ripped off a piece of the cooked flesh and began chewing enthusiastically. . . .

We will send you a free catalog on request. Any titles not in your local bookstore can be purchased by mail. Send the price of the book plus 50¢ shipping charge to Leisure Books, P. O. Box 511, Murray Hill Station, New York, N. Y. 10156.

Titles currently in print are available for industrial and sales promotion at reduced rates. Address inquiries to Nordon Publications, Inc., Two Park Avenue, New York, N. Y. 10016, Attention: Premium Sales Department.

QUEEN OF HELL

J. N. Williamson

LEISURE BOOKS NEW YORK CITY

A LEISURE BOOK

Published by

Nordon Publications, Inc.
Two Park Avenue
New York, N.Y. 10016

Copyright © 1981 by Nordon Publications, Inc.

All rights reserved
Printed in the United States

Acknowledgments

With gratitude to the influential women of my life: Mary, who doesn't mind possessiveness for she knows I am hers; my mother Maryesther, who couldn't have been more liberated; my talented sister Marylynn; my all-wise grandmothers, Bobby and Ethel; my valiant mother-in-law Ethel; my daughter Mary, whose wings spread daily; my granddaughters all, of unguessable courses; my teachers Vera H. and Jeanne G.; my editors, Nancy, Jane and Beth; my friends Marti, Debbie, Jean, Joyce, Karen, Pam, Connie; and those indestructible memories Marcia, Sigrid, Pat and Soni: My world, without you, would have been unutterably colorless, forlorn, flat. In your searches for the liberty you deserve please remember that one man loved you as you were, or are, and selfishly prays that you will not change too much.

Other Books by J. N. Williamson

THE RITUAL
THE HOUNGAN
THE TULPA
HORROR HOUSE
PREMONITION
THE BANISHED

"In our family we don't divorce our men—we bury them." —Ruth Gordon

"Woman is woman's natural ally." —Euripedes

"Thus the women of America raped the men, not sexually, unfortunately, but morally, since neuters come hard by morals . . . I give you her justice—from which we have never removed the eye bandage. I give you the angel—and point to the sword in her hand. . . . I give you Medusa and Stherno and Euryale. I give you the harpies and the witches, and the Fates. I give you the women in pants, and the new religion: she-popery. I give you Pandora . . ." —Philip Wylie (1942)

PROLOGUE

December 31, 1899. New York, N.Y.

On the lower east side, snow has stopped at last after drifting down for interminable, heavy hours. It seems to have paused, obligingly, to allow you here, inviting you to the slum-soul of mankind. It leaves as a frozen momento torn blankets draped like unclean morgue sheets across the incision-sized yard of the dilapidated tenement house. You pause. The building itself rises into the embryonic Manhattan skyline like a particularly repugnant, ripe tumor—or perhaps like a corpse protesting the chill autopsy scalpel with its last anguished wail.

Here, as you peep cautiously through the squealing door of the tenement, you realize at once that freezing coldness stalks the air like solid sides of beef, inside as well as out. Blocks from where they will say Irving Berlin grew up, and a host of dapper mayors, snappy comics, nimble dancers and doe-eyed chorines—thereby making squalid poverty picturesquely American—your outstretched fingers shudder away from a frigid railing, and all of the walls seem to close in, gravelike. Beneath you the antique furnace groans, tremors your feet as it starves on its paltry portion of coal. You shake your head. Surely the yowling, savage wind will blow this place down before the city fathers can give the order. And surely, you think, almost anything terrible could happen in such a place.

Start tenuously toward the stairs and become hideously aware of pestilential life celebrating New Year's

Eve—the death of an old century—by making more, and yet more, of its own repulsive kind. Scuttling brown roaches and waddling water bugs waltz across the steps as you climb, politely bringing *apertif* to their horrid ladyloves. Those avaricious and bristling gray rats which call the tenement home are wary shadows you scarcely see. *There,* one tumbles across your extended foot, weighty, to flee to its carnal corner of the unspeakable dank cellar—*there,* an immense black rat precedes you to the second floor, host-like in its grinning eagerness for you to follow it ... to see something truly unforgettable.

On the darkling third level your nerves are fully askew, when you pause for breath; you are absorbed, now, by this aged universe in which all macabre things seem possible, even likely. Already the teeming world outside seems distant, the end of your own century as remote as Ypres, Troy, Jerusalem. That *touch* on your temple—your hand shoots up to brush, frantically, at an obese black spider oozing orgasmic cobweb trails in the dark. *Now* you see, more with horror than relief, a faint light groping aura-like around the wood-frame door at the end of the hall. You move closer to the dim glow, floorboards squeaking with each shy step; you see, to the right of the door, a broken window leading to the rusted, unsafe fire escape. Yet even the frigid wind swirling inside like discarnate souls cannot fully disturb the aromatic cloud of uremic ammonia that has assailed you since you entered the tenement. Your own deepest self is now fully alerted, as it has never been; you will accept—you will believe—almost anything.

Even the man, the woman, and the sixteen-year-old boy who dwell on the other side of that door. . . .

Outsiders might have called this a "family," although each of them was as independently motivated, as disparate, as any gathering of nations. One, beyond that door, looked forward to Heaven and the rewards he felt would be provided there. One lived for temporal pleasures, where they might be found, and believed only—barely—in herself. And one, unknowing, lived only for the cruel rewards of Hell; his temporal pleasures were accursed things decent people do not discuss.

Alfonse Paradisio had taken his young wife to an early mass and, weary from a long day's labor on the docks, asked her now to come to bed with him. He even called it "making love." A good man, given the neighborhood to which he was held in bondage by habit and obligation, Al was of mixed Spanish and Greek ancestry, once a bull of a man whose overt strength tended to keep away both internal temptations and the many people who might otherwise criticize him for his innate decency.

Eighteen years ago Al married a naive young virgin named Bell. Through the passage of nearly two decades, she had become a lustily active thirty-three-year-old woman of individualistic morality. She did not think of her adulterous private life as immoral; to her it was a mild caprice which had nothing to do with aging Alfonse. In her way, she rather loved the old man, again mildly. For some people, extremes of any kind are forever foreign and so it was with Bell. She thought of her Al as a sturdy father-figure; when she was relaxed and mellow, after sex with a neighboring man, Al still seemed paternally full of good works, teasing affection, even sound advice.

But Bell Paradisio was not in a relaxed or mellow mood this New Year's Eve. During the twelve hours Alfonse had been working, she found herself promising a new lover that she would slip away from the flat at two A.M. to celebrate the holiday with him. There'd be laughter, he assured her, a good wine; for awhile she could forget everything in his muscular, smothering arms. As a consequence, her Al's unexpected urge for her was both surprising and ill-timed.

She supposed part of it was her fault since she had consumed several drinks with him before going to church. From experience, she should have remembered that the combination of alcohol and an hour of hearing the priest make recommendations that always reinforced Alfonse's good feeling for himself tended to bestir his passion. But Bell's, too, was aroused—for her young lover—and when Al was bold enough to express his holiday mood, Bell was bold enough to resist him. Passionately.

Neither could have guessed how bad his timing would prove to be.

In the other room lived their sixteen-year-old boy, Cristof-called-Crony, who often fed bread crumbs to the rats and had human friends of similar ilk. Crony's sociability was a fact that warmed Bell's heart as few things did. Bell, when Crony's age, had claimed only an aging husband. She did not know that her son was a key part of an especially proficient gang swarming through the slums of New York, the vital cog with the willingness to kill whenever a need for murder separated one gang from another.

Where other residents of the lower eastside were finding the knack of striking a baseball, or an aptitude for rising to the top in the garment district, Crony Paradisio's discovered talent was nothing more than an aptitude for providing death.

At sixteen, Crony topped six feet in height, was swarthy, inclined to outsweat and outgrow his homely clothes faster than Bell could mend them, or tailor Alfonse's hand-me-downs to the boy's always changing size. Yet often, during the daytime, she watched fondly as Crony went out to play with the Spanish or Greek lads who were polite to her, some of whom were appearing marvelously appealing.

She had never seen the cute things they did in their war games with the Irish, the blacks, or the Jews.

She did not see Crony slay one black with bare knuckles, just that past summer, or kill one little Jewish boy named Herman with a sickle that virtually severed the lad's curly head from his neck. She did not see Crony running until he felt his heart would burst, filled with self-awe and the dawning realization that not only *could* he take human life but he *liked* to kill, he was *born* to kill.

Nor did she see Crony, now, as he entered the bedroom of herself and Al, the special short-handled, jagger-toothed sickle Crony used in his war games honed to fine sharpness. Bell did not know that, in Crony's mind, his father was little more than old, inept, lastingly in his way, a fool for working so hard, a constant annoyance because of the way he steadfastly attempted to counsel, support, and direct his son.

No. What Bell saw with her red-rimmed eyes, as she lay boldly, blondly naked on her back, shrilling at teasing Alfonse in bleary irritation at his persistence, was her husband's pendulous abdomen, engorged organ and tightened testicles, hovering above her blimp-like and probing for an opening.

"Aw-w, cut it out," she yelled, not at all frightened but avidly looking forward to the younger man who was awaiting her. Bathing before going downstairs to him was a nuisance, and it would be painfully cold in this miserable tenement. She tapped her husband on the chest, twisting her head away from his trusting lips. "I wanna go t'sleep, Alfonse—d'jahear? C'mon, will yuh, Al, f'chrissakes? *Cut it out!*"

Crony regarded the tableau, from several safe feet away, with an arising sense of opportunity. Not for an instant did he deceive himself; he knew his mother was in no danger. Shit, he'd already seen her three times with other gross men bouncing up and down on her.

But *she*, he realized, might well *believe* that he saw her as a rape victim.

And *oh!* how he wanted to do it! The old man's fat ass was revolting, the short hairs and tiny pimples on his buttocks giving the impression of two enormous frogs staring dumbly out at him. The thoughts whizzed maniacally in Crony's tilted brain. Paw had work he wanted done the next day—on a *holiday*, would yuh b'lieve such a thing?—and Crony loathed labor.

But there was more going on in his small mind. A new voice throbbed there, whispering now, urging him on. It was like the voice that told him stealing and fighting were all right, that there was a *need* to kill in battle; but this messenger was stronger, more conspicuous somehow and more persuasive. It promised myriad pleasures of a kind available only to a Real Guy who did what he was asked to do.

Crony leaned forward, squinting. "Hey, *Paw!*" he called.

Startled, Alfonse Paradisio looked up, and out, with glazed eyes. He saw before him—death. The sickle in his son's powerful young hands whistled through the chill air of the parental bedroom, meeting distended flesh and passing cleanly through to the other side. Reflexively, Maw had muttered, "Cut it out."

Crony was obedient. When his eyes met his mother's, he smiled sweetly.

The old man slumped on his back to clutch anxiously at what should have been there and found fierce arterial blood pumping fountain-like between his shocked fingers. Alfonse turned to peer at the floor, incredulous, in shock; when his eyes saw what lay there, innocuous between his bedroom slippers, the old man gasped a final time and closed his eyes on a life that had really been too much to bear anyway.

It took awhile for Bell to regain her senses but Cristof was patient. Together, mother and son carried father, beneath a crimson-stained, tattered comforter, to the nearby, quite-historic river. Along their terrible way they had to stop several times. Alfonse's body was bulky, heavy; and the thing that Bell had folded into the blanket with him kept tumbling out to fall limply to the snow-covered pavement.

Finally, on the dock, perspiration turned to ice crystals on their foreheads, they stared dumbly, briefly, at the ebon oily silent waters just beginning to freeze over and then consigned the remains of Alfonse Paradisio to their turgid depths.

"I *know* you did it for Maw," Bell said back in the tenement, wiping away a genuine tear. "But it was *wrong,* darlin'—*wrong*. Now we can't never speak of this to nobody, y'hear? Not even them who comes around when he's found."

Crony felt both relieved and surfeited with a realization that fresh boredom would soon be coming in. "Sure, Maw," he yawned. He was tired now but one fact troubled him. He wondered why he'd had an orgasm at the moment the thing fell off his old man. And he wondered how soon he dared do something like this again. Shit, this was better'n girls. "It'll be our li'l secret, Maw," he promised, kissing her cheek.

And so it remained. Cristof-called-Crony was to have other little secrets during his life and he kept them assiduously well. Several years later, he married a reformed whore named Rae-Ellen who, mistakenly grateful, bore him five children. In a drunken rage Crony murdered them all in their sleep. Rae-Ellen, pregnant seven months at the time, escaped and gave successful, premature birth to a sixth child, a boy.

The boy proved to be strong, resilient, athletic. He helped form a leading labor union, barely lost in a mayoral run, fathered children who became influential in several cities of the United States of America and kept a little secret of his own.

When he was old enough to discover what Crony had done in his drunken rage, he strangled Cristof-called-Crony to death with his own hands. Afterward, the rest of the family lived happily ever after, all unknowing that they were no more than required elements of a reborn myth of vindictiveness, madness, and savagery that made the late Crony Paradisio's lustful habits seem tame by comparison.

January 2, 1900. Richmond, Virginia.

"I have something here that should pique your imagination, Professor Lord," the woman said coyly.

Her husband, who rather liked the way she referred to him by his title, peered up from his morning coffee. There was a full day's work ahead of him in his study—the University was closed for the holidays—but he was unfailingly patient and polite with his wife. "And what is that, my dear?"

"An atrocious murder in New York City," she replied. Then she folded the newspaper carefully and passed it across the table, touching his elbow with it. "On New Year's Eve."

"Alas, one of many, I fear." His smile was gently reproachful. He did not pick up the newspaper. "I'm not really fond of lurid tales with breakfast, my sweet. If you'll recall, I didn't even enjoy reading about the Ripper."

"But in a way, I think, this is *worse.*" Petite and round-faced, she had the expression of a woman who *thinks* she knows something fascinating that her husband doesn't know, but is unsure. "I've listened to you talking about mythology enough to pick up a smattering of information. Please, Professor. Just glance at that dreadful story and see if it reminds you of anything you've discussed."

He sighed, deciding to humor her. Whyever were they giving women so much freedom these days! He set his coffee cup down in its China saucer, the slight clatter symbolizing his protest, and retrieved the newspaper.

She waited patiently and then saw his knuckles whiten as his grasp tightened. "D'you see what I mean?" she asked cheerily.

For a moment he read on, before lowering the paper. And when he did, his face was whiter than his knuckles had been. "Good Lord," he murmured.

"It's *identical* with the myth, isn't it?" she prattled on. "At least, so far as it goes."

Professor John Lord stalled for time, trying to put a rein on his skittering nerves and upon an immense nugget of fear assuming grotesque proportions in his imagination. He scratched his tangled gray beard and, when he spoke, it was in the practiced manner he employed when teaching one of his classes. "There are . . . keen similarities. In Greek mythology, the story is told of a Titan named Heaven. He is married to Earth and they have a son who becomes infamous under the name Cronus. Hence, so far," he ticked it off on fingers that trembled, "we have a man named Paradisio—rather close to Heaven, isn't it?—found floating in Manhattan's East River. His wife, they imply, is quite earthy, their son named Cristof but called Crony."

"Close enough, I'd say," Mrs. Lord put in with an animated smile.

"Quite so. Now, in the myth," the professor continued, "the son finds Heaven and Earth in bed together and—*hum*—disfigures his father with a sickle. The Titan dies, but that isn't the end of it. There is no indication here that young Crony has been charged. But there is his reputation as a gang lad, and the notion that the murder weapon was a spade, sickle or hoe. They haven't located it."

"See?" the wife demanded triumphantly. "It's just like I thought! Is there anything more?"

Jabez Lord, professor of mythology, stroked his Van Dyke speculatively and accepted the fact, rather quietly, that the fear he was experiencing would probably never leave him. He glanced out the window of the kitchen and saw heavy frost on his favorite maple tree. The poor thing looked like a black pole with silvery sticks poking from it, almost as if they'd been shot into the tree. *Gad,* how he despised winter! And now, through the inadvertent attentiveness of his own wife, he was being plunged headlong into the deepest winter of his own life.

"Myth has it, my dear, that Cronus and the mother Earth carried Heaven's dead and maimed body to the sea. *This* poor chap, Paradisio, was found in the river." He sighed heavily. "Strange; it's fiendishly strange."

"Don't take *on* so, my darling Professor," Mrs. Lord persuaded, seeing for the first time the palpable tremor of her husband's hand where it rested, flat and pale, on the fateful newspaper. "It's only a myth—a legend, a mere *story*. It's all sheer co*in*cidence, isn't it?"

"I wonder." He wanted to believe her. He gaze wandered. That tree would have to come down in the spring. If there *was* a spring, for Jabez Lord. "It is generally agreed, you see, that every myth has *some basis in fact*. Without an ongoing written language, such tales were carried verbally for centuries. Whatever was true has been distorted by the masses of ordinary people, retelling the tale." He patted his mouth with a napkin and arose, rather unsteadily. "This—report—seems quite accurate."

Lord went into his study and closed the door softly, gently, behind him. That was his inviolate clue that he wished to be alone. He crossed to his precious, gleaming rolltop desk, a gift of his admiring colleagues on the Professor's twentieth anniversary at the University, and, twiddling his fingers, sat before it.

At last he pulled from the desk an oversized, gray-hued leather book on the cover of which was printed the legend: JOURNAL OF JABEZ LORD.

And there, nowhere else, he confided his terrified thoughts:

"Among professors of mythology, there has been a rumor—a virtual belief—that *all* myths of old will one day be reenacted. The trappings, of course, shall be modern; the glaring civilization of this new Twentieth Century will be reflected. And now, as I affix this press clipping to my faithful journal, I do so with the full realization that the reenactments have begun.

"The ancient gods are returning to Earth."

Professor Lord paused, the scientific aspect of his keen intellect aware that, in a lecture, he should need to provide evidence for his premise. But this, after all, was but a private journal. "Doubtless, in the years ahead, young Crony Paradisio will marry, have children, and slay all but one. That son will grow to maturity and be quite successful in America. When he learns what his father did, he will take Crony's life as an act of vengeance.

"In mythology, that surviving son's name was Zeus. And the grandchild of mighty Zeus—"

Again Lord stopped, looking vaguely across at bookshelves reaching from floor to ceiling. *I don't want to write it down,* he thought. *Surely I will never voice my beliefs aloud; for to do so might bring . . . her . . . upon me, and mine.* Blinking nervously, he plucked up his pen and completed the sentence:

". . . was the most evil creature who ever lived. *Hecate."*

Oh yes, others—even his beloved wife—might laugh. But Jabez Lord knew better than to smile. Thousands, who would deny knowing her name, still believed in her, in Greece and elsewhere. Even in his own fraternity of mythology experts Professor Lord knew men who blanched at her image, and would not speak her name. Unlike many gods and goddesses, who remained on Olympus, Hecate was frequently seen by mortals. The goddess of corruption, of blood and terror—of ghosts and perpetual darkness itself—Hecate was once *adored* by people, once lived amongst them in another guise, under *another* famous name—

Until, to save mankind from her insatiable hunger for watching men die, she was cast into Hades.

Until she was made, according to whispered Greek myths, the feminine version of Satan, with all the same capabilities, and with the identical gift of immortality.

Until she became Queen of Hell.

PART ONE

Soulless Laughter

"Men seldom make passes at a girl who surpasses."
—Franklin P. Jones

"The idea of progress is not merely a dream unfulfilled but an inherent absurdity." —Philip Slater

"But if God had wanted us to think with our wombs, why did He give us a brain?" —Claire Booth Luce

"Despite my thirty years of research into the feminine soul, I have not yet been able to answer . . . the great question that has never been answered: What does a woman want?"
—Sigmund Freud

"What we call progress is the exchange of one nuisance for another nuisance." —Havelock Ellis

"The fair girl, with a laugh of ribald coquetry, turned to answer (Dracula): 'You yourself never loved; you never love!' On this the other women joined, and such a mirthless, hard, soulless laughter rang through the room that it almost made me faint to hear; it seemed like the pleasure of fiends."
—Bram Stoker, "Dracula"

CHAPTER I

The Present. Southern California.

She tried hard to concentrate on her driving instead of beaten Mary, but the sunswept road winding up the coast was so familiar by now that her mind wandered. Like some insensate and blinded beast, it pawed clumsily out in several directions, finding nothing quite worth pulling to itself except those very things that were bad for it.

And Mary, these days, since the girl was raped—Carolyn could think the word to herself at last, without the nerves beginning to shrill—was bad for her to consider. Meditatively or deeply, that is. Bad to consider in an emotional way that allowed all the old hatred for men to seep toxically back in until she was again as impotent to act as her daughter.

Why couldn't her emotions accept the idea, once and for all, that it was Mary, her now-sixteen-year-old daughter, who had been raped and not her?

Dr. Carolyn Lord shook her head and the brisk breeze blowing through the open windows of the little MG wafted her soft, shoulder-length blond hair like a cloud of pretty smoke. Physically, Carolyn knew, she complemented this sports car with her modish new wardrobe. Neither of them was quite new, anymore, but both of them had style; neither of them had gone under. She'd bought the MG on something of a lark, making herself act on impulse the way Fred and Elna told her she had to do, now and then, if she was ever going to put her daughter's life and her own in some kind of perspective.

Thank God she still had a little summer vacation left, Carolyn thought, before she resumed teaching at U.C.E.V. and had to decide, once and for all, the subject matter of the new class she'd promised. The idea she'd had—vague and ill-defined, so far, but tied to the women's liberation movement—was doubtlessly linked to her own psychological problems. Probably the class would be cathartic, help her to get everything out in the open; but she was damned if she would teach anything but a first rate, imaginative course. It had taken too long to make herself return to teaching to throw it away in self-indulgence.

She switched off the radio and found herself remembering one of her early sessions with Fred Clinefort, maybe the best one-on-one shrink in Los Angeles, husband of her new, dear friend, Elna. "Quit telling me you know damn well you're not the rape victim and let it out. Care," Fred had urged. "Use me as a target for your resentment of men. Tell me every loathesome thing I, representing all men, have ever done to you."

For a moment it had seemed absurd, with Fred who he was—Elna's; an immense, sagging tree of a man with a face like a weepy sheepdog in its embrace of curling gray sideburns. But then he'd known enough to put a proprietary hand high-up on her thigh and somehow that triggered her. It became easy to tell him how her ex-husband very nearly robbed her of every chance of individual achievement, even self-understanding, made her believe she was no better than the indolent bigoted bum he was himself. Easy to tell Fred how her husband used her, never caring whether she was satisfied about the meal, the film, the program, the sex (she made *that* last on her list); easy to tell great, gallumphing, unthreatening Fred how she'd finally entered the liberation movement simply to locate friends who didn't—after her divorce—resent and see her as a threat to their own mates.

Easy, even, to tell Fred how Mary—not quite fifteen at the time—had crawled up the front yard to their cottage on the campus—that sunny, flower-bedecked new home that symbolized the hope of newfound freedom and return to the intellectual world which she had thought was forever lost—bleeding from every aperature in her heretofore virginal, child's body. And how she, Carolyn Lord, reborn English prof and awakened activist, had looked down at beaten, sobbing, hurting and humiliated little Mary and saw not her daughter in the gathering pool of blood, but *herself*. How Mary became, at that instant, the exact physical replica of how she felt internally about herself, before the divorce, and how she might *always* feel about herself: Psychically abused and bruised, defenseless, disgusting even to oneself, stripped of the essential personal clothes that covered the vital and not-to-be-touched places of the soul.

And how damnably guilty she felt because all those gallons of tears she wept then and later were quite possibly more for Carolyn than young Mary Lord. Even after Mary was locked, much of the time, behind impregnable walls of almost psychotic silence in an effort to keep it all *outside*, detached from her; even after Mary had had to be put in Bleeding Heart Hospital, twenty-seven miles up the coast from U.C.E.V., a secret from the rest of the faculty.

Gradually, over a period of tortured weeks, Fred Clinefort had helped her deal with the concommitant guilt and switch the direction of her sorrow and pain to Mary, enabling Carolyn to drive this now all-too-familiar road to Bleeding Heart once a week, adequately in charge of her own emotions to function more as a caring parent than as a recuperative victim. "Fred says it'll take quite awhile for you ever to relate to the opposite sex in a routine manner," Elna told her, only a week ago. "In a way, your mind has been telling you that you're as damaged as Mary and, like her, your wounds are too deep to be healed overnight."

Overnight! Carolyn touched the accelerator angrily with her toe and sped quickly and easily around a rickety fruit truck. It had been nearly *two years* since

Mary's rape, close to three since the divorce. Why couldn't she grow up and *face* things, like an adult? She was thirty-six years old, the great-granddaughter of one of the most prestigious university instructors in American History, Professor Jabez Lord. Ever since she was eleven, and read his fascinating books on mythology, she'd wanted to be a teacher at the university level, to follow in his shoes. Her marriage was only a diversion, a temporary departure from the path, however destructive it had proved to be. Now she was on the right track again and a mature adult would put things into perspective, not just intellectually but emotionally.

The familiar strip of pavement continued to unwind before her like some incredible bandage that, at its farthest tip, would again put her in the land of sickness and painful responsibility. She sighed, made herself think instead about what had happened to Grandfather Lord's journal. Many times, through her life, Carolyn had wondered what made the aging professor believe so deeply in the rebirth of an ancient legend. His notes were written with such conviction that it was hard, when you read them, not to think there was something to them after all. According to the family rumor, Grandfather had spent the rest of his years—after affixing that old newspaper clipping in his journal— trying to persuade his colleagues that he was right. He felt that danger lay ahead—danger for mankind. Many of his peers were tolerant, a few even accepting (the story went); but the majority of those whom Grandfather told thought he'd become senile or gone mad.

What was that line he penned? *"And the grandchild of mighty Zeus was the most evil creature who ever lived: Hecate."* Carolyn's hands tightened nervously on the wheel. Bleeding Heart Hospital was near, now, as the sun began to set and shadows swirled in exaggerated elongation across the road. Even after all these years the unseen image of Hecate terrified her. Off and on, during the course of her own education, Carolyn tried to study the ancient myth and was surprised by how little was written about the fabled Queen of Hell.

Even Grandfather's remarks, conveyed in the format of studied and formal history, presented slim data. Which was strange in itself, she felt, since the goddess' prominence was like the other darkly-negative side of supreme Olympus. Hecate was clearly a figure of towering significance thousands of years ago but the existing legend was only tentative, fragmented, wholly insufficient for her status.

Finally it had occurred to Carolyn, one long study night in Indianapolis, where she acquired her degree at Butler University, *why* there was so little recorded about the Queen: These tales originally were carried by word-of-mouth, for a period of many years. And the ancient messengers of Olympian mythology were clearly *afraid* to whisper Hecate's story—especially the parts that might well have been true.

In recent months, in Carolyn's uncertain and recuperative condition, the problem of Hades' Queen had been magnified by the disappearance of Grandfather's journal. She last remembered seeing it several months ago and Carolyn, who was meticulous with her things, could find it nowhere. But she had read the document so often that, even now, she recalled precisely what Grandfather Lord had written in his journal just before he died.

"They will not believe me because they are terrified to accept it. Even with the most awesome weaponry of this ultra-modern year of 1912, with the spectre of a war that may well engulf all men, there would be no way to deal with the literal rebirth of such a monster. And so I now must go to my lonely grave with the worst secret knowledge of all, the product of my feverish, culminating research on Hecate. The evidence is unshakeable that the Queen of Hell *will return* in the last quarter of this already-alarming Twentieth Century. And worst of all, dear journal, I fear to the depths of my tortured soul that she must have contact with my own descendants—my own family-to-be. May the loving concern of one dying student of the ages past reach out to comfort those dear ones of the ages yet to come.

Jabez Lord."

Carolyn still shuddered when she recalled reading Grandfather's final words, and when she closed his journal. Was it possible in some metaphysical fashion beyond her ken that the vicious attack on poor little Mary was involved with Hecate's return? The rape had seemed so improbable at the time! Mary was oddly waiflike, a foundling sort of girl with immense, sad eyes and a perpetually wan expression, a bookish and scholarly child who deeply wanted to be a writer. She was scarcely a prime candidate for rape and a beating!

Nearly two years had passed now and yet Mary wandered in and out of reality, generally lost in some safely private corner of her mind which no amount of therapy had been successful in reaching. Today, Carolyn was not scheduled to make the drive to Bleeding Heart Hospital but had received a phone call from a nun, virtually pleading with her to come. "I am most concerned, Dr. Lord," Sister Alicia Beth told her on the phone. "It is not a physical matter but something quite unusual that has befallen your daughter and I should prefer not to go into it on the telephone."

It was more than what Sister said then that alarmed Carolyn; it was her breathless quality, the tension of it—and a *last* remark Carolyn could not face. She assured Sister Alicia Beth that she'd come and, until now, as she drove the gravelly length of the shadowed driveway and approached the aging structure, she had managed to keep her worry for Mary's newest crisis at bay. The quiet as she parked her faithful MG in the visitors' lot, and turned to confront Bleeding Heart, was tomblike. She saw the now unused turrets that always brought to her mind some forlorn, hirsute madman muttering hopeless incantations to unreal gods on cell floors and felt her stomach tighten and her hands clench. The deep, vertical windows leading to the patients' rooms were not like the watchful eyes, of books Carolyn had read, but like so many rents in the body of the hospital—as if the building itself, burdened with misery and pain for so long, opened many mouths to cry out its collective agony.

Perspiration dotted her forehead and she patted at it with a handkerchief as she half-trotted up the chipped cement steps and in through the ponderous, multi-paned doors to the vast lobby. She was piercingly conscious of her footsteps on the terraza floor, and of the daunting, challenging nurse staring at her as she passed the information desk. Then the elevator, cranky, chugging, growling imprecations—

—Which seemed to Carolyn to say, very clearly, what Sister Alicia Beth had said, at last, before they hung up: "In some bizarre and terrible way I think your daughter has actually looked in upon a frightening event—of nearly one hundred years ago!"

CHAPTER II

"Your daughter, Mary, wanted to be a writer?"

Carolyn found it hard to keep pace with the briskly businesslike stride of Sister Alicia Beth. Clearly Sister had managed to regain her composure since phoning her. "Not just 'wanted,' " Carolyn amended the remark. "She *wants* to be a writer and, one day when she is well, I'm sure she will be."

"That's what her father said when he was here to see her last week." The incredibly light-blue, almost lashless eyes of the middle-aged nun washed like ice water across the teacher's face. "While we're bickering over semantics, Dr. Lord, perhaps it should be said this way: "Mary may *already* be a writer."

Carolyn stopped walking outside her daughter's room and took a quick breath. She was suddenly conscious of how she had been permitting the other woman, for months now, to have the upper hand. It had been a silly recall of her childhood that she tended to fear Sister Alicia Beth, a recall of a time when the teaching nuns at Sacred Lady of the East seemed to have the power of life and death over her. But this woman was merely a nurse, now, only as authoritative as Carolyn Lord permitted her to be.

And for someone as smartly dressed and successful in her own way as Carolyn to allow such liberties was absurd. "I think it's time we dispensed with all the mystery, Sister," she said flatly, folding her arms across her well-formed bust. "Before we go into my daughter's room, I believe you'd better tell me what has happened."

Something almost cunning crept into the nun's perpetually startled eyes. "You need have no concern about speaking in front of her. Mary has lapsed back into one of her episodes." Carolyn found her teeth gritting together at the sound of the euphemism. "Episodes," indeed! "But what she has written, presumably a form of communication with which her unconscious mind is comfortable, seems to me to be of professional calibre."

"Then I take it that *whatever* she's put on paper," Carolyn pursued, frowning, "you view as fictitious? I think that's an entirely different attitude than I inferred when we spoke on the phone." She paused. "Frankly, Sister Alicia Beth, you seemed almost hysterical."

The tall nun's fingers toyed with the edge of her collar, more a suggestion of stalling than of confusion. "I took the liberty of talking with Father about it. He assured me that your child has merely . . . written a little story."

Strangely, the remark caused Carolyn Lord fresh alarm. Father Brian T. Donnehy was a living miracle, because he was a priest and yet he believed, so far as she had been able to tell in their prior conversations, only that which he could see and touch. Privately, Carolyn was convinced that if Father Donnehy had discovered the sacraments of science and psychology before those of the Church, he would never have taken his vows. Hearing that the good Father was already involved in this mysterious literary venture of her daughter's and had already stubbornly proclaimed it fictional in nature predisposed the teacher to believe in the validity of what young Mary wrote.

"I appreciate your concern, Sister," she said shortly, opening the door. "Perhaps her mother should judge for herself."

Mary was propped up on the bed on a mountain of pillows, presumably the way Sister Alicia Beth had found her. A ballpoint pen with which she had managed to scribble a few largely illegible letters to Carolyn lay beside her outstretched hand. In her lap, Carolyn saw, was the manuscript Mary had composed; even a glance told her that Mary was in a vastly more logical frame of mind when she wrote it, because the letters and words were formed in the round, clear way she had written before the two-year-old rape.

And beside the girl, beyond the dropped pen—half-buried in the mound of tangled sheets—was the missing journal of Carolyn's great-grandfather, Professor Jabez Lord!

She was briefly stunned. Now she could calculate how it must have happened: Periodically, in an ongoing effort to arouse Mary's interest in the outside world—at the blessed moments when she was conscious—Carolyn had brought her bundles of magazines. Obviously she had rested a stack of them atop the old journal and then, on the day when she took the magazines to Mary, inadvertently brought along the ancient journal.

Why hadn't Mary mentioned it? What effect could it have had on these pages her daughter wrote? *Was* there a connection, actually; or was it nothing more than an impressionable teen-aged girl believing that the rich talent which once allowed a noted mythology professor to write several valued and published books flowed in her own youthful veins, as well?

She picked up the manuscript from Mary's lap and sat in a chair beside her, tenderly appraising the child's condition. "The child!" Carolyn rebuked herself. Why, Mary was seventeen now—almost a woman. A young woman who'd already had enough credits to graduate from high school before she was violently assaulted. Carolyn patted her daughter's hand. There was a spot of color in her high cheeks, for the first time. Asleep, her longish lashes and relaxed lips enabled her to seem prettier than when, awake, considerable shyness and self-doubt disturbed her features—caused them almost to appear to run, like a watercolor done by a gifted amateur. The sisters, she saw, had been brushing

Mary's brown hair differently, allowing it, as it grew, to frame her face in a way Carolyn instantly approved. It was odd to realize abruptly that Mary Lord, despite her troubled mental state, was actually becoming both more mature—and decidedly prettier!

She also observed with hope that this sleep of her daughter's appeared lighter, more natural. None of the nightmare frenzy that once twisted her sleeping expression into masks of untold terror—even as recently as two weeks ago—remained now. On the spot, Carolyn decided that *whatever* Mary had written—whether it was fiction or bizarre fact—should be encouraged. Clearly, getting back to her beloved literary effort was helping the girl.

Conscious of eyes on her, Carolyn glanced up. Sister Alicia Beth was mere feet away, a study in black and white, watching the teacher's every move. "I think I can manage to read this alone, Sister, perhaps more reflectively," she said softly, managing a moderating smile. "If you don't mind."

The nun grunted and turned heavily away. "Push Mary's button if you need me."

Absently, Carolyn nodded. She was already scanning the first few lines of the composition. And she was amazed. She wondered what Mary's father would make of it.

It was written for all the world as if Mary had *been there*, somehow, as if she had been an observer . . . at a bizarre encounter of more than *eighty years ago!*

She swiveled in her chair at the girl's bed, to encourage better lighting for the unusual manuscript, began at the first, and read it straight through:

December 31, 1899. Hindhead, England.

The gabled two-story, constructed of red brick and tile, perched comfortably at the end of a bush-lined, 150-foot winding drive and it was well worth the carriage ride. When one was asked in, it was pleasant to peer south to the toboggan hills covered with bracken and gorse. The view was that of the Nutcome Valley, one of the loveliest sights in that part of England.

Tonight, however, the house into which the master had moved with his family only two years before was dark except for the yellow illumination of electric lamps faintly shining from voluminous bay windows. Louise, the mistress of the house, was abed; most of the servants were off for the holiday with their own families.

But in the sumptuous drawing room, the famed author and spiritualist paced before his fireplace, occasionally stopping in front of his unwelcome guest to place a hefty hand on a wing-backed chair and gesture with the other. He was impatient to see the new year in with his beloved wife and hoped she would not yet be asleep. It was, however, growing late.

There were other and somewhat better reasons why the tall and powerful gentleman was obliged to draw with difficulty upon his well-known British courtesy. In May he had turned forty; and, always one who tended to work more prodigiously than the average man, he was suddenly conscious of age and all that it implied. He had always been a man who continued shoving his horizons back, one who extended himself and all his interests, and there was so very much to do before his journey in this vale was completed. It was especially galling, at times, to carry along his life-trail that detective he had made famous, that annoying creation with the hawk's nose, keen eyes, and wide range of idiosyncrasies.

Sometimes he would pause in the midst of more important work and wonder whatever had possessed him, just over a decade ago, to imagine such an impertinent fellow as Mr. Sherlock Holmes!

But the primary reason for the good doctor's impatience this evening was the particular guest who now warmed his toes at the fireplace, sipping good brandy over which he stared with two insolent, baleful and magnetic eyes.

This odd young man wore kilts and, knowing that he was not Scottish, the writer considered it showy and affected costuming. A bald spot that might have been intentionally shorn through his dark hair, so pronounced it was, also annoyed the author. Worst of all, this young man was insufferably bold—dropping *in* on New Year's Eve, great Scott!—egotistical without apparent warrant, and seemingly disrespectful of every decent custom.

The light from the fire played on Aleister Crowley's face. "When I was in India, earlier this year," said Crowley with an imperious tone that was a fraction subdued for his present purposes, "they were clearly impressed by my credentials. They can deny it, if they wish; but they were impressed."

"That may be, sir. But the fact remains you were rejected by the Order of the Golden Dawn all the same. Is that not the truth?"

"It is, Dr. Conan Doyle," Crowley acceded. "However, the reasons were jealousy on the part of those rank amateurs who call themselves magicians or metaphysicians. Why, damn! I've *forgotten* more magic—black *and* white magic—than they collectively possess in all their libraries!"

The man's brashness rankled. "For my part, I fail to understand why you should desire to be among them. Much of their work, I am told, is Satanic at best. And revisionary as well as plagiaristic at worst!" The author permitted a brief chuckle.

Crowley ignored the criticism and crossed his bare knees, tapping his long fingertips upon them. "I am prepared to give you a demonstration of my talents, if you wish. For example, I have seen that you will be knighted. Within three years, at the outside."

Conan Doyle's large face registered the mild pain of protest. "If it must be for naught but Sherlock Holmes, then I could not possibly care less. Better no recognition than applause for a minor creation."

"But accept it you shall. Perhaps something else I tell

you, shortly—concerning the astrological portents of this terrible night—will interest you more, sir."

The doctor seemed mildly curious. "Terrible night, is it, Mr. Crowley?—Or should I perhaps refer to you as the Laird of Bokestine?"

"You may call me anything, dear doctor, so long as you, *um,* invoke my name." The young egotist's smile became strangely beatific. "Some, including Mother, call me the Beast. I confess that I rather like that."

It did not charm Arthur Conan Doyle. "My dear fellow!" He drew himself up to his full four inches past six feet, shocked, even repelled. "I fear that I shan't be able to call you anything at all, much longer. Candidly, sir, your visit is untimely. I *do* wish that you had sent round an inquiring note, in advance. Kindly be good enough now to get to the point and inform me of the purpose of this evening's call."

"Elementary," replied Aleister Crowley, raising an eyebrow. "I wish to begin the Golden Dawn anew. On the continent, under my own regime."

"You were denied admittance in London, sir! Surely—"

"All the more reason to begin afresh on the continent, if I may say so. To do this effectively, sir, it should prove marvelous of you to lend me your support. Your name is known all over the world."

Conan Doyle laughed heavily. "As the man who so recently murdered Mr. Sherlock Holmes," he said. He fingered his heavy mustache, thinking of the letters of heated disapproval which had followed the appearance of *The Final Problem.* "Pray, tell me, Mr. Crowley: Why should I even for a moment consider supporting you, in any fashion?"

"You are deeply interested in spiritualism, sir," the mage remarked pointedly, lifting a finger that drifted effetely more than pointing. "You support many mediums and I can consequently discern no reason why I, too, should not receive your backing."

"Are you a trance-medium then, Mr. Crowley?"

The youthful black-magician spread two delicate

hands invitingly. "I am . . . what I please to be. For this night, kind sir, I am what *you* wish me to be."

Conan Doyle scowled, throwing a cigar wrapping into the fireplace. "Your temerity is unbearable, sir!"

"My temerity, alas, *is me*. I can do—almost anything." His eyes grew dreamy. "I assure you that spirits, among other less quaintly benign creatures, speak through me at my imperial command. I can summon anyone I please, to do . . . *any thing* I please." He beamed on the spiritualist. "Would you care for a demon, perhaps, to inspect? A ghoul? A sweet plaything of a banshee, then?"

Arthur Conan Doyle whirled away from Crowley to stare into the fire. "See here, sir. What I should really wish is your departure. But I shall observe the holiday season and tender an explanation. I am not impelled, you see, by every occult fancy catching the public's transient attention. I am sincerely interested in conversing with those on the other side—gentle Christian souls, sir, by means of respectable trance-mediums." He paused. "In the years remaining to me, I plan to establish the existence of these poor souls and the need to communicate with them. Beyond that—" Conan Doyle whipped round quickly, with alacrity for which Crowley would not have credited him, his oft-dreamy eyes full of ire— "I am bound to say that delving into arcane or evil mysteries rubs me—as a man of God— distinctly the wrong way."

"I am aware of that," said Crowley, smoothly.

"You are, ay?" The athletic doctor stared at him. "Since you claim to share the dark purposes of the Golden Dawn, I cannot possibly conceive what you would demonstrate in order to win me over."

"Curious, aren't you?" The Beast giggled. Then his face protruded forward and his head slowly oscillated from side to side in a curiously reptilian fashion. "Are you aware of the science of astrology, Dr. Conan Doyle?"

The tall host cast a slightly nervous glance at his mantle clock. Twenty minutes now until midnight, the end of a century and perhaps the end of a courtly, chivalrous age Arthur Conan Doyle had done his best to defend and preserve. "I have looked into it on occasion."

"Among my innumerable and extraordinary skills, sir, I am an astrologer as well. By means of astrology, I am able more precisely to foretell the future—to identify its more devious details and charming corruptions."

"Astrology appears rather intriguing through its avenues for character study," said Conan Doyle gruffly, starting to pace. "I am not for an instant willing to accept that it looks into God's own business, His privately planned future for mankind. His children."

"I *am*. You smile, sir, tightly though it might be. But I assure you, doctor, that it really is quite remarkable when one bends to study—makes the requisite, concerted effort. Sir Isaac Newton, upon entering Cambridge, I recall, was asked what he chose to study. He replied: 'Mathematics—because I wish to test Judicial Astrology.' And when Mr. Halley chided him for subscribing to astrology, Sir Isaac retorted, 'Evidently you had not looked into Astrology. I have.' So my little jest—'I *am*'—is not without dignified antecedence."

Arthur Conan Doyle pursed his lips thoughtfully. "Interesting. I do recall that a man in my own field of study, Hippocrates, declared: 'A physician without a knowledge of Astrology has no right to call himself a physician.' "

"Queer how that was left out of his Oath, is it not?" Crowley seemed almost to arch his back, catlike, in his purring delight. "I do think we shall become dear friends yet!"

"Do be plain, Mr. Crowley! Have you some proposal to make?"

"Ah, yes. Allow me, sir, to predict the future of the new century which begins at midnight. If I am able to do that—a simple task for such a genuine genius as I— then you, in return, will endorse my continental chapter of the Order of the Golden Dawn. And, as well, give close consideration to applying for membership yourself. I think you will find it easily obtainable."

Now Conan Doyle folded his hands together across his generous waist and his intelligent eyes gleamed in anger. "Once and for all, I am not accustomed to the obligation of entertaining strange persons who barge into my house at night—in the dead of winter, quite unannounced—and who insist, further, upon my entering bargains with them. I shall now hear what you have to say, Crowley, and then you must leave me. No promises."

Aleister Crowley arose from his wing-backed seat in a curious, sinuous motion. He seemed to stand in a movement, jointlessly. He unfolded a piece of foolscap from his pocket, rather ceremoniously, and held it beneath the nose of the older man. "This is a horoscope of the date. *Today*, sir. December 31, 1899. Are you familiar with astrological symbols?"

"To a degree. It is the Capricorn period, naturally; Mars in that sign." Conan Doyle squinted. "I say, this *is* rather unusual. I see there are four planets in Sagittarius, the confining Twelfth House to this solar period."

"Observant, sir, observant!" Crowley exulted. "Mercury, Jupiter, Saturn and Uranus are there. Jupiter in Sagittarius increases opportunities but does the same for opportunism and idealistic abstractions. Saturn here strives to *relieve* these, but for clearly *practical* purposes. It also seeks self-justification, and all this for the years *ahead of us*—as these planets progress. Yet Capricorn, where we find the Sun, this date, derives from . . . *the past*."

The physician-author glanced up. "Uranus here, of course, has contempt for things of earth. Nothing is too lofty for it to seek."

"Nor, from a negative application of the influence," said Crowley pointedly, "too—*low*. Are you aware, Dr. Doyle, of the curious matter suggested by the conjunction of Jupiter with Saturn—as we now find them?"

Conan Doyle considered; he shook his large head. "I

am not."

"Allow me, then, to make it clear. In the United States of America, under this conjunction, every president in office in 1900, 1920, 1940, 1960, 1980 and the year 2000 shall die before completing his term. A large percentage of these pretigious gentlemen will be, *hum*, assassinated."

"Good Lord!" Conan Doyle exclaimed. "And what happens *after* the year 2000?"

The sorcerer stared into the yellow flames of the fireplace a moment as if seeing the roll of future time. "After 2000, you ask? Why, *after* that year," he replied steadily, "there is nothing. *Nothing at all.*"

Conan Doyle reddened. "Of course," he said as he recovered himself, "it is easy for you to say these things to me. I shall not be living after the second half of the new century. Therefore, I cannot criticize any errors after the fact. Unless," he added, smiling, "you contact me through a trance-medium."

"Touché, sir!" Crowley smiled his impossibly magnetic smile. "But it has *already happened,* Doctor. Presidents died in office in 1860 and 1880. *You* will be alive to see it occur next year. Indeed, Doctor, you will see it happen in 1920."

Conan Doyle's face was gentle, even sad, in the golden flames reflected there. "And 1940, Beast? Shall I see it occur, then, in 1940?"

"Alas, no." The mage managed a quite artificial regretful sigh. "Not according to my progressions of your chart." He shrugged. "Dead, dead, dead!"

"You are an unrepentant rapscallion, sir. A cad."

"And thank *you,* sir." Crowley lifted the horoscope once more so that the light from the flickering electric lamp illumined it. "You'll perceive that the Sagittarian planets oppose Neptune in Gemini. A time of delusion, mental illness, even homicidal madness lies ahead, Dr. Conan Doyle." He smiled. "But worse than that?"

The spiritualist's sensibilities were again outraged. "And what could possibly be worse than that, Crowley?"

"With the Sagittarian factors opposed by Neptune during this particular period, the portions of the distant past which are *most* feared—most despised and dreaded by mankind—are to be . . . *reborn*. After all, the Sagittarius stellium points to the future—you must be aware of that—but with malefic Saturn symbolically ruling the Capricorn Sun, then the future, my dear sir, *must become* the *past*."

Conan Doyle, finding that he shivered, drew away from proximity to his bizarre caller, retreating to his fireplace. There, he warmed his suddenly cold and heavy hands against the heartening heat. "What, precisely, do you see?" he inquired softly at last. "What dreaded segments of the past do you believe are to be reborn in the new century?"

"The denizens of Hell, Dr. Conan Doyle."

The magician had approached the fire which painted his sensual face with scarlet shadows, hollowing the eyes, haloing the pursed lips as if in wait of a devil's kiss. Conan Doyle stared at him. "My dear fellow!" he exclaimed.

"A man shall be reborn in April whose motivation is that of demonic force. He dwelled here before, as the Hun, his hordes savaging the world. He'd had—*other* guises. In the Thirties and Forties, he will try again to capture the world on behalf of his . . . leaders. The Hun will rule Germany, and more."

"You speak of the distant future. What of tonight?"

"Oh, haven't I mentioned that?" The shaman's hands were so close to the fire Conan Doyle felt they must surely burn, yet Crowley left them there. "An atrocious killing in New York, America, occurs tonight. A maiming of father by son. I urge you to read the overseas papers when they reach you and then contact me in Scotland. I feel that you will believe my powers then."

The author-physician sighed. "You are incredible, Crowley. Incredible."

"With me to perform my magic, miracles the world has never seen—and you to authenticate me, to act as my Boswell!—we would become an unbeatable team!"

Conan Doyle roused himself and he had had enough. "Pray look at my face, Crowley, for you may be mad but you are not ignorant." He held the other man's gaze steadily. "All that I have to say has already crossed your mind."

"You stand fast?"

"Absolutely." With some hesitation, Arthur Conan Doyle offered his hand. "I am afraid that in the, ah, pleasure of this conversation I am neglecting business of importance which awaits me elsewhere."

Aleister Crowley was led politely down a long corridor by his taller host, knowing now that he had failed in his mission. At last he could not resist two final ripostes.

"You are going to bring Sherlock Holmes to life again, my dear Doctor," he observed with ringing certainty.

"In a play only," the author said with briskness, not stopping in his hostly pace. "I'm working on it now."

"There will be a return of your master sleuth in prose as well, sir—in an empty house, not upon a stage. You have my word for it." They had reached the front door and round its edges both men could feel the rough whisper of winter seeking sanctuary within. "A final point, Dr. Conan Doyle."

"Yes. What is it?"

"While the murder in America this night will go unsolved," said the Beast, raising his voice to compete with the wind, as Conan Doyle opened the door, "it will initiate the return of certain *other* of Hell's denizens. Specifically, I speak of those whom the Greeks worshipped. Bear in mind that a guideline for the new century shall be this: All that is fervently believed by sufficient numbers of people must come to actual being. It shall be given quite deadly, restored life."

Conan Doyle paused. "Do you speak, then, of Satan?"

"Not in this connection, Doctor, but of Satan's *woman*. The queen of the inferno, the temptress of sin; *Hecate*. She returns to full power in the final quarter of this new century."

Then he was gone. Arthur Conan Doyle closed the door on his visitor and an unaccustomed shudder curled up his long spine. He rubbed his hands briskly, then moved toward his staircase.

"Who was that, dear?" called Louise, sleepily, from upstairs. "Who was your caller?"

Conan Doyle laughed his barking chortle and began his ascent. "I'm not certain, my dear Louise. But I do believe I have just met Professor Moriarty!"

CHAPTER III

It was a very rare moment indeed when Dr. Carolyn Lord was filled with inspiration. By background as well as training, her approach was coolly scientific; if one had an idea by any process, one merely examined it for its value and accepted or rejected it on the basis of practicality. If she had been asked to express her feelings about unexpected, wild flights of imagination when one felt overpowered by some inner knowledge that a new idea was absolutely perfect, she would have replied quite sternly. Even angrily. She'd always subscribed to Edison's dictum that inspiration was ninety percent hard work.

Yet over the next week, after returning from her startling and disquieting visit to her daughter Mary at Bleeding Heart Hospital, Carolyn felt first that a marvelous idea was soon to surface and then, when the notion occurred to her, exulted with as much conviction and enthusiasm as any poet or composer: She would teach a class in which the young women students at the University of California at El Vista would learn about classical goddesses of the past, and then learn to identify strongly with them.

"I think it's just what my ladies need to develop true self-respect," Carolyn told her friend Elna Clinefort on the phone, twisting the cord and eager for an endorsement of her inspiration.

"Why?" Elna demanded in her usual direct way. She hadn't used to be that candid, that questioning.

Being married to a psychologist whose principal technique involved the asking of pertinent questions had hardened her in some way, emboldened her to force her friends to reason things through. *"Why will it help your students to develop greater self-respect?"*

Carolyn Lord paused and looked out the French doors at the farthest end of the front room. They led to a small balcony overlooking first the flower garden she'd cultivated since coming to California from Indianapolis, and, in the distance, the crisp white lines of the university itself. She was wearing a light-weight silk blouse and shorts, her customary I'm-determined-to-make-this-home-if-it-kills-me garb, and sitting on the floor beside the phone with her long legs outflung. Her gaze moved from the campus to her legs—still shapely, even sensuous, but not yet blessed with the tan she'd thought she would have by now—and back to the rather blockish main building of U.C.E.V. Suddenly it reminded her, for some inexplicable reason, of Bleeding Heart Hospital and she knew the primary reason for the course she planned.

It was intended to give other young women the brazen self-assurance, the inner strength, the sense of impervious superiority over men that would make any would-be rapist freeze in his tracks, every ounce of perverse and brutal yearning instantly dissolved forever.

"Let's face it, Elna," she said with soft determination into the mouthpiece, shaking back her mane of smokey-blond hair, "ninety percent of women are walking targets—and not just for men who are truly perverted either. I've read enough about the liberation movement, attended enough meetings, to face some facts that even other women are hesitant to mention."

"Such as?"

Carolyn tucked her pert knees beneath her chin, leaning forward in intense concentration. *"Any* man psychologically attacks *any* woman with whom he comes into contact during the day. If the woman wears a blouse open at the neck, the man virtually breaks *his neck* trying to look down it. If she wears a perfectly respectable sweater or blouse buttoned up to her *jawline,* the man's eyes sweep over her curves while he tries to *guess* what she looks like!"

"You exaggerate," Elna said coolly in her ear.

"That's an impossibility. If a woman drops something and stoops to pick it up, every man in the room *prays* that her skirt will ride up enough for him to see something. But it doesn't even stop there, El! Did you ever see a man watching a dancer wearing very few clothes, a go-go girl, someone like that? *Whatever* she has left on her poor, prostituted body, *that's* what the man is looking at—still trying to see every inch she has!"

"What about the men's magazines that show it all?" Elna asked lightly.

"With the newer ones," Carolyn continued, biting off her words, "the ones that *really* show everything, the men of the world won't be happy until one of those X-ray tube cameras is inserted in the vagina so they can see what women's goddam *ovaries* look like! What I'm telling you, El, is that every man is so damn curious about women that it makes the stories of our so-called penis envy look absurd by comparison. And that *knowing* this about them, facing the fact that they couldn't care less what's in our minds or what we're capable of doing, allows us to know *their* vulnerable areas!"

Elna laughed. "I accidentally got poor old Fred in his last night, when I turned over in bed and my knee came up."

Carolyn wasn't to be deterred. She shook her head. "I don't mean that. Their *real* vulnerable area is their *insatiable curiosity* about us—the fact that they don't for a minute believe we're just the rest of humanity, but a totally *alien force*. We're distinct and different from them—in their own minds—as if we came here from Jupiter or the 8th Dimension."

"How do you mean?" For the first time Elna sounded interested. Carolyn could see her tall, broad-shouldered and red-haired friend shifting her hips in her chair, really tuning in now. "How is knowing that an advantage?"

Carolyn smiled glacially. "By making ourselves *more* alien—in a literally different way, in a strong and self-reliant way—we become more different, more unattainable, and eventually, more superior. We shock their poor little brains into believing that we don't need them anymore—which we *don't*, by the way—because we have our identification *not* with the society created by men, *not* with man's masculine God and His standards of behavior, but with the tradition-honored society of ancient women who once were feared by every mortal man: the goddesses of old."

"You plan to teach your women students to *believe* in goddesses, instead of God?" Elna sounded thunderstruck, dumbfounded. "There's been some joking about praying to 'Her' instead of 'Him'—but few of us have been really serious about it."

"I'm deadly serious, Elna," Carolyn replied grimly. "In point of pure fact there's more evidence that the goddesses of old walked this earth, molded and created everything on this planet, than that God did. Goddesses existed in every ancient culture and society. While their names change, often just slightly, from culture to culture, their *identities*—what they did, what *made* them godly—remains essentially the same. And the fact is that men, of old, were *terrified* by what goddesses could do to them—or, if they were nice little boys and minded their mamas, what the goddesses could do *for* them." Carolyn lowered her voice, to complete the point she was making and show she was still in control of her emotions. "You see, I'm not advocating a Lesbian society; I don't happen to be a Lesbian, not even after what my ex-husband did to me and what some escaped lunatic did to my daughter. Homosexuality would mean the end of the world, not from a moralistic but from a sheerly pragmatic, biological standpoint. I'm telling you that my plan—beginning with the women who attend my class—

means *they* will do the choosing about who mates with them. *They* will do the looking, the chasing, the petting, take the lead in proposing marriage, take charge of their own bodies in *all* ways and never in the traditional form that somehow suggests a man has *rights* with *our* anatomies! This will happen for two simple reasons, El: First, that men are too curious, too hungry, to leave us alone; their need is immense, even if *they* seldom are! And second, my young women will have such self-respect and pride in their sex that they'll believe in their natural *superiority* and make it stick!"

"What do you mean, 'beginning with the women who attend your class?' Is your idea supposed to go on to something else?"

Carolyn inhaled sharply, then confessed it. "If I conduct my class properly, what I'm teaching can catch on. It will eventually spread to every needy woman in America, even the world. When others see how my students live—freely; in control—it'll be an object lesson to *all* women."

For a moment Elna was silent. "I can't say I'm comfortable with the notion of trying to eliminate God. Maybe I'm hopelessly old-fashioned, Care—Fred sometimes says I am—but I confess to *liking* the concept of a great, bearded Father Figure of the Cosmos. Someone who has none of the faults of my real father—he was a drunk, by the way—but all his virtues. His masculine shoulder to lie on, psychically. A God who cares yet holds rigidly to His plan, His scheme of things for us, who may be reached or contacted now and then and who will see to it that when our lives are over, we'll be genuinely rewarded for our good works." She hesitated, clearly not wanting to offend her friend. "I don't believe your plan—as good as it is, in general terms—will prove to be effective with your students if you insist that they abandon God."

"And I thought *I* was the ex-smalltown girl ruined by a crude and uncaring husband!" Carolyn sighed. "El, it's not that God is to be abandoned. I'm planning to put in the 'A' team, the varsity, because humankind is losing the ball game the way it is. I'm replacing God with the females who once were believed to rule this world, and apparently did in fact! It was the Hebraic and Christian male God who booted *them* out, who put *us*—women, everywhere—under the male thumb where he can crush or caress whenever he pleases. In a way, El, what I'll be doing isn't new or modern at all—it's a long-needed *return* to the way things were, and properly so, thousands of years ago." Now Carolyn's voice began to rise as she sought to convince her friend. "Instead of vague promises about the rewards of Heaven, I'm giving my young ladies an opportunity to *share* in the rulership of the entire universe—to bestride mountains and jump from star to star—to be as strong as the strongest man, and fully *in charge*!"

A pause. Then: "Carolyn, I wish you'd talk with Fred about this before you tell U.C.E.V. it's definite."

"Why?" Suddenly outraged, she scrambled to her feet, gesturing. "Why—so some threatened, long-faced, over-educated male can seek to solidify his status at my expense? So he can extend it, go on dominating even the female patients who come to him for guidance when what they all basically need is self-confidence? When they need someone to tell them they were right, all along, about their basic resentment of the opposite sex and their instincts telling them they're being raped by every wink, smile or touch? Not on your life, El! Not on your life!"

"But it may be on *your* life in the long run, Care," the other woman said at last, deeply concerned. "Honey, you've *changed,* so much, in such a short space of time! Why, it's only a few weeks since Fred had to see you before it was possible even to *drive* to Bleeding Heart! I—I wonder what's given you such awesome *conviction* about this since we last spoke. Please, Care. Give it a little more thought."

When she hung up, Carolyn made a glass of iced tea and carried it out to her balcony, her feelings ambivalent. It was possible that she'd been too harsh with Elna, particularly in criticizing her beloved Fred. The sun was angling down, its rays bathing the balcony, turning the day into a lazy-making afternoon. She sighed, propped her feet on the railing and then kicked off her sandals. For a few moments she remembered the handful of good days she'd enjoyed in her marriage, back at the start—days when her husband had relaxed his usual male pomposity and inclination to leave her all evening in preference to the neighborhood tavern, and shared things with her. A twinge of nostalgia made her frown. That was El's problem: Fred. She had a larger number of good times with Fred and because they were so much better than her friends seemed to have, El felt everything was basically the way it should be. He's all right, she's all right. So it wasn't El's fault at all that she didn't understand that *more* than equality, *more* than enhanced opportunity and freedom, was required for the mass of women.

Carolyn glanced from left to right. Her apartment was one of several with balconies, and housed principally single instructors from the campus. She saw no one in sight and no one beneath her on the grounds. Carolyn unbuttoned her thin print blouse. She wore no bra beneath it. The sun felt so good that she parted the blouse widely until it scarcely covered her breasts at all. Her blond hair rained on the colorful chaise in luxurious relaxation. It was good to have made up her mind, to have a new direction. Tomorrow she'd need to begin planning the course and lining up the books to be used. None of them, she thought, was apt to have been written before 1970.

For the first time she began to consider what El had said about her changing so much. Probably it was true, although the seeds of repugnance toward masculine aggression had been planted years before. Still, it was a good question: Why *had* she had this un-Carolyn-like inspiration and why was she willing to act upon it without more consideration? If she allowed her imagination to influence her, Carolyn mused, she might believe that the inspiration had somehow been *planted* there.

Undoubtedly reading that strange document of Mary's had played a part in her idea. Especially since the paper, or story, was clearly triggered somehow by Grandfather Lord's worry about the goddess Hecate. Eyes closed, the cool iced tea glass between her breasts, she smiled as the thought occurred to her. Old Professor Lord surely had every reason to fear the Queen of Hell! From what Carolyn had learned, Hecate despised all men. Her consignment to the lower regions, to rulership of Hades, had been partly spurred by the careless way she disposed of the mortal men who offended her.

There was, of course, no reason one Dr. Carolyn Lord should fear Hecate—no reason at all! *Whatever* it was that Hecate did which was so horribly frightening, they were still sisters separated by the centuries. For the first time Carolyn saw that her quest to learn more about the devil's Queen had not been so much to verify her grandfather's anxiety or his belief, but simply to learn more about a woman who once pointed and made mortal men jump. To learn more about the most respected, powerful goddess of them all. Someone whom a truly modern woman could admire, even serve.

She was beginning to doze off when *she felt the eyes upon her* . . .

Her own eyelids flew open. Cautiously, she turned her gaze to the right. She saw nothing, no one.

Then she looked up, at the higher story of the building—

—And saw him.

From this distance he looked small, ordinary, unthreatening, even wholly insignificant, the man who was peeping at her. Who *dared* to peep at her. She could just make out the side of his face as he squinted out around the curtain of his French door. He was seemingly hypnotized, she realized, frozen and held rigid in the grip of his secret, spying desire.

And he was clearly staring at her because her legs were bare, because her blouse was unbuttoned.

Carolyn's leg muscles tightened with the urge to leap to her feet and run, in shame, back into her own apartment.

Which was when it occurred to her that she had nothing to be ashamed of. *This* was her place; *that* was his, and she wasn't gaping open-mouthed up at him. The little male bastard, worse, must have singled her out weeks before, in order to know where to look. He might have been staring anywhere from his balcony, and missed her. But no, he'd already appraised her sometime when they passed in the corridors, studied her with his stupid, narrow little mind and had probably been losing damp sleep just *waiting* for her to appear, like this, in the privacy of her own home.

She wanted to run upstairs and scream at him, for his temerity and ignorance. How *could* men have such an abnormal lust to see, in a new woman, what they'd doubtlessly seen on a hundred others? It disgusted her—no, she thought, in a crazy way it *frightened* her—to think that she might have spoken amiably to him as a neighbor. And all the time his filthy little brain was seeing her naked and thinking he was getting by with it. Because that was the way they all were, Carolyn mused heatedly; they all thought they could outfox you, get by with their lurid little fantasies and stroke their florid little cocks and then tip their hats the next day as if nothing at all had happened.

Again she resisted the temptation to button her blouse and flee. Words—words she did not, then, even try to identify—flooded her mind, emboldening her: ". . . The most evil creature who ever lived. . . ."

Slowly, deliberately, but not so much so that her motions appeared intentionally sensual, Carolyn slipped out of her blouse. For a moment she made herself lean back on the chaise, the sun hot on her unaccustomed bosom.

She stood, then, languorously, cupping a firm breast in each hand, raising them as though generously to the eavesdropper but without looking in his direction. Great goddess, she thought, he must be ready by now, he must be in Seventh Heaven, thinking he's seeing all this and getting by with it. She lifted her arms high above her head, knowing the flattering ambiance this gave to her breasts, as though in a vast kittenish stretch. Carolyn had a good bustline; it was high and full, the nipples nearly pink and virginal in the afternoon sunlight. She kept her stomach tucked in, her bare legs posed just so.

And then she turned directly in the direction of the peeping man, looked up at him, saw most of his face vanish like a small boy caught with his hand in the cookie jar. And when he peered out again, she was raising her hand to him, the middle finger aimed straight up.

With a toss of her smokey blond hair, Carolyn retrieved her blouse and strode, defiantly but not swiftly, back into her apartment.

She had a normal, everyday American name and considered herself—most of the time—a normal and everyday American. When she entered puberty several years ago, she quite forgot the strange powers and stranger urges that had possessed her, often, as a small child. It was, in a way, similar to how children give up their imaginary playmates without ever giving them another thought.

But the bizarre skills and desires she once had were not imaginary, normal or American. They were far more terrifying, on all levels; and while she no longer knew how different she was—nor that she was the living reenactment of a lurid and superstitious past— her powers were only submerged, out of touch with her.

Temporarily.

Daddy had never entirely believed in them but he'd seen enough strange things to begin moderating what he said, in front of his girl, about the general uselessness of women. He went right on mistreating her mother but tried, most of the time, to live as if he didn't even have a daughter.

He'd thought it was safer that way, since she was "different"; he'd thought himself behaving prudently, as if it were his own idea.

What he hadn't known was manifold. A basically ignorant man, marred further by constant imbibing, he had no clue that his daughter was more than odd now, for that matter, that she preferred him to leave her alone. He didn't realize how sick she had become, hearing his earlier condemnations of her sex, seeing the way he mistreated her mother. And he had no idea that his daughter required far greater independence than any woman he'd known before. She'd gone her own way since she was a rather diabolical little girl and she meant for things to remain that way.

But several months ago she'd become pregnant during one of her experimental, independent actions, by a boy named Tom. Tom rode a motorcycle, lived well on the money he stole and the drugs he sold, projected an aura of excitement and had sworn to her that he wished to marry her. Unfortunately, that was *before* the girl became pregnant—not after.

Unfortunately for Tom.

The day Daddy had scheduled the abortion, to rid his daughter of the baby, Tom—with literally no idea now who he was nor why he was doing what he'd been told to do—put his father's revolver between his teeth and blew out the back of his skull. Even that was just as well, in a way; she'd told her parents that Tom raped her. And Daddy, after he and Mom saw the way she'd made herself look, fully intended to murder Tom right after the abortion, and his daughter was safe.

Although Daddy never was able to understand her and consequently wasn't fond of the girl, he was proud of his daughter's stoic courage that day. It was the same general time-frame when Dr. Carolyn Lord began to develop her idea for a special class concerning ancient goddesses and idly wondered where the inspiration had come from. Dr. Lord could not know that this young woman dreamed incessantly nor that the content of her dreams reached out, mysteriously advancing her conscious plans and desires. And when Carolyn spoke with her friend Elna Clinefort on the phone, explaining the idea that seemed to be her own, it was the same day that Daddy arranged for the girl to go to college. To forget the terrible thing that had happened to her; to begin a new life.

Just the way she had planned it.

Except she no longer had anything but a vague notion that she could *make* things occur the way she had envisioned them.

Outwardly, then, she was a normal, sometimes shy, teenaged young woman who had recently been ill. No one, not even her mother, knew differently.

After the killing surgery was performed, Dr. Peters drew Daddy aside, shaking his head a lot and nervously clearing his throat. It took the man some while to speak. "It's probably good that this happened now, sir. Instead of after your girl married."

Even though he'd been drinking for hours now, the father was startled to momentary sobriety. "Why d'you say that, doc?"

"Well, I don't know how to—to *explain* this, to make it easy for you, sir. And it is just possible that I shouldn't be telling you—about it—at all. I mean, there's no precedent for this. I have, um, no guidelines to follow."

The father had never been a pleasant or patient man. "What in crissakes are you talking about, dammit? Give!"

Dr. Peters wet his lips. "Let me tell you that the case is *over*, sir. Ended. No fuss and no publicity. It's all between us, and that's *all*."

"What 'case'?" the man snarled. For a moment it seemed that he would seize the physician by his lapels, "Publicity about *what*? What th'hell are y'talkin' about?"

"About the, ah, foetus we took from your daughter, sir," the surgeon replied finally, trying to get firmed up. He drew himself erect. "It wasn't far along, naturally; you know that. Nonetheless, sir, by some impossible . . . *genetic quirk* . . . well, that's why I said it's good it hasn't happened after your girl married. Honestly." Now Dr. Peters plunged. "Because it wasn't the foetus of a normal child, sir. Not at all."

"Will you spit it out?"

Dr. Peters took his last pause, wishing now that he hadn't opted for candor. He gripped the parent by the shoulder and looked steadily into his eyes. "The truth is, sir, your daughter's child—if it had gone full term—" now he could no longer look the father in the eyes; he averted his gaze—"well, it would have had . . . *more* than *one* head."

CHAPTER IV

By the time the weekend was rolling around, and another visit to Mary was scheduled, summer was definitely dying. Carolyn Lord scarcely noticed. Her new course was nearing birth, and it would not be aborted.

She had enthusiastically thrown herself into the details, her exuberance both rather dizzying and filled with feelings of *déjà vú*. It was sheer delight, for the first time since before a marriage that seemed to have lasted several lifetimes, to work again on her own class outline. She was keenly aware of how fortunate she was, to continue carrying personal acceptability on the basis of her kinship with the late, great Professor Jabez Lord, and to be allowed to introduce something entirely new at U.C.E.V.

Happily, it hadn't even been difficult getting the university to go along with her ideas. Day before yesterday she'd had a lengthy lunch with Dean Sybil Cronin, at a quiet little Chinese restaurant near campus, describing her plans and demonstrating the books and periodical bibliography she meant to employ. It seemed that Dean Cronin herself had experienced enough problems with male superiority, during her fifty-six years, that she was more than willing to go along with Carolyn's course. It was clear that she was safely in the fold when the distinguished dean leaned across the table to her to whisper, meaningfully: "I have no doubt that I would be president of this university today, had I been able to fill out the crotch of a pair of trousers."

Now, on an overcast day when it appeared likely that the fog would soon begin to stalk the highway, Carolyn headed for Bleeding Heart Hospital with a restored sense of confidence. Once more she had a future, not a husband's but one that no one else designed for her— one in which she sincerely felt that she might do some good, and perform a worthwhile service for her fellow women. Additionally, she would teach a freshman English class and be permitted to concentrate on women authors. Her head was full of those whom she wanted to teach. To Carolyn Lord, this afternoon, the sun was still shining and the air wafting through her beloved MG was fresh and regenerative.

But a large slice of her confidence and even more of her joy was sliced away after a brief discussion with Sister Alicia Beth.

"It hasn't ceased," the browless nun reported peremptorily when Carolyn drew within yards of Mary's room.

Suddenly the oxygen in the hospital corridor seemed to thin, and become tainted. A chill trembled along Carolyn's spine. "I take it you don't mean the way Mary moves in and out of awareness."

The tall woman shook her head somberly. "Your daughter has—*written*—again.

"Then why didn't you notify me?" Carolyn asked, worried and a little perplexed. "I would have come sooner."

Sister Alicia Beth's shrug was dramatic, and somehow hard. "It appeared pointless, Dr. Lord. Your last visit did not prevent Mary from resorting to her bizarre compositions and I doubt that this one shall." She paused. "For my own part, I do not like what is happening here, not a bit. I am not sure what . . . agency . . . is responsible for putting these peculiar thoughts into her head, and I am not sure I care to know."

"Please don't be ridiculous, Sister," Carolyn murmured, trying to see what the nun had hidden in her skirt, halfway behind her hip. "What's the nature of Mary's writing this time?"

"*Evil*, madam," the staring blue eyes widened. "I think the nature is evil." Something like a flicker of fear flitted across her stern, pale face. "And again, Dr. Lord, it's from . . . *that day*: December 31, 1899."

"It's not *from* that date, Sister Alicia Beth: It's merely *dated* then," Carolyn argued. "She might just as well put Easter Sunday, 1984—or All Martians Day, 2205, for all the difference it makes. Unless you're prepared to suggest that Crowley was correct, in what Mary had him saying to Sir Arthur, about the astrology of the date."

The nun crossed herself hastily. "The astrology? Heavens, no!"

Carolyn pointed to the papers nearly concealed by the folds of the nun's skirt. "Is that what you have there? The manuscript written by my daughter?"

"It is, madam." She raised her chin ponderously, dignity quickly regained. "I have just returned from showing it to Father Donnehy and he advised me to have you speak with him, after you've visited Mary. In his study."

"I'm not surprised," Carolyn retorted grimly. "Father doesn't hold with anything he *can't* hold. He probably wants to throw Mary out of here."

But Sister Alicia Beth had finished her remarks and did not see fit to reply. She placed the manuscript on the red plastic-topped table beside the mother and left her there, outside the girl's room, to read the report alone.

Carolyn sighed and took an uncomfortable seat, twisting her shoulders to encourage the inadequate lighting to illuminate her daughter's handwriting. She smiled, recalled her ex-husband's comment when she phoned to tell him about Mary's unusual literary efforts. "I always did think she was weird," he said. "I wouldn't come within a hundred miles while she's in a state like that." Carolyn thought again how well-off she was, without him, and read the opening line of the manuscript: *"December 31, 1899. Haiti."*

And as she read, her consternation grew.

The faithful were all on the beach this night of nights, all those who could walk or crawl or be carried, young and old alike. For those sufficiently educated to realize that the old century was dying, who could read or keep records and understand that a fresh ten decades of time began at midnight, it was the most important night of their lives. They had prepared for it over a period of energetic weeks, even months, praying in the shacks called *houmfors,* beseeching their Vodun gods to be compassionate and wise, *scrying* with time-tested stones and pawing blindly as well as bloodily through the complex entrails of presumably prescient chickens.

Some of the faithful believed in Umbanda, in gods who could be placated, reasoned with, appeased. They had read signs in the lakes and the trees that evil must rise as it had not been known for years; they feared the sacrifices that might be asked in order to live in peace and plentitude.

Others gathered at this end of the beach—those who had seen the same portents and omens, but craved evil as a sustenance for their dark spirits, as an encouragement of their terrible rites—saw that terror was proper, just as it should be. Glistening with perspiration, their skins glowing like a thousand trees emblazoned by mad fireflies, their faces adorned with the fierce masks of wolves or tigers, jackals and hyenas and great horned owls, they danced now until their naked feet were weighted with caked sand and their spirits clogged in mysticism.

First one, then six, *then* fifteen—thirty—*a hundred*—began to twist and writhe, as *loas*—the souls of the undead—crept in to possess them. This was not only permitted, but wildly sought; no exorcists needed apply. The possession would not be permanent but, while it lasted, they would be converted to all-knowing seers who might be asked evil questions that were unaskable under normal conditions.

Faces contorted in a passion of supernatural desire, they looked avidly from one to another, seeking to recognize the voice or expression of one who had already passed to Exú, lord of the underworld. Now, for the privileged few, they were again among the faithful—among and *in* them, chattering prophecies and helping to plan brutal murder or adultery, spewing words of accusatory torment—all of which was mingled with rich praise for Exú, for the dreaded/desired Baron Samedi, he-of-many-names who (they all knew) ruled masculine Hades.

None dared seek or address the ruler of feminine Hades.

Then the sky of glinting coal splintered as if struck a mighty miner's blow. Jagged bolts of lightning shot through the ebon night like so many warrior spears. A giant *despacho* at the edge of the ceaseless waters was struck, set afire, the immense offering aflame now like the angry eye of their god: insistent, unappeased, hungry for the sturdy nourishment of human souls.

Seeing the mighty pyre, once a mere token of respect, the rejected gift of Exú, screams of knowing anguish filled the night air. Bare feet ran on scorched sand. Pathetic appeals for mercy rang out like the bells of a crazed church.

From his perch on a throne safely up the beach, the *houngan* saw with his wise, tired eyes that the omen had taken place. The houngan understood it. He was weary now from all those whom he had ordered to death during his many years of reign, sick at heart that he hadn't placated Baron Samedi despite the hundreds it had been his responsibility to choose for death. Now the old man sighed, alert to duty, imperiously unhesitant, and very slowly raised two frail black arms. And his ruling head turned bleakly to those who waited.

"Exú has spoken," came the intonation in a crackling voice. Some heard its ring of genuine sadness. He gestured with his other arm to the burning and avaricious *despacho*. The command was reluctant, unbucklingly firm: "*Take the girl.*"

When she was drawn out, the houngan made no effort to identify her. She was honored to become the sacrifice. But briefly he saw the rolling, terror-filled eyes, the full lips parted in horror yet determinedly silent, the bare brown melon breasts, the muscled thighs that would now never rise to a warrior's thrust and later increase by one the faithful who were so willing to die.

To die for Quimbanda. And for the never-mentioned Queen.

The old man quickly saw the girl placed at the yawning mouth of the pit, too deep for her to climb out and so deep it was instantly, already a grave—already well on its fiery way to Exú. He saw to it that the oil was poured three feet deep in the waiting and readied pit.

Now the lovely virgin, who happened to be the houngan's granddaughter, refused to scream until the red-orange flames lapped hungrily at her feet and ankles.

Then she did not *stop* her shrieking until the flames had devoured the agonized support of her knees and thighs and dragged her at length into the burning oil.

The faithful chanted, mesmerized.

The old man did not move again until the roasting pig was hung above the identical pyre on a spit. One could not tell whether the sizzling smell of flesh came from the smouldering girl or the pig. Hungry faithful approached the pit to inhale and lick their lips.

"It is a bad night," said the old houngan wearily to his aide, the man who one day would supplant him. "It will be a bad year. A worse, troubled ten decades." He pointed to the rumbling, ominous night sky. "The gods are angry with the world—and something more."

"What, wise houngan?"

Deepset eyes like sad stone turned to the younger man. "They are—*returning.*"

Carolyn rested the pages in her lap and sat for a long

while, staring sightlessly across the still corridor at the painting of the Blessed Virgin. Without doing it consciously or even realizing that she did, Carolyn crossed herself.

It wasn't *like* the ravings or rantings of someone's unconscious mind, she thought, twisting the pages between nervous hands. Nor was it exactly like a story. God help us both, Carolyn thought, it's like something written by a person who was *there*—someone who could transcend the artificial boundaries of time and space to peer first at a famous author and then, on the same horrid night in the half-forgotten past, watch invisibly a voodoo ceremony no white man or woman would ever be permitted to witness.

She spoke aloud, then, her words soft and trembling like frightened butterflies on the quiet air of the hospital corridor: *"It's like—it's real."*

What could possibly be happening to Mary Lord's mind? She had never been an ordinary child, Carolyn knew that. Mary had learned to read—and well—before she ever began school. She wrote her first poem at the age of seven, and it was both mature and oddly grotesque. Even now Carolyn could remember a line from it: "Never mind the teacher, I see her face is Now; I could never reach her, in death she takes her bow." And Mary had laughed when Carolyn asked where she got such an idea and replied, "I couldn't think of anything else that rhymed!"

And then, those long altering years ago, it had seemed a child's understandable reason and Carolyn had gladly accepted it. After all, Mary was obedient to her, a bright and easy-learning child, always on her side when *that man* drank too much or tried to throw his weight around. She could still see Mary's sad, serious eyes awaiting a reaction from her mother and how disappointed the child seemed when the reaction was so mild, so agreeable, so docile.

For a moment Carolyn's old identification with the child was complete again and she felt, for that brief period of time, that *she* lay in that bed, victim of a vicious rape, a terrible beating.

Then she was shaking the mood off and on her feet, pivoting quickly to enter Mary's room before she lost her nerve and fled for the new sanctuary, the ivory-tower existence at U.C.E.V.

Mary was sitting up in bed, apparently trying to compose something new on the notepad resting against her knees, working at making-do with the sun's dying rays as they filtered feebly into her room. She did not look up when Carolyn entered nor in any other way show that she recognized her mother. Her pretty, somehow sad face was in shadows and, as Carolyn remained unnoticed, Mary appeared for a peculiar moment ineffably and inconceivably ageless. It might have been the face of an eager child, of a lonely teenaged girl, of an aging woman counting her beads, even of someone older than Time itself.

But as Carolyn moved silently to the foot of the bed she saw how foolish she was being to imagine such things and paused to smile in sympathy, even empathy, at the almost-woman who was her only child. There was nothing even faintly manic in Mary's expression; only something studied, alert, even—*listening*.

Yes, that was it; that was the fact of the matter: It was as if young Mary was intently listening to some voice only she could possibly hear; it was as if the seventeen-year-old was . . . *taking dictation*.

Dictation from beyond the grave, or from another time, perhaps another universe.

Then, to Carolyn's enormous relief, Mary was stopping her composing, putting down her pencil, and dropping the notepad at her side in the bed. She blinked several times, apparently losing all recollection of her work, and suddenly looked directly up at her mother with a genuine welcoming, quite normal smile.

"Why, hello, Mom!" she exclaimed happily, pert and pleased. "When did you get here?"

CHAPTER V

Carolyn chatted in a bright, maternal way for several minutes and then, as delicately as possible, asked Mary for the first time about the writing she was doing. She asked in such a way that it sounded like a compliment for her writing talent, attempting to treat the situation as if it were the most normal one in the world.

"I wasn't sure anyone else was seeing them," Mary replied, staring at her mother. *"That* explains why Sister Alicia Beth looks at me so funny. She must think I've flipped out entirely."

"I don't suppose she thinks *that*, honey," Carolyn inserted.

"I don't suppose she told you that I've been better this week, that I'm not sleeping nearly as much as before." She watched her mother shake her head regretfully. "Well, it's true. The psychiatrist says I'm much stronger, that I'm doing a super job of facing the facts about my rape."

"I'm so glad," Carolyn said, meaning it. "It'll be wonderful to have you home again."

Mary's expression was shrewd. She'd heard something in her mother's tone of voice that didn't ring true. "You aren't saying it all, are you, Mom? What happened? Did Sister think I'd really gone weird on her or something? Does she want to toss me out on my fanny?"

The modish blond smiled gently. She'd never been able to hide anything from Mary. While she was outwardly a strikingly average person, Mary had skills of insight that Carolyn thought were extraordinary. "All I know is that I'm supposed to see Father Donnehy before I leave here today." Thoughtfully, she crossed her legs and then reached to take the girl's hand. "Honey, I'd like to know how all this unusual writing began? So I have something to tell Father. And—and if you are *aware* of what you're doing?"

Now the shadows were long, lurching gray wolves crawling on their silent bellies through the room. Mary didn't reply immediately; she looked away. When she looked back at Carolyn one side of her face was hidden by shadow. "It's hard to explain to somebody, really, Mom. Usually before I awake completely—or before I fall asleep—I have the impression that someone—or something—has come softly into my room. Has somehow crept right into my flesh, my mind." She paused at her mother's expression of anxiety. "It isn't as scary as that sounds, because I—I feel that the presence means well. So I don't fight it, not everytime. And before long, I'm writing away on my notepad. Tales of the Gay Nineties," she added sardonically.

"Do you know exactly what you're writing?"

Mary's tongue protruded like a small pink creature and licked her lower lip. "I know enough of what's going on that I can sort of *read* what I put down, as I go. In a way, it's like a part of me really *is* doing the writing and not just the—the presence I mentioned. When I'm finished, like today, I have a good general *idea* of what's on the paper."

"Honey, you *do* seem to be vastly improved today. More like your old self. How *do* you feel, physically?"

Mary managed a girl's grin. "I could lick my weight in tigers, or rapists, for that matter. Frankly, I've thought about my improvement—tried to figure out why I suddenly began to get better, after so many months of acting like I had no character whatever—and I came up with a theory. I think it is the presence doing it, Mom. Or else it just makes me feel more like myself. I think in some way it's been good for me, actually, getting these thoughts out and into the open."

"Then you don't think they're genuine?" Carolyn asked anxiously. "That what you're writing really happened?"

The teenager paused, then laughed. Her light-brown, rather long hair danced on her shoulders. She snatched a lock of it and began munching on it. "You kidding, Mom? What do *I* know about 1899? I don't even remember 1965! Or what do I know about any of this heavy stuff I've been putting down?"

Suddenly Carolyn felt relieved, immeasurably lighter. "You're right, of course. It was silly of me even to think these strange tales could be factual. I must be entering menopause early," she said, managing a laugh herself. "But what does your psychiatrist say about all this?"

"Well, *I* wasn't going to say a word about it to him but Sister mentioned it. With her funny little naked eyes practically falling out of her head." Mary peered at a corner of the hospital room ceiling, musing, very much of a normal, bright teenaged girl. "He called it a 'hyp-na-gog-ic condition,' what happens to me when I begin wanting to write stuff down. He said lots of people have queer impressions, even things that are kind of like dreams, only very vivid, when they're ill or particularly neurotic." Her eyes met Carolyn's. "In people who are especially intuitive—y'know, like those psychic weirdos who go around solving crimes—they can even be factual. What they see *is* sometimes the truth."

"They can?" Carolyn asked, surprised.

"Sure. He says they sometimes predict the future with quite a bit of accuracy. But that's with psychic, not ordinary people." Her expression was almost teasing now. "Not nice kids like me."

"Mary, I don't want you to tell Sister about this—this hypnagogic condition. She could misunderstand it totally."

The girl heard the intensity in her mother's voice and appeared startled. "How could she misunderstand? I don't—" She stopped in midsentence, suddenly understanding. "You mean Sister Alicia Beth might think I was literally . . . *possessed* . . . or something?"

Carolyn looked away. "I think she's capable of believing something that archaic, yes." She glanced at the notes Mary had written, then back up to her daughter. "Of course, your manuscripts can't be psychic anyway. You're writing about the *past*—not the future."

"Well, according to the shrink," Mary said, musing, "sometimes things of this kind have an *impact* on the future. When a true psychic has them, I mean. It's like they're remembering something from deep in the past *because* it's *become* important, again, and may influence our future." Suddenly it was all too much to deal with and she gestured. "But go ahead and read aloud, will you? None of that predictive crap applies to me."

Carolyn smiled gladly and began reading: "It's still December 31, 1899. You're really stuck on that date, aren't you? But this time it's a small Russian village. And you say:

" 'He had not been home in Pokrovskoe long and the upwelling of ambivalent excitement that had infused him—an odd mixture of sadness for the complete absence of improvement in the village since his departure and a wild joy for the changes he knew would occur, and which glowed in the man's piercing eyes—was still with him. No one had cared how hard it was to leave here nor imagined the scope of his travels since he was fourteen. No one knew what the wagoner had learned.

" 'Grigori slept in the woods long enough to learn that he must somehow befriend the falling snow or it would smother and slay him, and his unorthodox improvisations had countlessly saved his life. He had learned, too, to speak with wolves and, beneath summer suns so blisteringly hot he went half-mad for awhile, Grigori had also learned to speak with the dead.

" 'He could not tell his friends, here, that he'd slept also in homes that were grotesquely ornate palaces, garish islands in the vast clinging ocean of poverty that was his Russia, performing his charming magic to the laughter of the mistress-queen's immaculate children and, afterward, performed his charming magic in the bed of the mistress." Carolyn hesitated, looked across at Mary. "I marvel at this, you know, darling. It's unlike anything you ever wrote before."

Mary nodded, herself surprised, bolt-upright in bed now and fascinated by words that seemed to have come from her own mind. "Thank you. Go on."

Among the many things Grigori had learned, and learned to accept, was the fact that he was unique among men. This did not make him conceited, nor did he imagine it; it was only acceptance of a fact. His uniqueness was a purposive, blessed curse that meant he would always be alone regardless of where his travels took him. Now, finally, they had led him home.

For sometime he'd worked industriously to renovate this, his old home, and to convert this single, large room just off the entrance way into a church. *His* church, Grigori thought with simple and rather shy pride, staring from his temporary pulpit to the chairs he had arranged. Home—and his church, desired since meeting the flagellistic Khlysty, at Verkhoture: At last.

Because his wife was a simple peasant child—he still remembered clearly the first time her calloused, gentle hand groped tentatively for his lantern jaw, the caress of a fluttering virgin-bird giving all the little she possessed, for the first time—she had not grasped truly, what Grigori strove to do. She neither intuited his inner certainty that he was marked for greatness, as the primal instrument of immense national change which would alter the world as well, nor grasped the soft words he used when hinting modestly at his God-given role. The little wife could not perceive that his travels and his prayers at Sarov had not only aroused wild imaginings and incredible visionary gifts but had taught him the mind control Grigori found essential to his formidable tasks. She would never see that this plain church within their home would be the final rung on the ladder before he was prepared to enter the capitol city, and capture it. Alone.

Now the handful of members of his flock—some kinsmen, some friends, some merely inquisitive about this tall and odd man who'd dared to roam the barren lands of the careless Czar and return here, impenitent—entered Grigori's church. There were enough that the few chairs were taken; some, with good humor, were obliged to take the floor.

The final day of the year, he told them when they were suitably hushed, is always a holy day. An extraordinary day. Time's inexorable march perpetuated itself and seared the frightened heart of man with its painful message. Yet now, at the brink of the new century, time lifted the people of Russia upon its broad, dauntless back and the precipice over which they passed would take them, gliding, to the land of liberty. Grigori paused, images forming in his busy mind. Behind tissue-thin eyelids which often caused him to appear awake even when, rarely enough, he slept, involuntary visions began.

He blinked them back. Just now, they were an imposition. There was much to say to these, his people, of the days of change which surely lay ahead of them. Because he, Grigori, had seen it plain.

He cleared his head, the bristling stubble of his first, still-emerging beard brushing his high ministerial collar. "As my testament to you," he said, the voice not loud yet carrying to every ear in the church, "are there those present who require the ministry of healing?"

Embarrassed silence. Heads wheeling briefly, flickering eyes meeting and lowering. A cough somewhere. Then the woman arose from the back of the room, bringing her baby forward.

His face was an angry red; his sleep unnatural, as if something darkly stealthy moved in his small form. The tall man's eyes saw quickly—the infant was far too thin, a fact true of many Russian infants, but *this* one was dying. His slender hands darted beneath the baby's head, raised it with rough certainty until the child started to cry. Even the cry was pathetic, a wail that appeared destined to reach to Heaven, trailing after until it pulled the child up with it.

Grigori made a clucking sound. The child's eyes snapped open. They were instantly caught; gripped. And the monk whispered his prayer, a litany meant for God and the infant alone. At the rude altar, beside the old leatherbound Bible, beside the candles, then—something . . . *moved.*

Those who were there swore to it, after. The motion grew, spread; it enveloped the twenty-nine-year-old monk and the baby in his arms—a strange, wavering motion that shielded them. Aura-like. And the crowd, like so many trapped leaves at a fence, rustled.

Only one other saw it. "The redness," said the child's mother. "The redness in my son's face—it is *gone.*"

Grigori gave her his rare smile, a benediction. "He sleeps, mother. He is well."

Mother and child sidled from the pulpit, with backward glances, wondering and grateful; afraid.

"Pierre," the monk called then. "The jewels your wife has lost? They lie between the bed and wall, trapped there. Try to be less athletic in your nocturnal zeal, eh, Pierre?"

All laughed, relieved. Except Pierre, who'd been anxious for his loss and had mentioned it to no one. His eyes were saucer-like; he crossed himself fervently.

Yet Grigori's visions would not cease, lurking frenetically beneath the monk's conscious thoughts, in wait. Those nearest him, knowing that he was peculiar, a man unto himself, merely sat, staring patiently as *silence* overtook Grigori. They saw a tall man who appeared taller, his slenderness accentuating his height. One's gaze was instinctively lifted to the extraordinary head of the man.

Grigori parted his hair in the middle above a wide and expressive forehead. Beneath it, two sleepy yet quite unblinking eyes beckoned, issuing beacons of promise. That promise heartened and lightened the load of some, who saw the fellow; the promise terrified and made violent those who would resist his intent, some of whom plotted against Grigori and would again. Already, one man had stabbed the monk directly between the shoulder blades only to see him slowly turn, peer with blazing outrage until the assailant fled and reach behind him to remove the knife. He had then walked steadily to the place in which he was staying, and no one saw blood on the fabric covering his back.

The monk's nose was long, the mouth wide and coolly sensual, his moustache a curling line of demarcation between the two which somehow seemed to seal the lips until they were well-prepared for speech, for prophecy or portent. Or even passion.

Now in his church, massively troubled by visions he could not disperse, Grigori Rasputin gasped in great gulps of air and then plunged forward suddenly from the waist. Before a soul could move to assist him, though, he was again straight and, in his intent, straight forward gaze, there was a look none of his friends or his family had seen before.

A few said, later, it had been an expression of fear.

Then, somehow revivified, he was himself again and telling of it to the waiters: "My people, I have seen clearly the purposes and motives of Hell." The eyes blazed. "I have seen tonight and tomorrow and yet the day beyond tomorrow. And for us, dear comrades, there remains much hope. Just as this infant was healed, another child will be saved by God, through my touch. His restored well-being will enable me—within scant years—to change the course of all your lives." He paused.

"For me, this anniversary holds specific meaning. On one such eve of the new year I shall be attacked by the *ochrana* and by a Prince, poisoned and shot, beaten and drowned." Rasputin smiled with irony at the shock on their faces. "Yes: *That* day, it will be enough to kill me. But more importantly, I have also seen that elsewhere in this chaotic world—*this* eve of a new year, a new century—another child who seems unimportant will sense in his vicious temperament and the tormenting seeds of his ancestry a calling for the propitiation and propagation of evil. Mark me: Generations of Hell proceed from that boy's murder of his own father this night."

At that moment, *other* motions swirled around Rasputin, movement that could not be seen with the naked eye but which was indisputably there, threateningly. Above it, the monk's somber and hypnotic gaze scorched and implanted the memory cells of all who heard him: "In a new century to be torn with revolution and war, the painful deaths of millions dying for a myriad of half-understood causes, the greatest evil of all—like the contrasting, simple birth of the Christ-child—will go unnoticed. For awhile."

"What *is* it you see, then, brother?" called one of the aging women from her seat, leaning forward with unhealthy perspiration on her sunken, toothless cheeks. *"Tell* us what it is?"

And Rasputin smiled benignly on her, then included them all in his brilliant, sweeping gaze. "My friends, only those the age of the infant I healed shall have the singular misfortune to live and thus see the return to our earth of Hell's most potent and destructive souls. First, a woman—unlike the Garden of Eden—and, at the last—the *very* last—something . . . *masculine.* The souls of those who never were but who have always been, who did not die because they did not live. The souls who have heretofore worked through the weak and the feeble minds of the living but who, at last, will find actual life themselves. Utter, evil annihilation comes to the world in the final quarter of this, the new century.

"Let us," Rasputin bowed his head, "pray for those who come after us."

"I wish to speak with you in my office, Dr. Lord," said Father Donnehy, who had stood quietly at the door—unseen—while Carolyn read it all, aloud. *"Now,* if you don't mind."

She looked up in surprise in time to see that he had crossed himself. His middle-aged face, customarily ruddy and glowing with health, was pale and stern. He did not look at Mary. "I think Mary is well enough to hear what we have to say," she said with more temerity and courage than she felt.

"I'd rather discuss it with you in privacy." Now he flicked a brief, unaffectionate smile at the teen-aged girl. "Afterward, perhaps, you will be able to tell her what we have decided."

Carolyn paused. Then, "Yes, Father," she said, quietly, and followed him out the door and down the corridor.

Neither spoke until they were safely esconced in his own quarters. He went busily behind his desk, then opened a cigarette box and pushed it toward Carolyn. Wordless, she shook her head and took the chair opposite him.

She was struck by the austerity of the office and by the fact that what did serve as decoration seemed businesslike, associated neither with Father Donnehy's faith nor his administrative position at the hospital. It might have been the office of a junior executive who didn't think he'd be buzzing around the corporate body for any length of time. A crucifix, behind his head, was the only sign of his faith. The chair in which she sat, her hands told her, was not even a genuine leather chair.

He lit a cigarette and leaned across the desk to her, a man with deceptively expressionless eyes beneath heavy brows. The only thing remarkable about his appearance was his rather large nose from which several bristling rows of tiny hairs peered in hirsute militancy. "I am very concerned about your daughter, Dr. Lord," he said at once. *"Very* concerned."

"I think she's coming along very nicely now, Father," Carolyn said quietly. "She seems better today than she has in ages."

"Physically, perhaps." The priest stayed where he was, bent across his desk. "Do you know that she is the only one I have ever known, personally, for whom I was tempted to perform the rites of exorcism?"

Since Carolyn was not surprised she was unimpressed when, having made his point, Father Donnehy leaned back into his chair to puff thoughtfully on his cigarette. "Unless exorcism serves to withdraw from a woman's brain the memory of the brutal things done to her by mortal man, Father, I cannot understand why you would consider such an archaic rite."

His lips worked, deciding between a frown and a derisive smile. " 'Archaic,' is it? And how many churchly rites do you see in that light, madam?"

She kept the words to herself. "I believe it's my daughter's faith in question, Father Donnehy," she said steadily, hiding her trembling hand at her side. "Not mine."

"Tell me, Dr. Lord." He had decided on giving her a faintly insulting smile. "Do you like history, biography—that kind of thing?" He didn't wait long enough for her to reply. "Let me be more specific. Has your daughter been exposed to the details in such lives as those of Sir Arthur Conan Doyle or the monstrous Aleister Crowley?"

"I have a complete edition of the Sherlock Holmes stories in the family library," she replied. "Whether Mary read them or not, I really cannot say."

"Would it interest you to know that her little, ah, 'creation' is entirely accurate? The place where Sir Arthur lived, the facts concerning Crowley's desire to begin his own accursed society bearing the name of an existing organization—the facts that Sir Arthur *was* home, that New Year's Eve, and that Crowley *was* in residence in Scotland?"

"It interests me, of course," Carolyn replied, flushing. "The source of my daughter's writing is unknown to both of us. I can't say that I'm exactly surprised that she has the facts right."

Donnehy's heavy brows lifted in astonishment. "You aren't *surprised* that a young woman who has been unconscious much of the time during her stay with us has somehow succeeded in doing *historical research* at the same time?"

"I only meant that, given the fact that these manuscripts *exist*, and that Mary is a practical girl and one who has done well in school, I would expect her to be factual when dealing with a realistic situation." She lifted her chin boldly. "I believe that knowing the difference between what is real and what is fictitious or fantastic *is* a definition of sanity?"

"I wonder if that's all you meant, Dr. Lord," the priest said shortly. "What kind of childhood did Mary have, before her alleged rape?

"Alleged!" Carolyn exploded. "How dare you!"

He wriggled his fingers. "Let it pass, let it pass. It happens that I know a little something about the history of Gregori Rasputin and his place in Russian history. It's been a fascination of mine, avocationally." Suddenly he reached out, smashing his cigarette in the ceramic ashtray, his eyes rising to challenge her. "That is *precisely* what happened to him—the wandering, the evil magic, that bizarre parody of a church, even the reference to how now he would save another child and change the course of history! Even the dating seems accurate! And I rather doubt, my dear Dr. Lord, that Mary Lord is an expert on the Russian revolution at the age of seventeen! Am I correct?"

With as much dignity as she could muster, Carolyn dragged herself to her feet. Her face felt hot; she found her hands were shaking badly and her knees did not want to support her. "I don't think I'm obliged to listen to these innuendos, Father—to accusations involving my daughter's soul, if indeed she happens to have one. She came to Bleeding Heart Hospital in desperate need of medical and psychiatric assistance, and it would seem that your staff has provided it adequately. I'll always be grateful for that, since I do believe she is almost herself again. But if you are personally too practical or pragmatic, Father Donnehy—too scientific in your method and approach to the *outré* inexplicable things of life—to remember how the Bible itself speaks of God moving in mysterious ways—"

"A person linked to women's liberation *daring* to cite Scripture to *me* is more than *I* am obliged to hear, madam!" the priest interrupted, half out of his chair, eyes bulging. "I am telling you plainly that your daughter may very well be *possessed* by Satanic forces, that at the very least she is obviously guilty of perpetrating some kind of disgusting *fraud,* that—"

"That's right!" Carolyn exclaimed with rich sarcasm, slamming both her purse and her fist on his desk in anger. "When all else fails, *shout* and *rant* at me! Try to *bully* me into submission! Those are the customs of your precious method, the *real* ancient possessions we need to exorcise—it's the way every man, whether he hides behind a collar or not, attempts to *possess* all of womankind and subjugate it to his will! Just because my poor daughter can't be *controlled,* using the methods you use to shove every other female patient into line, you—"

Both Carolyn and Father Donnehy became simultaneously aware they they weren't alone, that a third person was staring at them, whether with wonder for what she had to say or at this overt conflict between cleric and laity.

Sister Alicia Beth stood in the doorway. When she realized that she had their attention, she pointed helplessly behind her.

"It's Mary," she said in a quick gasp. "She's done it again, that eerie writing of hers. But *this* time she was conscious when she wrote it!" Her browless eyes shifted from face to face. "And—it's about a time *other* than 1899!"

CHAPTER VI

"Tell me, child," Father Donnehy began speedily, his voice warm syrup as he hastily beat Carolyn to the hospital room and took the chair beside Mary's bed. "What was it *like?* I very much want to help you but I must know if you felt that . . . *something* . . . came into you, possessed you?"

Mary was startled by the priest's sudden entry but had the presence of mind to hide her latest writing, dropped by the nun in her haste to report to the priest, on her other side. As she held his gaze she slipped the top of her bedsheet down over it. "It isn't like *that*, Father," she replied in all seriousness. "Not something *awful*, like that dreadful movie about the little girl and the priest." Her face brightened. "And this time I was conscious, entirely, while it happened. I sort of felt that part of it was my own writing." Despite seeming wan, she also looked rather pleased with herself. "And it's pretty good stuff! Exciting!"

Father Donnehy wagged his hands, indicating that the literary merit of her manuscript did not enter into this. "No, no," he said, glancing up as Carolyn first, then Sister Alicia Beth, filed breathlessly into the room. "It is not for you to judge the identity of the soul, or the demon, attempting to claim you."

Outraged, Carolyn rushed across the floor. "Don't tell him another word about it," she said hastily, plumping down on the bed next to her daughter and between Mary and the priest. "He'll hang you with your own words, baby."

For the first time, it seemed, Mary Lord was aware of the seriousness of what was happening to her. Parental, priestly and sisterly authority figures stared at her earnestly yet with varying expressions on their universally-older faces. "I'm so *t-tired* now," she said, scarcely above a whisper. "It sort of *drains* me to do this, at first. It's only l-later that I feel better."

Father saw the warning in Dr. Lord's eyes and took a deep breath, calming himself. "Very well, let's try a different approach. Everyone here wishes only to help you, child. What is the *purpose* of such peculiar literary endeavor? Do you assert that it is genuine, that it seeks to tell the truth?"

Before Carolyn could warn her, Mary was nodding and shifting her hips restlessly in the bed, the picture of sincerity. "So far as I can tell, Father, it's precisely what happened. In every report."

"A revelation," Sister Alicia Beth murmured, crossing herself. "A revelation, but one of dark evil."

"That," the priest said laconically, nodding and cocking a brow at Carolyn Lord, "would appear to be at the crux of our problem. If Mary was merely conjuring up harmless tales about people in the church—or even envisioning the Crucifixion, fantasizing it with a proper degree of reverence—this might be a different matter."

"Father, what it is, I think," Carolyn said softly, trying now to reason with the man, "is that Mary didn't rattle on orally in an irrational manner. You're used to sick people who see things that don't hold up logically, and people who never put it on paper. Please try to understand that Mary has *always* wanted to be a writer. It's as natural to her to *write down* what she imagines as it is for other sick folks to *say* it."

"That's a little pat and sophistic for my tastes, Dr. Lord." The priest rubbed a heavy brow with his little finger and momentarily peered out the window at the night taking shape there. There was dampness in the air, as if it might rain. His bad shoulder had begun to throb warningly. Again he sighed. "This girl's manuscripts all detail terrible, even monstrous things and, even worse, appear to portend still *more* dreadful happenings." He turned again to Mary and, despite himself, his tone was sharp. If this girl was truly possessed, he wanted her out of here, fast. He enjoyed a moderate position in the Church and intended to keep it that way. "Do you feel that present lives are involved, somehow, in what you believe happened in the past? Kindly tell me if you are, ah, a prophet as well?"

"Mary!" Carolyn cried warningly, but Mary ignored her, a paler version of her mother in spirit and candor. *"Yes!* I'd think it was entirely obvious! Don't *any* of you people understand that these—these messages are *warnings?* Warnings that a terrible, legendary creature from Hell named Hecate is *returning to existence soon?"*

Father Donnehy's eyes met Sister Alicia Beth's, meaningfully. "I think that's quite sufficient," he remarked, arising stiffly. "It may be best for Sister to see to it that Mary's release forms are brought up to date."

"At least, Father, give her a chance with the new manuscript she wrote," Carolyn asked, reaching out her hand to Mary. The girl looked doubtful, but placed the notepad in her mother's outstretched palm without a word. "Perhaps she's written something . . . *good,* good and decent, something that might—*benefit* humankind."

Father Donnehy looked doubtfully down at the thin teen-aged girl, considering. For a moment it seemed she would speak. When she didn't, he took the notepad offered him by Carolyn Lord and read aloud . . .

December 7, 1947. Southern England.

The pseudo-intellectuals' boarding house wasn't palatial—he'd lived in far more sumptuous quarters, visited and toyed with the forever-famous—but it was adequate, barely, for his present needs. When a man finds himself in his seventies he wants either more than he ever craved before or, as is thought to be common, far less.

For once this uncommon man was in the majority.

Part of it, too, was a realization that there was no way he could *have* more, unless it was just more of the publicity he adored and which, of late, had soured or slipped away. That old fuddy-duddy of a judge had made his lawsuit a farce, calling his magic blasphemous and abominable. While he knew that it was, he was troubled by the way the press made his failing suit sound like his last huzzah, implying that he wouldn't be hot copy ever again.

Today was the sixth anniversary of the bombing of Pearl Harbor, a date that continued to be special to many people in the civilized world. But for the aging Beast, the date was primarily notable for the moon transiting his own Sun Sign: Libra. Even cosmic life tended, with Aleister, to be reduced to a matter of personal importance.

Other than that, it was the Beast's practice that, when the final month of a year came around, he would take a survey of his past and cast horoscopes for the future.

What the old sorcerer hadn't realized when he started his astrological calculations today was that he would be shocked. Twice. Rarely had he been shocked by any idea conceived by man, god, or demon. His equability, his zodiacal sense of balance, enabled him to stand a bit apart from it all, adequately detached (even from the worst horrors imaginable), and aloof.

He was obliged to dig back into his ephemerides, checking and rechecking planetary positions, when the first shock occurred. Not fully believing, he re-examined his own progressions to determine that what he saw was, in truth, accurate. The work was no longer easy for the Beast. His aging hands were atwitch with ague, his memory beginning to slip.

But he worked hard and after he was satisfied that the first horoscope was precise, his evaluation true, he sank back into a worn chair with a heavy sigh and let his knotted fingers trickle like sand through the goat-like, snowy-scrub of a beard. Perhaps, he thought, the others were right when they told him he should spend more of his time in astrology. Perhaps he should have done it.

Because if he had, it wouldn't come as quite such a shock to learn that he would die this month.

Damnable Decembers! They'd always been monumentally important to him, one way or the other. He reflected on some, at times; now a chuckle lightened the burden of his shadowed memories. By Baal, he'd certainly shocked hell out of them during his career! They'd *had* to take notice of him, they'd been forced to confess that he was "the wickedest man in the world." Well, that was fine; fine. Better to have a strong impact than vegetate the way—

—The way he was now. The Beast sighed. Growing old was a worse penalty than dying, he mused. The horn pipe trembled in his grasp as he lit the latakia tobacco. Major effort coming up, will power required again, to resist another injection of heroin. Yes; he would make himself wait another hour, at least. He gave up on lighting the pipe but chuckled as he looked at the future world. Poor fools didn't even realize narcotics were the next big devil's toy, that the Beast himself was the brave forerunner of *all* man's evil, that he'd been the one who would try anything. Anything at all.

Still, he sighed, the fact was that heroin, combined with his whisky input, would surely be what killed him. Along with anhelonium, of course.

Shaking off an uncharacteristic burst of regret, the Beast began working on his second series of astrological charts. And then it occurred to the aging shaman that these predictions showed the way to one final, outrageous nose-thumb at the despised world—a final chance to get back at the dullards and dimwits who had jeered at him, stymied his finer advances. True; it was likely no one would know what he planned now to do, but that was all right. *He* would know. And he'd take that knowledge with him too when he left this place, laughing merrily all the way down. . . .

The horoscope for 1948, the new year, hadn't looked very promising. Little chance for genuine mischief there.

But when the Beast began progressing the charts planet by planet, ascendant by ascendant, midheaven by midheaven—finally stopping in the early sixties—he saw what gloriously *terrifying* possibilities existed. For the world; for *his* use.

What a shame he wouldn't be present to witness the fine chaos!

The scheduled rebirth could well be that which he had clearly envisioned almost half a century ago. But now he saw his slight error: The rebirth of Hades' hideous queen wasn't inevitable but stood as a sort of cosmic landmine, a viable imminent explosion of evil that awaited . . . a trigger. These marvelously hellish possibilities merely required the cooperation of someone who *wanted* it to occur, who *desired* the factual reappearance of Hecate herself in her awesome full flower.

And who in the world—this peace-questing chunk of stodgy, unimaginative placidity—would want the goddess of the inferno to return? The Beast smiled. Surely no one more than Aleister himself!

Now he knew that he could wait for his Scotch, even his heroin. The pervasive itch of old excitement he knew so well, well enough it had required constantly more diabolical stimuli to incite it, burned along his throbbing veins, tremoring at his pink and balding scalp.

First he would have to know the *exact date*, for verification. Astrology made mighty demands of precision, but the Beast was more at home with other methods. If *these* validated his findings, he could take steps immediately!

Wintry winds cackled like so many pale and friendly witches beyond the windows of his room as the Beast consulted two, then three ivory bone molds he'd procured years ago. They came from Egypt and had been employed most recently some two thousand years before Christ. Called *astragals,* they rolled clatteringly within the chalked circle he drew, like joking falseteeth. And at once they spoke to the Beast in affirmative voices.

Satisfied, he leaned back on his heels just outside the circle and considered summoning a devil for first-hand cross-examination. Reluctantly, he gave it up. The system itself was unreliable and he knew that he was so old he might be tricked. Besides, he'd live soon enough among those damnable horrors!

At length the old man dragged out his sandbox and puffed a little with his exertion. Suddenly he giggled, the pitch high and ridiculous. His countless foes would be delighted to see his crooked body crouching in a child's box of ordinary sand! "The bastard's gone round the bend," they'd cheer; "he's senile, completely mad at last!" Well, damn their eyes, he'd *always* been mad but he would never be senile, he could promise them that!

Performing as the *querant,* the mage let his wrist hang limp. The pencil in his liver-splotched hand finally began dipping, of its own accord, into the sand at his toes. The Beast asked his questions deliberately, knowing that a *"y"* scratched there meant YES, an *"n"* indicated a negative reply. Other marks stood for other things—some sacreligious, some obscene—and some were of a character he'd never revealed to anybody. Other shapes took form as the long-dead Navajo spirits grudgingly responded to the old man's queries.

And once more, Aleister's work was established. Hecate *would* become available.

The Beast then considered the Ouija board, resting it beside his chess game. Quickly, he decided against it. It worked best when *two* people placed their hands on the triangular *planchette.* Besides, the spirits he'd summoned so often—that doctor from Delhi, the Chinese prophet, even the silly fool who persisted that he was Uranian—were getting crotchety, were getting along, as he was. Twice the Chinaman had responded like a poltergeist, smashing everything in the room by telekinetic means.

Of course, the sorcerer thought, *pyromancy* would be lovely. He'd often found the obscure method of fire-reading efficacious. Regrettably, they'd throw him out of this boarding house if he set even a small fire. Briefly the Beast pictured his landlord in his mind's eye and muttered a particularly vile warlock's incantation.

Finally he arose, knees snapping like dry twigs, and went into the bathroom. Perching like a wasted white gull on the edge of the tub, he half filled it with water and left it running slightly. To create tiny waves. *Hydromancy* required exacting interpretation, even for the Beast. But it had occurred to him that since the study of moving water had been born in ancient Greece, it was appropriate to consult its omens on behalf of a Greek monster.

The Greek monster.

Soon he was assured that he would definitely die this month, even in a matter of days, and also that he was correct about Hecate's scheduled rebirth. By now he was so high on enthusiasm that he scarcely paid attention to the details of his own demise. . . .

Then it was on to *ceromancy,* a nearly forgotten art involving the droppings from a wax candle. He moved on to playing cards in a veritable library of tests climaxed, of course, by the Tarot itself. And finally he analyzed tealeaves.

Using a plain cup, the Beast held it in his left hand with the handle pointing south and swirled the dregs seven times, clockwise. Everything here depended upon the analysis, but Aleister had acquired his skills from an adoring gypsy woman whom he had once seduced and he dearly adored seeing the dregs take shape in the cup: There! the snake, symbol of temptation and evil, appearing repeatedly!

Yes, all his magic proved him correct. The Hades of Hecate was returning to the planet Earth.

It remained for him to provide the trigger, the release, that would enable her cruel and vicious spirit to pass the vale...

It took the old man several difficult trips to bring the correct books into his bathroom, where the shamanistic mystery must unfold. A single trip into the backyard proved sufficient. He was there some time, however, scraping aside patches of caked, gray slush to dig furtively in the earth. And then there was the visit to his actor-landlord's wife, a tawdry crone whom the Beast cheerfully detested and who sent his memory back to delicious torments of torture he might have invented for her. But he bowed, and smiled, and finally acquired the simple herbs and spices required for his task.

And at last, muttering imprecations in several languages, he returned to his quarters, refusing to shake the snow off his shoes but tramping peevishly into the bathroom.

Before the mirror the sorcerer caught a glimpse of himself off guard, as one sometimes will, not as we pose at our best for ourselves. He was stricken by the thin yet grim, tight-lipped, immensely lined face with the small nose looking back at him. His sometimes blithe, occasionally witty, frequently darkly sensuous face was no more. Even the intense eyes were dulled. Why, Aleister mused, someone had appended to his large ears—doubtless while he slept—the weary, drug-ridden face of a burnt-out and used-up old man. No one, male or female, could want him now.

Shoving back the self-pity, he began sketching a pentagram in red chalk on the wooden floor beneath the cracked bathroom mirror. On the chipped tile of the walls the Beast rubbed certain familiar herbs, periodically glancing at his evil books, until the room reeked. He labored energetically, perspiration flowing freely, and finally removed all his clothes. Getting naked, he'd always said, was one of life's little pleasures. Later, he felt, he'd do his Yoga to combat the debauches of his many years.

What was being done here was akin to *catoptromancy*, the art of mirror divination. Greeks, Romans, Egyptians, all used it when Time was fresh, peering into ornate silver and bronze mirrors to see images of the future. After glass mirrors were introduced in the Thirteenth Century, the Ventians made the art a near-science. But it had been beaten back by rationalism and by the Church; Aleister sighed as he realized that he might be the last man alive to know the secrets of this art.

Frowning, the aging shaman filled the basin with hot water and soon began dipping—*things*—into it. Tiny noises gurgled up; the water's color altered. They were terrible things, actually, some of them herbal, some merely dead; some had never had a name, and others had names sane men never used.

Muttering the proper baleful words, the Beast then threw onto the mirror small handfuls of the grotesque liquid from the basin. It stung his hands to do it, and it was scarcely translucent enough to see into it—even to recognize his own lip-moving image. The stuff stank; it twisted even the Beast's practiced nose. He tried to breathe shallowly as he worked.

And behind the old man, shadows *crept* from the closed bathroom door. At a glance, an eavesdropper would not have been astonished—until he saw that there was nothing within the walls of this quiet deathroom to *create* such curling, stealthy shadows. Especially the kind that now moved *toward* the Beast, breathing. Now they writhed faintly with a kind of vivid lower life, almost as if a hundred invisible, mad children were throwing tiny fists this way, and that, to tease or to provoke.

Meanwhile, the Beast completed his spell and waited as patiently as he could, his attention absorbed by what was occurring in his cracked mirror. Suddenly it clouded fully, lavendar and purple smoke drifting like silent mists of whorling time; behind it, too, swirls of sinuous sin began parting, slowly.

Slowly.

And then the Beast smiled above his mandarin beard.

Looking back at him was not his own face but that of an ineffably beautiful woman, young and graceful, projecting desire, her black hair draped long against her unclad, silken shoulders. Ah! the Beast sighed. Her breasts were full, high and bare, outthrust to him. The woman's sweet ambience drew the old man near the mirror, pulled his face close for a kiss that he suddenly yearned for as none of the millions he had taken in his seventy years. He shut his eyes romantically, extending his lower jaw, which reached for the lovely mirror— found the target, the splendid female goal—kissed. . . .

And shadow arms grasped him firmly from behind, dusky scraps of somethingful nothingness reaching to envelope him and hug him in deadly, suffocating, elsewhere-sexuality.

Aleister opened his eyes, bulgingly, startled by *the first sharp pain in his chest.*

He screamed.

For the woman was there, reflected in the mirror, dark hair still draped to still-bare shoulders.

But the breasts were ghastly, emptied bags like penisless testicles, limp yellow sacks suspended by strands of rotting flesh, the nipples two black holes into which a man might see no-time or all-time. Its body stench was overpowering, terrific; one's nostrils clogged with twitching maggots, made breathing itself objectionable. Above the bosom was a scrawny ropelike neck; above that, the face of a woman so old that she could not live and was therefore dead. Part of the forehead and nose were sliced off by careless Time, revealing bone of obscenely white clarity. Grainy, corrugated lips were edged by jagged fangs and split to one side, down the jaw, from putrefaction.

And yet: the eyes lived, twinkling hotly like galaxyswallowing lost stars beckoning the old Beast's magnetic eyes till they were caught, trapped, mesmerized by Sin far older than anything he'd managed to contemplate—and vastly worse.

The face of Hecate, he knew, her *true* features. The embrace was so frigid his teeth chattered. The pain in the center of his sunken chest was agonizing; unbearable.

But then, at once, the embrace was removed; the image had vanished. He stared, instead, at the face of a hurting, silly, sick, old human being who had dared to interfere with evil that was immortal—a foolish man who realized his own humanity too late.

Leaning against the wash basin, gasping for air, he realized abruptly what he had personally done *to* humanity, knew that he had willed that horrible creature to be reborn—*released* Hecate upon his fellow man.

After sometime the aging man acquired the energy to totter back to his sitting room. There, he sat in the one comfortable chair brought with him to this, his last house. Soon, he hoped, he would find the strength to locate his Scotch whisky. And he hoped he could force himself to flush the heroin and anahelonium down his toilet. He hoped he would be able simply to arise and return to the bathroom again, and to other rooms, to places beyond this boarding house.

He hoped he would not die, not that day, with the face of the goddess of Hell, inferno's queen, still etched clearly in his mind. And he hoped, finally, if he recovered enough to search his rooms, he might still find, somewhere among his books, a copy of the Holy Bible.

CHAPTER VII

There was a sickly, almost frightening silence in the hospital room when the priest finished reading. He had stumbled many times, almost whispering some of the words in Mary's report. For a moment, the four people in the room were frozen in silence. Then, very slowly, the priest's pontifical arm lowered to his side. After another moment, it raised; he tossed the manuscript unceremoniously in Carolyn's lap.

The mother looked anxiously up at the rather burly man, seeing how red his face was but trying anyway: "At l-least she says the Beast was l-looking for his Bible, at the last. Father, it can be regarded as a—a dying declaration for Christ. Almost," she added limply.

Father Donnehy turned to peer out the window. Night had come, quietly. It was of that particular pregnant-thick blackness that made one feel it would last forever. The arthritic ache in his shoulder was worse; there was a pronounced hint of dampness now. Quietly, he reached up to massage his shoulder and arm. "Mary does not belong here, at least, not any longer," he said without turning. In his tired voice Carolyn heard, for the first time, a hint of distant Irish brogue. "I am not the man for this task. I am afraid that she is either a fraud, or a blasphemer; or that some other *power* has taken control of her."

"Even if you should be *right*, Father, where *else* would I take my Catholic daughter but to a priest?"

He ignored her. "This is a hospital for people who

90

primarily have physical ailments. Broken arms or legs; gall bladders which need to come out. *Babies* are delivered here, Dr. Lord—innocent, infantile children. We have a psychiatrist on staff, as you know. But your daughter was allowed to come here mainly because of your great-grandfather and how much intellectual Americans still respect his work, his memory. How *shocked* he would be to see this distant grandchild producing bizarre, otherworldly memoirs and her mother condoning it!"

"It's also true," Carolyn said determinedly, "that Professor Lord tithed with admirable generosity, I believe."

The priest took a deep breath. "I think a large part of our debt to him has been repaid by allowing this . . . child . . . in our Catholic hospital."

"I'll get dressed," Mary said softly, soberly, sliding her legs over the edge of the bed. She tugged down her gown and averted her gaze but her lips caught in a fierce grimace of offended pride. "I'll be out of here before you know it."

"I'll begin processing the release forms immediately," Sister Alicia Beth said to the priest, her eyes darting at the recuperating Mary before she turned to rush from the room.

"Did you know, Father, that the primary fear held by my great-grandfather during the last years of his life," Carolyn said tightly, seeking to retain her self-control, "was that—according to certain mythological rumors—Hecate, the Queen of Hell, planned to return to earth late in this century? Can't you *see* that Mary's source, whoever or whatever it is, means to warn us—to help us *protect* ourselves?"

The cleric did not look back from the window. His stubby fingers continued to knead his shoulder as he spoke. "I fear that a large number of good men are given to wildly neurotic notions and imaginings as advanced age catches up with them." He shrugged. "We priests take that into account, try to make allowances and not blame them for their human faults."

Now Carolyn saw it was indeed useless. She went into the small bathroom to help Mary dress and get ready to leave. The girl had tears in her eyes and seemed a trifle unsteady on her feet, but her color remained good and she did not appear to be on the verge of collapsing. Carolyn zipped up the back of her dress, kissed her at the neck and hurried back out to the bedroom.

Hands on hips, she addressed Father Donnehy's immobile, broad back.

"It seems to me, Father, that the Church was founded for other reasons than to recite litany, conduct rituals or help people with the problems *others*—laymen—might help them with. Increasingly, I'm afraid, all churches are more interested in doling out free soup, pitching in after a fire, fighting for a priest's right to marry or giving a lot of social advice to people whose situations the ministry could not properly understand." She hesitated, furious. "Why don't we start a nice new church, Father?" The muscles in his neck tightened. "We can call it the Church of the Latter Day Roosevelt, or 'COLDR.' Think about it, please. *You* could earn a decent deaconship in that church in no time."

But strangely, after Mary was unpacking her things in her own bedroom at home, Carolyn was glad and relieved to have her daughter home. Perhaps, like Carolyn herself, Mary needed to come to terms with her problems and force herself to begin functioning well again.

She found that she was eager to describe her new course—now she'd decided to call it "Reemergence of the Goddess"—to Mary. Immediately, the teenager was enthusiastic. "If it'll make pompous asses like Father Donnehy stop treating us like we were third-rate morons," Mary declared, "I'm all for it."

"I've been thinking. . . ." Carolyn began, the second day Mary was home.

"About what?"

"About the possibility of your enrolling at U.C.E.V.,

perhaps even taking the course, along with other young women who want to learn some self-respect. You're young, but you had enough credits to graduate from high school. I'm pretty sure I could get you in."

At first Mary was excited by the idea. Then she shook her head uncertainly. "It sounds great, Mom, but I don't really know if I'm up to it."

"There'd be only young women in my course," Carolyn said pointedly.

"Well, let me think about it," Mary said, meaning it. "Okay?"

As the next couple of weeks passed, Mary seemed to get considerably better. She sunbathed on the balcony just outside the French doors of the apartment, once even went to a nearby beach. Unlike most states, California has very little real winter, and the warm sun began to bake out of her some of the stultifying effects of hospital life. At no time did she fade into silence, as she'd done so many frightening times before entering Bleeding Heart, and she was writing nothing more bizarre than a short story about two girls who liked the same boy.

From Carolyn's standpoint, increasingly, it began to seem a blessing that Mary had returned. Mary helped with the cooking, made the beds. But more than that, with this healthy version of her own flesh-and-blood, Carolyn found she was no longer reminded of the way she herself had been emotionally and psychologically raped by her ex-husband. In addition, Carolyn soon enjoyed bouncing ideas for the "Goddess" course off Mary, who proved to be a perceptive listener with ideas of her own.

For one thing, conversations with Mary began to give Carolyn a little more balance in her outlook on men. Mary had dated, before the rape, and truly liked boys. She helped her mother to see that the male sex was as tradition-dominated in its attitudes as the female sex. "If a guy's still a virgin by the time he's nineteen," Mary said, "it's a worse stigma than pimples or—or having no car. He'll be obliged to lie to his friends about girls he takes out. Why, Mom, they may have even *less* freedom to approach matters realistically—in a liberated way—than we do."

But two weeks before the new semester was to begin, there was fresh trouble.

Elna and Fred Clinefort, Carolyn's closest friends in El Vista, had been over for dinner on Wednesday night. Both of them hugged Mary, by way of greeting. They dined on clams and a good, inexpensive white wine, and Carolyn observed how Fred, the psychiatrist, addressed more and more questions to Mary. For awhile, she was glad; it was only Fred's way of welcoming the girl, she thought—of saying that he liked her. But the questions grew more personal and she saw how Mary began shifting uneasily in her chair when Fred asked her if she harbored a secret urge for revenge on the man who raped her.

And then Fred was alone with Carolyn in the little kitchenette of her apartment—she'd gone for cheese and been startled to find the psychiatrist right behind her—while Mary and Elna chatted in the front room. And the lanky Fred, his affable sheepdog's face earnest and concerned, was leaning close to her in a manner that she thought, at first, indicated a pass.

"I don't think she's out of the woods," Fred said under his breath. "And don't ask me whom I mean; Mary, of course."

"Well, *I* think she is," Carolyn replied firmly, reaching past Fred into a drawer for a knife. "She's behaving beautifully and I've had no trouble with her at all."

"In my opinion, that loonybin she was in has helped her bury most of her worst memories of the experience," he said, shifting to continue facing her. "Not clear them away, put them in a suitable category labelled 'Past Things I Can't Do Anything About.' And what's more, I think you know it."

Carolyn hadn't known it, hadn't believed it then, not for a moment.

But after they had gone, and Mary preceded her into the bathroom to get ready for bed, she heard odd sounds that she couldn't identify for a moment. She paused in the little hallway outside the bathroom, listening until she could.

Writing. It was the sound of a pencil being scratched across paper. *Mary was in the bathroom, writing.*

For a long moment, Carolyn stood with her hand on the doorknob, trying to decide whether to go in or not, whether to knock before she entered. Privacy was important for a girl of seventeen. For all she knew, Mary was writing some silly love letter to a boy she'd just met.

Carolyn shook her head, turned the knob and pushed the door open.

But as the door began to squeak open, she heard from within *furtive* sounds. Every mother knows them, has heard them, remembers them from when her children were small. Sounds of those made by someone who is trying to cover up—something.

"Hi," said Mary, cheerfully, raising a damp hand.

Carolyn paused just inside the door. Mary always liked her water as hot as she could stand it and the room was heavy with damp heat. Watergate, she thought inanely. The waterline was up to her daughter's rather compact young breasts and they seemed to float independently along the surface. The body beneath them appeared pink, disconnected or distorted by the gently stirring liquid, except for the dark, aggressive pubic patch between the girl's rounded legs.

Abashed, Carolyn's gaze withdrew.

It fell upon the white towel lying conveniently on the floor beside the tub.

She didn't remember any of the towels in the apartment being new enough to seem luxurious, thick and fat, the way this one looked. Without a word, the mother stooped to pick up the towel and look beneath it, hotly conscious of Mary's eyes on her a few feet away.

In recently purchased stationery with the initials "M.L.," something Mary had wanted wildly, perhaps to reestablish her identity with herself, was the girl's familiar scrawl. A ballpoint pen also lay on the floor by the bathtub.

And at the top of the damply thumbprinted page it read: *"Summer, 1968. The midwestern United States."*

"What's this?" she asked, as casually and lightly as possible.

"I think you know what it is," Mary answered, just as casually. It didn't even sound rude. Suddenly she bobbed fully, nakedly, into view as she stood and Carolyn retreated to the washbasin.

It was odd, looking at this all-at-once stranger, totally nude and built—as she was—like a woman. For some reason it was disconcerting; perhaps because, in her own mind, Mary was still a child. Carolyn cleared her throat. "D'you remember writing it, this time?"

Mary had the towel at her hips as she bent slightly; she patted her fleshy inner thighs. The girl's serious eyes lifted to meet her mother's. "Every word," she said deliberately. "I remember every word of it."

Feeling uncomfortable, unsure, Carolyn looked away. Her gaze drifted to the mirror above the basin. For a moment, in the steamy haze smearing its surface, she thought she detected . . . *something; a motion.* Perhaps a movement that couldn't be there. Then she remembered being young herself and tracing faces on such cloudy mirror surfaces and her eyes leaped nervously back to Mary.

Still bare from the waist down, her daughter was plunging her breasts into a brassiere. Carolyn didn't remember having seen it before. It was a new model, cut to the nipples, body-colored and lacy. Yesterday, it was just yesterday, she'd bought Mary a training bra. Now a young woman, one who, with renewed health, doubtlessly held considerable value in the appraisal of young men, had appeared in the stead of the downy-cheeked child. She knew she must speak before she grew dizzier. "What is this all about, then?" she asked, turning the manuscript over in her hands.

Partly clothed now, Mary gave her a quick peck on the cheek. At close range an expression of concern showed on her youthful face. What she'd been saying suddenly appeared sheer bravado. "Mom, I'm scared," the girl said. "Because if what came into my mind is *true*—what I wrote there—*I think Hecate is already among us.*"

CHAPTER VIII

Summer, 1968. The midwestern United States.

She was five or six, a child with immensely mature, serious eyes that alternated between seeing nothing, and everything. She had a somewhat pouting mouth at this age, an olive complexion that seemed nearly foreign, and a healthy appetite. Despite it, she did not put on weight and might have almost appeared frail. Her hair was dark now, straight, allowed to grow so that already it had reached the small of her willowy back and drew attention to her round, protruding buttocks. Her body and figure gave signs not so much of becoming tall but of growing suddenly, ripely mature; and it tended to embarrass people.

Men who saw the girl recognized her as very much a child yet saw her already disconcertingly on the threshold of distinct femaleness. Sometimes they had to avert their gaze to remember, hastily, her extreme youth. Women who saw her remembered their own chubby, ungainly child selves, gawky and awkwardly muscled boy-imitations, and many despised her on sight. Among themselves they whispered that if there was ever a potential rape victim, it was *this* child. Both men and women understood, though, that she was a child and treated her with exaggerated politeness and utterly feigned affection.

Neither sex fooled her, not for a moment. Yet something deep inside warmed to the essence of men, while disliking their inferred attitudes; something cooled to the women, even while it ardently wished to be *one* with them.

She had a brother, older, who was usually described as "really all-male, the All-American Boy type," and she sort of enjoyed his company. Appreciating her attention, he reciprocated in a masculine offhand fashion.

The children had a cat, but the cat had the little girl. By the time stealthy, furry Drusilda—she'd named the cat, carefully and self-consciously spelling its name for the parents—was no longer a kitten, it had attached itself to the six year old. And vice versa; very much, vice versa.

Not that she liked the cat especially. She even doubted that Drusilda loved her, either.

A few months ago it had dawned on her that no one loved anyone or anything very much. Certainly *she* didn't.

But unlike most maxims, there was some truth to the idea of like calling to like. The human female, obliged by upbringing to be independent young, and soon inclined to insist on it, viewed everyone warily because they saw her that way. She might have become bitter except for the small presence of Drusilda.

Drusilda fast became the only creature in the girl's life who seemed worth thinking about, studying. It was easy for the girl to admire the cat, and to learn from it. She knew Drusilda craved affection but understood that she would not get it much of the time and behaved as if she did not care. The child strove to live similarly. Left alone, Drusilda was docile; pressed, she became lethally violent. That characteristic too appeared enviable, admirable. Imitatable.

The relationship was born neither in heaven nor hell but in an unjust alienation or isolation that had always existed, traditionally, for such creatures as the cat and the girl. After awhile, neither bothered much to care.

At that age, she had no idea in the world that she was the reincarnation of Hecate, goddess of Hell, the embodiment of blood and terror, of what those who knew and dreaded her called "the parting ways." She remembered nothing of Sparta, of ruling, of killing, of the flames of Hades. Nothing of the vast powers at her command. Not yet.

But on this day in 1968 she *was* aware of hunger, that frequent visitor. She felt sometimes like she was always hungry. Mama, overweight, had begun regaining her figure and was slender now. She was absolute death to anyone near her who dared to overeat and the little girl knew it was Mama's way to fight back at Daddy, to release some of her pentup frustration.

Now, hungry and lacking the nerve to steal a snack, she watched Drusilda play on the lane in front of the house, reclined on one delicately fuzzy side while she batted in aimless menace at butterflies wafting past. Occasionally the cat turned her many-hued calico head almost around, a sight the child found comical, pursuing with her strange feline eyes the fluttering, colorful creatures. Drowsing on the steps, the child watched. A *Nancy Drew* book lay open, partly on the cement and partly on the emerald grass. She knew she'd really like mysteries, tales about crimes and killing, when she could just read a little faster. She yawned.

From the corner of her half-closed eyes she spied a fat ant climbing aboard her book and moving like a grammarian's semicolon across the open page. Above the ant and the book she saw, for the first time today, the neighbor's dog.

The animal had hated Drusilda forever, mainly because Drusilda wouldn't play with him. In breed, he was nothing in particular. In size, he was that of a fair-sized terrier, his coat curly with one ear apt to remain alertly vertical while the other lolled in good humor.

Now, however, *both* ears were laid back. The dog had lowered his legs till he was just off the ground, haunches set like fine steel springs ... and he'd maneuvered himself three scant feet away from the unaware Drusilda. "Jeff!" The little girl bawled his name, too late. *"Don't!"*

But the dog landed asprawl the much smaller cat, jaws clamping into her half-turned, bristling neck. A penetrating yowl of surprise, disgust and outraged pain sounded nearly human. Jeff, snuffling for air around his clenched jaws, issued a series of fierce growls. His sturdy jaws lifted the cat from the pavement and, in keeping with his kind, he began shaking the cat to and fro.

It's possible that Jeff was playing. It's possible that Drusilda's injuries were largely to her abundant pride. But it is definite that Jeff made a serious mistake.

Because the little girl's reactions were internal, inborn thousands of years ago, quite automatic—quite unplanned—quite lethal. She was on her feet suddenly, a cute child in baggy jeans and the old brother's shirt, snapping her fingers twice.

Then she pointed at the dog.

Jeff was instantly engulfed in a perfect ring of intense orange flame, somehow skipping past the cat, causing him to release it at once, yelping in acute pain. At once Drusilda vanished into the relative safety of the house.

Jeff, however, remained at the precise center of the fireball. *Toasting.* His frantic yelps were turning now to whines when he was abruptly flipped in a full circle, as though roasting on an unseen spit—then tossed rudely to the ground. Hard.

Landing on all four feet and propelled by pain and terror, the dog zipped toward the crawlspace at the side of the little girl's house.

She stood watching, surprised and faintly pleased. She did not fully grasp what had occurred but she understood it a little and approved. For a moment her pretty, dark head was cocked to one side in consideration.

Then, smiling to herself, she hurried up the lane and around the corner of the house.

Millions of tiny insects thrived there in the darkness beneath the house. They, too, had no need or yearning for humankind. It was moist and hot, shadowed, there; it was an infected womb of a place and she had always loved it. It was, in point of fact, the little girl's favorite place in this world.

Careless of her jeans, she knelt to peer cautiously

into the filthy crawlspace. Yes, there he was, his tongue dangling limply from the corner of his mouth, the tip in the dirt. Jeff's eyes stared back at her but saw nothing. The flies, other friends of sorts, already were on the scene like so many miniature reporters reacting to a newsflash. She squinted into the dark. A sizeable portion of the curly hair on Jeff's small form had been burned completely away and the six year old could tell—both from sight and from the pungent stench arising from his body—that Jeff was partly cooked.

Now she looked both ways, always wary. She crawled under the house to squat happily beside the deceased dog. As one, each and every fly arose and flew out into the clean sunshine, accident onlookers fleeing the authorities. Briefly, she regarded the steadily hardening creature and patted him, experimentally, with one small hand. Just to be sure.

There was no response. Not a twitch or spasm.

She sighed, fully relaxing. *It was always nice being here, especially on hot days like this, nice to get away from everyone, she thought happily, chewing enthusiastically and then ripping off a little more . . .*

After that, Drusilda stayed close to the little girl, apparently thinking of her as a protectress. In return, the cat seemed eager to *do things* for the child. It made the little girl giggle to realize that the moment she thought of something she wanted, good old Drusilda searched her eyes with a look of intent familiarity and then went after it. Even her folks noticed it.

"That cat's pure wonder," Daddy remarked at the supper table. "More like a dog, the way she fetches."

"She's *better'n* any ole dog," the girl replied. "I can get Drue t'do *lotsa* things—really *dif'rent* things! Wanna see?"

But Daddy's interest had wandered and Mama was concerned that her pretty daughter take some green food, so she was obliged to keep the *really* strange things Drusilda could do to herself.

That night they watched TV all evening. There was a political campaign going on and Mama let her children stay up to see how the primary procedure worked.

But Daddy got in a bad mood looking at the pictures on the screen of a rather youthfully good-looking man with a mop of dark hair. He was waving at the crowd in the hotel ballroom after making a speech which the little girl couldn't follow. He seemed friendly enough, she thought, reaching shyly out to take the hands of those cheering people beneath the stage.

"Lookit the senator!" Daddy snorted. "Shakin' hands with people like he don't have a enemy in the world! Well, he has," he boasted. *"Me!"*

Still anxious, at this age, to earn Daddy's approval and share his thinking, the little girl watched the TV picture closely, gripping Drusilda to her thin chest. Maybe Daddy was right; the senator-man was awfully slender and his front teeth gave him a sort of chipmunk look. Again she did not notice that her questions were disturbing her father. "Is he one of the bad men, Daddy?" she asked.

Annoyed at having his hatred interrupted, he scarcely glanced her way. "Well, yeah, he's no damn good for this nation, no more'n his big fancy-minded brother was. *Their* kind aren't satisfied with bein' rich; they want ever'thing and don't care how they get it."

Now the senator on the screen was leaving the stage, walking to the hallway behind it and disappearing from view. "I s'pose he shouldn't bother folks the way he was," she continued, seeking her father's adult logic. "Maybe they don't really want to shake hands with him."

"*Shouldn't* do it?" Daddy laughed harshly. " 'Course he should! This way, somebody'll blow his fool Irish head off someday and good riddance t' the whole family! Hell, even that Nixon fella'd be better'n *this* guy! Now, leave me be."

She caught a glimpse of the two enormously athletic-looking men beside the senator-man. "The ones with him look like nice men," she said again. "Are they just being fooled, or is it because—"

Daddy's arm shot out, exploding away from his body.

The open hand caught the little girl on her cheek and knocked her flat on her back with a loud thump. The blow hurt and, for a moment, her eyes blazed not with tears but searing hatred at her father. Drusilda arched her back, held her ground. Mama looked around, startled, anguished. The temperature in the room appeared to rise twenty degrees.

Then the man was out of the chair and quickly bending to the little girl with tears in his eyes. "Jesus, I'm *sorry*, honey," he cried, "really I am!" He assisted her to a sitting position, awkwardly patting her shoulder. "It's just that I'm a patriot and those people drive me *crazy* the way they're cuttin' up America, givin' it all to the Cath'lics and blacks with their hands out. It makes me sick!"

Now her gaze swept to the television set, staying. What had happened, well, clearly it wasn't Daddy's fault. It was the fault of that bad, smiling man on TV. He was driving her Daddy mad, making him sick, making him mean. A knowledge that had been hers thousands of years ago gathered and swirled within her with tornado-power, boiling over. When she acted it was again on sheer, innate instinct.

Standing, she braced her small legs, apart as though in a batting stance, eyes livid with rage. She pointed jabbingly at the TV as the word sprang to her furious lips: *"Die!"* she exclaimed. "Die, *tonight!"*

Daddy and Mom both stared from her to the TV, where the image of a hotel corridor on the screen violently flickered, over to the cat who was similarly frozen in fury and staring at the set, back to their vengeful child. Mama was speechless. On the stairs, her older brother blanched, turned and ran upstairs.

And Daddy was laughing, suddenly, wildly exuberant, his hilarity pouring out of him: "Hey, *lookit* that, will ya?" he shouted, glancing with pride at his little girl. "By gosh, she's puttin' the evil eye on ole Bob Kennedy!" He chuckled. "Now, where in hell d'you suppose she picked *that* up?"

The answer leaped to the little girl's mind without

any conscious understanding of it. From *the lower regions,* it whispered. *From the* lowest *regions.*

It was late at night, now, and Mary would not go to bed unless Carolyn lay next to her and watched over her. The teacher thought it odd the way Mary's first surge of confidence, when she lifted the towel and discovered the manuscript, had given way to growing apprehension. As if, at first, she had nearly understood the source of her knowledge and then, with the reality of the present growing stronger, Mary had again seen how bizarre the whole episode was.

But they had talked together at length and Carolyn had been surprised to learn of her daughter's decision: She would enroll tomorrow at UCEV, specifically to take her mother's courses, both the English class and that concerning the emerging goddesses. "I think it will be a triumph for you, Mama," she had told Carolyn with enthusiasm, "and I want to be part of your success, your new happiness. Just as I was part of your old unhappiness."

"But I'm not sure if it's wise," Carolyn had argued. "I mean, it isn't often *done,* a child being instructed by her mother."

"I've thought about that." Mary easily grew introspective. "Besides that, I don't really want everyone staring at me because of the rape thing. So I'll enroll under another name and nobody but *you* will know who I am!"

And do I know, truly, my daughter? Carolyn mused now, stroking the sleeping girl's forehead and wondering what dreams strolled through her mind, tormenting her, perhaps reminding her of things that were better forgotten. *Do I truly know you?*

At length, sure that Mary was asleep for the night, the blond instructor arose and went back out to the front room. There, she could not relax for a thought that continued to buzz around, stubbornly; and at last, with a measure of courage, she faced it head on: *It's almost as if Mary isn't being told these things. It's as if she . . .*

remembers. *And with every word she writes, Hecate seems truly to be—drawing nearer—drawing closer to us, nearer to . . . the present.*

PART TWO

Crisis at Hand: Converted Cannibals

"A science career is now almost as acceptable as being cheerleader." —Myra Barker

"When women kiss it always reminds one of prize fighters shaking hands." —H. L. Mencken

"Most hierarchies were established by men who now monopolize the upper levels, thus depriving women of their rightful share of opportunities to achieve incompetence." —Laurence J. Peter

THE FOLLOWING ONLY APPEARS TO BE A WOMAN'S DESCRIPTION OF MAN STRIPPING FROM HER THE RIGHTS OF LIBERATION: " 'I want you to hypnotize me!' she said. 'Do it before the dawn, for I feel that then I can speak, and speak freely. Be quick, for the time is short!' Without a word he motioned her to sit up in bed. Looking fixedly at her, he commenced to make passes in front of her . . . I felt that some crisis was at hand. Gradually her eyes closed, and she sat, stock still; only by the gentle heaving of her bosom could one know that she was alive. . . . Mina opened her eyes; but she did not seem the same woman. There was a far-away look in her eyes . . . " —Bram Stoker, *Dracula*

"With animals you don't see the male caring for the offspring . . . It's against nature. It is a woman's prerogative and duty, and a privilege." —Princess Grace of Monaco

"God made man, and then said I can do better than that and made woman." —Adela Rogers St. John

"A converted cannibal is one who, on Friday, eats only fishermen." —Emily Lotney

CHAPTER IX

Late August last year. A building on the UCEV campus.

High above the usually shining but currently scuffed hardwood floor, basketball backboards were pressed stoically into themselves like so many stylistic birds huddled for security in their own glass wings. Against the distant walls, the steep rungs of flattened exercise ladders seemed detached and spinal. Dangling things, barbells and objects on which one endlessly tugged, might have been the plucked birds' alien intestines. Occasionally a rumbling brown ball came tumbling out of the stitched bag near the corner and bounced independently through the crowded gymnasium body like something not quite properly digested.

From an open end of the great room Henry Parseval, the bald headed basketball coach, momentarily appeared to cast quickly dubious, dark glances at the students massing on his precious court. *This* year, he'd been sure, *They* would listen to him and make these children wear tennis shoes to registration or at least cross his precious flooring in stocking feet. When someone stumbled, falling forward a few feet in the crush of young bodies, it brought real pain to Henry's one-dimensional heart.

Once a tall man, at six-two, Henry worked in constant discomfort in a world of young men soaring toward seven feet and lived in a nonstop condition of love/hate ambivalence. He hated the way he'd failed, ten years ago, in an incredible attempt to build a speedily competitive team around youths not exceeding seventy-two inches in height. The failure taught him so well that his teams had won conference titles the past three years running. But Henry loved recruiting. Every time he met a spindly student graduating from high school, still growing as he ducked awkwardly beneath a doorframe, Coach Parseval prayed that he'd found the next Russell, the new Chamberlain, another Abdul-Jabbar. When they turned out mostly only to be tall, and awed by the world, Henry's ambivalence itself reached new heights. His favorite thing in the whole world was to dribble a basketball high and furiously in the air before his newest giant, tantalizing him, and dare the lad to steal it from him.

The one who succeeded, four years ago, spent three varsity years sitting on the bench. When he starred and went on to play pro ball with the Indiana Pacers, Henry boasted that it was his discipline that made the boy's success possible.

The coach's least favorite thing in the world, however, was registration when, as today, the university moguls seemed to forget that it was Henry's basketball program that paid the way—not these gawking, angular, besweatered children who, he knew, tended more to become enrolled in drama courses than subjects Henry considered meaningful. Like basketball, accounting, track, basketball, business, gymnastics, basketball, economics or basketball. Los Angeles wasn't that far away and it was a sore point with Coach Parseval when he remembered that the reason for UCEV's existence was a dead heat between Hollywood and the NBA.

Now Henry, who had been absent for as long as ten minutes, appeared at the *other* end of the immense practice gym, pretending to be there for the purpose of depositing a newspaper in a container. A slender redhead caught his act.

"Who in the world *is* that?" she whispered to the other new women students at her table, inclining her head. "He's beginning to give me the creeps."

The pert blond looked up from her packet of forms

and laughed lightly. "I don't know for sure. The way he glares at us I think maybe he's casting for a horror flick."

Across from her, a pretty brunette heard the conversation and leaned toward them. "That's Coach Parseval," she said in low tones, smiling. "Isn't he *something*? I thought for awhile he was practicing dematerialization—you know, like on *Star Trek*. Waiting for somebody to beam him aboard."

The blond, her eyes a startling dark, like bright and lively marbles beneath fringing golden hair, pursed her lips. "Who does he think he is? Knute Rockne?"

"Rockne coached football a zillion years ago," the redhead replied. "At Notre Dame. That character must be the basketball coach." She laughed. "I think his mother was scared by Red Auerbach!"

"Hi," cried the pert blond, putting out her hand. "I'm Soni Jerome."

"I'm Diana Stoker," said the redhead, taking the hand and shaking it. "Where you from?"

Soni retrieved her hand. "That's quite a grip, Diana—you must be athletic. I'm from Toledo. That's in Ohio."

Across the table, the brunette paused, looking shy. "I'm from the midwest, too. I'm Marcia Angell. Chicago is my town." She turned to the athletic girl. "Are you from out here, Diana?"

"It's like they say about New York. Nobody's really from California," Diana said, smiling. "No, I'm an Indianapolis girl. So! We're all little midwestern girls come to wide-open California to find fame and fortune." She lifted her eyes in comic mysticism. "Perhaps the gods already smile upon us."

"Not gods," Marcia replied softly. "Goddesses these days."

"Maybe that is the right word," Soni replied. "Anyway, fame and fortune will surely be ours. Right now, we're every man's dream come true: A blond, brunette and redhead."

"Don't forget brownettes," Marcia put in. "You sound pretty confident."

Soni twirled a short blond curl round her index finger. "I am," she said airily. "I'm into astrology and my horoscope for the day said I was making a new start. I thought it was pretty good, that it meant my registering for class. But maybe it meant finding new friends my first day on campus."

Diana's brows raised in interest. "I don't know that I believe in astrology, but it might be nice to see if we have anything in common but our origins. Does anybody have an invitation to the grand sorority whirl?"

The other girls looked quickly at each other, then away. Marcia said nothing. Soni's little chin jutted forward. "I don't doubt that we're *all* on everybody's list of prospects but I'm an independent kind of person."

"Good for you!" Marcia exclaimed.

"Why?" Diana asked pointedly. "*You* don't look like a terribly independent sort."

"Well, I'm working on it," the brunette said defensively, and the others laughed. Marcia paused, then returned the smile. "You two might be good for me."

"The last one who told me that," Soni replied quickly, "was a guy two years ahead of me in high school. I was just young enough to take it for a compliment."

All three young women chuckled. "Well, look. We've hit it off pretty well so far, right? If we're pledged later, we can always change the situation around. But for now, why don't we think about rooming together?"

Soni nodded. "Sounds good to me. We can be protection for one another, sort of, until we learn the ropes out here." She paused to peer across the table. "Marcia? What d'you think?"

The brunette hesitated shyly, for a moment, then gave a strong affirmative nod. "I think I'd like that a lot!"

"Terrific!" Soni declared, reaching out her hands to squeeze theirs. "Then it's settled. After all, friends are the most precious gems in the world—except for starring football players!"

Diana shook her head slowly. "I'm here for an

education, and like you guessed, Soni—athletics. I don't think I'll have a lot of time for dating. Not in my first couple of years anyway."

"I'm not quite ready to take the pledge, myself," Soni answered in her blithe, flippant manner. "I'm here to become the next Liza Minelli, to tell the truth of the matter. But I guess I wouldn't turn down Mr. Right if he came along." She glanced across the table. "What about you, Marcia?"

"I'm open ended about my major," she said with a shrug. "I like to write."

"No, I mean the subject," Soni went on, wagging her hands. "*The* subject of subjects, sweetie. Men!"

"All I can say for sure," Marcia replied tersely, "is that too many wrongs don't make a Mr. Right—just a lot of trouble for everyone concerned."

Diana studied the smaller girl, her eyes hooded in thought. "Don't tell me our shy one has a secret past."

"A mystery woman!" Soni exclaimed with delight, patting Marcia's hand. "Our little Marcia is a mystery woman!"

Marcia colored. "The only mystery about me is why they even let me in. I graduated sort of by myself. After I got sick."

"Then you've come to the right place," Soni observed, bending to scribble her name on the forms before her. "California's the right place to recuperate. I'll bet we all use it for a springboard to earthshaking accomplishments. Right, Diana?"

"Earthshaking accomplishments?" the redhead murmured, almost reflective suddenly. "Well, I wouldn't be surprised at all. Let's get a newspaper and then make the rounds of the boarding houses."

CHAPTER X

The trio of new student women straggled their way out into the California sunlight, talking animatedly and fairly freely yet with that infinitesimal hint of hesitancy an adroit listener catches in the voices of people who've just met. It seemed quite natural the way Soni Jerome took the conversational lead, one step behind the purposeful pace of Diana Stoker and two steps ahead of the quietly deliberate Marcia Angell.

Around them, three other sprawling structures comprised the major features of UCEV. Had one of them craned her neck and looked just beyond the nearest building, she might have made out the football field and adjoining track field. Instead, they perambulated to the curb where they paused, suddenly aware that they hadn't discussed the means of achieving their goal: renting rooms, somewhere in El Vista.

Instinctively, Soni turned to the others, her light hair reflecting the sun. Immediately she saw that Marcia had procured a newspaper but its presence seemed miraculous. "Where in the hell did you get *that?*" she demanded, pointing.

"I have my means," Marcia replied enigmatically with a scant smile, opening the paper to the classified ads.

Diana was bemused. "Marcia observed that Coach Parseval threw his newspaper away in a container at the end of the gym. She pulled it out on our way by."

"*I* didn't see that!" blond Soni answered, whirling as

if her new friend were trying to anger her. "And—and how do you know the coach is named Parseval?"

"I mentioned it," Marcia put in soberly, her gaze scanning the want ads.

"And if she *didn't*," Diana added, "you can see his name on the address label stuck on the corner of the front page. See?"

Soni blinked her outrageous dark eyes. "You gotta be *kidding!* What *eyesight!* I can't even read the headline from here." She looked from Diana to the studying Marcia and back again. "What kind of whiz kids have I got myself *involved* with, for chrissake?"

"Well, the kind who thinks it'd be nice to have wheels for our little hunting expedition," Diana replied. "Did anybody think of that?"

Marcia looked up. Her hand jiggled keys before her face. "I have a car, ladies," she said. "Interested?"

"So do I," Soni replied a trifle defensively. "But I'd rather ride with you geniuses so I can watch the way you do it."

"Over there." Marcia pointed. The three of them crossed the lot and waited while the softspoken brunette unlocked an aging sports car, instantly ducking her arms into the interior.

Something small and furry propelled itself forward and landed in them, purring.

"We've been invaded," Soni wailed, taking a backward step. "What the hell is that?"

"I think it's a cat," Diana remarked, reaching past Marcia's shoulder to scratch the animal's ear. It was a jet black cat except for its odd gray ears. "I like cats."

Suddenly there was a flurry of activity and Marcia was having trouble holding onto her pet. The cat twisted and stretched, reaching; then it was in Diana Stoker's arms, nestling quietly against her breast.

"I've only had Hercules for a short while," Marcia said softly, "but I thought he hated everyone in the world but me." She shrugged. "Well, you can hold him while I drive, Di. He's car broken."

Diana lifted the cat briefly to peer into its strange

eyes. "Don't worry. We'll get along fine." She waited as Soni slid into the insubstantial back seat, then sat in front with Marcia. "I have lots of experience with cats. Mine's with me, too."

"Didn't you guys ever hear of a goddam *dog?*" Soni called from the back.

Marcia ignored her, spreading the newspaper on the dashboard in front of the tall redhead. "Why don't you call out the addresses while I drive around and maybe Soni can help spot streets? Would that be all right?"

But Soni Jerome didn't reply for a moment. She was staring at the back of the two heads in the front seat.

She wouldn't have mentioned it for the world—not on such short acquaintance—but she'd almost swear one or both of them wore wigs. In Toledo, back home, the only ones who seemed to wear toups were middle-aged women who didn't want to put their hair up unless something neat was happening. Mainly, a wedding or a funeral. For just a second, without knowing why, Soni wished she were still in Ohio.

While they drove, the trio of young women became further acquainted discussing their homes. With less to do than the others, Soni got the ball rolling. She explained that she "got her gift for gab" from Mama Jerome, a woman of Italian descent who never even admitted her ancestry until Papa—Carlotto Jerome—convinced her that "wops are best." Since Carlotto played fantastic classical violin, and quickly became concert master in the local symphony orchestra, all Mama's latent Italian talent for cooking flowered. Soni remembered dozens of delicious evenings when the family sat around eating Mama's fabulous food while Papa entertained them with the most sentimental Italian melodies.

" 'Family,' you said," Diana remarked from the front seat. "Somebody else besides you and your parents?"

"A brother." Soni's dark eyes flashed as they met Diana's gaze. "But I don't talk much about him."

"You don't get along?" asked Marcia.

"I worship him," Soni admitted, flushing. "He's twenty-four, black-haired with eyes like deep dark pools, terribly handsome. But—"

"But you don't want to talk about him," Marcia finished for her, momentarily glancing at Soni in the rear view mirror. "Well, we all have our secrets, I guess."

Diana, however, remained looking reflectively over the seat at Soni. She had the most relentlessly direct green eyes Soni could remember having seen. They weren't cold, actually; just unblinking. Diana's tone was casual, though. "What; are you adopted or something? Is *that* the big secret?"

"Dammit, Di, I don't want to go into it just now!" The little blond slammed the car seat with her open palm. "Is that all *right* with you? Besides, why would you ask me if I'm adopted?"

"Never mind." Diana turned back to the front. "I certainly didn't mean to pry, Soni. It couldn't matter less to me one way or the other. Unless you're the daughter of a Mafia godfather or something."

"I asked you *why* you wanted to know if I was adopted?" Soni demanded, leaning forward, her face inches from the back of Diana's suddenly stubborn face. "Dammit, *give!*"

"Your hair, your coloring," Diana replied with a sigh. "You're a blond and I have a hunch it's natural. Most Italians are dark."

"Well, *I'm* not!" Soni half shouted. The cat in the front seat arched its back.

"Here's LaCaresta Avenue," Marcia said quietly, turning left. "What was that number again?"

Diana peered quickly at the classified page. "10755," she said. Her keen eyes swept numbers. "There! Across the street, a block down."

Marcia glanced admiringly at the redhead and slowed the aging sports car. As they stopped at the curb, she became aware of a snuffling sound from the back, and turned.

Soni Jerome was crying. Instantly Marcia's heart went out to her. "Baby, what's the matter? I'm *sure*

Diana didn't mean to hurt your feelings."

" 'Baby' is the right word for this performance," Soni snapped, immediately embarrassed and bristling. She sat up on the seat, ready to climb out. "The truth of the matter is, I've wondered for years if I *am* adopted. I—I always adored Mama and Papa and their old-country ways—everything about them. B-But Diana's absolutely right." Her hot gaze passed to Diana with a look of respect. "I *don't* look Italian or, for that matter, *feel* the way I should. About things. Shit, I'm a lousy Catholic!"

Marcia laughed and got out, holding the door for the tiny blond, filled with sympathy. "C'mon, Soni. I'll bet the three of us hit it lucky on our first try for rooms. Probably have an indoor swimming pool and the whole package for sixty bucks a month. Right, Diana?"

For a moment there was no reply as the tall redhead climbed out onto the pavement. She paused to make sure Hercules, the cat, was safely locked in and then came around the front of the car to Soni. "None of this explains why you don't want to talk about your handsome brother," she said pointedly to Soni, abruptly sliding her arm around the blond's shoulders. "But like Marsh said, we all have our secrets."

For a moment Marcia Angell held back in mild astonishment as the other women crossed the street. It was awfully obvious to her that Diana had just been outrageously rude to Soni a second time, yet the blond had *accepted* it, this time—even appeared glad to have the athletic Diana's arm guide her. Marcia couldn't decide if Diana was quietly appropriating her friend and converting her into some kind of emotional slave or if the athletic redhead merely had a different way of showing sympathy. While she locked up the car, Marcia stared at the two new friends climbing a steep flight of steps to the lawn in front of 10755 LaCaresta, musing about them.

Reflecting about people was nothing new for Marcia.

She had always been an independent person, in her quiet way, given to spending much of her time alone, lost in thoughts that she knew, intuitively, were rarely considerations of other girls. Blessed with a racing, inquisitive mind, she had been doing little word-portraits of others when she was twelve. Until her life had been severely upset by certain secrets of the kind to which she had alluded, Marcia had often considered becoming a writer. Even now she meant to take several English courses and eventually classes in advanced composition, English and American literature.

But they were secondary, just now, to the class that had really caught and fired her imagination. Whether it would be available for the first semester beginning in ten days was uncertain, but Marcia badly looked forward to Reemergence of the Goddesses.

Locking her side of the car, she noticed the difference in size between Soni Jerome and Diana Stoker. It wasn't just a matter of height. Although Soni was undeniably darling, her petite figure and rounded buttocks bound to be watched by the men on campus —especially with her brash brand of humor, which suggested a fun-loving disposition—there was also something utterly soft and vulnerable about the blond. Marcia suspected those immense dark eyes of Soni's had filled with tears many times in the past. She wondered, without a clue, what made Soni Jerome so deeply disconsolate.

But Diana was a very different matter. The redhead was nowhere near six feet in height yet there was something about her erect posture and the solidity of her quite womanly body—her breasts seemed to precede her by feet; Marcia wasn't small but she found herself envying the redhead's bustline—that suggested vast strength. Strength, and *more,* Marcia thought. A toughness of spirit, perhaps; a resilient zest for experience, perhaps. She was with Soni at the front door of the boarding house now and towered, in every respect, over the small blond. Diana, Marcia decided on the spot, would be a person to reckon with—a potential All-American, even Olympian—if Marcia was any judge of character.

And beyond that, she thought, hurrying after the

others, *two* things: Diana Stoker looked like a young woman who'd never shed a tear in her life. She would, for anybody unfortunate enough to cross her, make a positively lethal enemy.

The landlady proved to be a hefty, white-haired woman with hips that trailed after her like the train of a wedding dress. It would have been easy to dismiss her as "just an old-fashioned old lady." Her double-chinned lower face was grandmotherly; but the eyes and forehead, and the dignity of the woman, seemed those of a scholar. In her plump hand, when she let the girls in, she clasped a much-thumbed hardcover edition of *Bartlett's Quotations*.

"I recognize you by your device," she said humorously as Marcia rejoined them just inside the front door.

"Our what?" Soni inquired.

" 'All for one, one for all, that is our device,' " the elderly woman replied. "From *The Three Musketeers*. I take it you've come to see the rooms?"

Diana nodded and the others exchanged somewhat puzzled glances. "I'm Violet Hudson," the woman said, "Mrs. Violet Hudson. Follow me."

They did, climbing a carpeted flight of stairs to a landing where the old woman paused, one hand on her bent hip. " 'I am declined into the vale of tears,' " she said with a dramatic sigh.

Marcia warmed. "I know that one! Shakespeare, right? *Macbeth*, yes?"

Mrs. Hudson shot her a darting look before proceeding down the floor. "Shakespeare, yes; *MacBeth*, no." She shook her head disapprovingly. "How doth the taste of youth wither ere it takes form!' *Othello's* the right answer, dearie."

Diana, right behind her, called: "And the last one about the taste of youth?"

"Hudson said that," the landlady responded without pausing. "Mrs. Violet Hudson, that is!" She opened two doors. "These rooms connect and there's one bed in one, as you can plainly see, two in the other."

Diana entered the nearest room, Soni following.

Marcia peered into the adjoining room, carefully. "It's a little dark, isn't it?"

"I rather enjoy the dark when I want to rest," Diana called. "And that's mostly what I'll be doing here, I imagine."

Little Soni looked into a closet she had supposed was empty and something fell from the top shelf, startling her. She jumped back a foot before she saw it was only an old hatbox. "Woo!" she exclaimed. "That scared me."

Violet Hudson made no move to enter the room and pick up the hatbox. She looked at them from between narrowed eyes. "Look to what's in your heads, ladies, if it's scary things you fear. 'One need not be a chamber to be haunted; One need not be a house; The brain has corridors surpassing Material places.' "

Diana's gaze flickered to the older woman, a lazy smile on her lips. "The famous Mrs. Hudson again?" she asked softly.

"Nope, Emily Dickinson." The landlady paused, decided she'd put these young people in their place; nodded. "I'll let you look to your heart's content, ladies. If you want it, I want company and the small, precise amount I'll be needing for things. One fifty a month is it; not a penny more, not a penny less."

Then she was gone, closing both doors at the same time. "What a *char*acter!" Soni cried, replacing the hatbox after looking inside and finding no human head. "And her *name* is ideal! I remember Sherlock Holmes had a landlady named Mrs. Hudson, too."

Marcia sat on a chair, tentatively, the slipcover tattered and patched. Beneath it, however, she found the chair's material in excellent condition. "But she's more a Mrs. Danvers type, I think." She looked across at Diana Stoker. "Do you play the violin or do weird chemical tests, the way Holmes did?"

Diana was lying on one of the two beds, one knee raised so that it formed a triangle with the other leg. Her legs were exceptionally long, Marcia noticed, even sensual. She also observed that Soni was staring at the redhead. "I'm afraid I'm a very straight forward person, friends," Diana said, folding her arms behind her head and seeming perfectly relaxed. " 'Weird' always seemed devious to me, something of a cheat." Her gaze, as she turned her pretty head, passed slowly over Marcia and Soni. "When I want something, I just go after it."

Did she *mean* something by that, Marcia wondered, or was she simply introducing herself more thoroughly? Abruptly the brunette felt a great urge to turn the conversation in a different direction.

"What do you think of the place?" she asked, tapping her fingertips on the arms of the old chair. "D'you two think it's *too* Gahan Wilsony?"

"Frankly, I don't think we can beat the price anywhere in the state," Diana said quietly. "How about you, Soni?"

For a moment, the small blond didn't reply. She was still staring at the closet where she'd been frightened. The door was shut now. Then she looked quickly to Diana. "It's fine." She paused. "But how would we divide the rooms? Who'd be Odd Man Out in the second bedroom?"

Again, Marcia thought, there was a feeling of some *electricity* passing between the other young women. Although Diana hadn't spoken, she thought Diana's thoughts had passed into her own brain and spoke up. "Let me be Odd Man," she said, just to get it over with, to clear the air. "Like I said, I do a lot of writing. Often it's spur-of-the-moment, middle-of-the-night inspiration that looks god-awful the next day. But I like to do it anyway. If I'm in there, I won't disturb you two. Besides," she added, glancing in turn to the others, "this may turn out to be temporary anyway, if we're invited to the sororities we like. Right?"

Diana sat up, long legs together and slowly swaying from side to side. "Absolutely. Besides, Marsh, I suspect that old Soni here isn't the only mystery woman among us."

The blond colored, looked defiant. "What do you

mean by that, Di? What's mysterious about either one of us?"

"I'm only speaking of Marcia now, Soni," Diana said, smiling directly into the brunette's face. "Enigma Number Two."

Marcia flushed as well but tried to laugh it off. "I really have no idea what you're talking about."

"The thing is," Diana continued as if Marcia hadn't spoken, "if we're going to be lifetime friends and confide in each other, and like that, we have to begin by being upfront. Totally upfront."

"Diana," Marcia insisted, "I don't understand you at all!"

"It's simple." The tall redhead pointed toward the street below them. "If you're from Chicago . . . why does your car have California license plates?"

CHAPTER XI

There were a dozen stated or implied reasons for the delay, but what it boiled down to, Carolyn Lord realized with a taste of bitterness, was that she wouldn't be able to get her Reemergence of the Goddesses class underway until the second semester.

In a way, she told herself at the end of registration day, relaxing beneath a cool shower, it wouldn't be bad to have the time for a really fullscale, all-out preparation for the class. There was a great deal of research into ancient Greece that she could wisely do, in order to give the students better background atmosphere. Nor, for that matter, would it be bad to get easily back into the swing of instruction. Undoubtedly she was out of practice, the way the dean had suggested. Hence, teaching a couple of English classes as her entire classload for the time being would enable her to get acclimated—both to UCEV itself, and as a "reborn" teacher.

The water beating on her breasts and abdomen was more stimulating than she had expected. Carolyn moved away from the steady stream, slightly annoyed. It nagged at her incessantly that her impression might be right, and somewhere on the faculty—hiding behind a spadeshaped beard and a string of educational letters—was some man who managed to delay everything. Some male professor, dean or department head who didn't at all relish the idea of the women students learning they were every bit as good as the male students.

Or for that matter, Carolyn thought grimly, learning that women instructors were as competent as men instructors.

The gush of water on her body seemed almost irresistible. Without quite realizing what she was doing, Carolyn moved her hands upward until they cupped her breasts. The index fingers instinctively pressed in, partly covering the newly-erect tips of her nipples. When she depressed them, then released the pressure, they grew harder. She put her head back slightly, her lower body thrust forward, as she tried to think. It was depressing that Mary had decided to move into a rooming house with two young ladies she'd met. Not that Mary wasn't almost well by now, entirely capable of looking after herself. There'd been no more strange, peculiarly biographical messages from the teenager for weeks. Really, living life as a normal girl again might be the best thing in the world for Mary.

Carolyn's hands had drifted downward, over her breasts and across her still-flat abdomen until two fingers were entwined in tight, golden curls. She remembered momentarily the way her ex-husband had done that, before—going ahead. The wetness from the shower was almost like the sweet moisture of his lips, the few times he'd been carried away and knelt before her, to kiss. With the other hand, she parted herself; the fingers left the curls and *touched,* inserted very cautiously.

What's that! Carolyn's eyes shot to the mirror where, just once, when Mary was in the tub, she'd thought she'd seen *motion*—movement that couldn't possibly be there, with no one present to be reflected. Now one hand crossed her pubic patch, another arm shielded her breasts. She was conscious of her heart beating heavily as she leaned out, around the shower curtain, for a better look.

The mirror was clouded, fully clouded, with steam. There was no interruption in it, no design, and thank God, no *face* that she dreaded, just then, more than she'd ever dreaded anything in her life. The terrible, ugly, decaying face that had given the aging sorcerer in Mary's writing an attack.

There was nothing.

She dried herself quickly and went into her bedroom to dress.

Later, conscious now of how alone she was in the apartment, when the late-evening sun was setting, creating lengthy shadows that drifted sonorously down the hallway from the bathroom, Carolyn tried to forget the image in the mirror and could forget neither it, nor the impression it had left with her.

The impression that, in some incredible and unearthly fashion she could not even imagine, Hecate, Queen of Hades, was drawing nearer and nearer to her—and to Mary. *Nearer;* every day of the world.

It had been easy for Marcia Angell to convince the other girls that she only arrived in California before they, and that a friend who was an older student had bought the license plate for her.

Now, however, that the decision was reached to accept the quoting Violet Hudson's shadowy rooms, Marcia found it less easy to stop feeling that she had somehow made an error in judgment.

Undeniably that Diana was a sharp one, obviously blessed with an I.Q. every bit as high as her own. More than that, Marcia felt, Diana Stoker was perpetually wary—*suspicious*—as if letting down her guard, even for a moment, might release some frightful secret of her own.

Possibly, Marcia mused, there was some terrifying thing in Diana's own background—just as her own— that the athletic girl could not forget. Perhaps she simply handled it differently; maybe she'd succeeded in hardening herself against the torments of daily life by virtue of not quite *accepting* anyone until she was perfectly sure they could be trusted.

And just maybe, she confessed to herself, Diana was a Lesbian. The air was positively taut with tension, at times, when she and Soni spoke or looked at each other. Yet the funny thing was that Marcia didn't *really* believe that, couldn't *really* accept the notion that, of all the women attending UCEV, she'd been unlucky enough to fall promptly into a homosexual relationship.

After coming up with fifty dollars each, to cover a month's rent, the trio of young women paid Mrs. Hudson and told her they'd decided to stay. To their surprise and pleasure, the aging landlady neither asked for an extra month's pay—to protect her in the event that they destroyed the furniture, or left without warning—nor gave them any sage advice about the lack of wisdom of having men on the second floor. "I only hope that it will be this for you," said Mrs. Hudson, tucking the wad of cash in the valley-like cleavage of her bosom: " ' . . . The place of Peace; the shelter, not only from all injury, but from all terror, doubt and division.' " Her eyes drifted to Marcia, and then to Soni. "John Ruskin," she added, "1819 to 1900."

"I think she went downstairs and memorized that on the hope that we'd move in," Soni said, shaking with helpless laughter and lying down on the bed across from Diana. "Can you *imagine* the inse*cu*rities of a person who'd go to *such lengths* to seem intelligent!"

"Well, I'm sure we'll show some insecurities of our own here at UCEV," Marcia remarked charitably, lounging in the doorway between the two rooms. "Anybody want to help me move my crap up from the car?"

"Sure, let's just *be* the Three Musketeers Mrs. Hudson talks about—all for one, you know. Three liberated, female musketeers." Soni jumped agilely up, tugging her blouse down. "After that we'll go back to my car and wherever Diana has her stuff stashed— okay?" She turned to the redhead, bluff and busy now. "Where *is* your shit, Di?"

Diana smiled. When she rose, it was almost a languid motion, Marcia noted; she moved with athletic grace. "It'll be here day after tomorrow, I think," she murmured, taking the lead in heading toward the door. "My Dad wasn't—altogether sure I'd fit in here. He wanted me to get registered first, meet some people. And I've done that, haven't I?" Diana lifted a finger of warning as she moved lithely down the hall. "The rest of that story is *my* secret, chums. I've got a toothbrush and all that kind of crap in a bag in my locker, plus a change of clothes or two."

For nearly two hours the three worked to get their meager belongings into the rooms on LaCaresta, then drove back on campus to the Distant Vista, a downstairs cafeteria in a building adjacent to the sprawling Theatre Arts complex. Over cokes—Soni impulsively ordered a BLT, too—they chatted idly about their new scholastic careers.

"What I can't quite figure out," Diana said, sipping from a straw, her long red hair prettily framing her face, "is what a trio of brainy broads like us is doing at this place at all. After all, it's only marginally at the university level. Damn near half the students come here for drama, just hoping to crack into movies so they can buy coke at quantity prices."

"You can't really blame them for being here, though," Soni argued quietly, nibbling on a piece of lettuce and suddenly looking, to the watchful Marcia, like an especially pretty rabbit. "Bigshots come over from Fox and Warner's and the TV networks to hold workshops and make speeches. Sometimes they grab somebody right off campus and haul them back to fame and fortune." Her eyelids flirted humorously with Diana. "And topgrade Colombian!"

"But it's such an odd combination," Marcia put in, glancing out the window at two joggers passing by in full uniform. "Lots of the male students go out for sports. I never *saw* so many athletic, jock types on campus anywhere! UCEV seems to be half-dramatic, half-athletic."

"You're forgetting UCLA and USC," Diana replied quickly, looking a little irritated. "A lot of the guys here end up transfers to the big football factories. They get a reputation here and do what's called 'red-shirting,' because they're just as anxious to catch on with an NFL team as the movie-minded kids want to be noticed by the DePalmas and Spielbergs. You see, basketball and football are the big sports for men in college and the cream of the crop want scholarships to play with the Bruins or Trojans, with Notre Dame, Alabama, the Big Ten schools—like that."

"Why don't they go there to begin with?" Soni inquired, puzzled.

"For the same reason film-oriented students come here," Diana said patiently. "There's terrific competition in Hollywood and also at the football factories. So you come here, or a place like this—down the line from the bigtime—and try to be so impressive that you get another shot at a major university."

"You sound sort of irritated," Marcia noticed. "At me?"

Diana shrugged her broad shoulders. "Only in the sense that you make fun of what you don't understand, like everybody. This is a very competitive world and it's harder in sports than most places."

"You're really into all that sweaty stuff, aren't you?" asked Soni. "Which sports are yours?"

The redhead hesitated, folding her plastic straw and watching it snap back. "Actually, I'm not absolutely sure. I—well, I like most of them."

Marcia smiled as she studied Diana's intent expression. "A streak of modesty there, I believe. Soni, what Diana is saying is that she's good in *all* of them." She found herself rather liking the redhead. "I'm sorry if I sounded condescending about sports. Do tell us a *little* about yourself, Di."

"There's not that much to tell." She shrugged again. "I have an older brother named Gordon who's twenty-three, settled down in Indianapolis with a wife and kid. I—had some trouble not so long ago, like Soni, and afterward it sort of straightened out my thinking." Now she lifted her strong, lovely profile to peer silently out the window for a moment. The students drifting by were like characters in a silent movie. "I knew I wanted some kind of career, with or without a man—something to help me learn just who I am, and what I'm capable of doing."

"I'll bet that's a whole lot," Soni said without looking up.

"Maybe," Diana whispered. "I hope I can make my name in the world. I don't have any virginity left to barter with anymore and I didn't find sex that fabulous anyway. I think I can discipline my emotions, draw *within* myself for skills that have nothing to do with sex." Her mouth hardened in a line. "Frankly, I'm galled that there aren't outstanding career possibilities in sports for women, the way there are for a man. I think I can do anything the average guy can do. And, if I fail," she looked up at them with a laugh, "I'll switch over to drama and become a kind of female Incredible Hulk!"

Diana-watching remained Marcia's favorite game only for a short while into the Freshman year. Indeed, in a matter of weeks, all three young women were too involved in college life to do more than exchange brief confidences when they met in their rooms at night. To her own amazement, Marcia found herself dating a junior instructor who had appeared worldly, safe, gorgeously brainy and competent. But when she refused to sleep with him, he dropped her immediately.

After that, Marcia concentrated on her grades and the first report indicated satisfactory progress: She produced nothing but B's. To her further astonishment, when she asked Diana how she was doing, Marcia was given a glimpse of the redhead's computerized gradesheet—nothing but A's. Again, she thought, she had underestimated the capabilities of her extraordinary new friend.

Soni struggled her way through the first semester, managing a string of average marks and avoiding probation but privately living in a topsy-turvy world that concerned both Marcia and Diana. To them, she confided that she'd had an affair with an offcampus, professional trumpet player who was into narcotics and whom she desperately wanted to salvage. In the process, the little blond gave him her heart and much more and was then brushed aside when Matt went back east "to be closer to my supplier."

For her part, Diana hadn't been allowed to go out for sports until the completion of her first semester and Marcia noticed, with some mild resentment, the apparent ease with which Di fitted into university patterns. The few dates she reported having were uneventful, barren of the matching-up emotional concerns conveyed to her by the others; she seemed to take them in stride, even seemed to be genuinely more interested in where she went with her dates than what they were like. Marcia observed that when Diana wasn't studying or dating, she appeared almost to be appraising her rooming house mates with a curiosity that was strangely detached, perhaps faintly amused at times.

Yet she had to admit, too, that when either she or Soni really needed a friend, Diana was unfailingly there. Her advice was sound, when they asked for it— the athlete rarely volunteered it anymore—and if they simply required somebody to listen, or relax and share some grass with, Diana was perfectly willing to curl up barelegged on her bed and hear them out. "But I have to take it easy on drugs, chums," she told them one November evening. "I wouldn't want to blow my chances in sports."

She didn't. As the second semester began, Diana moved into first gear. Neither Marcia Angell nor Soni Jerome had the free time or the athletic interest to watch their girl friend in her efforts, but Diana informed them, with uncharacteristic excitement, that she'd made both the archery squad and the woman's track team.

"Is it tough, competitive?" Soni demanded, firing questions enthusiastically. "Isn't track a whole bunch of things? Listen, what are you gonna be doing, specifically?"

"Hold it, little one!" Diana was returning from several hours at a beauty parlor in El Vista and hadn't yet removed a cloche hat that hid her hair. She laughed. "One question at a time! To be honest, I found that it was surprisingly easy. They told me that I set a new team accuracy mark the first time I used the bow. As for track, well, they say I sort of pose a problem for them." She turned to Soni and Marcia, whipping off her hat. "I qualified for all the events, but the speed stuff seems a natural for me. How do you like the new Diana Stoker?"

Marcia's brows raised. Soni gasped. Diana's hair was short, now, the flowing locks disappearing into a beauty parlor dustpan. More than that, however, she was no longer a redhead.

"Why did you dye your hair black?" Soni wondered, aloud, staring.

"That's the wrong question, my girl," Diana replied, peering into a mirror and fiddling with short hairs at the nape of her neck. "It should be: 'Why had you dyed your hair red?' This is my real color."

For a moment Marcia didn't speak, simply watched the athlete from the door connecting their rooms. Something—some faintly remembered, largely forgotten wisp of *something*—moved in her mind. Something that bothered her, almost *frightened* her. She cleared her throat. "Why *did* you dye your hair red, Di?" she inquired at last.

Diana laughed merrily. "Would you believe? I don't even remember now." She shrugged, and began changing her clothes. "At the time, it seemed like a good idea to have a new personality, since I was coming out west. To look like a *different* girl entirely. How do I look to you, Marsh?"

Marcia didn't answer at first. She couldn't, because *other* associations were making tingling electrical connections in her memory; *other* pictures she had seen were being recalled.

Diana stood not far from the window. The sunlight flooded her figure from head to toe, bathing her in golden rays. She was marvelously sexual just then, the image perhaps of what every woman would care to be. Already the athlete was superbly tanned by the California sun and, clad in bra and thin panties alone, her conditioning was inescapable. Glaring. Diana Stoker, Marcia realized, was a tremendous physical specimen—but rather more than that. While her shoulders were broad and, when she bent her arms, surprising bicep development became visible, Di's breasts were full, wide, high—precisely what every man was said to desire. Her legs didn't appear muscular so much as ideally proportioned. Her buttocks looked flat in the flimsy white panties; her stomach was covered by a sheen of soft, downy hair, without the hint of a bulge.

And when she stooped to kick her skirt away, her newly short-cropped, ebon head thrust forward, Diana's uncanny similarity to something in Marcia Angell's memory became entirely clear.

She said nothing, not knowing how Diana would take it. Suddenly and oddly—unreasonably, she knew, unfairly; for Diana had never shown a hint of anger or violence—Marcia was *afraid* of the athlete's reactions. And so she kept her thought to herself. . . .

. . . That, half kneeling and barely clothed, bathed in sunshine that made her powerful feminine musculature gleam, Diana Stoker looked like pictures Marcia had seen of long-gone Amazon goddesses stooping remorselessly and coldly to their kill.

CHAPTER XII

Early December. Last Year.

It probably would not have surprised Marcia, who tried to be even-minded and fair about the way she regarded her companions on LaCaresta, to realize that Diana Stoker was growing genuinely concerned about both Marcia and Soni Jerome—and, for that matter, herself.

For the first time in the athlete's young life she found that she cared deeply about someone other than Di Stoker. She had always been a loner by preference, but in the process had also succeeded in making herself lonely. Only the three cats she'd owned, since she was a little girl, had provided any kind of friendship. Diana had come to UCEV largely with the hope of learning more about Diana Stoker—or developing her own mind and considerable abilities in order to become more comfortable with herself. It had been easy, at first, with a completely self-centered goal, to appear detached and midly curious about others.

But that was months ago now and Diana had come to realize that Marcia and Soni filled distinct, once-aching voids in her life: The voids of sisterhood, and of friendship. These facts grew increasingly important in her life as she realized that participation in athletics was providing her with no more insights into a role in life that she felt was confusing and which had begun giving her a series of downright ghastly nightmares—dreams in which she felt enveloped by walls of flame, the searing heat fantastic yet somehow not quite touching her even as she watched other people burn to screaming, shrieking cinders before her coolly alienated eyes. The nightmares seemed oddly more informative than her athletics.

Not that she didn't enjoy the respect, even the envy, with which other young women on the archery and track teams treated her, even the burning, selfish interest the coaches had in her daily prowess. She did.

But the physical side of Di Stoker, she felt, was pretty well handled by itself. The gorgeous and smoothly functioning physique was a gift of nature, not really her own doing. It was basically an outer shell, of no more importance than that, except at the times her body called out in the dark for some sexual release from the opening pit of loneliness that always threatened to overcome her. Ever since childhood, Diana had felt peculiarly apart from her family, out of the mainstream, "different." While she had blocked from her conscious mind many troubling incidents back then which even now sought to rise to the surface, during moments in her frightening dreamworld, a key part of Diana desperately sought answers that might give her a clue to what she *really* was, what she *really* should do with her life.

In the meanwhile, Diana was both so relatively inexperienced and so intelligent that she was shocked to see the mistakes her friends were making. She sensed that Marcia wondered if she, Diana, was sexually different and did not know how to explain that there was a chameleon-like strain running through her that automatically responded to and emulated the latent, generally negative qualities which she intuited in other people. That innate, chameleon side had seen something at once in Soni that Soni didn't even know about herself, and sought to conform to it.

But of late she was learning herself just enough to know that it was a man that Diana Stoker needed, and wanted—and that Soni was on the verge of stepping over a boundary line without truly knowing *her*self or *her* needs. She had made a friend of a senior girl from the debating team. Instantly Diana had sensed that

Pam Garnier was a Lesbian, that she was seeking to lure Soni into her own way of life. And poor little Soni, warmly responding to the attentions of an older classmate, still disturbed by early memories which she could not manage to convey to Di or Marsh, was fast becoming Pam's special prey. If Soni had been steady enough on her own feet to make an adult choice, it wouldn't have mattered to Diana. But now she sensed something undesirably masculine in the aggressive attention Pam gave Soni, and it troubled her.

Tonight, however, it was Marcia Angell who concerned Diana. Di had agreed to a double date only after the bare bones of a skeletal plan had become firm in her mind. In Diana's opinion, Marcia was little more equipped to make a mature decision just now than Soni. The junior instructor who earlier rejected her, after Marcia refused to sleep with him, was clearly on Marsh's mind a lot these days. Anxious for male companionship, she had rebounded to a junior basketball player and all-round athlete named Burt Starr—

—And Burt Starr, Diana knew, had the worst single reputation on campus. He'd never been faithful to any of the young women he dated, despite a line of persuasive gabble that his friends envied, and yet he'd succeeded in bedding most of them. Soon after, of course, he was on his way; worse, he bragged openly of his conquests and yet convinced his next-selected victim that he loved only her in the whole, wide world.

Burt's latest selection was the freshman, shy Marcia Angell.

Happily, Marsh had insisted on doubling tonight and Burt, who had never met Diana, fixed her up with a young socialist named Ray Ellis, who was similarly tall but only the basketball team's manager. He was also, according to rumor, the best bowler on the UCEV campus, of nearly professional calibre.

When Diana was asked what she'd like to do, she chose bowling. Marcia concurred. Burt and Ray looked at each other above the women's heads, an expression that clearly said, "Here's our chance to show off."

Which is precisely what happened during the first game in which the two young men defeated Marcia and Diana by bowling games well in excess of 200. Diana noticed that Marcia was adequate, but barely; her first game score of 120 was fourth among them. Midway through that game it was as if the men had gone alone to the Shamsky Bowling Lanes; Burt would roll a strike and instantly call out to Ray, "Let's see you match *that,* hotshot!" When Ray did, Burt—coolly confident that he remained popular and adorable with his carryover reputation from basketball and romance—applauded wildly, slapped Ray on the backside and then snuggled close to Marcia for a kiss.

At first, Diana was off her game. She hadn't bowled since her junior year of high school and, while she had shown talent in that sport as well as all others, she was content just now to watch what was going on around her. Ray Ellis, for example. Six-two, handsome, with soft brown eyes that danced and a firstrate mind given to experimentation in everything he did. She was beginning to like him until, in the first frame of the second game, he came up to the line after her. The shoes she was wearing, rented from the lanes' management, were tight and she lost her balance when she rolled the second ball. An easy spare was lost. That brought Ray to the line in a timorous pose, wiggling his hips in an exaggerated imitation of her, impossibly shifting the ball to his left hand and *still* succeeding in knocking down nine pins!

Burt Starr was immediately thrown into howling hysterics, chortling with glee even as he hugged Marcia to him and surreptitiously cupped her small breast in his big hand. Her protesting twist away was halfhearted. "Terrific idea, Ray baby!" he called. "Left-handed we can make this easy shit real *fun!*" He peered down at Marsh from his six-seven, his handsome, boyish face flashing with his next double entendre. "I always *was* ambidextrous!" He winked at Ray.

It was Marcia's turn to bowl. Diana watched her. It annoyed her to see no reactive evidence of irritation in the shy brunette's attractive face. Indeed, psychologically smothered by Burt's masculine attention, her face was rapturously twisted into an expression of such limpid adoration that Diana knew Burt must soon add her to his collection. Di's lips became a grim line as she watched.

Marcia guttered her first ball, and giggled—something she never ordinarily did. The basketball player reached out to pat her buttocks, fingers lingering. "Don't y'all worry, little gel," he cried in a western accent intended to be amusing. "Ole Lonestar Tex Ellis'n me'll bowl southy from here on out jest t'show mercy on you cute little heart-rustlers!"

With her second roll, Marcia picked up two pins. Burt and Ray's applause was gleeful, manic. Burt, sitting at the scoring table, murmured with elaborate carefulness: "Let's *see* now. *Two,* added to your combined score of sixty-*eight*—" he looked up with a wild-eyed expression of mock anxiety—"why, Raymond, they's pulled t'only one a hunnerd-and-twenty-five points *behind* us! Ah do think we's in *ser*ious danger!"

Marcia sat gingerly beside him. Immediately his broad palm was high on her leg, the fingers gripping, closer. Marcia's hand convered his as she gave a small gasp, partly of anticipation, partly of a surprise akin to fear.

Diana arose. Dressed in a mesh yellow sweater and tight-fitting crimson shorts, she knew she looked great and had been periodically aware of how both young men had stolen glimpses of her long, well-curved legs. "Breaktime, okay?" she murmured casually. "Let's get some cokes." Now Ray was seated at the scoring bench. "Burt, give me a hand with the cups, will you?"

He wouldn't drop his phony western accent. Burt seemed to find his humor entrancing. "Leetle gel, it's m'pleasure, hear? Treat's on Ole Deadeye hisself." Burt hauled his muscular six-seven after Diana, up the steps, his eyes devouring her legs as the thought occurred plainly to Di: *I'm supposed to be next. First*

Marcia; then me.

She stopped before reaching the concession stand, turning to rest a palm on his deep chest. "Burt, I have something to say to you."

"Y'crave my fantastic bod, right?" he asked, only half teasing.

"You are no good for Marsh. You really aren't." Her eyes held his. "I don't know what kind of promises you've made to her, but they're sheer bullshit. You know that, and I know that. Let's be candid."

He wasn't even startled. He'd obviously heard this before. Girl tries to protect her friend; how boring. "Go ahead and tell her that, why don't you?" he challenged from a foot above Diana. His smile was the coldest thing she'd seen in years. Despite his tanktop and jeans, Burt suddenly did not look like a boy anymore. She saw him clearly as a mature, calculating, grown man. "Tonight, okay? Tell little Marsh Ole Deadeye just wants to get her bones in the sack. And see how far you get, baby!"

She shrugged. "I thought it would be that way. Look, you're an athlete like me. Right? I mean you dig honest competition and all that jazz?" She watched as he nodded, slowly, his handsome eyes narrowing. "Honor in sports means something to you—a little something anyway. Right?"

Suddenly he began to get the drift. "It does," he admitted, taking Di seriously for the first time. "I never cheat in basketball. What d'you have in mind?"

"This." From a pocket in her shorts she pulled a note, holding it up for him to see. "This little note needs your signature, stud. It says, quite simply, that if I—'I' is *you*, Burt Starr—lose the second game of bowling on tonight's date, I—that's *you* still, Burt—will inform Marcia Angell of the truth, and stop dating her. Stop calling, stop seeing her; for good." She smiled and produced a pen. "I'd like to trust you, Honest Competitor, but I'd rather have you sign the note."

Slowly, deliberately, a wide, even warm smile passed

across the athlete's face. "Fascinating!" He said it not without admiration. "Your score against mine—is that what you mean?"

"No." Diana shook her tight-cropped head. *"Our score against yours and Ray's."* She paused. "You wouldn't understand this, but it's important to me that we *both* defeat you—*together.*"

"You gotta be outta your skull," Burt laughed. "You just heard our score a minute ago. We're killing you, *totaling* you! Y'haven't a chance!"

"Fine. Sign the note." She pressed the pen and paper in his palm.

"Hold it." He took them, then looked steadily down into her dark eyes. "A bet is a bet so what do *I* get out of it? I mean, sure, you can't possibly win. So the logical question *is:* What do *I* win?"

Diana placed her fists on her hips and spread her legs provocatively, her bust forward. *"Me,* All-Star. That's what you win. Me, wherever you want, doing *whatever* you want. All . . . night . . . long."

He looked down at her full lips, her high breasts pressing against the thin material of her sweater, her broad hips and impossibly long legs; he released a slow, admiring whistle. "This is the best Christmas present I ever got!" he exclaimed, swiftly scribbling his signature on the note and returning it. His blue eyes glowed with open sensuality. "Marcia to screw tonight, *you* tomorrow night! Hot shit, what a parlay!"

This time Diana returned the note to her cleavage, watching Burt's brows raise as he followed the note mentally between her swelling breasts. She wore no bra. She hoped he got a good look.

"Your turn up. Di," Ray Ellis called as they returned. "Where're the cokes?"

Diana patted his head as she looked for her ball in the rack. "Forget 'em, Raymond," she told him, inserting her fingers in the heavy black sphere. "They're bad for superstars like Burt and me. Almost as bad as the other kind of coke."

Two steps, three, four; arm back, forward; the ball

released, rolling; *strike!*

"What turned *you* on?" Ray asked with a mild laugh. "Nice ball, Di."

"Thanks." She paused beside Marcia with a confidential smile, her eyes glittering at Ray. "You ain't seen *nothin'* yet!"

Burt Starr was all business now, the athlete who was All-Pac 10 in basketball, the one they said would be a First Round draft choice in the NBA. He retrieved his ball numbly, bowled it. He was tense and it narrowly missed being a strike. A single pin remained and, when he released his second ball, it briefly grazed the pin, yet left it standing. Only nine points. He glared at Diana but said nothing as he returned to the bench and sat beside his male friend.

"Marsh," Diana said, as offhandedly and amiably as she could, "don't try to bowl it so hard. Okay? If the ball's weight is right, it doesn't take a lot of strength. Just accuracy. Look for your spot and a good follow through."

Marcia nodded, glanced at her friend. The match meant nothing to her but if it was important now to Diana, she'd try.

Eight pins down. When she stepped back beyond the line, mildly dissatisfied, Ray Ellis stood and approached her with the friendly, expert smile of someone who is really good at something. Diana decided she was right about him; he was essentially a decent person. "If you girls are going to try," he said affably, "let me show you how to pick up that spare."

"Ray!" yowled Burt, looking at his pal and seeing Benedict Arnold instead. His face was scarlet. "What the fuck y'*doing?"*

"Relax, All-American," Ray replied without looking up, bending to his pupil. "This is just business. Okay, Marsh—like this, see? All right?"

She nodded.

She also picked up the spare. Burt squirmed irritably, uncomfortably, on the bench.

Ray followed with a pretty strike but when Diana

again took four sure paces forward, she bowled another strike of her own.

Now the lead dwindled. Burt blinked several times as he stood. "Somethin' in my eye," he growled defensively. He took several deep breaths, looking like a giant crane. This time he stood nearly half a minute at the line, a picture of studied concentration. Then, in three long strides, he was releasing the ball—

—And watching it hook impossibly to the left, skitter along the edge of the lane for several wobbly feet and then fall heavily into the gutter.

"Son of a bitch!" he exclaimed angrily, whirling to glare furiously at Diana Stoker. *"Damn* you, you witch-bitch!"

Ray was beside his friend in a moment, frowning. "Cool it, man," he commanded roughly. Ray was only a couple of inches shorter than the basketball player and somewhat more muscular. "I don't dig language like that in front of ladies, okay? Take it easy! This is just for *fun*—remember?"

Impotently, unable to explain, Burt glared at his friend. He badly wanted to tell him the truth, that there was not one but *two* broads in bed at stake, and much more than that besides: his pride as a lover, his pride as an athlete, his pride as a man. But when he glanced at Marcia, he realized that telling the truth now would lose her; when he glanced at Diana, his eyes gone mad, she patted between her breasts. There, he knew, where *he'd* like to be—teaching her a lesson, *showing* her how much a man he was—rested the note.

When he rolled his second ball it was just off center. Instead of a second-ball, all-pin spare, he knocked down only six pins.

From there on, it got easier for the women. Marcia, still coached by expert Ray Ellis, steadily improved her game. Two frames later Burt got one more strike and felt a surge of renewed hope.

But next Ray, thinking more about Marcia's game, blew a spare—

—And then Diana struck out, the rest of the way, her

swing a perfect, flawless stroke, her power startling in a woman. Ray applauded wildly. Her individual score was over 260, best of the evening.

Added to Marcia's 168, it edged the men by three pins.

The ride back to LaCaresta was silent except for Ray, who was driving but continued to look back over the seat at Marcia. It had dawned on him that she had qualities he appreciated in a girl: she was attractive, tractable, bright without showing off, and fun. He wanted, he thought, to take her away from Burt Starr. How that could be done, he had no idea.

For her part, Marcia seemed surprised, even confused, by the way Burt Starr kept his distance from her. In front of the rooming house, he got out and led her up the steps where he spoke briefly, curtly to her. "I think he's breaking it off," Ray said to Di in the car, astonished. "She's going right inside."

Diana patted his arm. "Thanks for a fun evening, Ray," she said softly. She gave him a quick kiss on the cheek. "Maybe you'll never know *how* much fun."

When she climbed out of the car she met Burt on the street. Her voice was sweetly feminine. " 'Night, Burty," she purred.

"*Twat!*" he said under his breath, pausing just briefly. "Fuckin' queer goddam *bitch!*"

Her face was within inches of his then. "I'll tell you one thing, All-Star," she said under hers, her hand locked on his wrist and squeezing until he wanted to cry out. "If you *ever* call me that again, I'll break your back for you. And if you don't think so, *try* it."

He didn't reply. She let him go. Then the car door closed with a mighty slam and she hoped he heard her tinkling laugh floating back down the steps to him.

CHAPTER XIII

Marcia stopped on the steps leading to the second floor, tears in her eyes and her shoulders shaking involuntarily. When she looked back to Diana a glance told her that Di knew, that it was all over with Burt Starr.

Instead of wondering why, she went into Diana's arms in a quick little rush, sobbing.

"Did you love him so much after so short a time?" the athlete asked, not hugging back but allowing Marsh to cry it out.

"N-No. I don't suppose I really *loved* him, or anything l-like that," replied the timid brunette; "but he was so *beautiful!*"

Di nodded soberly. "The ones who hurt the most always are, it seems. And they're so goddam *aware* of it!"

"At least," Marcia murmured, pulling her face back a little and mustering a smile, "you didn't insult me by telling me I'm better off without him."

"You *are*, though," Diana retorted promptly, smiling back.

Mrs. Hudson, aroused by the talking on her stairs, appeared below them with a questioning expression on her oversized face. "You're back early," she remarked, keeping her index finger in the ever-present Bartlett's. "Is anything wrong?"

"A minor case of broken-heartitis, Mrs. Hudson, thank you," Marcia answered, drying her eyes on a handkerchief. "Or the wrong guy for the right girl; something like that."

"Well, well, I shan't criticize your affairs, dear," the old woman asserted. "I remember the verse by Busch: 'Youth should heed the older-witted when they say, don't go too far—Now their sins are all committed, Lord, how virtuous they are!'"

Mrs. Hudson beamed upon them with merry wisdom, waved a plump hand and disappeared into the downstairs sitting room as Marcia and Diana stared after her in astonishment. "How does she *do* that?" the former asked in amused wonder.

"I think," Di replied, leading the way to the second floor, "that she memorizes what she wants to say, and then uses black magic to *motivate* the situation until it's applicable!"

Both girls were laughing with relief when they barged into the first or nearest room—the one shared by Diana and Soni.

Both girls stopped in their tracks, gaping, as Diana's cat Mercury fled into the hallway.

On Soni's bed was a tangle of bodies which, for a moment, couldn't be mentally separated. Diana and Marcia weren't expected back for at least another hour and the two young women in the bed were oblivious to the presence of anyone else.

It was Soni and the senior debating girl, Pam Garnier, the two blonds locked together like golden shears. Soni, below, turned her face abruptly to peer toward the door and an immediate look of horror contorted her features.

Atop, Pam's face continued to work energetically between Soni's legs. In the shadowed room her naked, straining body appeared oddly hilly, the buttocks and shoulders forming the major mounds, the bobbing head a minor one.

In three swift steps Diana was beside the bed, reaching down with only one hand to snatch the long, scraggly yellow hair of the Lesbian, yanking her, bare, to her feet. Pam staggered and her fingers flew to her panting mouth in consternation; her eyes were at once glazed with passion and nearsightedness from the close contact. She was a rather pretty young woman except for a somewhat hippy ambience below the waist and rather heavily thighed legs.

"*Damn* you, you don't give a good goddam about Soni Jerome," Diana accused the older girl, still gripping the blond head and shaking it now and then. "It wouldn't be any of my affair, what's gone on here, if I didn't realize what you're doing—how you're taking advantage of someone younger and more helpless than you."

Pam batted feebly at Diana's hand locked in her hair. "I don't know what the hell you're talking about," she blustered, trying to pull away.

"I'm talking about the way you behave no better than most of the men on this campus," Diana retorted, letting go now and scooping Pam's hurredly discarded clothing into her arms. "Here, get into these and then get out!" She hesitated, glancing down at Soni. "So what do *you* have to say about this?"

Soni had pulled herself to the edge of the bed and sat there now, trembling, obviously startled and confused. She was a natural blond, the way Diana once had guessed. Her breasts, flattened and scarcely discernible when she had been on her back, were strangely childlike as she leaned forward; they looked new, unused. Her knees turned in, like those of a timid, small girl.

"I'm sorry I d-disappointed you and I s'pose you're right, Di," she said, deep in embarrassment. "Pam told me she just wanted to interest me in the Reemergence of the Goddesses class." Soni lifted her pert face up, forlornly, first to Diana and then to Marcia. "Next t-thing I knew, she was—holding me. I guess maybe I'm just a big baby but it seemed n-nice . . . getting affection from somebody. . . ."

By now Pam Garnier had replaced her bra and shoes and stood stork-like on one stout leg, trying to get into her panties. Her face was fiery red with anger. "I'll *get* you for this, Stoker!" she swore. "No freshman, female jock does this to a senior and gets by with it!"

For a moment Diana did not reply. Sudden silence filled the room, instantly became stifling. Marcia, watching the scene with amazement, felt something like—*electricity*—dart from her friend to the Lesbian. "That's twice tonight people have called me names and threatened me," Diana said thoughtfully, her voice soft and yet menacing. "It's also twice *too* often."

As Marcia's eyes widened in astonishment, Diana reached for Pam Garnier. What happened next was so quick, so powerfully dazzling, that she couldn't quite follow it.

But Pam Garnier's half-naked body was soaring from beside the bed through the open bedroom door. It collided with the wall, hard; there was a little scream of terror and pain and then Pam was on her feet, running for the stairs, her yellow hair streaming behind her. Marcia ran to the door with Diana, who threw Pam's other clothing all the way to the stairway. They watched, seeing the way Pam looked back up in total fright before disappearing into the night.

Marcia turned to gape at her friend. "My God, Diana," she said in a breath, "Pam's no little child—and *you threw* her *all* the way across the room—and out into the hallway!"

Diana ran a palm across her close-cropped dark head and dropped before Soni, handing her clothes with almost maternal gentleness. "I was furious, Marsh, that's all," she said softly. "Sometimes anger gives you the strength you don't know you have."

Marcia Angell nodded, speechless now, and sat down across from Soni on Diana's bed. *Oh, yes, Diana Stoker,* she thought with fascination. *You knew perfectly well how strong you were—and somehow I don't think that display even scratched the surface.* Then the other thought occurred to her, unasked. *"I'm sorry I disappointed you," Soni had said to Diana. Was it possible that poor little Soni was just swapping* one *authority figure, even* one *bully, for another?"*

Carolyn Lord knuckled the sleep from her eyes as she went into the living room of her apartment to answer the phone "'Lo?" she said, and added, before hearing the caller's identity, "This'd better be important! D'you know what *time* it is?"

"It's Mary, Mom," said the voice in her ear. "Sorry to call now but *I* think it's important."

"Are you all right?" came the perpetual query of the mother.

"I'm fine." Mary paused. "I wanted to tell you that it's all settled. We're enrolling in your Goddess class, all three of us."

Carolyn, conscious of a chill in the apartment, pulled the bathrobe closer around her breasts. "I'm glad to hear it, of course," she said, yawning. "But couldn't that have waited until morning?"

"There's more," Mary said. She seemed to be gathering her nerve to speak and, for a moment, fear hung like a tangible thing in the air between mother and daughter. "Mom," she said at last, "I think—*I think I know who Hecate is, and s-she's right here on campus!*"

CHAPTER XIV

Christmas break, last year. The school cafeteria.

"I asked y'here to be *reasonable,* y'know?—to try t'iron-out Diana Stoker's problems for ya," Coach Henry Parseval said persuasively to the strong-faced, orange-haired woman across the booth from him. He could not know how they were separated by far more than sport or sex. "T'see if her coaches can't make the decision for her."

"You asked me here, Henry, to screw me out of the finest archer I've ever had," she countered in affable tones. "To take Diana away from me for your full utilization on a track team you got *stuck* with coaching when Eddie Conroy died."

He spread his hands, still seeking to appear reasonable. "Look, Betty, I'd *like* t'do that. God knows, I would. There ain't nobody from ole Eddie's last team and I just don't unnerstand track and field the way I do basketball. But I figure gettin' Diana completely away from you is just as impossible as the things that broad does in sports."

She paused to look languidly around Distant Vistas, dismayed and a little nostalgic, the way the cafeteria had made her at this time of the year for the past five years.

It was almost deserted and clicking cups or saucers sounded booming, echo-chambered. There were some kids present who needed to spend every minute boning up for crucial test, plus a few who didn't have the money to go home and return in January. Several

Jewish boys and girls played bridge at a table near the door. A handful of foreign exchange students were seated yards up from her, their bright native costumes somehow deepening Betty's negative feelings.

A few weeks ago, festive with red and green streamers, the place's merriment had engaged her, but now the cafeteria was lifeless. It had an after-the-raid, bombed-out demeanor and the gay strips of colored paper were getting tattered, reminding Betty Haggert of the way her own middle-aged life was fraying out at the ends. She sighed deeply without looking back at Parseval. It was nobody's fault, actually, and she wondered woefully if anything was. The only companion she'd ever had since Daddy died in '56 was her mother and it was no one's fault that Mother grew senile, five years back, and now existed—deeply esconced in a molasses past—sad light years away.

It would be impossible to get this pragmatic, balding man across from her to realize that she *lived* for a chance to coach someone like Diana Stoker, not only because Diana could single handedly give her a good season but because—well, because all her girls were the daughters she'd never had and the brilliant ones, like Diana, required special attention.

Her gaze trickled over Parseval's seamed, ex-athlete's mug and she realized that even if she *could* get him to see all that, Henry Parseval wouldn't give a single damn. "You can't have her to yourself, coach," she said flatly. "I won't allow it."

"Shit, Betty, let's face it. Di Stoker is the best athlete ever to hit this campus, male or female. And more'n that, archery ain't a major sport; never will be."

"Track and field, of course," she replied coolly, "has millions of avid fans. Professional track and field stars earn top dollar, right?"

"Well, they do better'n *archery* people, f'God's sake!" he snapped, wondering what it took to reason successfully with this broad with the sturdy back and shoulder muscles. "I really believe Diana can get t'the next Olympics, win maybe two, three gold medals."

"And put her coach's name in headlines all over the world, right?" Betty patted his hand fleetingly. "Glad to see self-interest still hasn't gotten the best of you, Henry." She lit a cigarette with perfectly steady hands. "I want her as my archer, full time. She can't possibly be better in your sport than mine."

"Oh, yeh?" he growled, reddening. He put his sandwich down. "Let me tell you, lady, that Stoker dame is—is *weird*, she's so good! I can't pay her a higher compliment than to say she's athletic the way a guy is—incredibly competitive, strong, great endurance, smart enough to know when t'pace herself, always something left." He leaned closer, trying not to cough over the smoke from her cigarette. "Lemme tell you something, in confidence, okay? I had Fred Enders, our miler, take her on last week. He's been unofficially clocked at close to four." His eyes gleamed fanatically. "She beat him. I had a watch on her, and she ran it—I *think*—in *under* four minutes." Parseval stopped short and caught a breath. "The amazing thing is, Diana wasn't even sweatin'—and I think she was holdin' something back! When she gets her form down, Betty, Diana might break the world's record in the mile—the man's world record!"

"That's almost impossible," Betty Haggert said flatly. "She told me she's never *run* the distances before!"

"I know." He nodded sagely, tapped his coke glass. "Sometimes, well, I think Diana isn't quite human."

Betty Haggert jumped, blinked. Then she bit her lower lip. "I wish you hadn't said that."

"Said what?" he demanded. "That she can do the mile in under four minutes?"

"No, no." She shook her head. "That Di isn't quite human. And that other thing you said—that she's 'weird, she's so good.' I, um, I sense something very... *different*... about Diana. Something I've never seen in another student, female or male. For that matter," she blinked, embarrassed, turning from him, "in anyone else."

The most metaphysical Henry Parseval ever got was

on Easter, when he made his annual visit to his Baptist Church and tried not to believe that the pastor was talking about him. "Waddaya mean?" he demanded. "*How*, different?"

Now her eyes met his levelly. "*Inhumanly* different. Look, you brought it up, Henry." She rapped her knuckles once on the table. "*You* said she was weird."

"Yeah, I did." Parseval had always been an honest man, a fair man; he prided himself in that. Now he sighed. "Maybe I could go along with you in what you're sayin', Betty. Part way." He pointed his finger at her. "What *are* you sayin'?"

The cafeteria seemed tomblike just then. Most of the scant student patronage had quickly departed as night came on and the counter girl, with nothing to do, had retreated to the kitchen. Silence etched its unseen dark lines in oval shadows that peaked in the booth of the two coaches.

"Do you know any mythology, Henry?" Betty asked quietly. "It's been a hobby of mine, for a long while now. I've even thought of monitoring the new class Carolyn Lord will be teaching."

"Go on," he encouraged her.

"Henry, I don't think anyone's done the things with a bow and arrow that Diana Stoker can do since . . . since Diana, the Huntress."

"The *goddess?*" he demanded. "From Olympus?" He chuckled drily. "Jeez, that's kind of far out, Betty. Whaddaya sayin' to me now?—that *this* Diana is the—the *reincarnation* of some ancient myth?"

She put her cigarette out with a sudden darting motion, then waved her vertical hand to suggest indecision. "I don't know, really. But Henry, I've really gotten *into* mythology since Mother . . . got sick five years ago. A lot of free time on my hands, know what I mean?" She smiled. "Well, a great many experts believe that Diana, the Huntress, and a hideous creature named Hecate, *were one and the same person.* That the prototypes of the Olympian gods and goddesses actually existed, and that Diana's name was changed when she was—was—"

"Was what?" Parseval pressed her.

Betty frowned. "When she was consigned to the rulership of Hades."

"You believe in *that?*" he demanded. "In Hell, as a real place, somewhere down in the center of the earth somewhere?"

Betty colored. "I don't know just what I believe, except that there are plenty of mythologists who claim to have evidence that the Olympians *lived*. Among them, Diana and the perfectly atrocious Hecate." She hesitated. "You've heard all the talk about the possibility that the Earth was seeded by visitors from other planets? Well, if so, the gods and goddesses were among those visitors. So Diana, or Hecate, was *never* human—never one of us. But she *did* live."

The coach grunted. "Gotta admit it's interesting. Tell me more."

"So much of this was handed down orally for generations," she continued, "that it's hard to separate fact from fancy. Maybe impossibly so. But the *facts*—"her eyes flashed sternly at him—"are there. A school of thought claims that Hecate was actually *trioditis,* three entities. Goddess of the Parting Ways."

"But this was so long ago," Parseval argued. "Nobody believes this shit now, do they?"

She nodded. Affirmatively. To her back, a cafeteria window was filling with blackness as the day drew to an end. A tree branch tapped against the window, eerily, forming moving shadows. "Today, Henry, among Italian witches—some say the most potent and uncanny witches left on earth—it is *not* Satan who is their leader, but Hecate—a cat-goddess of ghosts; cannibalistic; sheer evil; mother of a monster named Scylla who had more than one head and who still serves at the other entrance to Hades. Hecate is also known in all *chtonic,* or nocturnal, secret sorcery around the world—but always *whispered* of; rarely is she directly invoked."

"Lemme have one-a them cigarettes," he said nervously, taking one and lighting it, glancing toward the moving shadows at the window. "Keep goin'. If I go home now, Peg'll have me helpin' clean the joint for Christmas Day. Look. How did this Diana, or Hecate, *get* to Hades? I'd think that might be tough for a living goddess who wasn't a simple sinner like me."

Betty smiled. She realized that Henry was only curious; she also realized he probably thought her mildly mad. And that he was trying, hard, to make friends and get her cooperation. "A society of devilish women called the Sybils guided and served her, and also Lucifer, god of Hades. When the Sybils went into trances, they were possessed and used by Hecate or Lucifer." She paused. "For unspeakable things."

"Okay. What's this . . . 'trioditis' you mentioned, the three forms of Hecate?" he inquired, puffing unfamiliarly on his cigarette and trying not to look out at the darkness behind Betty. "Who else *was* she, besides Diana?"

"*Trioditis* coincides with three lunar phases, the new, full and old moons," Betty said. "The ghosts of those who died before their times are Hecate's special companions and, in that connection, she's sometimes called *antaia*, 'the meeter,' by those who don't wish to use her name. Or even *einodia*, 'she who appears on the way.' The way to Hell." Behind her, thunder suddenly rumbled and lightning winked in the window. "But to answer your question, Henry, according to authorities such as Cavendish, Bullfinch and Huson, Hecate's other or third person was Apollo's sister, Artemis—Lady of Wild Things. In the *Iliad* she even appears as a beautiful virgin huntress, Mistress of Animals."

Henry's brow raised. He had seen her hesitate. "So was Artemis a nice little goddess?" he asked jocularly. "And how can anybody livin' today believe in someone—even an alien from outer space somewhere—being *three people?*"

"Haven't you ever heard of multiple personality?" Betty asked softly. "I believe that's what the case was, that the goddess we call Hecate, *whatever* her origins, was driven mad by the evil within her." She picked up her purse and edged her way out. "Artemis, in answer to your question, was regarded as good and decent for some time, until she condemned her lover, Admetus, to death. And, well, there was one incident even worse than that."

"What was it?" he asked, suddenly uncomfortable despite himself.

"A Greek named Actaeon inadvertently saw Hecate bathing naked. It's said that Artemis—or Hecate—turned him into a stag and summoned the hounds, which she rules." Betty tried to smile. "He was run down by them, killed and eaten."

Parseval pushed back the cold remnants of his sandwich and made a face. "God, that's *gross!* I got to hand it to you, Coach Haggert. Y'know a lot of interesting things."

"And one more of those, before I leave," Betty said, standing at the end of the booth and smiling down at him. "I appreciate the rapt attention you gave me but I will *not* share Diana Stoker with your track and field squad. Understand? I'll fight you for the exclusive right to her skills. So I suggest we leave it up to Diana herself and forget all this nonsense. Yours, as well as my little fairytale."

He glanced up at her and saw that she meant it. "Okay." He fumbled to shake her hand. "It's up to Diana."

After he heard her heels click away into the distance, and out the door of Distant Vistas, Henry Parseval sat for another moment with the cigarette he'd taken and thought about the things Coach Haggert had told him.

Finally he put the butt out and stood, much less at ease than he'd been when he arrived. He put his sweater on; the night grew chilly, for California.

It had just occurred to him that maybe it would be just as well if Diana Stoker stayed with the archery team. Because, even though he could never say this to Betty Haggert and would never say it to another man, not for the greatest basketball center since Bill Walton—because Diana Stoker scared the living hell out of him!

PART THREE

The Reemergence of the Goddess

"I asked a Burmese why women, after centuries of following their men, now walk ahead. He said there were many unexploded land mines since the war." —Robert Mueller

"Male domination has had some very unfortunate side effects. It has made the most intimate of human relations, that of marriage, one of master and slave instead of one between equal partners." —Bertrand Russell

"A woman is but an animal, and an animal not of the highest order." —Edmund Burke

"The history of mankind is a history of repeated injuries and usurpations on the part of man toward woman, having in direct object the establishment of a tyranny.
—Woman's Rights Convention: Manifesto, Seneca Falls, 1848

"They came close to me, and looked at me for some time, and then whispered together. Two were dark, and had high aquiline noses... and great dark, piercing eyes... There was something about them that made me uneasy, some longing and at the same time some deadly fear... They whispered together, and then all three laughed—such a silvery, musical laugh, but as hard as though the sound never could have come through the softness of human lips."
—Bram Stoker, "Dracula"

"At dead of night in front of the dark cavern on the bank of the somber lake she slaughtered four coal-black bullocks to Hecate, the dread Goddess of Night. As she placed the sacrificial parts upon a blazing altar, the earth rumbled and quaked beneath their feet and from afar dogs howled through the darkness. With a cry to Aeneas, 'Now will you need all your courage,' she rushed into the cave ... They found themselves soon on a road wrapped in shadows which yet permitted them to see frightful forms on either side, pale Disease and avenging Care, and Hunger that persuades to crime, and so on, a great company of terrors. Death-dealing War was there and mad Discord with snaky, bloodstained hair, and many other curses to mortals."

—Edith Hamilton, "Mythology,"
Little, Brown, Mass., 1940

"Hecate of hell, Mighty to shatter every stubborn thing.
Hark! Hark! her hounds are baying through the town.
Where three roads meet, *there* she is standing."

—Homer

CHAPTER XV

January of this year. Muriel Kane Hall.

There'd been no flashy announcements that the Re-emergence of the Goddesses course would get under way on the 7th of January, nor any statement to the effect that students would be given immortal life. No one promised them so much as certain graduation, or eventual triumph over the male of the species. But word-of-mouth excitement so successfully spread the news—plus copious hints of how youthful Dr. Carolyn Lord planned to approach her hot topic—that attendance at the first session astounded everyone concerned. Over two hundred young women filled with a religious conviction that life could be much better, enrolled within the first ten days that the course was available. By itself, that was a reception that heartened and enthralled Carolyn.

But by the afternoon of the 7th, last-minute enrollment incredibly swelled to nearly five hundred brash and eager female students. They milled about outside room 401 like so many multihued birds of prey, bickering and squalling for space—especially for entry to the normal-sized room—with the mindless mob viciousness of strutting pigeons scrambling for a handful of breadcrumbs. A security officer or two lounged, perplexed, on the outskirts of the mob, fingering nightsticks like so many sensitive phallic symbols. There, a male instructor could be seen bobbing precariously above the avian tide, moving his arms in what was sometimes a literal breast stroke, calling unheard commands, only to go under again. One security guard later said wryly that he was sure some of the valiant monitors never surfaced again.

As a consequence of this unparalleled enthusiasm, Reemergence of the Goddesses—swiftly acronymed ROTGOD, with possibly more subtle indication of how this course might evolve than anyone consciously intended—picked itself up, bag and baggage and birds, to move from Room 401 to the more capacious Muriel Kane Hall. The way the students flowed inside gave the impression that a giant vacuum sweeper had sucked them into the hall.

Despite her own extensive preparation, the svelte Carolyn Lord found herself momentarily smitten by nerves. The restless sea of fertile faces before her might have unhinged a more experienced instructor, and Carolyn had only the prior semester of her sedate English class behind her. She picked out her daughter, Mary, with some difficulty, concluding that the girls on either side of her were her friends from LaCaresta Drive.

She took a deep breath and plunged. "The goddesses of old—our first arbiters of law, theology and morality; our first heroines—are not dead, because the divinity *cannot* die. They only sleep. But soon, sooner than anyone knows, they will awaken, they will reemerge— through each of *you*."

Immediately she had the rapt attention of her audience, and it seemed to intensify with everything she said. Midway through the fifty-minute class, it occurred to Carolyn with surprise that part of her task would not be to persuade or convince, at all. These young women were so anxious to participate in anything linked to the women's liberation movement that they would believe *whatever* she told them! For a moment she would remember, Carolyn stopped talking to look out at them—bright, often lovely, alertly intelligent faces—and felt unprepared and unworthy to perform the rites of education in the midst of such uncritical, strangely mindless acceptance.

In that transient instant she realized that she had misjudged the urgency, the feverish desire of many young women to abandon an entire world of traditions, mores, cliches and general public and social accommodations to the concept that civilization was primarily operated with men at the throttle. More, she had not accurately gauged the fury and violence with which some students clearly viewed all such accommodations nor how fully they intended to revoke these customs, at *all* costs. Yes, Carolyn thought in a quick feat of intuition, that was it! *She* had recognized with annoyance the domination of man, felt it was a silly custom; but *these* young women saw it as nothing short of slavery. For her it was a periodic irritation that simply found its focus usefully in the Neanderthal attitudes of her ex-husband. For them, well, it was a perpetually occurring, ceaseless version of psychological rape.

And she thought at the outermost fringes of her blinding moment of understanding, of frankly apologizing to them and quietly pulling out of the class until she could reappraise her own position, learn if *she* was right, or they: occasional annoyance or ongoing brutilization.

What she had meant to use as a means of persuading them to become as disturbed as she—by almost-satirically invoking ancient goddesses as a temporary substitution for God, or the Godhead—could only be taken *literally* by such people as they, and made no more sense then trying to talk the New York Yankees or Notre Dame into taking sports seriously. *Did* what she was meaning to do amount to intellectual incitement to riot or—

—A hand up, two rows from Mary's. "Yes?" Carolyn asked, relieved to let someone else speak.

"Are you honestly proposing that we supplant the concept of a male God with the goddesses of old?" asked a stringy-haired and obese young woman. "Is that what you're really suggesting?"

Carolyn stared as long as she could before answering, blurting it out: "Yes! That's exactly what I'm urging. It must be done for us to be free."

Slowly, like thunder rolling up a beach and seeming to fill the sand itself with sound, applause rumbled from all sides and culminated in something like a booming shout of agreement. She felt dazed, and dazzled by such open endorsement of what she'd planned to use as an exercise tool in logic and in persuasion.

And she smiled back into that thunder, allowed herself to be bathed by the storm of reinforcement. Finally Carolyn raised a palm and the noise immediately diminished to murmurs of joy. "Isis, Athena, Demeter, Hera, Astrae," she intoned the ancient honor roll of goddesses, "they strode this earth and mortal man bowed beneath them, humbled. *Their* sex is yours, *their* blood flows in your veins. *Think* of the total liberation I'm holding out to you, ladies!" Somehow she was back into her lecture, uncertain of just where but aware that it didn't matter in the least to them. "Why do we need men at *all*, in our lives? When Hera was angry with Zeus, and refused him a child, she conceived an infant of her own—totally *without the aid* of Zeus or indeed *any* man! *That* was the first virgin birth!"

Another hand shot up. Carolyn Lord did not recognize the beautiful young woman but she sat between Marcia and Soni and her name was Diana Stoker. "Please tell us, Dr. Lord," she began, her voice forthright, easily carrying, "if Eve wasn't the first woman—and if, in the beginning, there were only gods—who *was* the first real woman on earth?"

Carolyn was pleased by the question. "The first woman's name is not recorded, which shows how our generally careful storytellers of old felt about a mere female. In that sense, I think I may say, she is *you*—*each* of you, seeking your own special identity." Now her gaze roamed around the room, challenging the students who, to a woman, were on the edge of their seats. "She was the fatherless infant to whom I just alluded. She was formed from clay by the goddess Hephaetus, alone, was later adorned by the goddess Athene and was finally displayed by Zeus both to the gods and mortal man—for according to legend, man was here first, *without* woman, and Zeus apparently wished to punish unruly mankind by sending them women." The instructor smiled, but it was wry and humorless. "Already, then, we were being exploited. Our maker, a supreme and divine woman, made us as an *equal;* but a male god cast us down. I fear it is further recorded, clearly by male scribes, that this mythical first woman was presented to men as Zeus' 'punishment' for demanding the gift of fire for human beings." The professor's cool eyes narrowed. "And so we see that it was woman who created woman, who earned for civilization our sex's first useful knowledge—fire, ordinarily considered the tool of man—and woman who was obliged to defy a man who was the mightiest of gods in order to secure fire for the humankind of both sexes."

The interest level remained where it was but here and there Carolyn saw smiles of passing disbelief, smiles that said to her, "It's always been this way and we can't fight it." Again Carolyn raised her arms above her head; again they fell quiet.

"I wonder if that legend I've read you will remain as amusing," she went on, "when I read more of the *exact words* of that male scribe." She glanced down at her notes. "He said that 'when they saw that which was sheer guile'—meaning of course, the lowly and deceptive creature called Woman—'it was not to be withstood by man. For *from* her is the deadly race and tribe of women who live amongst mortal men to their great trouble.' Think of *that,* young women! 'Deadly,' he called us; full of 'guile;' all 'great trouble' laid promptly at our doors, right from the beginning of civilization! And *that* attitude hasn't changed in *thousands of years!* If any of you should wish to consider goddesses nothing but myths, you must still confront the fact that ancient human beings, who founded civilization, *believed in* goddesses and *began* everything we continue to oppose today!"

Now, mingled with the strong burst of encouraging applause, there was a murmuring note of sharp anti-male resentment. Brief, fiery retorts were whispered; the few young men who had ambled into the class from curiosity quietly arose, then tiptoed out of Muriel Kane Hall, like reds at a KKK meeting.

"But kindly note, my new friends," Dr. Lord picked up the thread as her voice rose with authority, "that there is *an operative clause* in the remark of that ancient male scribe: 'It was *not* to be *withstood* by men.' In short, they couldn't beat us! Man could not withstand—*he couldn't cope with*—our so-called 'guile.' And what's more, students, there's not a man alive who can, even *today*, withstand the intellectual vigor and splendid moral courage of womankind! Because—" she finished, having to yell now above the emotional calls of "Right on!" and "E.R.A.!", herself afire now with revolutionary zeal—"because *men* were merely born or put here, but *women* are the *direct descendants of goddesses!*"

There was tumultuous applause and frantic note-taking. Here and there, a young woman stood, her hands energetically flailing one another. Eyes that had been too long dimmed by the physical, looming threat of Man sparkled or wept.

At that moment, had students voted for the next President of UCEV, Carolyn Lord might have been elected by acclamation.

She closed her class that first day over shouts of "no, no!" by dramatically stepping back from her lecturn, folding her arms across her bosom, and speaking the lines she had memorized: "Let us begin learning *today*, young women, how to invoke the famous Muses of Olympus, the daughters of Zeus. Begin by committing to memory these words from the *Theogony:* 'Shepherds of the wilderness, wretched things of shame, mere bellies! We know how to speak many false things as though they were true; but we know, when we wish, to utter true things.' And so, ladies," Carolyn finished in a whisper, "and so we do, indeed. They shall be uttered here twice each week."

Then she was gone, appearing almost to vanish.

"Did you like her?" Marcia asked as the three women from LaCaresta Drive found themselves, almost stunned, on the cool sidewalk outside Muriel Kane Hall.

"I'm impressed," Diana replied softly, almost unable to walk. She appeared flushed. "That's more a political rally, in some ways, than a course. Or else," she added as an afterthought, "it's the way the university and college classes should *always* be taught!"

Soni had been in bad sorts for days now, inclined to quarrel, as if embarrassed by what had happened to her and determined to think her own thoughts. "Isn't it a little extreme," she wondered, "to lump all boys or men in the same category? Aren't there *some* decent men around, somewhere?"

"I think she's absolutely right," Marcia Angell replied stoutly. "We're goddesses in the making with centuries of husbanded, unbeatable power coursing in our veins—just ready to be used."

Diana had been thinking. "Yes, it's unfair to lump all men that way. But why should we care about that?" she asked defiantly. "It's the same thing *we've* had done to *us*, by them, all these thousands of years. The big lugs have it coming."

By now they had walked as far as Distant Vistas and they seemed to be drifting down the steps to the cafeteria. "Speaking of coming," Soni put in, "my older brother David is coming to campus for a visit in February."

Marcia glanced quickly at her but Soni averted her eyes. The mystery brother, at last; the one who seemed somehow to have caused such anguish for little Soni.

"Could you fix me up with him?" Diana inquired, her tones light and low, falsely carefree. Privately, she wanted to solve Soni's enigma. "I'd like to get to know him."

Soni said yes, sure, as she hurried toward the cafeteria line where other young women students were already discussing Dr. Lord's outstanding lecture.

She'd only hesitated for a moment.

CHAPTER XVI

ROTGOD, Carolyn Lord's daring new course, became the talk of the entire campus in no time at all. Even students who had no interest in the women's liberation movement at all spoke of it incessantly between classes and at sorority and fraternity houses.

Privately, the dean who'd asked Carolyn to return to teaching believed that the fascination with ROTGOD would diminish as swiftly as it had grown. Fads came and went, always had and always would. She remembered, from her own distant college days, special courses in leftwing or liberal politics that delighted her friends and engaged their attention yet made no lasting mark on the university curriculum. But even the dean had to admit that ROTGOD seemed a special case, both in terms of enthusiastic enrollment and the way the whole student body was discussing it. She was wise enough to know that even people who, like many of the male pupils, derided and joked about a subject might do so in order to keep from being fearful. Already she'd heard that a number of the men planned to enroll for the next semester, for whatever reasons they might have.

Ray Ellis, the handsome bowler, had taken to stopping by the rooming house on LaCaresta to visit Marcia. Sometimes the two of them went somewhere, but often Ray, who was serious about his studies, simply settled for sitting around talking with all three girls.

"I'm one hundred percent in favor of women learning how to be themselves, how to demand liberty and freedom from the ridiculous demands we men make on them," he said from a chair in Violet Hudson's sitting room. "The notion of any human being having to be considered nothing more than an object nauseates me. Guys like Burt Starr are cool to run around with, but they think like dinosaurs."

"I can just hear the word 'but' on the back of your tongue like something that needs to be spat out," Marcia told him, frowning and glancing at Diana and Soni. "And I can't imagine why that should be there if you're really as open-minded and mod as you claim."

Ray crossed his long legs and approached his answer with care. "It's hard to explain, but your Dr. Lord has a different approach than other women's lib people, I think. She seems to be taking you in a different *direction*," he said at last. "One that involves more than commitment to your sisters."

"What are you saying?" Soni flared. "More of that junk some of the guys are spreading, like shit?"

He chuckled. "The idea that Dr. Lord is converting you all to Lesbianism?" Ray laughed. "From what I've heard about Carolyn Lord, that charge would make her madder than it does you. Actually, she's a damned good-looking woman."

"She is, isn't she?" Marcia murmured. "I mean, you don't have to be gay to notice that."

He laughed again. *"I'm* not gay and *I* think she's gorgeous. No, Marsh, I was referring to the way she wants you to discard an entire element of your lives—the religious one. From what I hear, she's taught that the Bible endorses a paternalistic society under a male God, the Father, and that you must throw that stuff aside. Instead of worshipping a single godly figure, she wants you to return to a polytheistic faith, right? Worship of the goddesses."

"Well what's wrong with that?" Soni demanded. "Isn't it all true?"

"Truth is what I'm talking about," he replied calmly, thinking that the little blond had changed the most, outwardly, of the three of them. Although she remained pertly pretty and he could understand that many men would find her desirable, there was a hairtrigger temper there, and a certain emotional instability, that turned him off. "Y'see, this *is* a society in which the majority has expressed at least a token conviction that there is *one* God. Christians argue over whether Jesus was literally His Son or God in the flesh, but the same basic concept of One divinity in charge held true. If *half* the population wound up believing in something new—the divinity of several female figures—the best that would happen is a complete division between men and women. It could crack this nation down the middle."

"I thought *you* were a socialist and an atheist!" Soni retorted incredulously, slamming her feet on the floor and smiling evilly. "Are you a hypocrite too?"

"I'm an agnostic," Ray answered easily, "but that's just my point: It doesn't *matter* what I believe as an individual. In America, I'm permitted to believe what I want but it's *still* majority rule. And what Carolyn Lord is promoting could change all that."

"But *you* want to change society," said Marcia, going over to sit on the sofa beside him. She held his hand. "I don't get it, honey. Why is it all right for you socialists to change America around, and it isn't okay for women to do it?"

He patted her hand. "Babe, I want a gradual shift to a socialistic form of government for economic purposes," he reasoned. "And we were headed that way, straight as an arrow, until Ronald Reagan was elected President."

"And you know what kind of chance women who think the way we do have under him!" Soni said across the room.

"Religion is at the heart of our lives even when we don't *belong* to a given religion, even if we don't *like* it," Ray argued. "A complete split on the basic thing that *everybody* religious agrees to—Catholics, Protestants, Jews—would be devastating to American society."

Suddenly it occurred to him that the usually voluable Diana Stoker hadn't said a word. "What do *you* think about all this, Di?" he asked. "Let's get the All-American vote counted!"

The athlete was curled up, wearing shorts and a track warm-up sweater, in a corner chair. He could barely make out her olive-complected features because she was deep in shadows, stroking her cat, Mercury. She looked up languidly when Ray called her name.

"I think," she said slowly, her voice carrying easily, "that everything Dr. Lord has taught us is absolutely true but that it only scratches the surface." She paused and, as she turned her face and light from a lamp beside the sofa lit her lovely features, reflected an expression of determination Ray Ellis had never seen before. Yet there was something inescapably dark and brooding there, too; something she could not manage to say. "I think that the goddesses actually lived, and that we are all direct descendants of them. That we have experienced the wars and poverty and miserable lives we have because we went astray, and stopped praying to our divine goddesses."

"You're serious, aren't you?" Ray asked quietly, intrigued. "You really mean that."

"Oh, yes." Diana took the cat's head between the palms of her hands and turned it so she could look in its enigmatic eyes. It purred back at her. "But I don't just believe it, I *know* it. Something . . . is triggered in me by what Dr. Lord teaches, and what I'm reading in our books. Something . . . that *knows*."

Ray studied her without remark for several seconds, oddly drawn to her even while it occurred to him that the same emotional instability he sensed in Soni might be true of Di. Her black hair was beginning to grow back, he saw; it was tangled, a wiry bush of ebony hair that looked as strong as everything else about Di Stoker. "Weren't all three of you brought up to believe in God?" he asked mildly, glancing to the others and back to the athlete. "Doesn't it bother you at all to give

Him up?"

"Don't you dare talk about how I was raised!" Diana was suddenly on her feet, furious. Mercury, the cat, landed on all fours; he faced the young socialist instantly, hissing and raising a menacing paw with the claws bared. "What has God or my family done for my sex except make us slaves!" she exclaimed. "The more I hear Dr. Lord and the more I study, the more I realize that *all* the true progress that's ever been made on Earth is the work of women! It isn't *us* who invent doomsday machines—it isn't *us* who go to war, who murder our children—it's *men!* And till we destroy the religious foundation from which *all* our misery springs, we're stuck with *staying* psychologically dependent upon puny mankind!"

"I didn't mean to upset you, Diana," Ray said gently, placatingly. "But I'm entitled to my opinion."

"No!" She screamed it at him, took several steps toward him. "No, Ellis, you're *not* entitled to your opinion—you *or* the Burt Starrs of the world! Not in the new society we're creating!"

"Diana!" Marcia cried, shocked. Ray had scrambled defensively to his feet.

Now Diana was fully in the glaring light from the lamp, her vivid green eyes ablaze, her sensuous lips twisted in rage and hatred. "Oh, we'll still need men for purposes of sex, I suppose; most of us will. But that— that *something* dawning inside me, that sudden *knowing* that Dr. Lord is correct—it informs me that women have a great deal more to do than merely become your social *equals.* We must assume our goddess-given role of *superiority* and *rulership! We* will dictate the uses of our bodies; *we* will decide when we wish to propagate the race—there'll be no more 'accidents' that you little boys run from like so many timid rabbits!"

Now she was inches from him. Although he was well over six feet tall, Diana appeared, with her muscular strength and the righteous anger coursing through her, quite nearly his match. "I think you need help," Ray said in low tones, turning away.

"From a *male* psychiatrist, I suppose!" Diana yelled. "Let's *test* that male superiority of yours right now, Ellis!" She shoved his shoulder. "Come on, big fella! Fight me!"

He looked back at her. Her eyes flamed furiously, viciously; he knew she would stop at nothing short of killing him, if she could. At last he looked away. "I'm leaving," he said softly. "I'm a gentleman. I don't strike insane women."

"Go ahead!" Diana shouted, hitting his shoulder now. The blow traveled only inches but it numbed his arm to the elbow. "Try it! Try fighting someone your match!"

But he didn't reply, or flinch. Instead, he bent to kiss Marcia on the cheek, and saw how dazed she looked. He smiled, then walked down the hallway to the front door and out into the night.

For a long moment the three young women did not speak. Marcia wished Mrs. Hudson would come back from the grocery. The old fear she'd felt for Di Stoker surged, now she knew Diana could break her in two, if she wished.

Then Soni Jerome broke out in a round of gay applause. "Leadership!" she cried, joyously, giggling a little and slapping her knee. "By Hera, we have *real leadership!*"

The next day, Diana Stoker dropped off both the track and archery teams and began spending all her free time in the apartment of Dr. Carolyn Lord.

CHAPTER XVII

February, this year.

"I've never advocated physical retaliation," Carolyn Lord said to Diana Stoker, pouring tea for them and for Marcia Angell from a gleaming, steaming pot. "I'm pretty sure of that. Nor do I believe that it's quite natural to try to do *without* men entirely—at least, not for women whose actual, adult preference in sex *is* men." She smiled, in full command of the situation. "I do understand that men have been known to turn you on?"

Diana colored faintly, and nodded. "They have, in the past. Lately I've become pretty ashamed of it. I've tried to fight it. That—and a lot of things."

"Why? Basically, Di, you only have two choices. And I don't think I'm striving to start an order of goddess-believing nuns."

Carolyn put the pot down and returned to the sofa. *This girl is like putty in my hands,* she thought with amazement. *It may be like the blind leading the blind, but this is heady stuff I've begun. I really believe that if I told this strong girl to kill the president of the university, she'd try!*

"I suppose I was offbase trying to egg Ray Ellis into fighting me," Diana confessed, feeling confused. She sipped tea from her cup, conscious of how fragile it was in her hands. "Especially when I sort of *like* him, at heart. All at once he just became the embodiment of everything I've hated about men."

Carolyn sat beside Marcia, who was drinking a coke.

They exchanged glances. "There are elements of what is called 'ladylike behavior' that I feel must be retained. If we begin by threatening to outfight them, I fear we'll wind up losing the few privileges of courtesy that we're accorded. But some of it may well have been my fault."

Diana's brows raised. "*Nothing* could be your fault, Dr. Lord," she said in a breath. "Nothing bad."

"The idea is goddess-worship, not *heroine*-worship," Carolyn murmured. She passed a plate to the athlete to remove the sting. "Try my cookies, hon. Unless you think that baking them makes me altogether too feminine?"

Again Diana flushed. "I guess I have a great deal to learn before I can be the kind of leader you want me to be."

Carolyn considered for a moment. "Perhaps not so much. There are all kinds of leaders in a peaceful revolution. But you *did* appear to ignore an implied question of mine. So let me be candid: Isn't it true that your friend Soni fixed you up with her brother?"

Diana put her cup on the coffee table with immense care and nodded. "Yes, ma'am. We were supposed to go out, David and I, with Soni dating a boy named Bill Acton. Tomorrow night, when David gets in. But I—I wasn't sure I should go."

"Of course you should, if you want to," the blond instructor replied encouragingly. "And on that date and all others, dear, follow your *own* good judgment, your *own* instincts and moral values. Don't be blackmailed or cajoled into anything more." She shrugged. "If *you* like a young man and there's no reason not to sleep with him, it's entirely up to *you* how you decide how far to go. It's that simple, Di—or that difficult."

After speaking in more general terms about the effect goddesses of old had on civilization, with Carolyn dipping into the knowledge she had gained from her grandfather's writing and special insights gleaned from the past few months of study, Diana noticed her wristwatch and remarked that she was nearly late to another class. "Are you coming?" she asked Marcia.

"Not quite yet," the brunette replied. "There are another few points I want to clear up with Dr. Lord."

Diana stooped in front of the teacher impulsively. "I think you're the most wonderful woman I've ever known in my life," she blurted. "Please don't ever let me down."

When Diana had gone, Carolyn turned nervously to the remaining student. "Is *she* the one?" she asked her daughter, her voice filled with tension. "Mary, is *that* the one you suspect?"

Mary Lord nodded somberly. "I don't think she realizes it yet," she told her mother, "but, yes, from what we've discussed and what I implied in my writing, I do feel pretty sure Diana Stoker is the one." She paused. "The real Hecate, Queen of Hades."

"My God," Carolyn whispered.

"Watch that, Mother," Mary said with a nervous laugh. "It's 'goddess,' these days."

"I know she hasn't—literally 'become' Hecate yet. But even the way she is now, if that girl ever suspected I had feet of clay, or thought I'd betrayed her in any way," Carolyn said with awe, "she'd rip me in two. Mary, I've seen a few real zealots before and I believe Diana would literally *kill me* if she was crossed. And if she . . . *became* Hecate. . . ."

"What are we going to do, then?" Mary inquired. "Do you think I should stop dying my hair darker than it is, tell her I'm your daughter but that it was just to avoid trouble—not directed at her, as an individual? She'd only be a *little* bit tricked that way. Di can still show signs of a sense of humor."

"No, no, that won't do," said Carolyn, biting her lip and shaking her head. "Honey, it's just too risky. I think that the only way I can continue the class and still manage to get Diana out of it—and the other students not to take themselves quite so seriously—is by becoming absolutely outrageous." She nodded in agreement with herself, eyes flashing. "Yes, if I play more to Diana, ask more of her—harmless, silly things, but things that make me appear ludicrous in her eyes—

she might drop out of the class. Along with some other zealots. And then, you see, she *might never find out* who she really is." She squeezed Mary's hand in mutual optimism. "Maybe, if we're very fortunate, honey . . . maybe Hecate will *never* be the goddess who truly emerges!"

It was a wonderful evening. Soni's brother David Jerome, twenty-four, was exceptionally small but he was also exceptionally handsome. He had jet black hair which he brushed straight back, and gleaming, intelligent eyes that positively danced with wit and style.

Yet the way the evening ended was rather worse than a fiasco.

Instead of going to a movie, the way Soni's date Bill Acton proposed, they closed up the Distant Vistas and then went to an all-night eating spot, the Hungry U. Wine went down easily, along with pizza. There was a lot of good-humored banter which primarily engaged David, Bill and Diana, who was trying hard to relax into normality and enjoy herself.

But Soni seemed strangely out of it, shy or remote from her brother. She looked away, at a menuboard or other people in the restaurant, whenever he spoke. Again Diana wondered why the little blond continued to trace her personal unhappiness back to such a charming young man. Despite his height, Diana already could envision sleeping with David; if circumstances naturally worked toward that, she wouldn't refuse.

They closed up the Hungry U too and, when Bill drove the four of them back to LaCaresta, Di was surprised and disappointed when David didn't try to kiss her goodnight. Instead, while Soni clung in Bill's arms, her tiny brother was content to look out the window and remark to Diana on how marvelous it was to be warm and comfortable during the winter. Later, when Soni and Di alighted, David said that he had rooms in town and wouldn't be staying with them.

"He's so wonderful, Soni!" Diana exclaimed after

they were in their room. Marcia's door was closed but Diana was so excited she found herself speaking loudly anyway. "Great goddess, David is actually a *gentleman!* I didn't know they made them that way anymore—or that they were genuine conversationalists!"

Soni only grunted, sitting disconsolately on the edge of her bed. She kicked off her shoes, avoiding Diana's enthusiastic gaze.

"I wonder. Is there any reason David couldn't stay here longer than he originally planned?" She unbuttoned her blouse, pulled it free of the skirt. "I mean, if *that* lovely little hunk of a man needs coaxing, I'll do what it takes to make him stay for years and years!"

Soni stared at Diana as she stretched her arms above her head, her large olive-complexioned breasts rising. The nipples remained hard with excitement; a little vein in Di's throat was pumping hard. Soni looked away, unhappily.

"Hey, Soni, I'm talking to you," Diana called. "Why didn't you tell us David was such a great guy?"

Suddenly the blond burst into tears. She hurled herself flat on the bed, sobbing. "It's not fair, Jesus, it's not *fair!*"

"Soni?" Diana ran across the floor to her friend and stooped to stroke her shoulder. "Whatever is the matter? Do—do *you* have a crush on David?"

"No, I just love what he *used* to be, that's all." Soni sat up, her dark eyes redrimmed. "Di, you couldn't persuade David to stay here if you were the greatest lay in history. Don't you dig it, baby? Di, David's *gay!* Hell, *I'm* worried about leaving him alone with Bill!"

It was so like a physical blow to the belly that Diana blinked several times and stood, leaning forward slightly, hurting everywhere and fully unable to reply for another moment. "He can't be," she whispered finally. "He just *can't* be!"

"David's a *gentle man* all right," the blond went on, sniffling. "Oh, they still make *plenty* of 'em—and David's tried them all: football players, ballet dancers, music teachers—wherever he's been able to find his own kind." She stood, staring defiantly at Diana. *"That's the real reason I let Pam Gernier 'do' me, Di—to find out, once and for all, if I was my brother's kind, too! To find out if I really wanted it, that way, or i-if it was just my imagination and m-my desire to be allowed to be close to my brother again."*

"Look, it may just be a rumor," Diana said pleadingly, sitting beside Soni, her face anxious, persuasive. "Maybe it's just a rumor. Maybe he's just a s-slow starter with women, shy like Marcia."

Soni blew her nose into a handkerchief. "No way, honey. I found out the hard way. That's wh-why I came all the way out here to California." She finally met her friend's intense gaze. "You see, I found David in bed with another guy, two years ago." Her face clouded anew. "The guy happened to be the first boy I ever d-dated, the *only* one I ever thought I loved! And dammit, Diana, the son of a bitch was *David's* lover—not mine!"

Diana was on her feet, moving to her own bed, bending. When she stood, it was with the bed—mattress, springs and all—high above her tangled, wiry head, raised there as easily as Soni lifted her handkerchief. The little blond stared in astonishment.

Then Diana threw it to the ground—not dropped it, *threw* it down—and the collision was like that of a boulder which raced down a mountainside to crash into the sea. Beneath the faded carpeting, Soni was sure, the floor itself surely cracked. Already there were the footsteps of Mrs. Violet Hudson rushing up the stairs. Marcia threw open her door, stood in the entrance in shortie pajamas, gaping.

"The bastards, the filthy *bastards!*" Diana cried, hitting her palm with the other fist. "Hera! Isis! Strike them down!" Her face turned skyward, anguish written in every working muscle. "Great goddess, even when they behave *halfway decently* to a woman they tear us apart! Even male *queers* have the power, the—divinely given right to hurt us!"

"What is it?" Marcia asked Soni, anxiously. "What's wrong?"

But Soni was at Di's side, comforting her, an arm around her friend's waist. "They aren't going to hurt us anymore, Di," she said softly. "We won't let 'em, you and me—we'll *fight back*, Di, we'll stop them from crucifying us!"

Diana took a long deep breath and smiled down at Soni, striving for self control. "You're right, little friend," she said, nodding. "I swear it by Hephaestus, I pledge it by Demeter!" She shook her fist at the ceiling. "Look out from now on, men—be on guard, *whoever* you are and *wherever* you are. From now on, Diana Stoker is your *sworn enemy*—and I'm going to ruin *every one of you I can!*"

Later, when Mrs. Hudson was consoled (and told that it was only an accident) and Marcia was asleep in her own room, Diana arose, naked, from her bed and crossed the floor to where little Soni lay. "Move over," she whispered, climbing in beside her friend.

Sex was the farthest thing from the mind of either young woman. Instead, they lay in one another's arms, seeking some intimate moment to replace the bleak loneliness each of them felt was becoming her tomb, the final resting place of her feminine soul. And: "You really liked David, didn't you, Di?"

For a long while there was no answer. "Yes," the athlete said at last, trembling. "I think I could have loved that man—could have loved *someone*—for the first time in my life." Her eyes almost glowed in the vagrant light from the window. "But I'll say this, Soni. I swear it to you on whatever you hold sacred. I'll never allow myself to love anyone again. No one, I promise you, *no one*." her passion was almost a physical thing; heat rose from her body in waves. "From now on, Soni, Diana Stoker is looking out for Number One!"

CHAPTER XVIII

Mid-April, this year. Dr. Lord's apartment.

Because her husband had demanded it, Carolyn Lord had tended to sleep in the nude and, in a climate that was nearly always warm, she continued the practice even though the bad, old days were swiftly receding into the merciful past.

Lately, because of the excitement greeting her ROTGOD class, she had found it difficult to get to sleep. With the realization that an inadvertent remark might bring the demonic creature Hecate to the surface of one of her students, falling asleep was even harder.

Tonight she tried taking a long, hot bath before retiring and succeeded in making herself sleepy. Yawning and stretching, she perched momentarily on the edge of the bed and her eye fell upon the sleeping pills prescribed for her, months ago, by her friend Elna's husband Fred. Tomorrow she would be trying to implement her plan for weaning the more fanatical students away from ROTGOD, especially Diana Stoker, and a good night's sleep was essential. Even though she did not really approve of them, she quickly swallowed two of the white pills and lay back on the bed.

Carolyn had decided to introduce the idea of her students selecting a *personal* goddess to supplicate and with whom to identify. It seemed to her that a bright girl like Diana would instantly recognize how insane it was for a twentieth-century young woman, brought up on Carol Burnett, Kiss, the Muppets, Watergate and the Fonz, to put active, ongoing faith in goddesses who might or might not have lived but were certainly *dead* thousands of years! It was unreasonable, in Carolyn's opinion, to expect any but the most gullible to go along with the idea—at least, in the sense of investing genuine faith in them.

Turned on her side with her clasped hands folded beneath her pale, sloping breasts, Carolyn had a twinge of regret that she could no longer hide from herself. Never again in her entire life would she have the chance at such power, at literally leading a human avalanche of earnestly protesting womanhood down society's massive mountain until it smashed headlong into the headlines, perhaps even to the White House and Supreme Court. It wasn't hard to imagine that the name Carolyn Lord could soon become one to reckon with, that she could be a famous name among those who sought the final liberation of her sex. Yet because of one remarkably athletic young woman, she had to throw it all away—perhaps even becoming a laughing stock on the UCEV campus.

Of course, that wasn't the sum and substance of it. She was doing it—making this considerable sacrifice—to keep something monstrous from emerging on unsuspecting society, something that had been feared and expected for a very long while. The reemergence not of some constructive goddess like Hera, but of hell's feminine ruler. Hecate.

She twisted, finally turned over. Pill induced alpha waves were beginning to soothe her brain, lull her to sleep, and suddenly she didn't want to go. How reasonable *was* it, she wondered, groggily, for a well-educated modern woman—dwelling in the same world with Billie Jean King, George Bush, Norman Mailer and George Brett—not to mention the Fonz!—to accept completely such an incredible reincarnation as that of Hecate? Could she possibly be wrong in the way she interpreted Professor Jabez Lord's writing, or that of her own daughter? Wasn't it just conceivable that both of them had been irrational, and that she was infected by the same nonsensical bug?

Now the thoughts simply would not form into logical patterns; her will was being sapped by the imperative need to sleep. Fleetingly she thought of forcing herself to rise, to go slap cold water on her resistive face; and then, throwing her head from side to side in brave protest, Carolyn was asleep.

It didn't come, not immediately. At first, there was a certain comforting nothingness—a spreading, soothingly cottony blackness that wafted and billowed her, and told Caroylyn that everything was all right.

It lied.

Because she was *not alone,* in her mind, not any more. It had been invaded, effortlessly, the controls that were already relinquished to her sleep centers now slipping easily into the commanding hands of . . . *another.*

For a moment something inherently decent, something that had once been strongly self-reliant before its gradual daily erosion by events in her life that were much more farflung and injurious than any simplistic designation of Man as the enemy, sought to fight back. She moaned, her lips twisted into a grimace that might have been sensual to another, more normal kind of intruder. She scratched at her pale, rounded breasts, then at her belly, as the invader moved to assure total command. Her naked hips lifted from the bed almost orgiastically, thrust upward not to meet the understandable invasion of an urgent lover but to strive to repel the attack of a force quite as female, ultimately, as she.

Her outflung arms revealed a network of working veins and muscles as her fists first tightened, then opened to spread clawlike and the fingers dug into the sheet. Now Carolyn's eyes shot open, staring in dumb unknowing animal terror but seeing neither an imaginary lover nor her own ceiling above her—seeing, instead, with a *shared* and *distorted vision* as the remorseless and irresistible will of the other seeped through her bare body.

Seeing, now, the vaulting, searing flames of Hell

licking at the walls of her apartment and, even as she sought to gasp and move away from them, finding her body transfixed, immobilized. The fire leaped for the ceiling, hungrily spreading, as she felt her entire body break into immense *gouts* of perspiration, as the sweat soaked the sheets beneath her and dimly—as if from unfathomable distance, a distance of cosmic proportions that, pray God Himself, was uncrossable!—Carolyn heard the indefinably mournful wail of creatures who could *not* escape these blast-furnace flames. . . .

Yet even as she stared at them the perspiration and massive heat dwindled, an adjustment being made inside her; and while the flames continued to mount the walls and the agonized sounds of Hell's constant victims groaned in her ears, she knew that she *must listen,* now, *must hear* the words that directed her destiny from this moment forward—that told her, plainly, she must do their bidding or descend defenselessly into the abyss for eternity.

Eleusian rites, the message whispered, its passion and command unmistakable . . . *the rites of lustration must be performed. Soon I shall claim my regal, rightful court and it shall comprise the resistless whole of womankind . . . and you shall see that it is done, you shall be my servant and my tool—the Eleusian rites of lustration at last shall mean for me my ultimate release—from the flaming bowels of Hades, to my proper, promised rulership of humankind.* Something like mad, chaotic laughter squealed in Carolyn Lord's mind before the message ended: *It shall be the liberation* not *of mortal females, my servant sisters, but of their Queen from now to the end of time*—Hecate!

When Carolyn awakened in the morning, her conscious mind remembered nothing that had happened.

But her unconscious mind, withdrawing and reeling from the onslaught, recalled it all and accepted it, as the unconscious mind must do; unquestioningly.

From that point it was only a matter of time until Carolyn would consciously conclude that her change of plans was entirely her own. That she was quite capable of handling Diana and had no intention of abandoning such a marvelous opportunity.

There were only seven weeks to go before the semester ended and Diana, Soni and Marcia had yet to make any firm plans for the summer. They were far too absorbed by what was happening at UCEV, especially in the ROTGOD course which was increasingly becoming a way of life for them and many other female students.

At first, Carolyn Lord had seemed open to the three girls dropping by, at the end of the day, but not particularly anxious for them to be there. Mary-called-Marcia knew, of course, that her mother was not a single-celled creature but a person of many interests and with a growing number of friends. Thus, she was surprised when Carolyn began seeking not only the company of Diana, Soni and herself but of the entire ROTGOD class.

When even a fraction of the huge enrollment showed up, of course, it was impossible to get everybody into her apartment so Carolyn frequently took advantage of the superior California weather and threw little parties on the expansive grounds surrounding her complex. Increasingly, these get-togethers became the place to be for at least one hundred of the young women enrolled in ROTGOD and Marcia began to feel distinctly uneasy about the change in her mother.

A few days ago, for example, Carolyn spent a large segment of her monthly salary on dozens of lawn chairs and even installed a brick barbeque with the grudging permission of the UCEV administration. It quickly became a customary sight for neighbors to see a trail of young women in and out of the apartment building, bringing out a nonstop assortment of soft drinks and snackfood for the gatherings on the lawn.

But it was more than her mother's total absorption in the class and the students that began troubling Mary-called-Marcia. For one thing, Carolyn showed no inclination toward approaching the students with literally fantastic ideas that would turn them off to ROTGOD—and with them, hopefully, Di Stoker as well. Instead, she seemed to be couching her for more far-out views in the most convincing language available to the instructor, appealing to the ego of the girls and making them feel more and more important. It was as if the conversation mother and daughter had had never occurred at all.

Worst of all, from Mary's view, it might be her imagination but she felt that her mother was treating her no differently than any of the others! There was no special light of private recognition in Carolyn's eyes now, no added wave of warmth passing between them. When Carolyn addressed the girl, she called her "Marcia" without an iota of obvious difficulty, and yesterday, when Mary wanted to speak privately for a moment with the teacher, Carolyn gave her a cool professional smile and murmured, "I don't think that would be polite to the others just now, do you, dear? Telephone me sometime."

Today Carolyn Lord was seated at the center of a wide, attractive circle of her special students, on the wide complex lawn, holding court and obviously enjoying it. For Mary, it was amazing to see how naturally commanding her mother now seemed to be; it was growing hard to remember how both of them had once bent and finally broken. The teacher's young women were either seated in lawn chairs or comfortably sprawled on the warm, spring grass, magnetized by what their leader was telling them:

"You young ladies are the fervent soul of this revolution," she intoned firmly, praising them. She no longer resorted to notes at all; it was as if the facts, theories and fancies were firmly implanted in her mind by some outer source prepared to whisper answers to her. Carolyn had taken recently to wearing all-white costumes—dresses, skirts and blouses, or tennis garb, like today and her smoky blond hair accentuated the lack of color. Nonetheless, the intense brilliance, the *heat,* of her green eyes made her appear individualistic and prominent. "But you are like a soul entering a body at birth, for the first time. You need to learn both how to *use* that infant shape and precisely *whom* you are.

"Very soon now, we shall begin to learn how your new women's bodies are to be used to bring freedom for all women closer and ultimately closer. In time, I promise you, you are going to experience something *extraordinary,* indeed: The famous Eleusian rites. That, my friends and students, will be the penultimate moment in your life."

"I thought the Eleusian rites were no longer known to anyone," Mary-called-Marcia remarked quietly, seated on the ground beside Diana and Soni. "That they were lost for all time."

A queer light twinkled distantly in the instructor's eye. "Many people believe that, but I enjoy—*secret access*—to them. You are going to be thrilled by what transpires."

"When will that be?" asked a plump redhead from her well-squeezed chair.

"When school resumes in the Autumn, Belinda," Carolyn replied. "In conjunction with the Homecoming football game." She paused. "I think our rites will have considerably more impact than that boy-child's sport. Now, I want you at present to begin thinking about something truly important; the other question I raised." Carolyn's gaze swept the circle. *"Who,"* she asked, *"are you?"*

Diana Stoker's firm body seemed to prickle with electricity. Mary, beside her, felt the athlete squirm in anticipation; even Soni glanced at Di.

"Because it it *no accident* that you are all here, today," Carolyn Lord announced, her chin raised importantly. "You have been *motivated* to be a part of the Reemergence of the Goddesses—by the goddesses *themselves."* Her cheek muscles worked with passion. "I did not speak rhetorically, at our first class together, when I said that you contain the seed of divinity. And one day soon, my friends and students, you must decide *which* of the goddesses dwells within you. *That*, in short, is what I meant by finding out who you are!"

There was a frenetic burst of buzzing, enthusiastic conversation. Mary shook her head slightly, worried. This approach would not deter Di Stoker; it would appeal to her, attract her mightily, just as it was doing with most of the other girls in the circle. *Everyone* wanted to feel important, wanted others to consider them important, unusual in some way. It was an approach that couldn't fail—if Carolyn Lord was working one-hundred-and-eighty degrees away from their plan.

For God's sake, she wondered with an angry surge of fear, for her mother and all of them, *what* did she think she was *doing*?

Soon talk turned to wider discussion of ancient goddesses. When Soni boldly demanded to know how there could possibly be "enough of them to go around," Carolyn seemed neither to pause nor to be irritated. She explained that she would pass out lists of them, before the end of today's gathering, numbering in the hundreds. She also added that it was conceivable for more than one woman to share a given goddess since it was a teaching of ancient Greece that, through reincarnation, soul division sometimes occurred and several newly born people could possess elements of the same divine Oversoul. "And for those of you who cannot quite accept the miracle that is happening on this campus," Carolyn said, her soft voice rising until it reached every attentive ear, "it can be simply viewed as a new function of a *symbol system*, something which many of you modernists know well from your other courses. Those of us who *know*, however," she added quietly, slyly, "view time differently and understand that several thousand years is no more than a century in the gaze of a goddess, and that a century is only a manmade construct."

Some of the contributions of the goddesses were

amiably, almost off-handedly discussed, with Carolyn Lord always at the center, easily fielding questions asked of her. Again Mary was amazed, this time by how much her mother had learned and how readily it rested on her tongue. They spoke of Demeter, who gave birth to Plutus; his divine assistance could make one rich. Now Dr. Lord's eyes sought out those students who were not pretty to see, who were overweight or had slight figures. "Yet Demeter was not herself lovely, at all. She achieved beauty through spells which lasted long enough for others to see her inner loveliness. In time, she was called by all 'the greatest of joys and blessings to gods and men.' An example many of us may cherish."

They spoke, as well, of Astraea, the pure goddess of justice, a daughter of Themis and Jupiter. She so sought that which was fair for all that she became the last immortal to withdraw from earth at the close of the Golden Age. "Her spirit is with us now," Carolyn whispered, "as *we* seek to invoke justice for womankind."

Some righteous, pleased laughter arose when they spoke of Isis, ancient Egypt's principal goddess. It seemed that when she mourned the murder of her husband Osiris, who was slain by forces within man's royal city, she trimmed her hair short and worked as a servant girl in order to gain admittance through the royal walls. There, surrounded by her late husband's murderers, she removed her cloak to show herself as a goddess and was instantly surrounded by thunder and lightning. Everyone in the city was justly destroyed, and Osiris had been avenged.

Diana, Mary-called-Marcia saw with concern, listened with fascination to that story. Her nostrils flared with excitement when she learned now vengeance had been enacted. What, Mary wondered, did her mother *mean!*

Before they left, as Soni, Diana and "Marcia" paused to say farewell to Carolyn Lord for the day and thank her for the snacks, another incredible thing happened:

The instructor paid special attention to Diana and pressed into her eager hand a slim volume. "It's about your namesake, Diana, the Huntress," Carolyn murmured. "I commend her story—her *entire* story—to your attention."

The athlete accepted it with effusive appreciation and genuine gratitude, failing fully to catch a glimpse of Marcia's expression. At home that afternoon on LaCaresta, Diana eagerly began reading the book given her by her heroine, carefully taking notes as she proceeded.

The original Diana, she learned, was not really that person at all. She was told that to become chief among goddesses she must first become a mortal, and experience what ordinary women experienced. Her name, before this transformation to humanity, had been Artemis. Now, in human flesh, she assumed the role of Diana, a mighty huntress who also taught magic and sorcery. She was the earth's first mage, its first witch. "All that is like man," she was said to have told those who inquired, "—yet *not* mortal." In that manner Diana brought the occult and paranormal to humankind, as a mixed blessing.

Yet Diana was subject to the urges and needs of mortal women, and craved the experience of sex. Even more, she yearned to return to her original form as a goddess, just as much as she wanted to become chief among the immortals. Hoping to achieve some of her goals, Diana took the form of a cat and then slept with her Earth-brother, Lucifer. Lucifer had innocently enough taken her to his bed for warmth; but there, in the darkness, Diana assumed her own sensual form and, though Lucifer knew she was woman, they yet had sexual relations.

Both Diana and Lucifer were seen because, in the form of mortals, they had forgotten it was impossible to deceive the gods and goddesses. For punishment, Lucifer was dispatched to the underworld as its ruler, while Diana was sent with him to become its queen. Because Lucifer was human, his name was not changed; but Diana became the most mysterious of all

Olympians, the dark and evil Hecate.

She laid the book down, thinking. Her joints ached from sitting so long on the ground at Dr. Lord's but she wanted to figure it all out. What *happened* to Hecate? What were her powers, now that she had become part-good goddess, part-mortal, part-evil goddess?

To relax, Diana decided to take a nice soothing bath. Resting the slender volume on the floor beside the tub, she began undressing. Of late she never wore a brassiere, not only because it was a symbol for some women of masculine oppression but because, increasingly, *all* the clothing Diana wore seemed uncomfortable to her. She had no idea what clothes she'd prefer to wear, but current American garb seemed confining as well as ludicrously garish.

For a moment she paused at the tub with one knee raised, her full-figured body naked and the freedom from her usual garments oddly luxurious. She reached down, between her spread legs, touching. A thrill coursed through her body. Her face tilted slightly toward the place where the wall met the ceiling as she touched herself again, and again. The third time the fingertip was damp. She realized that she was trembling faintly, her heavy breasts rising and falling with emotion, with desire and need—*and with something entirely new to Diana Stoker:*

A dawning feeling, no, a realization, that like Artemis, she was strangely . . . more . . . than just Diana Stoker, more than a woman who yearned for an ordinary man to satisfy her, who required much more for the kind of climactic, orgiastic release of which she now knew she was capable—a blinding, fulfilling explosion of release could be hers, if . . . if . . .

It had taken him a long while to reach his decision but partly because of that he now knew that he was right.

He cared deeply for Marcia Angell, and he had to get her away from the influence of that Lesbian-to-be, Soni Jerome, and even more, that lunatic athlete, Diana

Stoker. If Marsh continued staying with them, he felt, something perfectly *terrible* was going to happen to her.

Something from which Ray Ellis might not be able to extricate her.

Violet Hudson let him in, telling him, that so far as she knew, none of her girls was home yet. "But you're welcome to look," she called after him. Ray was already taking the steps two at a time.

The first room on the second floor, where the two crazies lived, was clearly empty; they'd left the door open. The second one was shut and Ray knocked softly on it, not wanting to startle Marcia. No reply, so he rapped again.

Nothing.

Where could she be? Ray was decisive, now; he'd made up his mind to get her away from Diana and Soni and he meant to do it.

In six quick, purposeful steps the young, socialistic bowler—a good-hearted man—had covered the length of the hallway to a door that was ajar.

Without giving it a thought, he threw it wide.

And shouted in abrupt, instantly hysterical alarm, taking a quick backward step as he threw his arms across his face and half-cowered against the doorframe, trembling.

What he had seen was almost beyond description. He could not believe his eyes, nor did he wish to. It would, something told him at once, be preferable to think he had simply gone mad. Because such defiled, inexplicable ugliness—such an image of grotesquerie, as if ultimate Sin *had developed a face and body of its own— could* not *exist.*

Yet Ray's shocks were not at an end.

Because now, to his extreme shock and embarrassment, he was looking instead at one of the most beautiful, wholly desirable young women he had seen in his life. Di Stoker, exotically formed, her bare body fully exposed to him, stood at the tub with knee lifted, her rarefied sexual beauty hypnotic. He stared at the thicket of jetblack hair, up her indrawn stomach and narrow waist to the globe-like heavy breasts, to the familiar beauty of Diana Stoker's face—and finally to the aroused, violent hatred pouring almost like molten lava from her eyes.

Her arm shot away from herself and toward him, the finger imperious, commanding—*unbearably* commanding. Not a sound escaped her lips; she did not even seem surprised; only malicious. His thoughts awash with confusion, fear and embarrassment, Ray mumbled an apology and turned at once, *compelled* now, to run down the hallway to the stairs.

He took the steps in two great bounds with the urge to be *away* from this impossible house greater than any he'd ever experienced; he rushed through a small corridor, kicked the front door open and shot into the street, heading for his car.

From Di Stoker's bathroom window, curtains parted; she looked down. But her mind—not *yet her* mind, actually, but an element that began slowly to merge, deliberately and unremittingly to join with that of the original Diana Stoker—reached *out*—groping, and *finding. Summoning*. Beckoning; insisting; calling; *summoning* those creatures who had always belonged to her, which involuntarily did her bidding.

Below the window, Ray Ellis had stopped, trying to get into his automobile only to find the door unaccountably jammed. Panicky now, heart surging, he yanked fiercely at it, desperately tugged it open—

—Even as he heard them—from the distance— baying. Baying and *coming*. Coming for *him*.

Soon the sound became a din, then grew deafening, as they poured from everywhere and nowhere—Ray Ellis their exclusive target, the lost prey on which they focused—in obedience to the strident summons of their ruler from Hell.

Now he *saw* them, with incredulity for their numbers . . . and yet, as well, he saw them with an immediate leap of paralyzing perception that *knew* why the creatures came and *knew*, too, *who* had beckoned them.

Dogs. Dogs of all sizes: German shepherds, poodles, bulldogs and dachshunds, terriers of every breed, Great Danes, wolfhounds, Scotties, English Sheepdogs, Pekingeses and chows—dogs that were large, and small, bounding like streaks toward him and yappingly trailing after—the dogs of an entire town, *dozens*, no, *thousands* of dogs, their barking, boisterous and inchoate numbers propelled by Diana Stoker and *hurtling*, almost like a single fantastic and immense juggernaut, toward only him.

Something *else* of ghastly quiet, its motion that of a death-silent gray spirit, loped easily at the side of the canine ranks, leading them. Ray observed it with shock-dulled eyes, witnessing the flecks of saliva springing from his muzzle, oddly red as blood and staining the sidewalk as he came. Unlike most of the others, this dog had no collar, no tags—*this* monstrous parody of a pet, surely five powerful feet above the ground at his muscular shoulders, the head three times Ray's, was free and took no orders from mortal man. *This* great beast was no friend or kin to man or, for that matter dog, as its almost slow-motion, silent speed continued bringing it closer, looming larger as he came. *This* animal allowed others to bark for him, his evil mind clearly directly focused on the human being he must soon reach. Ray stumbled back another step, thought of running; its *eyes*, the man's soul moaned, *God*, its *eyes* had the calculating wisdom of a human—and a hatred no man ever allowed to shine from his eyes.

Now the sound made further thinking impossible as their thousands of nimble feet clattered near. The canine smell filled Ray's nostrils, clogged them and choked him. *Must move*, Ray told himself; *I* must *get into the car*.

That idea, too late. *Now*, oh *now* they were upon him, knocking him caromingly off the car's side and to his squirming back, wave after wave of attacking, snapping, growling, clawing dogs-gone-mad, dogs-under-direction. He screamed, once. Its lingering note of terror and pain quivered on the air.

The man was down and they stepped back, allowing the lead dog—that gray ghost, half-again the size of any other dog present—to step forward. His wise eyes coolly appraised the pack. Ray looked up at it; their eyes met, held. And the enormous head lowered to Ray Ellis, massive jaws opening, then shutting, as Ray died in agony.

"Good dog, Garm!" came the cry from above. *"Good dog!"*

Garm raised his great head to look up, the human's throat dangling and dribbling from his jaws. His gaze met that of the naked young woman at the window above; his massive tail wagged, puppy-like, brushing in the pool of gore forming by his feet.

"Finish, Garm," ordered the lovely girl with a nod of encouragement.

Garm's sharp toenails dug; probed. With some difficulty he finally extracted the eyeballs, one by one. He let them roll for a moment on the sidewalk, like marbles. Again Garm peered up, questioningly; again Garm looked down, picked one of the eyes up with his mouth. *Crunch,* the sound rose to the possessed and naked girl; once again, *crunch!* Wet stuff oozed from his mouth.

Meanwhile the others waited, necks and tails stiff, circling the tortured body and, on the outer edge of contro, wanting to feast.

But the equally controlled woman above them spoke a last time: "Garm, good leader; all good dogs," she praised softly, gently now. *"Go."*

Instantly the smaller dogs became friendly house pets anew, yelping and whining their confusion in a nightmare of noise; they were unaware how they had gotten there, and how to get back. None of them paid attention now to the dead young man; to the average animal, death is seldom interesting.

Garm growled and they turned to him at once. For the first and only time, he sounded his mighty voice. It was a cannoning boom of a bark, a guttural command breaching no argument or pause. Ears back, the other dogs ran quickly away in every direction. Soon they were dispersed; gone.

All except Garm. The gigantic canine looked up again at the window and saw, instead of she who ruled him, an unfamiliar, silly human being staring down with a startled and stunned look of anguish and horror on her pretty girl's face.

Disgusted, Garm took three swift, dignified steps, and vanished.

CHAPTER XIX

June, this year.

Diana, Marcia and Soni were only three of the many ROTGOD students who decided to stay in El Vista for the summer. Numbers of Carolyn Lord's young converts felt that they had found a new home there, and that more could be accomplished by remaining together and meeting frequently at Dr. Lord's during the three summer months.

Besides, as Marcia wryly observed to her friends, there was something about taking a definite stand—about maintaining a viewpoint, passionately, which was at odds with general social attitudes—that not only tended to alienate a group from others, but also made that "in-group" a close knit, surrogate family. Diana had replied, with simple partisanship, "Our place from now on is together. Until we have finally won." Marcia did not make the mistake of asking her, "Won what?"

After the honestly mystified Di Stoker had telephoned the police, shakily reporting that she had chanced to look out the bathroom window and see the mutilated body of her friend Ray Ellis, the UCEV campus was thrown into an uproar. Marcia Angell was distraught, for she had been fond of Ray and regarded him as the only decent man she knew. For awhile it was rumored that a wild-eyed madman secretly inhabited the university grounds, probably dwelling deep in the wings of the Theatre Arts complex, a contemporary Phantom of the Opera. Some suggested that the latent resentment of the El Vista townspeople of the sometimes lurid activities of the brash UCEV students had finally gotten out of hand, that some senile assortment of aging radicals had learned of Ray's earnest participation in socialist politics and decided—as the students put it these days—to "off" him.

But police investigation quickly revealed the existence of innumerable pawprints left by the packs of savage dogs, in the area where Ray's maimed corpse was discovered. In conjunction with the Humane Society, an intensive search was mounted for the roaming, presumably mad animals. Although countless citizens of El Vista privately admitted that their own pets mysteriously disappeared for an extended period, on the day of the young bowler's hideous death, they kept it in the family. Eventually, authorities were left to conclude that the dog packs had wandered out of town, and notified adjoining cities. In the end, Ray Ellis' passing went unavenged and the only half-constructive outcome was a city-wide campaign to get every dog inoculated and tagged.

Alone now, except for her friends, Marcia joined them in spending most of their leisure time at Dr. Lord's apartment. In a way, of course, it was literally "going home" for the real Mary Lord; but Carolyn continued to treat her as if she were no closer, emotionally, than the others.

Early on a Thursday evening, delayed by a homework assignment from another class, Marcia arrived at her mother's apartment complex and heard chanting coming from behind the building. They had frequently chanted before, of course; but there was a greater intensity of purpose to this noise, and it was much louder than usual. She hurried down a walk separating the two apartment buildings and emerged in the terraced area between the structures themselves and a small lake.

Marcia stopped short, staring in disbelief.

It was a scene from another day, another nation, another culture—one that believed in alchemy, in spirits that inhabited flowers and stones, in dark nights of the soul when man might be driven to death by a muttered spell. Not for the first time it occurred to Mary-called-Marcia that there was something Druidic or smacking of the witches' coven about this cult which her own mother found herself leading—and something, as well, of madness, of base depravity.

Sweeping tree branches hovered above some hundred young women of the ROTGOD course who had shown up for this final get-together, before the summer break; and each of them had removed her shoes, blouse or sweater and now paraded, half-nude, in a precise circle around Dr. Carolyn Lord. They had joined their hands in a camaraderie of sisterly familiarity and seemed oblivious to the presence of anyone else. As Marcia watched she realized that the circle was not complete, that it was actually led by Diana Stoker, her marvelous breasts glistening in the dying sunlight and her long, strong legs moving in a way that indicated absolute defiance, absolute commitment. She saw, too, that the others' eyes were glazed and wondered, briefly, if her mother might actually have procured marijuana for the enhanced cooperation of her students. It would not be the first time, she knew, that a university professor had provided drugs for his class.

Embarrassed for them, Mary looked quickly around, half-expecting to see hundreds of avid male eyes watching her friends. Instead, she saw only Pam Garnier and another woman she did not know, fully dressed and standing at the distant entrance to the court, arms folded across their bosoms like military guards. It was semisecluded here, except for those tenants who might look down in wonder from their apartment windows; obviously Carolyn Lord didn't care, anymore, about such simple concerns as modesty.

"The goddess is here," half the marching women cried; and the other half replied, "The goddess is us!" The chant went on in a ceaseless, hypnotic rondo, the first chant serving as the incitement to a wildly screamed second, responding chant—over, and over.

Mary had just spotted Soni, the tiny blond looking like an out-of-place child amidst the sometimes Amazonian stature of her friends, when Pam Garnier seemed to realize that she had left the entrance unguarded. "It's too late to get in the fun," she said to the girl she knew as Marcia. "You can help me guard the place from any horny male bastards who might try to get in."

"Don't worry," Mary replied with a shudder. "I have no desire at all to run around naked in the backyard." Pam gave her a resentful, studied glare and returned to her own post.

Now the group of young women had stopped, at some imperceptible signal from Dr. Lord to Diana Stoker, forming facing ranks and throwing their hands over their heads in an exultant cheer that was joined by all: "Goddess, come *back!*" they pleaded, two hundred breasts rising and falling. *"Return,* goddess!" And, finally, "Goddess, *be us!"*

The passionate plea was strangely moving, Mary realized, a chill running down her spine. Without realizing it, her hand went to her own button-down-the-front sweater and parted three buttons. In most women, she thought, there might be this kind of exuberance if, indeed, they dared release it—if they had the *courage* of the ROTGOD women, and the *leadership* of Carolyn Lord. It occurred to Mary that this act of semi-nudity was a way of linking them all, a way of saying, "We'll do *everything* we must to achieve our goals and we'll *win* because we're united."

She recalled a book by Mary Daly from 1973, *Beyond God the Father,* in which Ms. Daly pinpointed a spiritual vacuum which was said to exist for many women brought up in a basically patriarchal society. Despite herself, even Mary, who liked and sometimes craved men, who was raised a Catholic, found that she vibrated harmoniously with such sentiments.

When first Carolyn and then her lieutenant Diana signaled the end of the chanting, the hundred or so young women breathlessly collapsed on the yard or the terrace, laughing slightly in the way that people do when they have exhausted themselves in having a good time. Diana saw Mary on the sidelines and then Soni did, too. Lacking all self-consciousness about their partial nudity, the two girls jogged over to their friend, breathing hard and grinning. Soni hugged Mary and Diana plopped down on the ground, using a handkerchief to dab at her perspiring breasts and abdomen.

Before they could talk, however, Dr. Lord clapped her hands for attention and instantly got it. Carolyn was beautiful herself, today, contrastingly fully dressed in a new white suit with white, high-heeled shoes. She was permitting her smoky-blond hair to grow, now, and it fanned over her shoulders in a nearly haloing effect.

"Homer wrote," she said, and there was no longer any need to raise her voice among these students, "that there were so many persons who wished to be initiated into the mysteries of Eleusis that it was necessary to build a special temple, in ancient Greece, simply to house all the candidates! Possibly my humble home will suffice, when we are all together again in September."

"What are the rewards for becoming an initiate?" Diana called, and Mary felt that this was prearranged.

Carolyn's face was beatific. "The unimaginably happy afterlife pledged for all of us by Demeter—a far better existence than mortal mankind has known since the Eleusian rites were lost." She paused, smiling radiantly. "As I told you, they were found again by one of my relatives and have come into my possession, so that I may share them with each of you."

"Can you give us a hint of what will be involved in these glorious rites?" Diana asked on cue.

"Yes, Diana, the process of soul-cleansing called *lustration*. Through these rites, my dear fellow women, you shall finally, *truly*, merge with the goddesses you have selected. You shall find them come to you, and become *one* with you, filling your spirits with feminine godliness. Forever, you shall be freed of men and their repressive dominance." She lowered her voice and her gaze passed over each of them. "But today, *this moment,* the time has come to announce the goddess of your selection."

"I don't like this," Mary whispered roughly to Di and Soni. "It sounds like—like demonic possession!"

"We aren't *really* going to be possessed by them, Marsh," Di replied in her most patronizing tone. "It's largely . . . symbolic. Actually, your own identity will be strengthened in the process, I'm sure."

"Every man you know will *pant* for you," Soni said, smiling joyously, "do *anything* to get you. That's when we make them the worthless worms they really are!"

"If there is one here who is not prepared to take this step, to invoke the name of a goddess," Carolyn Lord called, looking directly at her daughter, "I must ask you now to leave us. When you change your mind—as you surely will—you will be free and welcome to rejoin us."

Mary swiveled her head, looking at the ocean of bare breasts and legs, saw the lusty, avid expressions on the faces of the other young women. It was like a religious crusade; these girls were *soldiers*—but not of the Lord. Wasn't one of the Ten Commandments something about "having no other God before me"—or was that only what she had picked up as a girl? Mary was confused; she felt indecisive, part of her tugged by civilization's most powerful false urge—the urge to *belong.* There, her mother continued patiently staring at her—but *was* it her mother, really, anymore?—and now the others also turned to look where their leader stared. Directly at her.

Mary scrambled to her feet, brushing away grass. "I don't k-know," she mumbled, trying now to avoid Carolyn Lord's unveering, penetrating gaze, "I just d-don't know. But, not now," she added, turning to begin a near-run out of there, "maybe l-later, but *not now.* . . ."

She had reached the passageway leading between the buildings and out to the safe, sane street when she heard Diana Stoker's eager voice behind her:

"Hecate, Dr. Lord," Di called, her tones almost reverent. "I choose to be . . . *Hecate!*"

CHAPTER XX

July, this year.

"I feel more like Daphne all the time," Soni Jerome murmured from her bed. "I've read every word I can get about her, and I'm sure that the Eleusian rites will really make me her."

Diana and Mary-called-Marcia were studying at their desks in Diana's room and didn't answer for a moment. Diana's nameless cat and Soni's cat Mercury were playing with a sock. "Who was Daphne, exactly?" Di inquired without looking up from her book.

The little blond plumped her pillow, to get more comfortable. "Ovid told her story. She was a tiny huntress and very independent, even afraid of marriage. Her father, the river god Peneus, wanted her to marry, however, and even recommended mortal men to her. But she would sigh and tell him"—at this Soni looked directly at the person whom she admired so much, Di Stoker—"'Father, dearest, let me be like Diana.' And then she'd run into the woods, where she was happy."

Mary, who had not yet decided whether to go along with her friends or not, put her Advanced Composition book aside. "Did she escape marriage, then?"

"Only by being more independent than almost *any* of them," the tiny young woman answered with pride. "You see, Apollo badly wanted her because he found her enchantingly lovely. But she ran from him, even when he called, 'I am no mere farmer or shepherd. I am the Lord of Delphi, and I adore you,' But Daphne resisted still, running until she reached the river of her father, Peneus. She screamed for help, with the horny Apollo *right* on her heels, and something marvelous happened: Her feet took root; leaves sprouted; bark began to enclose her. Daphne's independence had transformed her into a lovely laurel tree."

Diana glanced at her young friend. "I'm not sure that's so cool," she offered. "Who wants to be a tree?"

Soni's dark eyes were immense. "But that's not the *end* of it!" she exclaimed. "Because Apollo loved her so much that he made Daphne *his* tree, and announced that all his men—from that time forward—would wear her leaves at times of victory. And so they did, for these were the famed laurel wreaths that have always been a symbol of achievement and triumph."

Mary's smile was tender. "How very romantic," she said; "I understand perfectly."

"But it isn't just a story!" Soni exclaimed. "That wondrous tree still stands, somewhere in Greece! And her soul—*Daphne's* soul—will be one with mine!"

"Of course," Mary answered softly. "Of course."

For a moment the three were silent. Then Diana looked at the other two. "I think I need your help," she said to Mary and Soni. "As you know, I chose to invoke Hecate." She frowned. "But I've found out in this book that it isn't quite as easy as it will be for Soni."

"What is that book?" Mary inquired, looking over at Di's desk.

"A personal journal by a grandfather of Dr. Lord," Diana replied with pride, raising the cover for Mary to see. "She's allowed me to use it for research," she added proudly.

Mary-called-Marcia blinked and her lips parted. It was one of great-grandfather's journals. The one she had had with her at Bleeding Heart Hospital and which so alarmed her mother. Yet Carolyn had *loaned* it to Di, knowing whom they both believed Diana to be, with all the private research and unprinted data greatgrandfather had acquired about Hecate. She couldn't answer Di for a moment.

"We'll help you if we can, Diana," Soni said; "won't we, Marsh?"

"Of course," Mary replied. "But if I understand it properly," she continued, cautious now, "Hecate wasn't a terribly *nice* person, was she? Why did you select her?"

If she had expected Diana to be angry or resentful, she was wrong. "Well, we all are seeking power over men, aren't we?—Power to do without them or, if we have to live with them, to do it on an equal or better footing. And Hecate, you see, had more power than any god or goddess in the long run. She could do many things, fantastic things, like drive people mad, or—or cause her enemies to acquire dreadful diseases. As queen of the underworld, she had an immense wolf-dog named Garm who guarded the living from entering, the dead from leaving."

"Who would want to *enter?*" Mary asked with a light chuckle.

"Lots of people," Di said vaguely. "To acquire her power." She stooped to retrieve her cat and began stroking it behind the ears.

"I thought you didn't even *like* dogs, though," Soni put in, puzzled.

"I don't, as pets." It was Diana's automatic reply. Something flickered in her memory, something largely forgotten; she could almost *see* mighty Garm just then, and he had something in his mouth. "Anyway, she also could summon ghosts and have them haunt people—all kinds of neat stuff like that."

Mary paused. "I can certainly *see* why you admire her," she said sarcastically.

"But by *day*, Marsh, Hecate was beautiful! Euripides even loved her, I think; he called her she 'who dwells apart, the flame of flames, in my fire's inmost heart.' *That's* romantic, isn't it?"

Soni grinned. "In a yechy sort of way," she said, making a face. "How can we help you invoke your goddess, honeybun?"

"We must follow the proper ritual exactly," Diana

explained. "we must get a dog . . . and then go to a joining of three roads by night. We need honey and—"

"If we're going to eat a dog," Soni snapped, "count me out."

"We aren't going to *eat* it, silly," Diana replied with a laugh. "Just—sacrifice it."

"Kill a dog?" Soni demanded, incredulous. Her eyes met Mary's, who added, "I never killed *anything*."

"That's all right," their friend said softly. *"I'm* the one who has to kill it. At the time of the new moon. Medea explained to Jason that to invoke Hecate three women must bathe in a running stream. Then, by ourselves at midnight, wearing very dark clothes, I must slay the animal and pour honey over it. While we pray to Hecate, of course." She fumbled in the pocket of her dress for a scrap of paper. She held it up, eagerly. "I have the two major prayers—they're absolutely *ancient!*—right here!"

"When?" Soni asked, moved by the excitement of it now. "When do we do all this?"

Again the athlete hesitated before answering. "There's a new moon tonight." She put her cat on the floor and clearly beseeched them for assistance. "I looked it up on the calendar, and tonight is *perfect*. Please? If we don't do it tonight, I'll have to wait a whole *month* before everything's right again. Please—*will* you help me?"

Mary considered before answering. She'd felt rather like an outsider for weeks, ever since she walked away from Carolyn Lord's place without selecting her own goddess. "Okay, I'll say the words along with you two," she agreed reluctantly. "And I'll even catch your dog for you. But I don't know about the 'nude bathing' part."

Diana stood, squeezing Mary's hands with joy. "I didn't say it had to be nude, babe," she pointed out, exultant now. "We can wear our undies. Marsh? Soni?"

"A deal," Soni replied, and Mary nodded. "Done."

"What do we do for that joining of three roads?" Soni inquired, anxious now to get started.

"There's an ideal place just two miles west of here.

It's almost on the ocean." Diana's eyes were huge with anticipation. "Along one road, you see, there's a woods. One road leads back into town, another to the beach. And the *third* road"—she grinned impishly—*"that* one leads to the cemetery."

"I think I just changed my mind," Soni protested, sighing. "Just what a nice little laurel tree like me needs! A goddam cemetery!"

"You can't change your mind now," Di said kiddingly, leaning down to hug the pert blond's shoulders. "I'll put a killer hex on you if you do."

Mary stared at the athlete, and thought: Why do I have the feeling she's not *kidding?*

At 10:45 that night, the three young students were crowded into Mary's old sports car—the one loaned her by Carolyn Lord when Mary enrolled at UCEV—and heading toward the intersection of the three designated roads.

It was pitch dark now and Mary thought it was strange how driving only a few miles from the busy campus plunged them into such a feeling of isolation. Instead of the incessant drone of voices, cheers or radios playing rock and disco, they moved now in a vale of utter silence that quickly engulfed and unnerved them all.

Ahead, up the turn in the road at perhaps two hundred yards away, an aged farmhouse stood atop a rise. Garbed in shadows with the windows unlit, it looked dementedly haunted. They stopped far short of the house, beside the creek Di had described, leaving the car between two gnarled trees. Then they were walking in a tangle of grass and weeds, Soni instantly bitten and pausing to scratch energetically.

The creek looked black and shallow. When the practical Mary prodded its depths with a tree branch, it wasn't too deep but she wondered what *things* lurked at the bottom. Overhead, a sliver of pasty new moon looked like the blade of a pirate cutlass. Then a series of gray clouds meandered across its face, and the blackness of night in the woods closed in on the girls like a chill and clenching fist.

"I don't like this," Mary muttered, standing tossing the branch into the woods. "We're sitting ducks for any carload of guys who want to cross over the line to genuine rape."

"Everybody at school, practically, has gone home for the summer," Soni reminded her, skinning out of a tanktop. She had no bra. "And the men in town seldom come out this way. They're more afraid of us than we are of them!" She slipped off her jeans and threw them in the general direction of the car, shivering in nothing but bright-yellow panties.

"I wouldn't let *two* carloads of men use us like objects for their simpleminded pleasure," Diana promised. She unbuttoned her shirt-style blouse and shrugged out of it. She, too, wore no brassiere. Then she slipped out of both her scarlet shorts and bikini panties and stepped boldly into the creek. In one hand she held something, carefully holding it out of the water.

Mary looked at the two of them another moment, went back to the car, and returned in only her black bra and panties. She looked thin, beside Di, almost scrawny beside Soni. With enormous reluctance Mary took an experimental step into the creek, found it cold but not unbearable, and stepped all the way in.

"We must be quite a sight," Soni remarked, giggling a little. She scrubbed at her small breasts with water, pretending to take a bath. "I feel positively *evil!*"

"Maybe that's appropriate," Mary responded with a frown, shivering and wishing Di would get on with it. "Hecate is supposed to *be* the very incarnation of evil. What's next on the agenda, Di?"

The athlete paused. Above her, and over her shoulder, the moon was emerging again and her tangle of wiry, black hair—both on her head and between her legs—seemed to glisten. Even her green eyes were ebony here. "I don't want either of you to misunderstand," she said, "but the next part is necessary."

First she turned to embrace Soni, lowering her head to kiss the blond on the lips as she cupped her small, perfectly round breasts in her hands. Despite herself, Soni was beginning to respond when Diana released her and approached Mary-called-Marcia. "This is part of the ritual," she said soberly. "A farewell to earthly desires." Then, like Soni, Mary felt Diana's palms gently squeezing her breasts. What was she *doing* out here, she wondered with fury at herself for going along with this; why was she *allowing* this? Did the part of Hecate already dwelling in Di have some *hold* on her?

She was interrupted in her thoughts by the sudden yapping of the dog she had found begging at the Distant Vistas rear entrance. A skinny, starving mongrel, he was tied by a rope in her backseat. "Shut up, can't you?" she called, *sotto voce*. "You'll bring Farmer Brown down on us."

"—And give the old goat the thrill of his life!" Soni added, giggling. "What's next, Di? Are you supposed to cast a spell or puke in the water or something?"

"Only one more thing before we go to the cemetery," the athlete replied, unfolding the note in her hand. "These are the Latin words of the famous sorcerer Jerome Cardanus. Each of us must read them. Aloud." She spread her legs in the creek water, steadying herself. Mary, watching with fascination, thought she had never seen anyone who looked either more beautiful or self-reliantly powerful. Diana seemed to have memorized the note, because she looked skyward, almost reverently, to intone: "*'Execratur illis precibus, Hecate dicante, primum adorandam.'*"

Soni took the paper which Di passed to her, wordlessly, and tried to imitate her agile friend. Immediately she staggered, losing her balance and crying out comically; but the athlete caught the small blond and righted her. At last Soni read it, aloud, stumbling over some of the unfamiliar words.

"What does it mean, Di?" Mary asked cautiously as the paper was handed to her.

"I don't know, precisely," she said, hesitating. "Just

sort of a . . . welcome to Hecate, I guess. It's not all that important." She looked down at the smaller young woman. "Go ahead," she urged in an inflectionless command. *"Read it."*

Mary neither spread her legs nor lifted the note. She simply turned her shoulders slightly to encourage the moonlight's cooperation, and slowly intoned the words on Diana's scrap of paper—the third and last one in the rite.

Suddenly, inexplicably, the moonlight was gone and they were plunged into total darkness. It was almost like a literal plunge; the bottom seemed to fall out of the world, leaving them in the absolute dark, unable to see each other or even their own hands. Some flying night-creature flapped over their heads, close to them, squealing—is that a bat?—and Mary felt some squiggly thing writhe against her bare ankle. Then, for a frightful instant, it was unbearably, impossibly hot in the creek; the lapping water seemed to become hungry tongues of flame. Soni shrieked; her fingers dug into Mary's arm in terror.

Then the slice of moon was there again. Three young women shuddered close to one another, huddling for reassurance. "Wh-What the hell *was* that?" Soni demanded.

"Clouds," Di replied, blinking. "It must have been clouds hiding the moon."

But Mary was scanning the *back* of the paper scrap Diana had given to her, reading it aloud: " 'Goddess of darkness and the dead, blood and terror, spirits and witchcraft, Hecate wanders among tombstones to find and drink the blood of corpses. To summon Hecate is to summon *einodia*, she who stands at the crossroads to Hell—a dog-devouring spectre of all that is corrupt.' Good Lord, Diana, let's call this thing *off!*"

The athlete snatched the paper away. "Don't be absurd! Those are just superstitious words by someone who didn't understand Hecate's origins." She laughed. "You don't believe every word of this, do you?"

"No, I don't," Mary said deliberately, getting out of the

creek now and looking for her clothes. "But the pathetic and frightening part is, *you do!*"

"Sure." Diana laughed once more, following Mary onto dry land. "And I believe in the Easter bunny and the Great Pumpkin, too! Let's get over to the cemetery and finish this up."

Mary spun to face Diana, a hand raised against the brunette's thrusting bosom. For a moment they were eye to eye, Mary Lord finally so alarmed that she dared confront her powerful friend. "If it's not really important, what happens if we *don't* finish these rites? What would happen if I decided *not* to go with you?"

For a second their eyes locked, each face shadowed from the other. Finally Di laughed, and shrugged. "Okay, then. I've had friends betray me before. If you don't want to keep the rest of your promise, we'll just skip it." She pulled on her panties, then the red shorts over them, and straightened again to Mary. "But I won't forget this, Marsh. I *never* forget it when I'm crossed."

"C'mon, Marsh," Soni pleaded, miniature in the moonlight with weeds to her knees. "Don't chicken out *now*."

At length Mary nodded. "All right; you win. We'll do it your way." She finished dressing. "What's the next step?"

"All three of us slip on these dark coveralls," Diana answered quickly, parceling them out. "Remember, it said to wear dark?"

Mary nodded, anxious to get it over with. The three did as Diana wished and then got into the car where Mary resumed following her athletic friend's driving instructions. Passing the farmhouse, she thought she felt *eyes* peering at them from behind the shadowed windows. Ahead of them now, the sports car headlights picked out the heavy marble pillars between which hung an ominous bronze legend: GOLDEN LIFE cemetery. Mary shuddered.

Easing the car to a halt, she paused instead of shutting off the beams. Through the entrance all three girls could see row after row of tidy headstones occasionally separated by huge, solid mausoleums rising like spectral linebackers on a darkened football field. Here, roads broke away in different directions and, in the gloom of isolation, seemed to extend merely a few feet before falling off the bottomless edge of the earth. Somewhere to the west an owl hooted; Mary bit her lip. If this was as bad an ordeal as the creek's, she doubted she could see it through. Her nerves were afire with anxiety. For the first time some of the words she had written, herself, about Hecate, came to mind; for the first time in months she remembered vividly what it was like to be mentally ill; nonfunctioning. And she wondered how close her friend Di Stoker was now, to the same disabling condition. Behind her, the mongrel dog she'd trapped began to whine and Mary wondered if she had done the right thing at all.

"I'll get the mutt," Soni said, reaching over the backseat.

Wordless, Diana strode ahead, vague and preoccupied. She mounted a slight rise to the cemetery entrance, Soni three steps behind her. When Mary, leaving the headlights on, joined them, Diana produced two neatly typed sheets of paper from her coverall pocket. "Here," she whispered, handing them out. "I'll take the dog now and remain here at the entrance with it and the honey." He face was lovely with excitement. "After he's ... gone ... you two begin reading the spells. Aloud, like before. That's when I pour the libation of honey. Before you know it, this'll be all done."

Soni handed over the dog. The minute it was in Di's strong arms, it began struggling, its eyes rolled back in terror. "How're you gonna kill him, Di?" Soni demanded, a bit breathless. "With a k-knife?"

"No, you jerk." Di laughed harshly. "With ether I stole from the lab at school. You think I'm some kind of monster?"

Neither Mary nor Soni answered her. By now, Soni, too, was wondering. She wanted to withdraw, to forget the whole thing, as much as Mary did. But it was *just possible*, Mary Lord mused, that seeing how this nonsense failed totally might bring Di *back* to herself. In fact, it might well be the only chance she had left.

Costumed in black, Diana's lovely figure was highlighted by the car beams and Mary saw with relief that, while her face was twisted in a grimace of distaste and determination, it was *still* Diana's strikingly pretty face. She got the ether from her purse and, at arm's length, poured it carefully on a handkerchief, coughing a little. Even at the other girls' distance of yards the smell was overpowering. Di knelt to the cowering animal at her feet and held the handkerchief over his nose and mouth. The dog put up a brave fight, trying to pull away, alternately growling and yelping. Di had to straddle his small form with her legs to hold on, and Mary looked away.

As if in answer to the deadly peril of one of their own kind, several *other* dogs began to howl somewhere beyond the cemetery. Mary's and Soni's flesh crawled as they listened to the awful racket. To her, it seemed that the other dogs *knew*—in some fantastic, long-distance, telepathic manner known only to creatures—*exactly* what was happening to one of their own. More dogs joined in. They bayed now, the young woman felt, in fearful sympathy—and respect.

But at last the poor mongrel lay still at Diana's feet except for one spasming hind leg.

Soni nudged Mary's ribs. Dutiful, almost frantic now to get this over and return to the rooms at LaCaresta, Mary squinted against the ebony night to read the typed sheet Di had given her: "Three-headed, nocturnal, excrement-eating virgin of Hades, holder of Persephone's clanking keys, Koré of the underworld, Gorgon-eyed terrible dark one; *come* now! we *beseech* ye!"

Soni heard it out, quivering, eyes huge. Then they shifted uneasily, scanning her own paper: " 'Infernal, terrestial and celestial Bombo, goddess of the crossroads, guiding light and queen of night, sturdy enemy of the sun, friend and companion of darkness,' " Soni read, getting more into it as she continued, beginning to call out the ancient words with authority. " 'You who rejoice to hear the barks of dogs and see red blood flow; you who wander amongst the tombs in the hours of man's late night, thirsty for gore, and the terror of mortal man—Gorgon, Mormo, Bombo, black moon of a thousand forms—*do* as we seek! *Enter our friend!*' "

A thunderclap, staggering! Mary and Soni shrieked their fear as the sky over their heads was sundered by a glowing dagger of enfuried lightning that illumined Diana's figure where she stood in the entrance, the still cemetery at her back. *Two* unhuman forms, at first enormous, seemed to rise from the very earth beside Diana Stoker, shimmering in a shortwave-like series of livid flashes, their features impossible to perceive even as the figures swiftly shrank to human size to stand, palpitating and mesmeric, like risen ghouls.

Each vibrating figure looked feminine at a glance; each was dressed in a long, thin gown trailing to the earth; and each gown was splotched with wet human blood that dripped noiselessly to the ground. From all around the bizarre party of three at the entrance came another, nearly canine cacophony of yelping, thunderous, anxiety-ridden barking that washed out *toward* Mary and Soni as if unseen dead dogs loomed nearby. Diana issued a single sound—a tentative scream that might have been the muffled shriek of woman-in-orgasm—as her friends shrank away from her. Then a *second* rippling bolt of lightning carved the black meat of the heavy night—

And the forms on either side of Di Stoker seemed to be absorbed *by her,* flowed *to and smoothly merged with her into a single,* nightmare *form.*

Soni, transfigured and aghast, half-turned away, her hand raised defensively. Mary screamed, ran for the car. Before either the blond or the altered Di Stoker could move or even speak, Mary was throwing the car into reverse, spinning, *peeling* rubber as she careened wildly away from the cemetery, and away—she prayed, *forever*—from the reemerged and quite literal, living form of Hecate, Queen of Hell.

CHAPTER XXI

Same night.

She had headed frantically homeward, at first—back to LaCaresta—intending to lock herself into the room, barricade it, possibly never come *out* of it again.

Then it occurred to her that Diana would go to the same place, if Diana she yet remained; and if she now was Hecate, principally, she would also know exactly *where* to seek her out. . . .

For awhile Mary Lord drove aimlessly, still terrified, grateful for the lights on the street. Momentarily she considered driving to her mother's apartment. But the way Carolyn was behaving lately, herself, it wasn't safe to conclude that she was not already under Hecate's influence. Perhaps mother was no longer mother, in any meaningful way; perhaps she'd forgotten Mary ever existed. The girl sobbed, blinked back tears.

Besides, judging from what she'd heard of Hecate's awesome power, a rooming house door or one in an apartment building wouldn't keep her out if she *really* wanted in.

Mary tried to think, not cry, as rationally as humanly possible. There *had* to be a way out of this nightmare!

The police!—But what could she *tell* them that would make them help her? That she and two other girls bathed naked in a creek and then went to the cemetery in order to summon some ancient goddess? That she'd seen two ghoulish shapes seem to rise out of the earth, stand beside Diana, and then sort of *ooze* their creepy way into her young body?

214

The notion of telling this to down-to-earth police brought a genuine, half-hysterical smile to her lips. No police department in the world could accept such nonsense; she'd be lucky not to be locked away for good. A sitting duck for the vengeful Hecate.

Without realizing it, she'd driven back onto the UCEV campus and now putted slowly through its darkened streets, her own aging car ghostlike on the deserted campus. Now Mary began trying to come to grips with the problem, to confront the reality of her situation.

Mass hypnosis, she'd read, was not as uncommon as people believed. She remembered reading about a town, two or three hundred years ago, which became afflicted with a "dancing sickness." Before it ended, half the town had dropped dead of exhaustion or coronaries! Viewed in that light it wasn't impossible to think that she'd imagined *both* the hellish blackness, when they stood in the creek, and the rising, decaying forms that seemed to merge with Diana. There was no reason to think she and Soni hadn't been *seeing* things, put in the mood by the surreal nature of their occult reason for being there.

And come to think of it, *Soni hadn't run away* from the cemetery! Maybe it was only *she*, herself, who'd seen the spectral bodies! And maybe they had encountered in the creek, some bizarre manifestation of weather or atmosphere! After all, people were forever mistaking little-known, natural weather phenomena for UFOs!

For a moment she thought of returning to the rooming house, even turned one dark corner in that general direction.

But Di and Soni would be rightfully *furious* that she had left them marooned at a cemetery miles away. Good heavens, Mary thought, nibbling her lip, they might drop her as a friend, forever! Now she thought of driving back to the land of the dead, perhaps to pick them up on the road along the way; but the image of what she'd seen at the Golden Life entrance reappeared vividly in her mind's eye, and she knew nothing on the face of the earth could get her back there that night.

Well. Better to confront them both in the morning. If they *were* both there, and themselves, she would apologize endlessly for her childish fright—they knew how timid she'd always been. And if they *weren't* there in the morning—if her original conclusion was correct, and Diana Stoker was transformed to Hecate—she'd have the daylight on her side. Someone had said something about the Queen of Hades being principally a nocturnal creature, like Dracula.

Having decided to stay away from home, Mary looked for and found a lover's lane known to the dating students of UCEV. Here, indeed, poor Ray Ellis had taken her one night. She wished now, in a way, she'd given herself to him, that he'd been allowed one transcendently pleasurable experience before the pack of wild dogs got him.

Not even the campus fuzz knew about this parking spot, Mary imagined. It wasn't down a side road at all but between two large trees through which a car could just barely squeeze, turn sideways and be unseen from the street. Mary switched off the lights and found a study pad she always kept with her; she began to doodle cartoons, and yawned.

Funny. How could she be so sleepy after such an incredible night? Surely she hadn't been so frightened that she was in *shock?*

For a moment she was asleep, then shooting her eyes open and staring out at the night. All she could make out was a protective canopy of trees and a certain amount of grassy growth remaining where myriad cars had parked before. She managed a smile at the thought that she was probably the only *single* person who'd ever stopped here. Anyone seeing her might conclude that she had some rather strange personal habits!

Again, heavy eyelids, a murkiness of the mind that she knew, from her reading, appoached the psychological hypnagogic state. Without fighting it, she began to write on her study pad, to scrawl words that made sentences, and sentences that made paragraphs, and . . .

Mary-called-Marcia slept.

The cold touch of a hand on her arm, lying on the lowered window, yanked her into abrupt and stunning wakefulness. Afraid and rather disoriented, Mary blinked into the shadowed night, tried to make out what had touched her.

At this level she could see a shirt-style blouse and scarlet shorts. Female-like, she recognized them instantly. "Diana!" she called out, still too sleepy at this point to react in other than a customary way. The events of the night were still lodged in another chamber of memory. "How did you find me here?"

There was no reply. Crickets chirped in the thigh-high grass encircling the isolated sports car. Something slithered, close to the ground. The shirt-style blouse and scarlet shorts were frozen there, unmoving. No sound came from the figure.

All the night's terrifying experiences flooded Mary's mind at once and she cried out, terrorstricken now. "D-Diana, are you okay? *Answer* me, Diana!"

Silence. Even the crickets had stopped singing now. Nothing stirred; nothing in the night moved except her own frantically pounding heart.

Hand trembling, she reached out desperately for the ignition key—

—And found it gone.

She pulled the handle of the door and shoved against it, deciding to run; she tried to open the door—

—And found it rudely, powerfully slammed shut against her pressing leg. Mary winced and cried out in minor pain.

Again, the silence.

The shadow outside the door huddled, folded in on itself; the figure's head sought now to look inside the car. It was dark there, too, however. The figure outside the car could not see Mary Lord either.

And so it *opened* the door, itself, and the ceiling light flooded the interior with phlegm-yellow illumination.

Now the thing could see inside.

Now Mary could see *outside* . . . and screamed in blinding horror.

It might, once, have been Diana Stoker or perhaps partly Diana; someone with a vivid imagination could have discerned something human in the face, possibly—or someone on an LSD trip that went bad.

Or someone who was cursed with the reasonless imagination of the mad, or of the damned.

The creature's face seemed more eaten by worms than by time, and inch-long, pale, *wriggly* things moved in and out of the mooncrater pores—those that weren't covered, instead, by green pustules and hirsute moles. The nose was a thing that dribbled out roughly from the center of the face, bending down at the tip until it overhung a sadist's thin mouth devoid of all but three or four snaggly yellow teeth. It was the face of an old age that *could not be,* controlled by a mind of such advanced malice and indefinable sinfulness that it *should not be.* The rheumy, antiquarian eyes were mesmeric, tinted a hellish blood-red that, once fastened on one as now they fastened upon poor Mary Lord, seemed to suck out all personal will like a particularly disgusting leech sucking the juices from a fertile egg. The cross patch network of harsh lines and broken veins which passed for a face was encircled by torturous, brownish-green strands comprised entirely of writhing, avaricious snakes, their tiny multiple mouths open to permit miniature tongues to lick avidly toward Mary's panic-stricken face. She sought to scream with the intention, perhaps, of going on screaming till there was no breath left in her lungs.

But with her will draining away Mary could only sit limply in the bucket seat and stare in horrid revulsion as the hairy back of the ancient crone's hand moved in nightmare caress, down her soft cheek and throat, across her shrinking breasts, over her outraged lower body. Vomit rose in Mary's mouth, stayed. The hand turned round, then, reaching for her once more, cupping Mary's head like a vise, its touch icy, unbelievably clammy. Mary made small, disgusted noises in the back of her throat but the scream of terror would not come. Even now the ghastly crimson eyes transfixed her, even now the message was transmitted from the aged bitch's mind to her own: *As I told you, I never forget it when I'm crossed.*

The immeasurably old creature made a single, cackling sound as her drooling, snaggled mouth dipped toward Mary, drew near, the breath gagging by its foulness and searing heat, the toothy remnant fastening unerringly in the soft flesh at the side of Mary's breast. There was a swift, sure snap and the pain of hell when the teeth met and tore away a bite. Hecate nibbled on only part of it, holding the rest daintily between her cracked and scabrous fingers.

Blood streamed from the awful rent in her flesh and pain soared as the young woman, fighting faintness, turned her pleading, anguished eyes up to the lunatic parody of a female which crouched just beyond the car, quietly chewing. Their eyes met and the crone understood the terrible query in Mary's glazed eyes, and chuckled.

"Oh, I'm not going to *eat* you, dear," she said. The voice might have been Di Stoker's, if Diana had been three thousand years old. *"That* little bite was just to *begin* your death." She paused, mental fingers roughly, carelessly penetrating the girl's stunned mind for the question rising there. "To begin *what?* Why, the dread disease, child! The dread disease!" It strangled briefly on the flesh in its mouth, chuckling. "When they find you tomorrow, you see," the red eyes danced evilly in their sunken sockets, "they will know right away what killed you. It will be perfectly clear to everyone, my girl . . . that you died, *riddled with cancer."*

After that, only the sound of the aged apparition's steady munching broke the nightmare silence. When it moved away, satisfied, licking its fingers and hurrying back to LaCaresta, the young woman left behind was already unconscious. Unseen, the rancid cancer cells multiplied with cheerful abandon in her dying, decaying body.

PART FOUR

"Our Lady of Pain"

"Look: the constant marigold Springs again from hidden roots. Baffled gardener, you behold New beginnings and new shoots." —Robert Graves, *Marigolds*

"The god of the cannibals will be a cannibal . . ."
—Ralph Waldo Emerson

"The isles of Greece, the isles of Greece!
Where burning Sappho loved and sung . . .
Eternal summer gilds them yet,
But all, except their sun, is set." —Byron

"Nature has no principles." —Anatole France

"Or bid the soul of Orpheus sing
such notes as, warbled to the string,
Drew iron tears down Pluto's cheek." —John Milton

"Her legs were such Diana shows,
When tuckt up she a-hunting goes
With Buskins shortened to descrie
The happy dawning of her thigh." —Robert Herrick

"It often seemed to her in the first eight months of her fifteenth year, that all males were nasty louts, and that she would have to live and die an old maid for her fastidiousness. She faced the prospect cheerfully." —Herman Wouk, *Majorie Morningstar*

"What ailed us, O gods, to desert you
For creeds that refuse and restrain?
Come down and redeem us from virtue,
Our Lady of Pain." —Algernon Swinburne

"Even God cannot change the past."
—Agathon (447-401 B.C.)

"And many more, whose names on Earth are dark,
But whose transmitted effluence can not die,
So long as fire outlives the parent spark,
Rose, robed in dazzling immortality." —Shelley

"As you are woman, so be lovely;
As you are lovely, so be various,
Merciful as constant, constant as various,
So be mine, as I yours For ever." —Robert Graves,
Pygmalion to Galatea

CHAPTER XXII

Next morning. The LaCaresta rooming house.

"Goddess, I'm tired!" Soni said, sitting up in bed and slapping her alarm clock into silence. Achingly, creakingly, she moved her legs to rest her bare feet on the floor, and stretched. "Tromping around in the woods had made me an old lady overnight!" She laughed self-deprecatingly. "My Catholic upbringing is fighting back at the idea of nude bathing. What are you doing up already, Diana?"

The figure at the window remained silent a moment. A cat was clutched in its arms. "I've been up for hours. I couldn't sleep worrying about Marcia."

"After leaving us that way, she's just too ashamed to come home. You'd have thought she saw a ghost or something!" Soni yawned and stood, her rather oversized pajamas giving her a clownish demeanor. "Don't stew it, babe. I'm sure she'll show up at Dr. Lord's apartment this afternoon."

The figure at the window turned back. Diana Stoker, pretty in turtleneck sweater and tight-fitting skirt, smiled at her roommate but her lovely eyes were sad. "I hope so. I'm terribly concerned."

"We'd better get going. Two new working girls have to learn how to be on time or get sacked early in their careers."

Since deciding to remain in El Vista for the summer Diana had found work in a sporting goods store, Soni at a McDonald's restaurant and Marcia at a local office. The missing girl was a temporary file clerk for Dr.

Claud Mauser, and when Diana telephoned him later to see if Marcia had arrived safely at work, he almost snapped Di's head off.

"No, she certainly hasn't," came Mauser's nasal voice. "You college girls think you can come and go as you please. Next time I'll try to find a man to fill the job."

Diana, holding the phone so Soni could hear too, instantly told him, "If you paid a woman what you'd pay a man, maybe she'd have more interest in your damn job." Then she hung up, her expression puzzled and still confused as she shrugged at Soni.

Around ten that morning, however, the mystery was solved. Police detectives called on Di, at Sichting Sports, and Soni at her McDonald's, separately breaking the terrible news that Marcia Angell's body had been found, separately interrogating them to learn what they knew.

Each young woman told the obvious facts in the matter to the mixed amusement and disgust of the police. When Soni was asked why Marcia left them at the cemetery the little blond shook her head tearfully. "Something spooked her, officer, that's all I know." "You didn't see anything frightening yourself, Miss Jerome?"

"It's '*Ms.*' Jerome," Soni corrected him. "Well, the whole thing was enough to make anybody edgy. It *was* kind of funny, but when Di was bending over the dog, to pour honey on his body—I couldn't look anymore at all. Next thing I knew, Marsh was screaming and driving off."

In her interview Di, leaning faintly against a counter full of expensive tennis rackets, gave her opinion that Marcia had fled when she realized the *trioditis* was a perversion of the Holy Trinity. "Marsh wasn't quite one of us, really," she said feebly, "and I d-doubt she'd have continued with Dr. Lord and the others much l-longer."

"Well, now, I don't know about that," demurred the plainclothes detective, a burly mustached man named Abbott. His eyes burned into Diana's as he spoke: "Didn't you know that Marcia's *real* name was Mary Lord, and that her mother *was* Carolyn Lord?"

There was no need for Di Stoker to act. She was genuinely astonished. The *implications*, given the way Carolyn catered to her, yet with what the instructor doubtlessly realized about the way her actions were being subtly controlled, were profound. "No!" she cried. "I d-didn't know." She had to grip the counter hard to steady herself. How much control would remain now that her own daughter had been killed—and how much would Dr. Lord figure out? "I—I'll have to go to Dr. Lord immediately. She needs a friend now."

"She knows," Lieutenant Abbott said laconically, closing his notebook. "We went to her first."

Appalled, Diana informed her manager of what had happened, then phoned Soni, who had just learned the same dreadful news. For her, of course, there was only the fact that a teacher and a friend was in grief. They decided to drive immediately to Carolyn's apartment to console her, Di's mind abuzz with conflicting emotions and fears.

Several other students had arrived by the time they got there, along with Dr. Lord's friends Fred and Elna Clinefort. The lanky psychologist was trying to persuade Carolyn to accept a sedative when the newcomers arrived.

Carolyn looked up through her tears to identify them, and her face twisted in horror—and more.

"Oh, Dr. Lord, we j-just found out about Marcia," Soni cried, hurrying to her and dropping to her thin knees. "I mean, about—M-Mary."

"You." The smoky-blond instructor struggled to her feet, not seeing Soni, staring past her at Diana. Her mouth worked; she wanted to say more, but clearly it was a battle. Only one other person understood how *much* a battle it was.

By now the athlete remained only *part*-Diana; that which was not her own groped anew for Carolyn's mind, strove to reinforce its instructions, and encountered iron resistance. "Something's happening to me," the real Diana murmured, trying to explain.

"You—*witch!*" Carolyn managed, blinking her eyes

and staggering slightly. Fred's hand went out to steady her, his expression amazed. *"You* did it to my poor girl! *You!"*

"Carolyn," said the psychologist, patiently, "you don't mean that. The police informed us, remember? That it was cancer?" He smiled apologetically at the athletically lovely young woman before them. "This girl couldn't have had anything to do with Mary. Life was just too much for her, she was too *frail*...."

Carolyn Lord made the supreme effort. She swept her long hair back from her face and charged the few feet separating them, grasping Diana by the biceps, shouting into her face: "Mary *just came* from a hospital only *months* ago—remember, Fred?" Her eyes, furious and too wounded for fear, challenged Diana's. "It takes *years* for a cancer to develop, I know that—and they said it was *everywhere* in her body!"

"A terrible, isolated victim," Fred said soothingly, placing his hands on her shoulders, urging her away from Di. Beside them, Soni looked in bafflement from face to face. "These things *happen* sometimes. Don't blame it on—"

"You fool, where do you think Mary got that awful *bite?* Can't you *see* this is no mere girl?" Carolyn's gaze locked with the unprotesting Diana's. "Tell us the truth, Hecate—come on, admit it! Damn you back to hell, you fiendish bitch, I have *proof* that you were *expected*—Mary *knew* you were coming; so did great-grandfather and I have *proof* that you're here! You didn't know that either, did you, Hecate? That my Mary was *on* to you a year ago!"

"I'm sorry," Fred apologized for his friend, his patient. "Care, let me give you something. *Please.*"

Her mouth was frothing now; spittle flew in her anguish. "So you'd better *finish* it, Hecate, I mean it! You'd better take *me* out, too!"

"You're hurting my arm," Diana said gently.

"Act the innocent, then, bitch!" Carolyn's face was inches away, her eyes maniacal in their stare, "but I *will* expose you! I have *all* the papers safely hidden, including the ones Mary wrote *just last night,* before you attacked her! Shall I tell my friends where they are?"

Easily Diana broke the hold and put her own arms around the hysterical instructor. Quietly—as sweetly as a mother tucking in its child for the night—she kissed Carolyn's jawline, just below the cheek. *"Poor Dr. Lord,"* she said with profound sympathy.

Soni made a muffled screaming sound. Carolyn Lord had taken a single, stiff-legged backward step; she'd thrown her arms up, not in fear but in pain. A terrible expression of agony crossed her attractive face. She blinked, tried to speak; nothing came out but a ghastly strangling sound.

Then, quite slowly, like a collapsing doll, Carolyn slipped down the slippery side of the normal world to her knees, then fell over on her back, paralyzed and staring speechlessly at the ceiling.

"A stroke," Fred Clinefort said in dismay and concern. He gestured furiously at Soni. "Quick! Phone for an ambulance!"

When it came, Diana and Soni stood helplessly by as Carolyn's still, unmoving form was tenderly raised on a stretcher and pushed gently into the rear of the vehicle.

Tears were in Di's eyes as she groped for the little blond's hand. "She was the finest woman I ever met," she remarked with quiet sincerity. "What a terrible tragedy to see her this way."

Soni nodded at the athletic woman beside her and delicately, carefully withdrew her hand from Di's grasp. She studied her expression another moment, heart pounding heavily.

That evening, without informing anyone, Soni packed her things and moved into the women's dorm.

Mrs. Violet Hudson took it badly when she learned what had happened to the girl she knew as Marcia Angell, and when she found that only Diana was left in the two rooms upstairs, she shook her head sadly. "Horace had it, 'Brace thee, my friend, when times are hard, to show A mind unmoved; nor less, then fair thy state, A sober joy.' Bear that in mind, Miz Stoker."

"It's only my heart that's sad," Di said easily. She smiled frigidly. "My mind *remains* unmoved."

Alone in her room, the aging landlady laid aside her Bartlett's for the first time in months, replacing it with the Holy Bible.

Alone in *her* room, the last of the suite's three tenants, Diana Stoker found Mary Lord's cat sulking and hungry in the corner. Her own, larger cat was facing it, defiantly, apparently trying to threaten the smaller animal.

With a sigh, Di retrieved the cat food and put a small quantity in each of the two bowls. Mercury, Mary's animal, promptly went to his bowl but Diana's bounded toward Mercury and scratched it away from the food. Fascinated, the athlete watched from a chair to see what would happen next.

When her cat was finished eating Mercury's food, it turned to the other feline and, without an ounce of warning, knocked it down and then fell upon it, scratching fiercely, clawing rips into the other's belly.

Diana threw back her head to laugh. "Silly kitty," she purred. "You don't have to do *everything* that Mama does!"

CHAPTER XXIII

August, this year.

There had been no decisions reached by UCEV about whether or not to cancel Dr. Carolyn Lord's class for the semester beginning anew in a month. Word from the hospital was that the intelligent and lovely blond showed slight improvement; she might be well enough to resume teaching, she might not. Their indecision was based on the constructive fact that Carolyn was quite youthful for a paralytic stroke, and the negative fact that she showed no signs of recovering from her daughter's terrible loss.

But sheer economic considerations, on the part of the UCEV registrar's office, demanded a decision be put off until the last possible moment. Hundreds of young women students *cared* about Carolyn, now; hundreds of tuitions amounted to sums of money worth considering.

Left to her own devices now that she occupied space in the women's dorm and rarely saw Diana, Soni Jerome began dating men again. She told her new friends that she was happier then she'd ever been before at UCEV and told herself, privately, that she'd been even more neurotic than usual about Di. People simply didn't become goddesses or give others cancer and strokes.

Without the excitement of Dr. Lord's guidance and the ROTGOD course to occupy her time, unwilling to return either to the track or archery teams and yet filled with a lurking suspicion that *something awesome* would soon happen in her life, Diana also began to date.

She described her feelings and what she'd come to know of herself in a perceptive diary which she might have killed to keep private: "Clearly, I am not in control of my own thoughts or deeds; just as surely there are times when I am. Loosely speaking," she confessed to her journal, "I'm a little like someone with a dual personality complex. But *I know who else I am* and integration with Hecate is more difficult than it was for the fabled 'Sybil' or 'Eve.' I've read that every human mind is a compendium or amalgamation of all its inherited traits, all its environmental or social experiences, all it's been taught.

"So in a way," Diana wrote, conscious of a dull headache that told her her *alter ego* was registering a mild objection, "I've always been Hecate while it's also been a role to which I've been *growing*—continually growing. Just as a fat little boy tends to become an obese man, or a girl who loves painting or piano playing because her mother painted or played and she is molded to *become* a painter or pianist." She paused, biting her lip till it almost bled, before writing the next line. "In my case, I was always meant to become a female monster."

At that point the building headache, stretching from her temples to the front of her head, became intense and she had to lay the diary aside.

The next night, however, almost eerily alone in the old house on LaCaresta, Diana gritted her teeth and wrote on: "Because of the way society leavens and moderates, the way mother sought to guide me and even my terrible father in his way, I'm not entirely evil and fundamentally remain she who was given the name Diana Stoker. It's just that I have a new, internal roomie—Hecate—and when I feel Randy's arms around me, I begin to doubt that I want her there anymore." The pain, from the blue, laced through her skull and she had to grip the pen with all her extraordinary strength and determination. "I am still me, but I seem to be losing more and more control by attrition. And what I cannot detect is how much I think or do with Hecate's unspoken permission, or because she's influencing me subtly, or—worse—some of the things I do because Hecate is then *fully* exerting herself. What I'm laboring to say is that I cannot be certain all the deeds I regard as my own are, in point of fact, mine. Until Randy Duncan came along, happiness—especially mine—wasn't much concern to me because I had never experienced joy before. Now, though it may have come too late, I have found that men can be truly wonderful. I pray that I may, somehow, retain my sensibilities enough to share joy with him . . . soon."

When Soni heard that Di was seeing Randy, a UCEV acting major who, more than any other, was regarded as having an excellent chance in Hollywood, she swallowed her latent fear and went to visit her old roommate.

It was a scorching summer day and Di was wearing a bikini top and shorts, sitting patiently in a chair she had brought from Mary's old room. Outwardly, Di seemed glad to see Soni and the latter felt suddenly foolish that she had ever believed her old friend capable of monstrous acts. She sat on the edge of her own old bed, and tried to be as forthright as she could.

"You really tried to help Marcia—I mean, Mary—and you also tried to help me," the little blond said. "I know she appreciated it, the same way I still do. Your quick thinking prevented me from becoming a Lesbian and now, with several nice guys to date, I'm grateful."

"But there's a point to this, isn't there?" Diana inquired stolidly, fingertips strumming steadily on the arm of her chair. "And that point is Randy, I'm sure."

For a moment Soni simply couldn't bring herself to continue. Her old friend had changed in some major respects, since . . . what happened to Dr. Lord. Her face was rather drawn; there were hollow shadows beneath her beautiful, expressive eyes. Yet the odd fact was that, if anything, Diana also seemed lovelier and more self-reliant. Something inside the tiny blond snapped its fingers: *Yes*, by Hera, that was it—she'd never seen *anyone* so self-reliant as Di Stoker today. One day, perhaps, that pretty, shrewd face would be little more than a mass of harsh, vertical lines from the way it had formed and expressed the words, *No,* and *I don't care what you think,* for a lifetime.

And yet, Soni thought, pained by the notion, *now* Di was saying "Yes" for once—to the slickest, most corrupt conman on campus. Randy Duncan. And it was her fearful task to change the athlete's mind, or heart.

"Come on, Soni!" Di was snapping. "Out with it. I'm not going to bite your head off!"

Not the way you bit Mary to poison her? came Soni's wayward thought. She inhaled, said her piece: "Di, baby, we're friends and I gotta say it all. Your actor friend is worse than Burt Starr ever was. I mean that. I'd really like t'see you be happy—enjoy some normal experiences at UCEV. But sweetheart, Randy Duncan is your standard, amateur actor-type. D'you remember hearing about the late James Dean, the way he 'collected' people, tried to *feel* their moods as a sort of laboratory? That way, he could try to act out everything they felt. And sometimes, Di, *sometimes* he wanted to know what it felt like to be conned, to have your heart broken." Soni gulped. "Randy's—like that. Worse, he *talks* about it. He shoots off his big yap about every conquest. Female *or* male."

Diana smiled. Astonishingly, warmly. "Bless you, Soni, for caring," she said, reaching out to pat the blond's flinching hand. "But Randy *confessed* all that to me. He even said he'd tried to make it with you but struck out. That he's now ashamed as hell because, well, he never *cared* about any of the others. Not the way he cares about me."

"I see." Soni spread her fingers, peered studiedly at them. She was amazed. Di was very much still human, in the most dangerous of ways. Dangerous to herself. "You, ah, *believe* all that jazz?"

For a moment Di's eyes glistened. "I have to, babe. Sometime in my life, I have to put my faith in something or someone—other than . . . "

"Other than Hecate?" Feminine superiority?"

"He's different, Soni." The athlete held her head up. "I can tell that. Randy's changed. And if he can, so can I." She hesitated. "We have a date tonight, pal—right here in my room. I'm going to show him how human I can be."

For any objective onlooker it would have been obvious that Randy Duncan accepted Di Stoker's offering of herself in a grand style, a grand manner, as his just reward for having dated her at all. At twenty-two, he was a perfectly proportioned six-two, blondly handsome in a manner reminiscent of Robert Redford, his eyes skyblue and miraculously clear of both guile and his rather ribald living-style, a dimple in his cheek and a matching one on his chin. In his easy serious attitude he even managed to convey something of the comforting father-image. But his most important operating tools were a mop of sandy-golden hair, and the practiced hands of a sexual surgeon.

From Randy's viewpoint, the conquest of Diana Stoker was, at least, a major one. He'd heard stories of her athletic prowess, how she'd broken two coaches' hearts by dropping off their teams, and that told him she'd be something special in bed—a physical match for him, if he was lucky. He'd also heard some rather bizarre tales which he instantly dismissed. He knew that most of the men on the UCEV campus lacked the simple courage to ask her for a date, fearing both rejection and her unsurpassed feminine strength; but he knew, also, that if there was one coed in school who figured in the nocturnal fantasies of his friends more than any other, it was Di Stoker. Her very inaccessibility was legendary. Randy had the reputation among males on campus that, just as Soni told Di, he painted graphic pictures of those he bedded but more than that, never, *ever* lied. If he told his cronies that he'd slept with Diana, they would accept it as fact.

Besides, he thought as he finished undressing her

and slipped off his own T-shirt, icy-calm and controlled, it was important to learn what made this one tick. The complexities of Diana's emotional makeup and of the keen intellect which he almost respected were nearly as important factors in his conquest as any other motivating forces.

Or they were until he turned to look down at the gorgeous ambience of the naked young woman on the bed beside him. Even Randy Duncan caught his breath in admiration. His arousal was instant.

There was something savage about the close-cropped black hair and her lips, already parted as her eyes closed, were full and sensual. Although she was flat on her back, Diana's breasts were upswept and full, the nipples incredibly tiny with erect centers lifted hungrily a good half-inch from their soft beds. The plunge of a powerful chest to a narrow waist which his hands could almost encompass emphasized both the breasts and the generous, waiting hips. Instead of the pubic hair being wildly tangled, spread to her trim thighs and creeping up her lower belly, it was surprisingly sparse but short, wiry, and jet black. The legs, he thought with the appraising admiration of the true collector, *oh!* the legs were just what he'd envisioned—long, firm, muscular, without an iota of surplus flesh and, even as he studied them, beginning to twitch in anticipation.

Eager now, he kissed her upraised nipples fleetingly, planning to return and allowed his lips to swirl almost like moving water down the length of this prized object to the warm, wet, waiting femaleness between her incredible legs. With the experience and subtlety of a connoisseur, his tongue gently inserted, the blond god rested his cheek against Diana's inner thigh and went to work.

To his astonishment, he suddenly found himself literally in midair and then flopped like a fish, flat on his back. He was more stunned by the unexpected aggressiveness of his chosen night's target then he was by her considerable strength, looking down with amazement to see his member disappear between Di's hungry lips. In the seconds that he had been disengaged from both her vagina and his self-accepted position as aggressor Randy's penis had begun to wilt; but now that it was sheathed by her eager lips and drawn down her throat a distance that he would have considered improbable, his prize tool was functioning with its customary rigidity. Chills of passion soared like tiny jet planes from temples to toes and back again, dropping happy warning flares. Briefly, he lay back to accept the unanticipated pleasure as just another tribute, entirely understandable under the circumstances.

But, *"Hey!"* he cried, wincing as her teeth raked him, and "Di, for God's *sake!"* as they momentarily closed in an avaricious bite. He lifted his head rather more in concern than pain, to look down at her—

—And realized that he had never seen a young woman so hungry for sex. As a general rule—one that certainly had never been broken until now—Randy was delighted to encounter such people.

But it went through his mind, at that moment, with more horror than he'd ever experienced in his young life, that this crazy woman might literally bite his member in two! He struggled to sit up, got on one elbow with some difficulty, and was instantly shoved on his back again by a jarring Stoker straightarm.

She was being more careful now, though, and he might have relaxed fully except that with the realization that his penis would survive the encounter came the understanding that he could not long prevent a premature climax. Several times before, he had enjoyed this particular sexual treatment; but never, he was sure as his head began to spin, had he met such unbelievable enthusiasm. Suddenly he shouted, in warning, "Di, *dammit,* I'm gonna come!"

She was off him in an instant, a blur of motion as she swung one long, strong leg across his body to impale herself on him. Now all fears were gone; *now* there was only the fact that the most beautiful and the most sex-starved girl he'd ever encountered was mounted above him and surging backward and forward so swiftly he could not even catch and hold her outthrust breasts. Deliciously, his hips rising to meet her, his climax came; *gallons*, he thought wildly, madly, I'm shooting *barrels* into her! And she was still moving, draining every drop he had.

And still, incredibly, a blur of motion continued above him. The lights had remained on and he saw her lovely face upturned with the mouth suddenly agape with imminent ecstasy, the skin over her cheeks taut and her green eyes pressed tight. *Two* thoughts occurred to Randy then, in quick succession: He'd never seen anything lovelier in his life—

—And if she did not stop, soon, she would hurt him after all. She would hurt him badly. Already spent, his penis sought to withdraw but found itself trapped as if between avaricious jaws that would not relent and which began somehow to tighten, increasingly. Then her hand reached below and between them, instinctively knowing fingers at his scrotum, gently squeezing his testicles; and he was hard again, himself eager, miraculously ready and cooperating with her. It took longer this time—much longer—and it hurt, Randy thought grimly, it hurt goddam *bad*—but finally he reached another climax that seemed to scald every internal inch of his body and to turn his proud penis into quivering mush.

Her hips swiveled, somehow began to *revolve*, sweat from her great breasts feeling boiling hot as it pelted his chest. *She was going on!* Oh, *Lord*, Randy thought, close to prayer for the first time in fifteen years, she's *not stopping!* Instead, she raised her lower body above *him*, pulling his member with it, little more than an elongated string now, and *slammed* down on him. He groaned, whined, "Get, *offa* me, will ya?" and was either unheard or ignored. Diana twisted her powerful body until she was virtually lying on her back, the great thigh muscles vividly thrust out before Randy's tortured eyes. Massive moans began to escape her dry lips as she grasped for what she sought—

But I can't give it to her, Randy realized with awful honesty and a terrible sense of emasculation; *I do not have it to give her.* Just then every ounce of urge toward sexuality, experimentation, toward the act itself or its eventual release, was as foreign—even frightening—as the possibility of feminine rejection might have seemed to him before coming to LaCaresta tonight. With more passion than he'd expended Randy simply wished, devoutly, that this Amazon behemoth of a woman—this incredible, sexual *machine*—would get *off* him before she ruined him for life.

Now she struggled and sat up again. He saw with his practiced eye that she neared the climax she needed. With his desperate fingers he tried to help her, but that only prompted a choked out, "Yes, *yes!*" and the *redoubling* of her killing efforts. He thought he might be bleeding and *again* she was in motion above him, first backward and forward, then up and down, while Randy's stunned penis shrieked for its master to stop. To him, it was no longer the tool of conquest and personal delight it has been before tonight; it was a searing, half-devoured noodle that was beginning to tatter and fray. Even his testicles, too, began crying out in pain and nausea; now he *knew* she would surely leave him dead, *knew* that Everyman's dream of being fucked to death was just another lie whispered from generation to generation.

In absolute desperation, Randy swung his fists, left then right, *smashed* them against her marvelous, sweat-drenched breasts. At that moment—he never knew whether he caused it or if it was synchronistic—Diana came, screaming loud in a manner he feared would summon the old landlady he'd met. For a moment it was almost as if she had exploded, he thought, her whole body turned into an holistic organ of fulfillment, her arms outflung, her hips welded to his, her head so impossibly thrown back he feared her neck was broken.

Then she was quiescent, collapsing across his chest,

and he was wet everywhere from her grateful body including the tears that poured from her lovely eyes. "It was fantastic, marvelous, incredible, *everything* I wanted!" she said in a gasp, hugging him with surprising affection. And then she added, unbelievably, her voice a tiny whisper of total femininity: "Was it okay for you?"

Later, they bathed together and when she saw what she had done to him, the empurpled pulp of his proudest possession, she bathed him with the soft touch of an expert nurse. With difficulty, Randy bit his lip and kept from crying. He'd always liked the hollowed-out feeling, the impression of airy lightness sex sometimes gave him; now he felt literally emptied, as though every functioning sexual organ had gone beyond pain and rupture to plain nonexistence. Exhausted, psychically castrated, he lay in the tub against Diana's broad shoulder, soothed by the warm water and her patting fingers and her softly repetitive, "There, there."

And when they had gone to bed—he badly wanted to go home but feared he could not drive—her arms went around him and he heard, like the tolling of a bell denoting his passing, her whispered command: *"Again. But this time, your way. Gently."*

He'd have considered it impossible, but this was a *new* Di Stoker now, he realized, more like the one he'd expected. Besides, he still did not know exactly what made the brunette tick and had begun to wonder, for the first time in his life, in his boastful young manhood, what made *him* tick.

This time her fingers were excruciatingly gentle, subtle and teasing on his scalded and bruised member; this time her lips parted to his questing tongue and her breasts yielded beneath his shifting male weight; *this* time he encountered a different facet of the fabulous athlete and realized, for another First in his double-handful of self-pleasing silly years, as he modestly reached out a trembling hand to switch off the bed lamp, that it was true that women were many things and that the most marvelous creation in the world was, indeed, Woman.

He raised up to enter her and saw her face in the new dark, trapped by revealing moonlight from the sultry California night.

Her head was wreathed in coiling serpents, a thousand tiny strands of snakes wrapping round her throat, stirring as if awakening, with uncounted miniature eyes seeking him out. Below the serpent hairline was the face, eyes closed demurely in the midst of a living nightmare from Hades.

Sometimes it is possible to become so stunned, so agonizingly shocked, that one does not cry out and isn't frozen in place but merely *runs*, mindlessly, away from that which has brought with it the clammy spectre of death, disease and utter destruction.

The ultimate castrate, Randy snatched his pants as he sped naked through the door, light as air and dimly conscious somewhere in his whipped brain that his flight was like that of some hyperventilating eunuch, running from the snarling touch of sensual perdition even as Pam Garnier and Ray Ellis had done before him.

Unlike them, however, he was not to be further tortured. The creature Diana Stoker had become, slept on.

That is, unlike them, for the time being.

Soni told Diana what happened after that, visiting her the next morning—how Randy Duncan came banging tremorously at her door, barging in to warn her, his eyes liquid with fright, that her friend was something unreal, something monstrous. "Inhuman, honey, that's the word he used," Soni said sadly. "He also called you a nymphomaniac gone beserk, a—a *maneater.*"

For a period Di Stoker was unable to speak. Disconsolate, she finally looked up at the little blond who had again proved her friendship and said, through her uncontrolled weeping: "Oh, goddess, *I gave* him *everything I had*—I turned myself *loose* for him, *showed* myself to him." She added, wailing, "I th-thought it was what he *w-wanted!*"

"Di, darlin'," Soni said with her heart pounding, "that's probably what no woman can ever afford to do. But it's true, isn't it? You can tell ole Soni, hon." Now she *had* to know. "It's true that you *are* Hecate, too. *Aren't* you?"

Diana could only nod, then hurl herself into her friend's small, generous arms, sobbing. Soni, from duty and a sort of repulsed affection, held her close and remembered what she'd read that Sir Frederick Treves wrote about John Merrick, the Elephant Man: "He had no past to look back upon and no future to look forward to. At the age of twenty he was a creature without hope. . . . He was a wanderer, a pariah and an outcast." Diana Stoker, she saw, was like Merrick; she was that kind of monstrosity—except that his ugliness was *always* worn on the outside. Womanlike, Diana's was kept within.

Soni lifted her reflective, somber gaze above the weeping woman's grasping arms, thinking with a chill, suddenly—there are *other* differences, too. Hecate would never permit herself to be kept in a hospital room, carefully shielded from the public. It was the public who needed to be protected from her.

Then, too, the Elephant Man was a gentle person who never harmed a thing in his life. He could never have done the things done by this monster whom Soni now held in her arms.

But instead of pushing Di away, instead of concluding that she was in danger, Soni's eyes filled with tears and she hugged Diana closer. With a quantum leap of maturity Soni, always an honest woman, saw that it was more dangerous to lie to oneself. It occurred to her, then: *Was* Di Stoker, even as Hecate, really worse than any other vindictive, vengeful feminist who put her own hypothetical liberation brutally above everything else? Wasn't it possible that what had happened was actually *symbolic* of the fight all women waged; that much of what Di—even Hecate—did was done *because* that twofold Beast from Hell mirrored a segment of womankind and was *simply able to do it?*

On occasion a woman may speak with wisdom to another woman, if no other, when jealousy is stilled. Soni held Diana at arm's length. "I think you mean to punish Randy," she said with directness, "and I don't blame you. Not really; because *I* can't. I might, if I were a man," she added thoughtfully. "And one other thing: I think you know, too, how all this is meant to end."

"What do you mean?" Diana whispered, drying her eyes.

"Think about it awhile and then, when you can see it clearly, go see Dr. Lord at the hospital." Soni's dark eyes held her friend's green ones; for the first time, she saw clearly that not one but *two* astute minds soberly looked back at her. "Will you do that, Di?"

Diana nodded.

Carolyn Lord was better but spent most of her time sleeping, these endless days. Sometimes she had nightmares but they were better than most of those she experienced while she was conscious.

Now, abruptly, she could not tell which was which, as the face of Diana Stoker peered down. When she figured it out, still unable to speak coherently, she pressed shrinkingly against her tear-stained pillow and a single partially paralyzed arm inched out, groping for the button that would tell her nurses she required help.

"That isn't necessary," Di said softly, moving the buzzer out of reach. She sat on the edge of the high hospital bed, smiling sadly and shaking her head. "I came here for a different kind of purpose, Dr. Lord."

Carolyn's terrified face sought to retreat into itself. Her eyes were enormous with fright. "Don't . . . *kill.* . . ."

"No. No, not you." Di took a deep breath. "I want you to go ahead with the Eleusian rites. At Homecoming, just as you planned. I want you to start up the ROTGOD class for the new semester, teach us just as you intended *everything* we must know in order to become *truly* and *completely* the goddesses we've chosen to be, so we can be prepared for the Eleusian paradise you promised us."

Paradise was at that moment farther from Carolyn's mind than it had ever been before. *"Can't,"* she managed the word with difficulty. Wasn't it obvious to this monster? Couldn't she *see* what she had done to her, that she was a wreck of a woman; that her life—like Mary's—was over?

"Yes," Diana corrected her, bending forward with her eyes hot, "you *can.*"

The kiss on the pale cheek was that of an extraordinary, but human, intelligent young woman.

Vitality—*healing* vitality—flooded Carolyn Lord's tortured body. Her arms and legs stretched by themselves in relief. Blood pumped energetically through her veins. Her heartbeat briefly accelerated, then settled, where it was meant to be. She stared at Diana's lovely face, speechless now because she could not find the words to use. It was as if Satan had said a prayer.

Only at the door did Di Stoker, herself, speak again just then. She paused, turning back in a swiftly agile motion reminiscent of the Di whom Carolyn knew, her emerald eyes flashing. "It's going to end the way it's *supposed* to end, Dr. Lord. I promise you that."

CHAPTER XXIV

September, this year. Muriel Kane Hall.

The reappearance of Dr. Carolyn Lord on the UCEV campus, outwardly unscathed by her terrible ordeal of ill health and the loss of her only child, seemed to her enthusiastic students the very embodiment of the class name—the reemergence of the goddess-like woman who had come to mean so much to them all. When she again stood before her people in Muriel Kane Hall, statuesque and pale, both the women who had been her original students and those who were now enrolled for the first time came to their feet in admiration, in sustained applause.

After all, they knew, Carolyn had been literally at death's door; yet here she was, blondly beautiful and miraculously youthful, with none of the halting traces expected of a woman felled by a stroke.

From such as this, Carolyn thought wryly, bowing to their cheers, personal *mythos* evolve. It was easy to see herself moving from this lectern to a national platform, her every sarcastic comment duly recorded by the nation's presses, her influence reaching all the way to the White House. But there were two things these loyal young women did not know and which she did not dare tell them; for one, she no longer felt that men were responsible for every tragedy befalling her sex. The reemergence of Hecate, however fleetingly, proved that. And for the other, Carolyn Lord knew that the spectre of death sat smiling in the midst of them.

Without needing to search, the instructor knew that

Diana Stoker sat in the third row from the front, two vertical rows over, listening intently to her every word. But now Carolyn knew that, with a touch or a kiss, that beautiful girl was capable of sending her reeling into another paralytic stroke, into madness or even into death itself. Briefly Carolyn felt dizzy, confronted with the fact of Di Stoker's awesome power; for a moment she couldn't go on.

But go on, she must. The smiling young athlete hanging on everything she said *desired* that it go on, *insisted* that she proceed with her plans for the rites of *lustration* as if nothing at all had happened. Now Carolyn wondered achingly, looking over the hundreds of eager faces before her, why it had become so important to Diana—wondered *what evil madness* Hecate, through Diana, intended for the Eleusian culmination of this torturous year. If she could only deduce the plan, Carolyn thought with immense longing, possibly she could foil it—perhaps she might somehow sacrifice herself and, by doing so, put an end to a nightmare that had been building in the world since the turn of the century, and which had already cost the lives of her great-grandfather, her daughter, and untold others.

She pulled herself together. "Some of you know," she said steadily, "that I have talked of a reenactment of the Eleusinian rites of *lustration* during Homecoming—the celebration of our football team's return. Some of you may remember that I said I was the *only one alive* who knows the details of this ancient celebration, since I encountered them in certain writing of my famous ancestor, Professor Jabez Lord.

"Now," she continued, speaking into attentive silence and intently uptilted young faces, "I will begin to give you some of the details—for *all* of you will have the chance to take part, and participation will be a requirement for your grade. Let me tell you some of the fabulous history of these rites." She cleared her throat. "Eleusis, which was located in Attica, some 14 miles west of Athens, was the home of the first great tragedian, Aeschylus, who was born about 525 B.C. It was he who said, 'A state that is prosperous always honors its gods,' and that is what we will be doing during Homecoming Week.

"But the rites of Eleusis go back well before Aeschylus, to at least *two thousand years* before Christ—at a time when all civilized people believed in gods and goddesses. This national worship endured for countless centuries, and all *ephebi*—or youth—was expected to be part of it. Anything else was irreverent, not only sacrilegious but antisocial. It consisted of a wondrous procession along the Sacred Way between Athens and Eleusis led by an official called the *mystagogos*, lasted two nights in the Telesterion, or Hall of Mysteries, where there was a dazzling contrast of light and darkness. That 'light show,' as you might call it today, engendered in the initiates the extremes of joy and grief, of hope and despair. The purification rites following involved cleansing in the sea, a sprinkling of the blood from pigs, a sacrifice and, at last, a *terrifying* wandering through an *underground passageway* in which there was great *peril*."

Carolyn paused as she realized the students were stunned, frightened. She gave them a reassuring laugh. "Oh, no pigblood—porcine or police!—will be sprinkled on you." A few giggles. "The sacrifice will be a token gesture, and, of course, you will not be in any *actual* peril."

"Thank Persephone for *that!*" muttered Soni, aloud, seated beside Diana in the third row. Several other young women tittered.

"It is from that point *on*," Carolyn continued, "that much of what transpired is either fully *mysterious* to most people or a matter of conjecture. *I* know what happened, however, and—it will happen *again*." She paused for full dramatic effect, again the absolute center of attention before her hundreds of followers. "For one thing, I want volunteers before we part today—volunteers for dancing choruses. You'll be fully costumed in traditional garb and Rhonda Brauberg, the choreographer, will work with you for a week on some meaningful steps as well as a pantomime. The latter will include the rape of Koré."

Diana frowned, curious. "The rape of Koré?" she asked without raising her hand. "That sounds familiar, Dr. Lord."

"Koré was referred to in your own, ah, private ceremony for Hecate," Carolyn replied levelly. "Now there will also be symbolic potions, which Professor Hartings in Chemistry will contribute—nonalcoholic, I assure you"—several students groaned their mock dismay—"and I will provide the Golden Key with which to open an ancient basket imbedded in a chest. The latter is a *key* part of *lustration,* and it happens that the basket and the Key are genuine—left to me by my great-grandfather. *You,* Diana," she turned again to the athlete, "will be our *hierokeryx* or sacred herald and be asked to carry the chest. It's—rather heavy."

Diana flushed, conscious of envious eyes turned to her. "It will be my honor," she said with more certainty than she felt.

"And Soni Jerome, one of our earliest and most dedicated students," continued Dr. Lord, "will be our official *daidouchos.*"

"I only use 'em once a month," the little blond quipped, and was greeted with laughter. "What the hell is that?"

"Torchbearer, Ms. Jerome," Carolyn replied, sharing in the smiles. "Nothing more than that, but in the passageways *we* will all be traversing, your role as *daidouchos* is essential."

"*What* passageways? Are they really all subterranean-like?"

The speaker was an excited, tall and very slender black student. Carolyn turned to her. "Since you, also, decided to speak up, I'd like you—because of your excellent height—to be our bearer of the *backhos,* or mystic staff. Please tell us your name and if you'll do that for us?"

The girl, a freshman, beamed happily. "I sure will, Dr.

Lord. And my name is Ardenna Wilkinson but they call me Denny."

"In answer to your question, Denny, many of you do not know there is an elaborate and complex new storm sewer system running beneath this campus. I've been assured that it is entirely safe and will not be used *as* a sewer until late November. It happens, ladies, that the wife of Mayor Chandler is a feminist." Carolyn smiled. "When I told Kay what we had in mind, her only demand was that she be permitted to come along as an observer. In the meantime, since it's supposed to be the Hall of the Mysteries described by Plutarch, *I* will see to it personally—with some help from Brownie Kerlan in the Art Department—that the sewer is properly intriguing for you."

Another young woman, heavyset and sweatered, her light-brown hair short-cut, held up a hand. Carolyn nodded. "Doctor, if these ceremonies were once so important and so many people believed in them, what happened to *stop* the rites?"

"Good question. A man happened to them, Sarah," Carolyn said grimly, "a man named Alaric I, King of the corrupt and destructive Visigoths in the Fourth Century, A.D. He murdered the ancient faith the way such men always destroy that which is good and decent." She paused, eyes widening. "He conquered peaceful Eleusis, and burned it to the ground."

Here and there, resentment for Alaric showed; here and there, a shadow of fear crossed a face as the Hall of Mysteries filled an imagination. For the most part, however, she saw a reaction that was one of mingled curiosity and rich anticipation.

Now she leaned to them, earnestly. "There'll be many things for many of you to do. For example, there are special vessels used in the rites, called *Kernos,* consisting of a terra-cotta standard with several small receptacles resembling candlesticks—these must be carried, along with garlands of flowers. I have *another* feminist chum at Rosenblatt's Florist, Sylvia Rosenblatt. She's donating the garlands. We will have a great deal of pleasure, ladies, I assure you.

"But you must *never* lose sight," Carolyn pressed on, "and I shall not *let* you forget, that we are doing something quite unique: for the first time in *thousands* of years, we will literally *reenact* the secret Eleusian rites—using some of the identical props, and the *actual ritual* itself—and it is not impossible that we shall witness the *literal reemergence of the goddesses whom we revere!*" She stopped to see the expressions of awe developing before her. "This is, in point of fact, a serious religious experience which none of you will ever forget. Many of you, I think it's safe to say, will be forever . . . *changed.*"

Diana Stoker's arm snaked langurously up, a calm pillar that caught Carolyn's attention immediately. For a moment she had forgotten Diana, and the evil goddess emerging within her; for a moment her passion was again genuine—

—And as she nodded for Di to speak, she remembered something else left her by Professor Jabez Lord and began, for the first time in months, to hope.

"How," Diana asked, her tone colorless, uninflected, "how does all this end?"

"In deepest, darkest mystery," Carolyn replied, her eyes locking with the athlete's. Only Soni, of all the others present, sensed the current of electricity between the two women. "The way it's *supposed* to end."

Diana's smile was teasing, deliberate. "Well, could you be a little more precise than that, Ma'am?"

Carolyn paused. She felt, again, the literal, searing *heat* Di Stoker exuded in such confrontations; it was something heavy, pregnant, *palpable* between them. At last she drew herself to her full height. "Kurt Seligmann once remarked: 'Many students of the occult have stated that the Eleusian rites contain the one great magic secret, kernel of all wisdom. . . .' And with him, my dear Diana, I believe it was a mystery of faith more than a mystery of knowledge." She managed a brave smile. "Until *lustration,* I alone shall know that secret."

Because they shared their *own* secret, now—and because Diana had, in a queer shift of influence based upon need and trust, come to look to Soni Jerome for help—the two young women were again often together.

Not that they were friends, exactly. Whenever Soni felt that she might somehow overlook the fact of Di's multiple personality—might, indeed, try to persuade herself that the queen of Hades was not actually functioning in Diana's twisted mind, from time to time—she had only to remember what had happened to the mutual friend they'd called Marcia. Whether Di knew what was happening when Mary Lord was infused with swiftly destroying cancer cells or not, she had been Hecate's instrument of death and *never once*—not even with their acquaintanceship renewed—had Diana spoken of trying to banish Hecate from her mind. In some perverse fashion, Soni thought, Hecate fulfilled a dark need for Di Stoker; or perhaps it was only that the seeds of evil were planted so long ago that Diana knew nothing in the world could eliminate them.

"There's so much Dr. Lord *didn't* tell us today," Di said to Soni, over Pepsis in the Distant Vistas club.

"Sure. Secret stuff to show us all at Homecoming," the little blond replied.

"More than that," Di argued, shaking her head. Her hair had come back in by now, a mop of jetblack hair that grew, untouched, in the form of a dark, rough-edged halo. "Much more than that."

"How d'you know that, Di?" Soni asked quietly, disturbed.

"You forget," Diana answered, sipping from her straw, "that she loaned me Professor Lord's old journal. According to the ancient myths, Demeter was mad because her daughter, Persephone, was carried down to Hades by the God of the Underworld. Demeter left Olympus to wander among mortals, searching for a way to find Persephone and bring her back. She worked as an old maid for King Celeus, who was kind enough to teach her the sacred mysteries—mysteries that, even then, were tens of thousands of years old. Eventually Demeter worked out a deal with the Underworld: Persephone had to spend one-third of the year below, but came back with her mother—in the world of light—for two-thirds of the year."

Soni shrugged. "That's part of the 'light and darkness' myth Dr. Lord mentioned, then. Greece is barren from June to September so that's when Persephone dwells beneath the earth." She hesitated questioningly. "What are *you* thinking?"

For an instant Di didn't reply. She peered out the cafeteria window at the rush of sunlight, and blinked. Lately she'd taken to wearing strong sunglasses and now she tugged them from her purse to slip them on. "I think, Soni," she answered readily enough, "that Dr. Lord thinks of herself as Demeter and of poor Mary Lord as Persephone. That she's here at UCEV, as wise King Celeus, and quietly—on her own, researching the *other* journals and things the old professor left her—looking for a way to bring Mary back. Or at least, to strike some kind of deal—" she looked full in Soni's face now, the gorgeous green eyes shaded and tortured behind the sunglasses—"to rid the world of me."

The piquant blond was sobered and did not comment for a moment that became swallowed in the unknowing commotion of the other normal, happy students milling around the cafeteria. Someone dropped a tray and Soni was so taut with nerves she didn't move, taking the clatter internally and wincing there. "What," she asked finally, "do you plan to do about it, Di?"

"Do?" Again there were *two* minds functioning methodically behind the facade of brilliant eyes. "Why, nothing. I've done nothing myself in any case. I have, as Diana, *no* recollection of harm coming to Mary Lord. So I won't do a thing, Soni." There was a flicker of a pause. When she spoke next, Soni felt that a single mind was in charge. "Until Homecoming, and the Eleusian rites."

CHAPTER XXV

September, this year. The eve of the rites.

Every man must learn truths about himself, however hard he runs. As they are acquired—not like nuggets of gold, which one eagerly hoards, but more like gashes in the spiritual hide—there are some that can be easily tolerated, even assimilated, and some that cannot.

In this particular day and age, which is no more than a transient indication of time's passage and of no special or enduring significance, a man may be outworked, outdressed, outcharmed, outgambled or outconned, and live with it. He may encounter better students of life, yet feel that in his own realms *he* is the instructor. He may suffer job loss, divorce and the opprobrium of his friends and rise again to seek new positions, loves, companions.

But "rising again" has its limits. In no era treated by historians, to date, can any man be outsexed by a woman, filled with terror and put to hysterical flight, and tolerate the situation. In order to look himself again in the mirror and fancy how debonair he is, how exquisite to the feminine eye, a man so humbled or frightened must return to the frontlines again and, if necessary, again and again.

Fortified partly by beer and partly by self-inflicted lectures in which he explained lucidly, to himself, that he must have been too weary after several nights of hard acting rehearsal to remain sexually abreast of her and consequently given to wild imaginings that beauty could become the beast, Randy Duncan mounted the stairs to Diana Stoker's apartment to try again.

He was operating under a seriously mistaken assumption typical of many vain young men and hadn't bothered to find out if Diana wanted to.

His Redfordish hair shiny, pleased by the way he'd charmed the overweight landlady into admitting him to the house, humming a nameless little tune, Randy rat-tatta-tatted on her door. Although he had succeeded by now in blanking out most of the facts concerning his bizarre night with the gifted athlete, he still retained, male-wise, vivid memories of Di's remarkable body and a general nostalgic recollection of how hard she'd labored to please.

"Hi-i," he greeted her softly, saccharine in the midst of his alcoholic buzz, and wriggled his fingers.

Diana, preoccupied by the handful of last-minute details which were her concern for the next day's Eleusian rites, frowned. She retreated a discreet step from Randy's booze breath. "What do you want?" she asked.

"You," he intoned without apology for his lack of originality, and reached.

Promptly, he found himself flipping past her side, turning once in the air, and crashing against her chair.

Not especially injured but considerably more sober, Randy sat up with a wry, boyish grin that always wowed them at UCEV. He rubbed a sore shoulder and tried not to seem grudging or afraid. "Judo or karate?" he asked easily.

"Muscle," Di said flatly, arms akimbo. "What is it you expect to get from me now? I'm very busy working for the ROTGOD rites tomorrow, at Homecoming. You already tried to ruin my reputation, telling my friends ridiculous tales about me. I'd have thought you did enough damage."

He stood, brushing his knees, seizing his advantage. "You're absolutely right. They were ridiculous stories and I've come to apologize."

Some old, warm feelings stirred within her. *Damn!*

he was good-looking! She'd been right about that if nothing more.

"So you gals are gonna put a little pizazz in the old football rally, huh?" he asked, drawing nearer. "It's about time. All those jocks give me a pain. I hear you're gonna try to turn yourselves into goddesses or something, right?"

Diana sighed. "This is hopeless. You'd never understand." She paused, then added meaningfully, "But I think you'll get it when we're through. Now, I'm very busy."

He was appraising her, trying to get close, desire building in him. Di wore, so far as he could tell, nothing but a man's white shirt, XL, her gorgeous legs and feet bare. He was reasonably certain there was something beneath the flapping shirttails besides Diana but equally sure it was his duty to find out.

"Look, I really deserve another chance. I'd been workin' hard on a play at the Theatre Arts Center—I'm Christian in *Cyrano*, y'know?—and I was out on my feet when I came here." He gave her a lopsided grin, one he often practiced in his mirror. "Maybe I performed like the old guy himself, instead of bold, brave Christian, but I can make it up to you. 'Diana, Diana,'" Randy intoned, within arm's reach, "'your name is like a golden bell hanging in my heart; and when I think of you, it swings, and rings, along my veins . . . Diana.' Not too shaggy?"

This time when he reached for her, she let him get close. Then he was kissing her, his hand groping first beneath the shirt for her left breast and then quickly sliding down to her shorts, moving sinuously beneath the waistband. Diana gasped as his hand found and cupped her, then retreated slightly, the fingers working. His mouth was on hers—hot—the breath sweet. Instinctively her own arms went around him, her own hand slipped down his front.

"You sure don't feel like any damn witch," Randy muttered. "And you don't *need* any damn goddess inside you when a young god can be there instead."

If he had looked at her face, at that moment, he'd

have known how mistakenly he chose his words of love—how they had bypassed the mind of Diana Stoker and registered on the mind of *another,* instead.

But the only thing that Randy Duncan knew was that the hand reaching down his body had stopped, grasped and begun to squeeze. Hard, and harder. It would be the only thing he knew for the rest of his life: excruciating masculine pain.

CHAPTER XXVI

Revival of the Eleusian rites. Homecoming.

Color the crowd huge and color it loud, Dr. Carolyn Lord thought nervously as she awaited her turn, from the back of the raised platform, to address the pep rally. Tomorrow afternoon was the Homecoming football game for which the majority of these people present had come, to honor it, some of them from many miles away. It was strange, after speaking before hundreds of students, frequently, to feel a surge of stagefright that bordered on fear; but Carolyn experienced it.

A pat explanation, she supposed, would be that this was a mixed crowd. In addition to young female students there were dozens of racously shouting, derisive young men; more than a few dozen members of the pep rally crowd were other instructors and their guests; while a number of Old Grads had returned for the Big Game, wreathed in aging smiles and bleary-eyed from pocket flasks. Overall, the crowd seemed a single, living organism in its incessant small movements, Hydra-headed in shadows occasionally illumined by torches that cast angry red birthmarks on a hundred faces and made them at once marred and demonic.

Any intuitive person, Carolyn thought, sensed that a crowd like this was a veritable, unleashed juggernaut capable of enormous damage. It growled there in the almost-dark like a mighty beast, pawing the ground and muttering to itself, stirring up ancient animosities and, in the true spirit of any mob, united against a common foe. Carolyn thanked the Lord she had begun again to respect, since she was hospitalized and certain of remaining paralyzed, that this carnal crowd hated the USC Trojans—not her. Tomorrow would be the first game ever with the famed rival; Keith Jackson and ABC Sports would be there to record the event and put every jarring tackle or quarterback sack in several million living rooms.

A part of Dr. Lord's nervousness stemmed, she felt sure, from realizing the distinct possibility that the crowd would laugh when she spoke or when her young goddesses-to-be came forth. It would be embarrassing and demeaning but, if they somehow drew Hecate from her lovely, lonely confinement in the spirit of Diana Stoker, it might also prove fatal. Carolyn accepted it as her responsibility to get these people to understand.

And so, when it was her turn, the microphone handed her by the grudging and condescending, balding head coach, Carolyn carefully and eloquently expressed the reasons for her Goddess class and what they intended to accomplish in the traditional two days of festivities eternally entitled the Eleusian rites.

"No one wishes to mar your pleasure in anticipating tomorrow's game," she reassured them, noticing the crowd begin to break into clusters of half-hearted listeners, many of them shifting their feet. "After all, sport was born in ancient Greece and competition between males—as well as activities between females—is almost as old as time itself.

"But after these thousands of years," she continued, heat from the nearby bonfire toasting her cheeks, "only a handful of athletes are truly liberated: the men. With the Reemergence of the Goddesses course I teach—commonly called ROTGOD—I have attempted to come to grips with the problem, indeed, to liberate the ladies I teach."

On a cued signal from slender, pretty Denny Wilkinson with her *bakchos*, or staff, the participating members of her special class paraded onto the

Rembrandtesque dark earth in front of the football stadium—more than three hundred young women dressed in the traditional gowns of ancient Greece, a single shoulder bare, the dress tied by a cord at the waist, the white skirt reaching the ground. Each young woman carried either an ear of dried corn as a totem, or a small statue of the goddess with whom she identified. The parade wove silently through the great crowd, the students both beautiful and utterly solemn in their new religious fervor. Even those randy male students who began to essay good-humored or patronizing quips ceased quickly, immersed in the loveliness and serious order of the weaving women. Their legs, peeping through the split skirts at the front, captivated the men and their carefully coiffed, rather short hair—occasionally wreathed—intrigued the women in the crowd.

"In effect," Carolyn said softly, confidently bolstered by the evident approval of the pep ralliers, "we are all *Eumolpedie*—those who celebrate the rites of Euleusis, just as it was done dozens of centuries ago. Tonight, while you disband in joyous preparation for tomorrow's football contest, we march to the interior of the fieldhouse and to the pools for the next step in our initiatory procedures. And tomorrow—" she raised her chin, proudly—"while you are in your seats in the stands, rooting for old UCEV against powerful USC, *we* will be walking *beneath* your feet—beneath *the field itself*—in a solemn Homecoming of our own: the re-enactment of civilization's oldest, most honored rites."

Now Diana Stoker joined the teacher on the platform, the football coach blinking. Many of the male students, and not a few of their fathers, sucked in their breath and gaped at her.

Di was costumed in the garb of Diana, the Huntress, her thrusting breasts obviously naked beneath the thin fabric separately covering each of them, her skirt short and pleated, her arms bare, her feet encased in the finest modern running shoes. Oddly, on her they were not incongruous. Scarlet highlights designed by the flickering firelight moved on her pretty face; the softly curving strokes and the strong skeletal angles of her youthful woman's body were bathed in subtle shadows. At that instant she was—almost literally—breathtakingly lovely.

"This young person, Ms. Diana Stoker," resumed Carolyn Lord, still discreetly avoiding the girl's slightest touch, "might have become the greatest athlete—female *or* male—in this school's history. Had she continued participating, that is. Instead, she cast her lot with us. For that and for the reason that we couldn't possibly *order* someone more ideal, I've asked Di to be the focal point of tomorrow's events." Now, carefully, her gaze sought and found Diana's. "We've agreed that she will begin, at once, as the *hunted*—running from us, hiding in the incredible maze of complex tunnels comprising the vast, subterranean storm sewer system beneath us."

"But it's dark down there," called the archery coach, Betty Haggert. "She could get lost—injured, and never found."

"Precisely," replied Carolyn, though the other woman's interest in a former team member wasn't lost on her. "She will, however, have a torch—not in the British sense of a flashlight, but a simple torch or faggot. This portion of the rites must endure at least twenty hours. After that, it is *our* task to find Diana, symbolically to catch her and bring her with us for that magic moment when *all* our young ladies are filled with the spirit of the glorious Olympian goddesses. Until the twenty hours expire, Di is permitted any trickery to escape capture, creating an element of fun for everyone." Carolyn paused, then stooped to a heavy chest containing an ancient basket not unlike that in which Moses, as an infant, traversed the Nile. The chest was not large but clearly was heavy. "Diana is our *hierokeryx*. She must bear this with her, partly as a balancing or compensatory factor for her tremendous athletic prowess. What is in the basket, within the chest, represents our penultimate moments tomorrow and she does not know what is in it. I, alone, possess the fabled Golden Key"—Carolyn's index and middle fingers touched the string—"at my throat. I, alone, can unlock the chest to display the basket's significant contents—and relieve Diana of her heavy burden."

It was astounding, Carolyn thought, even as so much that was unsaid passed between her and Diana; but most of the crowd—charmed by the still-parading, solemn young women, who began softly to chant, *"We are the goddess! the goddess is us!"* in the background, and dazzled by Diana—was listening intently. Those who were not had simply wandered off, deeper into their myopic fealty to Today.

Now she turned back to the intrigued crowd for her own final public message: "The Greeks always had a resentful feeling about the horrors of futility, and of meaninglessness. They demonstrate it in the legend of Sisyphus, who had forever to roll a rock uphill and watch it roll down again without moving." A few listeners chuckled. "*We* have shared the feelings of futility, because we are women. The impression that life bypasses us even though it lacks purpose *without* us. We know that life seems to go nowhere until the latent goddess-spirit of any woman is brightly revealed at the time of marriage, the moment of birth or in the guise of a respected, wizened yet wise grandmother. Confronted with a wedding, a new child, or the hallowed maturity of womanly age, the coarsest male pauses to wonder. But these times, my friends, are *not enough*," Carolyn proceeded, firmly, raising her voice, "not nearly enough for that modern woman who, in common with the women of ancient Greece, *knows* that civilization may go forward, but it *cannot remain static*. Don't you hear her plea, even this moment, ringing down through the centuries—her demand to be *part* of civilization, and *part* of the changes to be made?

"Di Stoker, here," the teacher began her concluding remarks, "symbolizes for us all the White Goddess of poet and occultist Robert Graves, who pointed out that the triple moon-goddess he sometimes called Leucothea was *universal* in pre-Christian poetry as well as mythology. Graves respected her far-reaching legend, saw that she symbolized the faith of us all—and he feared her. Her fabulous record remains in Greece, Rome, the Scandinavian nations, among the Africans, the Celts and the Hindus." Carolyn's eyes glittered. Only those who were in the first row of spectators might have seen *fear* lingering, along with awe, and acceptance. "She was known also as *Diana.* Among . . . *other* names. And so, tomorrow, we pursue *all* the things that Diana is, that the White Goddess represents—good or evil, noble or ignoble, but unmistakably . . . *woman.* Woman: liberated and *free."*

In a brief little motion Diana Stoker extended her face, sudden tears in her green eyes, to kiss her mentor's cheek—once on each side. When Carolyn's eyes met hers, it passed the tortured mind of the athlete that this would be the *last* time either of them met as instructor and pupil, as mortal and immortal, as—friends.

She burst off the platform in a mighty, soaring leap and began sprinting with uncanny, fluid ease for the distant fieldhouse, her knees raised high and dappled by night, her pace and form unequaled. *When next we meet, Carolyn Lord,* she thought to herself, entirely unsure whether it was entirely *her* thought or shared, *it shall be for the* final *time, too—and with the perfect ending* all stories *of mortal-contact-with-immortal must surely have. It need not be a happy ending, only . . . suitable.* Regardless *of who is left to whisper the myth's incredible details into the ears of any posterity fortunate enough to come* afterward, *fortunate enough to* remain.

CHAPTER XXVII

Last rites.

"We must be cleansed," Carolyn Lord gently instructed them, aware of the hundreds of eyes awaiting her leadership. "Before we dare descend into the earth."

She avoided the gaze, carefully, of the mayor's wife, Kay Chandler, who had watched the ceremonies thus far with obvious approval. Kay was in her middle fifties, a well-girdled, handsome woman with hair turning nicely—with her hairdresser's epicene aid—light turquoise. The two women stood at the head of the fieldhouse indoor swimming pool, watching.

The ROTGOD students knew what to do. With the mayor's lady staring incredulously, each of the young women quietly removed her flowing Grecian gown and dove or dropped into the pool, naked. Because they numbered nearly three hundred, because this was a serious rite, there was no swimming and very little room. Only a reenactment of the dim past. Very little chatter, embarrassed or otherwise, transpired just then. Pressed almost breast to breast, Carolyn's girls waited for their next orders.

"This is outrageous!" Kay exclaimed, her lips bubbling. She was unable to remove her gaze from the scene. She had the distinct impression that all womankind had gathered in the UCEV pool, incredibly and defiantly, even gloriously, nude. "I d-didn't agree to *this!* What about the boy students—" she stared at the distant, closed door, half-expecting a thousand foaming rapists to burst through—"what if they f-find out what's *happening* here?"

"The door's locked. Besides, the men are telling obscene jokes with their pals, drinking as much as they can to prove *their* sex worthy. Tomorrow, they watch their little football game with bad headaches." Carolyn smiled, slipped out of her customary white blouse and skirt, folded them carefully and laid them on a dry area. She paused. "If you're going with us, Kay, and you fail to participate in this vital cleansing ritual, you may be in danger. I urge you to join us."

"Madam!" the older woman expostulated, reddening. The very suggestion made her feel naked, and hence obscene. "How *dare* you!"

"It's on your head," Carolyn said with a shrug.

She removed her underclothes and paused for a moment on the edge of the pool, still lovely and blond. Feeling more self-conscious than she'd care to admit to the mayor's wife, she bobbed into the pool, brushing against Soni Jerome and giving her a friendly grin.

Kay Chandler hesitated, thinking about leaving, thinking about having the whole lot of them arrested.

Then she sat down on the edge of the pool, took off her shoes and stockings, and waded into the shallow end. "I'm having the time of my life!" she called to Carolyn moments later.

Diana stopped running at last, breathless, dropping to a catcher's squat and resting the torch on a ledge extending, apparently, the full length of the sewer. Thank Hephaestus it was just as dry down here as it was supposed to be, she thought gratefully, and looked around.

It was hard to see very far ahead, down that apparently endless tunnel, with any clarity. She had the disconcerting impression—and a rising vertigo—of peering into a bottomless pit. She put out her hands instinctively to steady and remind herself that she was actually kneeling on a flat, cold surface.

While this was the most modern of sewer systems, electric lights sporadically twinkling like fireflies along the walls, placed there for the benefit of workmen, the miniature bulbs were both infrequent and of low wattage. Doubtless the city had spent hours arguing the budgetary question of how well-illumined this place should be. The dim results, she thought, indicated what certain city fathers felt for their laboring forces.

It was actually so poorly lit that Di felt it was like stepping into some constant, obscure twilight land—a world of trolls and possibly ghouls, a country of the depressed spirit where dark night was always only a heartbeat away. The mentally ill must feel like this, sometimes, about their world, she thought; for shadows conceal—*things*.

And this place, for her tutor Carolyn Lord's personal purposes, was now the Telesterion, the secret Hall of the Mysteries, a fabled place of the ancients. Diana knew that Dr. Lord had come here first, alone, "preparing" it. For the first time she felt a thrill of fear for something Carolyn might have done to her. Although Dr. Lord hadn't dared to mention the death of her daughter, Mary, Di realized that Carolyn privately blamed her for it—not without some justification. To someone with Di Stoker's turn of mind, it made perfect sense that the instructor would have to crave and seek vengeance; and this was an ideal place for it to lurk in waiting.

If only communication skills had been a gift of hers, the athlete pondered, the ending toward which they all were plummeting might be very different. None of those who had died so hideously met their ends while Di was truly, entirely, in control of the body labeled "Diana Stoker." It was true that from somewhere in the corner of her mind, she had watched, seen, even *enjoyed* what transpired. But sometimes the hands themselves were no longer anything she claimed as her own; sometimes they were gnarled, potently clawed things with a life belonging to another. *Always* the impetus to rend, to maim and to kill, came from that other she knew as Hecate—and wasn't it true that psychologists claimed an urge to murder, to erase or expunge from the face of the earth, dwelled even in the most tranquil and peaceful of beings?

But what Diana could not yet face, as she got to her feet, retrieved her chest and torch and slowly began to peer into the Hall of the Mysteries, was the fact that control of her own mind was slipping away with constantly greater frequency, that confusion of *who* was in charge was vastly greater now, and that, worst of all, that cowering corner of her mind was beginning to long for the moment when the Queen of Hell would take *total* control—and take whatever loathsome steps she had planned for nearly three thousand years.

"I had thought, for awhile, that the *mystai* or initiates were blindfolded before descending to the Telesterion," Carolyn Lord said, hearing a few fearful groans, then smiling; "but that would appear to defeat the purpose, wouldn't it?"

Everyone was clothed again, Carolyn herself wearing the ancient Grecian costume but in the pure white of the *mystagogos*, a corsage at the shoulder which was covered. She delighted in the eagerness of their expressions and that of Kay Chandler, who was now fully into the spirit of the rites and bearing a tall stack of floral wreaths. They would be donned at the culmination of *lustration*, by those girls who played a leading role in the panoply.

"There are several more things you ladies should know before we descend into the Hall of the Mysteries," Carolyn said quietly, warningly, everyone hanging on her words. "I do not intend for any of you to be harmed—*below*—but the huntress-who-is-hunted, our *hierokeryx*, is strong and earnest in her dedication. She could, conceivably, become . . . overzealous. For that reason, I urge you to stay together, occasionally clasping hands and calling out to the initiates on your left or right."

Soni Jerome, who knew the dangers posed by her friend Diana better than the others, stood near a small, stocky girl named Lucy Marasco, who touched her arm for comfort. Each girl had a lump in her throat, a pattern of goose bumps along her bare arms and the legs protruding from the traditional gown. The night had passed, early California sun reaching brightly intrusive fingers of light across the quiet campus; yet they were about to return to the darkest night of all.

"We shall pass slowly through the Telesterion," Carolyn continued, "trying—within another few hours—to capture Diana. Her mere apprehension is sufficient; she will go with us then. Toward her discovery I shall send forth a chosen handful of huntresses who *must* remain together and who will use this ball of yarn—" she lifted a vivid golden ball— "with which to trace your path back to the main body of the party. When we are reunited with Diana, we proceed to the Greater Eleusinian I have prepared magnificently for you, in the heart of the city itself. We will have dancing, pantomimes, and—most especially—the unlocking with my Golden Key of the chest Diana now bears with her."

There was absolute silence when Carolyn paused. Even Kay Chandler, the mayor's wife, shifted nervously from foot to foot.

Carolyn's gaze moved silently from face to face among her hundreds of followers, severe and pregnant with meaning. "At that point, ladies—when we are in the unnamed, secret room that culminates our ritual—I will only be *partly* in charge. If we have properly recreated the Eleusinian procedures, each of us should be imbued with a spirit of the farthest ages, of divine goddesses, and—*most important of all*—each of us should then receive unto us the *most profound religious truth ever recorded*. A knowledge of how the universe was formed and why, a knowledge of why we are here, and where we are going. We may learn, in fact," Carolyn Lord finished, her voice no more than a whisper, "the *deepest secrets of immortality.*"

Then she threw aside the sewer cover to reveal a new steel ladder, leading downward—it seemed—a million miles. Carolyn smiled, boldly, her arm shooting valiantly into the air. *"To the earth's heart, ye mystai!"*

The underground passages, Di Stoker found, first with some consternation and incipient terror, then with growing amusement, were bedecked with richly imaginative posters, lifesize cutouts, optical illusions and hideous drawings that leaped out at her with the utmost of ingenuity. Some dropped from above, released by some nearly invisible cord she had accidentally tripped; others slapped from around a corner against the wall she approached.

Diana had some faint notion whom the vivid pictures portended to be, but only a faint notion. Some of the better-known gods and goddesses were easily identified; others, more obscure, were also more frightening when they seemed to materialize before her. She had to give Carolyn Lord—and her artist friend, Brownie Kerlan—credit for enormous cleverness.

But with the gathering, growing emergence of Hecate within her, Diana promptly laid aside any further trepidation and, as the remaining dummies and props vaulted into view, brushed them aside without further consideration.

When she had passed, they sprang quickly back into position, clearly in readiness for pursuit by the other ROTGOD girls. Undoubtedly the fantastic art display—especially those lifesize cutouts or actual, stuffed puppets rigged with ghastly lighting—would terrify Soni and the others. The part of her that remained Diana smiled with humor, in an amiable, nearly sisterly fashion.

But the smile was short-lived and soon replaced by another expression.

An expression—indeed, a *face*—at the times when these subterranean shadows were stygian enough to reveal the disturbing truth—that was vastly more chilling than anything depicted by the university art department.

She lifted the torch high, tucked the heavy chest beneath a powerful arm and moved on. *Soon,* the female creature thought, *they will try to capture me.*

That should prove amusing. Most amusing!

"You must realize," Carolyn Lord said, her voice ringing hollowly in the long sewer corridor, "that as initiates you are not permitted to discuss anything that happens down here—anything at all."

"We know that, Doctor," remarked Denny Wilkinson, the lanky black student. Her face appeared carved from coal despite the torch lifted high by Soni, the *daidouchos* or torch bearer. *"We're* on *your* side 'cause *you're* on *ours."*

Carolyn, trailing the leaders in line as the young women moved deeper into the tunnel, many hand-in-hand, smiled gently. "I only meant to caution you all that this shouldn't be considered a game of any kind. It's a serious, traditional ceremony. The rest of what I must tell you now is this: None of you will be permitted to go back, not now." Silence greeted her remark, a feeling of many girls being stunned. "You cannot be allowed to leave until you have received the complete impact of . . . *whatever* is to happen, here and at the Greater Eleusinia—where arcane knowledge has always been taught to the *ephebi.*"

Several of the students glanced nervously at one another. Others cast curious looks at their teacher and leader, trying to determine if she was only teasing, perhaps heightening an atmosphere already growing heavy, taut and tense.

"I have my reasons for feeling as I do about obeying the rites fully," Carolyn remarked, as if reading their minds. Ahead of them, the corridor veered to the right, its sharp right angle disturbing angular, moving shadows. "And I'll try to explain those reasons now. In Europe, ladies, the word 'Eleusis' eventually became perverted to 'Alaise' and then, over a period of many years, the word 'Alaise' was shortened, in old Britain—shortened to the term *leys*. Do any of you know what *leys* are purported to be?"

A thin, freckled red-headed girl who seemed little more than a child answered from behind Carolyn. She was barely visible from where the teacher walked but her bold, brazen young voice bounded off the darkling walls. "I've read about leys."

"Tell us what you know, please," Carolyn urged.

"Well, it seems there are whole areas of England crisscrossed with straight lines—tracks of olden times that link sites of ancient worship." Startled by the sound of her own voice, the woman-child spoke in a harsh whisper that reached all their ears in this silent place. "Some say *leys* are everywhere in the world. In China, they're called 'dragon paths.' In Britain, they sort of link up places like Stonehenge, King Arthur's Glastonbury—sites of early Christianity."

"Excellent, Glenda," Carolyn praised, continuing to push forward. "Ancient *barrows*, or burial grounds—places where mounds and megaliths stand other than Stonehenge, sites of great churches and cathedrals, famed cemeteries as well—*all these places* appear to indicate natural places in the earth where its magnetism is powerful, even extraordinary, and able to do—strange things. Almost as if the gods themselves deemed such areas sacred, and special. Here, some say, the influence of the heavenly bodies on earth's simple forces is at *maximum intensity*—and that, on the places where leys *intersect,* astonishing—often *inexplicable* events—sometimes occur. Messages are imparted, great leaps of psychic knowledge achieved. Dowsers locate water; hunters find treasure—or insanity. Hauntings occur."

"What d-does that have to do with where *w-we* are?" Denny asked her, her tone mirroring her gathering fright.

Carolyn's reply easily extended to all of them. "A large, impressive megalith—a great and impenetrable, enigmatic stone column bearing exotic words—resides in Eleusis to this day. It is called *Omphalos,* with hushed breath, though no one still alive knows what that means. Nobody knows what it was built there for, nor *who* placed it there. They do know that it is all but eternal, and that the megalith is sacred." She paused, lifting her voice. "I have learned from my great-grandfather's researched journals that *Omphalos* marked the entry-point of the ancients to the subterranean land where Eleusinian rites originally were held. I have learned that beneath *Omphalos* stretches the Hall of the Mysteries. And I have learned that, in terms of it as a *ley*-site, *Omphalos* is centered at thirty-five degrees, thirty minutes—and *we, my friends, presently walk beneath the ground at precisely the same north latitude!*"

Compelled by the implications of what she said, the others were too stunned for a moment to speak. Soni, blinking in the savage heat from her torch, looked back at Carolyn, fear blending with shadows in the hollows of her cheeks. "You knew that all along," she declared wonderingly to her mentor. "You knew, from the start, that we women of ROTGOD had . . . *close, geographical ley-connections to Eleusis herself!*"

Dr. Lord nodded. The front of the marching column of women swept left now, continuing its passage through the underground system. Here it seemed to narrow and, with the narrowing, it seemed darker as well, more threatening. Carolyn glanced at the mayor's wife, saw the look of fascination—and more—in her middle-aged face. "Yes, Soni, I did. More even than that, we have *precisely* the correct, mystical number of women here to invoke the goddesses at our destination. Three-hundred-fourteen, a three-plus-one-plus-four for the number '8,' the digit of life and death, of birth and rebirth. It was for this reason that I asked Kay Chandler to accompany us—to become the single individual we needed to *assure* us that something incredible will happen, when we finish." She stopped walking, raised her hand and called out to those ahead of her. "Let's halt now and begin the search for Diana, the huntress-to-be-hunted. I'd like to select you, Soni Jerome, as a friend of Di; Glenda, you; Denny, your friend next to you there—Alice Quentin; and Kathy Nolan. Soni, while you're our official torchbearer, we *do* have more torches and you'll need to take yours with you. *Four* of you, the number of the Family—to bring Diana back to the fold."

Soni paused, unwilling to leave. But when Carolyn passed the bright yellow ball of yarn to Alice, she turned to leave the main body of the group without another word. Perhaps Diana was partly her responsibility, now; perhaps Carolyn Lord even knew that she, Soni, was also fully aware of what was happening to Di. She led them down a corridor to the right, the end of the yarn left in the teacher's hand, for no reason better than it being the nearest corridor.

When they were out of earshot, Carolyn turned to the others with a smile. "Obviously, I can't leave them by themselves in a place as complex as this. Kay, you have a map of the system, I believe. How do we circle around, *ahead* of Soni's party?"

Kay had toted along an expensive attache case and snapped it open, fumbling inside until she came up with the map. She spread it open and studied it several careful moments, then looked up, beaming. "We go straight ahead some sixty feet and take another right turn," she said happily, delighted to be of use and to feel like one of them. "It will take us out around two hundred yards southeast of them. Tell me, Carolyn; why do you want to do it?"

"Just so we can all watch their faces when they run into some of the little *surprises* I've arranged for them," the blond instructor answered mysteriously, giving Kay a conspiritorial wink. "Come on, then! We'll all need to walk faster than they are to arrive ahead of them!"

The she-creature lurking in the shadows of the interior tunnels had worked out a logical procedure for its pursuers to follow. With an intuition almost as old as Mother Earth, she knew, somehow, that she was right: they would come this way, for their final parade.

She was not yet, quite, one hundred percent herself again. If she did not fall fully into the dark she would appear, at a glance, a beautiful, rather demented young woman who seemed to be fighting valiantly, now, against that which threatened to overcome her. *Let the girl fight*, she thought. *I can conquer the world.*

It had occurred to her that, if she could somehow retain the good looks of the human-thing in which she was encased, she might use her wiles, her magic, her manlike drive to become Queen of *all* this world. The real world, and it would finally bow to her. There would even be a place for this *Diana*, with whom she found herself strangely closeted, if she would again lie quiescent and stop her useless struggling.

Now she could hear their whispers, scant yards distant. There wouldn't be many—an advance party, that's all it was—and they were frightened of nothing more terrifying than the complexity of the corridors, and the threat of darkness which was held at bay by the torch in the little blond one's hand. She laughed, not loudly, her sides trembling with amusement. How foolish human beings were, when it came down to that—how *silly* in their fears, when the world on the surface and beneath it as well was absolutely *full* of horrid things beyond their worst nightmares!

She should know, after all.

She had spent innumerable centuries in a land far deeper, and darker—far more complex, more mind-numbing in its soul-death convolution of maniacal satanic regulations and terrible enduring punishments—than this.

She hid her heavy chest at the end of the tunnel and arranged herself, just so, beside one of the childish spring-out *papier-maché* constructs of amateurish horror with the condescension of a consummate professional, and waited.

Hungry.

"What's that?"

Alice, a homely black girl with a cornrow hair style and the highest I.Q. in her junior class, turned to Glenda with a good-humored smirk. "Why, that's the football game goin' on above us, Red," she said, drawling her words. She'd always been afraid that displaying her intellect would suggest that she identified with the white world. Alice felt big-sister-mature to the more juvenile Glenda. "Can't you *tell* that, girl? It's the most distinctive sound in the world!"

The others, deep in fear, had not heard the sounds. They stopped walking momentarily to listen.

Kathy Nolan, who meant to assault Hollywood with a personal glamor that was largely self-delusory, became the next to identify it.

The sound filtered to them like a blend of thunder and seasound, like water splashing against staunch rocks. How strange it was, Kathy thought, to be all this way under ground and yet—'way up there, on the surface—twenty-two young men were knocking each other silly. Hard to believe the whole lot of them, crowd and all, wouldn't break right through the earth and squash them!

A shout went up from the avid UCEV crowd, the underdogs. From the duration and volume of the joyous shouts Soni was sure what had happened. "Touchdown!" she exclaimed, filled suddenly with a certain, strangely out-of-place pride and a growing urge to be aboveground—to become just one more besweatered blond yelling her head off, hanging helplessly on the condescending arm of a boozy, wisecracking date. "Why, we just scored a touchdown on mighty USC!"

She said it abruptly, in a flood of passion: "I wish I was up there." Kathy shuddered, disturbed by a new flush of feeling that danger was near, possibly irrevocable and irresistible. "I wish I was doing a play right *now*, even with old Randy Duncan, hands and all!"

"Me, too," little Glenda confessed, as they resumed walking. "This was fun t'begin with, but I—I don't think I like living my life in a horror novel!"

When they approached new turns to left or right they crept on tiptoe until they might raise the torch, peer into them. There was no sight of Di Stoker. Prudently, Alice let out another length of yarn. Then they followed the corridor when it suddenly veered to the left.

All four girls shrieked in alarm. Soni nearly dropped their torch.

A gigantic monster was dead ahead, mighty muscled as it swung to and fro, topped with an immense, angry dog's head. The eyes popped; foam spread across its fierce muzzle. Rather than hands or even paws the thing possessed ugly flippers which, even as they gaped in fright, waggled in a mixture of seductive invitation and subtle threat. But the waggle, they saw soon, was mechanical.

"Sirius," murmured Alice, getting her breath. "It's nothing but a cardboard imitation of Sirius, the dog star legend."

"It's j-just something Dr. Lord made, to s-scare us," said little red-haired Glenda. She added, passionately. "I've made a mistake. She's plain *crazy*. I want out of here."

In a way, she was—quickly. Glenda didn't hear the screams of the other girls as they turned to get away, didn't see the living she-monster vaulting toward them, smashing her friends to the sewer concrete, two unconscious and the other instantly killed. Because Glenda also hadn't felt it when the strong hands shot out from beside plaything Sirius, snatching her throat and, in continuous motion, snapping her spine at the base of the skull.

Hecate reviewed the scene, her black hair wild, her psuedo-girl's face twisted into a mask of malice, of madness. When the *papier maché* Siruis momentarily brushed past her, briefly cloaking her in darkness, the face was that of something normal life does not allow to exist.

For just a moment there was near-panic as the girls at the front of the march spun to run away and other artistic creations and inventions of terror flashed into view, almost the entire length of the corridor.

When they realized, just in time, that these inhuman,

surreal countenances were endowed only with the most transient life—by string and rubberbands, by clever but simple mechanical means—the students of Carolyn Lord laughed, first with embarrassment and then with genuine humor. They turned to look at her with renewed appreciation for her genius, and her thoroughness.

"Standing before you ladies, is a visual panorama of some of the most important gods and goddesses of the ancient world, yet some of those with whom you may not be familiar." Carolyn was again the teacher, perils in the complex system forgotten in the opportunity to teach. "This is Glaucus the Gray-Green, who taught divination to Apollo and who established the oracle at Delphi. Beside him, you see the amphibian god Proteus, whose name has proved useful in certain adjectival connotations recently. Proteus was the first Old Man of the Sea and possessed the mutability with which to change his shape and, in the process, see into the future. He was a brilliant oracle."

Denny stood across the way, in control of her emotions again but clearly still shaken. "Who's this dude?" she asked, pointing.

"That isn't a dude, dear," Carolyn murmured. "It's the Syrian goddess Atargatis, who was born from an 'egg' that dropped from heaven into the River Euphrates. You'll notice that she has a certain, *uhm*, 'outer space' demeanor in consideration of the fact that certain contemporary scholars believe her 'egg' was, in point of fact, an Unidentified Flying Object. Now, on past Atargatis—" her arm swept their troubled eyes on—"you will see an image of the Telchines, a diverse group of gods with magical powers whom Zeus sought to destroy since they interfered with the weather." She paused, hearing the rumbling sound of the football game above her. "Perhaps they are interfering with *today's* weather, as well. I should add that—as you'll see, in the picture, from the way their numbers begin to change shape drastically—they eventually became the fabled fifty hounds of Actaeon, a cohort of one

Hecate, known as the Queen of Hades."

Her own reference to the monster seemingly possessing Diana Stoker caused Carolyn to pause, her pretty eyes flickering uncertainly.

A lanky Lesbian named Audra Galloway, once a friend of Pam Garnier, had stopped near the end of this corridor, where it angled to the right. She was pointing with a finger that seemed to tremble, and Carolyn approached, studying the two swinging *papier-maché* contraptions at which Audra appeared to point in terror.

"Those two?" Carolyn mused, drawing near. "The first one is Eurynome, the goddess who dwelt under the sea. Pretty, isn't she? She was described absolutely eons ago by Pausanias as being half-maiden, half-fish. And beyond her—" Carolyn continued to move forward —"is Sirius, the dog star god." Now she saw how pale Audra Galloway was, how she was insistently pointing *beyond* Eurynome, and *beyond* Sirius. "That, Audra, is—is—"

But the blond instructor couldn't finish. Instead, she was on the verge of fainting. Kay Chandler, the mayor's wife beside her, did.

That was not an artificial monstrosity of cardboard and paint but the broken-necked body of red-haired, frail Glenda.

And leaning seated against the far wall, cowering in apparent despair and terror, with the mangled and partially decapitated corpse of Soni Jerome held tight in her arms, was Diana Stoker.

"I w-wish you'd found me s-sooner," Di called in a tiny voice. She looked sadly down at the body she held, almost tenderly. "My f-friend might still be alive."

The braver of the girls began edging closer, both horrified and, as at an automobile wreck, fascinated. One of them stooped to the athlete. "For God's sake, Di, what *happened?*"

"I don't k-know," Diana replied, her expression tormented as she looked up, her gaze sweeping across all her companions' faces. "I—I heard them coming, looking for me, and decided I was tired, that it was t-time to end the game. But just as I got c-close, there were these awful noises and—" she glanced down again at Soni, and across the corridor to the similarly slain Glenda—"and I *found* them. *This* way."

The spectre of death crowded them, cold and clinging, in the close air of the complex system of tunnels. Carolyn tried to think what to say or do. She had her plan, but it wasn't for *here*. The last thing Mary Lord ever wrote indicated the way it was meant to end, *how* it would all climax—but in the Greater Eleusinia, not out here. Confronting Diana with the truth as she saw it might only trigger the monster dwelling within the powerful athlete, release her as she obviously was released upon these poor, dead girls. Although the other students outnumbered Hecate three hundred to one, Carolyn doubted that the odds were great enough.

Behind her, the twinkling, tiny lights in the sewer wall did their apathetic best to illumine the macabre scene while the still-swinging *papier maché* inventions, some of them lit from within, cast multicolored light and mingled it with uncanny shadows on the concrete floor. Staring at a gathering pool of blood, Carolyn recalled the fun her ladies had had, moments ago; she remembered how this place, her Telesterion, was intended to create a dazzling contrast of light and darkness to instill in all their imaginations alternating moods of joy and grief, hope and despair, immortality and sheer terror. It had done all that, and more; *she*, Carolyn Lord, had encouraged it, had *let* it happen— and she was determined to make no more mistakes.

"*Where*," she asked as the thought stunningly occurred to her, "are the *other* two girls?"

Diana shook her head. "I didn't see them. I have no idea where they are. I—I s'pose they saw what was h-happening to Soni and Glenda, then just took off."

Carolyn considered a moment. "Well, they didn't come down our corridor, and you didn't see them pass this way." She turned to the mayor's wife, who was standing shakily now, deathly pale. "Kay, I think we'd better just go on to the Greater Eleusinia now. The other girls must have run there. I'm sure we'll find them waiting."

"I'll bring Soni," Diana said, brokenly, getting awkwardly to her feet as she lifted her little friend's broken body in her strong arms.

"No, you still have the chest to carry," Carolyn reminded her. "You four women standing by the Eurynome device; please be so good as to conquer your own repugnance and carry both our fallen warriors with us on your shoulders." She felt a new constriction in her throat, tears hot in her eyes. "The least we can do for Soni and Glenda is to see that they are properly, posthumously initiated."

"You're goin' ahead with this?" demanded Denny Wilkinson, jet eyes wide in amazement. "After what's happened? Lady, we need the *fuzz* down here—there's crazy people runnin' wild!"

Carolyn blinked, swallowing her words. Badly, she wished to tell them all that *this* was the final journey, for Diana and for her, as well as Soni and Glenda; that they were only minutes now from that ideal ending Di promised, and Mary predicted, in her last written words. Somehow, clearly, it had to come to an end. Helplessly, she turned to Denny. "We'll get the police from our place of final rites. But beyond anything the rest of us have done, Glenda and Soni have won the right to their goddess identities. In their behalf, we *must* complete lustration."

She didn't wait for an argument. With a trembling Kay Chandler, at the front of the line, indicating the swiftest passage to the transcendental room of Great Eleusinia, Carolyn Lord led the procession through the last stretches of dank, shadowed corridor. The young women were solemn, eerily quiet, terrifyingly aware that someone maniacally murderous was nearby. Diana, a few feet behind the leaders, struggled with the chest as she maintained her role as *hierokeryx*, sometimes glancing sadly back at her dead friends as they were borne high on the shoulders of the living, would-be immortals.

They were passing well beyond the football field, veering toward the outskirts of the town of El Vista. Now the enthusiastic rumbles of the football teams and raucous crowds faded away, and ceased; even for those who had not been consciously aware of the normal noises from above, the subterranean tunnel became hellish in this silence—a silence broken only by their sandaled feet scraping on concrete, by the frightened sobs of a few anguished girls, by breaths that were half-held in anticipation of yet another culminating horror.

Almost unnoticeably, the tunnel floor sloped upward, now, until they saw the steel ladder leading up to a huge iron door. Inside, perhaps, lay safety, sanity. The mayor's wife, Kay, climbed up to unlock the door. It creaked, warningly, then fell back.

Within they found themselves in a capacious flower- and streamer-bedecked room which would, one day soon, be used by workmen in the sewers as an office and quick bypass to the tunnels. Denny stared at the incongruous coke machine across the room, ready to kiss its metallic ordinariness. Here, too, electric lights were in readiness; one of the students threw a switch with a feeling of thanksgiving, flooding the room with light. There were a few desks, some graphs and diagrams of the sewer system on the walls, a typewriter or two. Photographs of President Ronald Reagan and Mayor Chandler smiled down upon them. Normality, of a sort.

But the streamers and flowers seemed woebegone, even incongruous, after what had happened. The bearers placed the dead girls' bodies on the couch, shuddering. Once they were all crammed inside, with little room to spare, Carolyn Lord climbed atop a desk covered with gay party-paper and sought their attention, clapping. *Lordy*, Denny thought incredulously, *this crazy broad's goin' on with it!*

"First, let me ask Diana Stoker to join me here," the teacher said. Her tone of voice, many of the women realized, did suggest that she, too, was eager to complete the rites and return to the living atop the ground. A few girls, more astute, heard another quality in Carolyn's tone of voice and identified it as fear. "Bring the great chest, please, *hierokeryx*."

Without hesitation Diana hoisted the chest atop the desk, then leaped lightly, lithely, to stand near her mentor on the desk. She saw, at once, that Carolyn had no intention of touching her or of staring into her extraordinary emerald eyes.

"I guess we'll have to phone the police. The other girls, the remaining two from the group that went in search of you," Carolyn said pointedly, courageously, to Di. "They aren't here after all."

"That isn't my fault," Diana said simply, coldly. Her muscles tensed in readiness. *Soon,* she thought; *soon I will act.*

"I believe it is your fault." Dr. Lord turned to the mystified onlookers, raising her voice. "She killed Soni Jerome because she knew that only a few people remained who, ladies, were aware of a terrifying fact. That Diana *already* achieved unity with a goddess of old." She saw their astonished faces. "More correctly, perhaps, she is *possessed* by that evil demon, a cannibal and carrion-eater, the murderous, monstrous Hecate, Queen of Hell."

"You're absurd," Diana said coldly, matter-of-factly.

Carolyn had only Mary's writing, and her plan, but knew that this *had* to be instigated, that someone *had* to make the plunge and lead them all to the ideal conclusion she was pledged. Why *else* would Diana have brought her back from the certainty of crippling paralysis and the brink of death? Still avoiding the younger woman's gaze, she spoke as emphatically and forcefully as she could. "I am aware that some of you think I've gone mad today, and that this accusation of mine proves it. But I must tell you that the ruler of the Underworld stands before you now, in the guise of lovely, capable, mortal woman—and what happens *next* will either prove or disprove my claims."

Diana indicated the chest on the desk between them. "I think we should get on with *lustration,* Doctor," she said quietly. "And summon the police. You alone have a key to the chest, I believe. Which means, by the way, that only *you* could get into it. Why not open it, now, according to the rites of Eleusis?"

The soft tones of the athlete's voice didn't deceive Carolyn but, as she risked a quick glimpse of Diana's face, it occurred to her that Di, too, doubtlessly wished this ghastly farce to end at last. Probably, like many people who did awful things, Diana welcomed capture, welcomed the truth. Her hand flew to her throat to retrieve the Golden Key passed down to her by her great-grandfather, Professor Jabez Lord.

She knelt quickly, to unlock the chest—*and begin to initiate her own plan, as well.*

Inside the chest, she knew, were special garlands with which to adorn the three hundred students of her Reemergence of the Goddesses class, something they could retain as souvenirs, use in their endless battle for liberation. She knew, as well, that something *else* rested among the colorful garlands, the means of defeating Hecate, for achieving salvation itself. She'd told *no one* it was there, hidden in the weaving of the basket within the chest—

—the fabled *hekakontalithos,* an occult, magic stone of ancient Greece. That it had survived at all, as small and precious as it was, to reach her after the countless centuries, was itself a miracle. While Carolyn did not know its properties, or what it might do for its possessor, she had come—through her suffering over her daughter's rape, and illness—to regard the *hekakontalithos* as her final hope for life.

Consequently, as the chest flew open, her hand dove into the weaving of the basket, the fingers closing round the magic stone—

—Before she staggered *back* from the chest, screaming in a horror that the terrified students had never imagined in their collective lives. She stared down, down inside the chest, unable to speak, helplessly pointing.

Instead of lovely garlands filling the basket in the aged chest, Carolyn saw crammed there instead the severed heads and partly eaten bodies of Alice Quentin and Kathy Nolan, the missing girls who'd gone in quest of diabolical Di Stoker—

—And atop the poor, mangled remains were the dismembered, proud penis and testicles of Diana's macho lover, Randy Duncan, ripped out by the roots.

Carolyn's fright was so great that her upswung hands struck the chest and emptied its macabre, repulsive contents on the floor before the horrified eyes of her students. One head rolled all the way to the coke machine and stopped, *grinning*.

Diana Stoker, still somehow beautiful in her seemingly justified wrath, shouted above the panic to gain attention: *"Remember, girls! Only Carolyn Lord had the key to the chest—no one else—only she could have put these terrible things in it! Nobody else!"*

"Nobody else," Carolyn whispered, breast heaving in emotion, shocked by Diana's duplicity, "by means that were . . . not *magical*."

"Magical?" Diana repeated the word, taunting her. She'd anticipated this and folded her arms across her own outthrust bosom, her expression derisive. "Magical, indeed! How much *more* of this antiquated nonsense—this neurotic *bullshit*—do you expect us to *buy*, lady?" Now she dared laugh, hoarsely, aloud, aware that hundreds of terrified eyes were fixed on her. "We've listened to you till now, dear Dr. Lord, because you showed us a *new* way to seek our freedom as women—a *fresh* means to righteous liberation. But you can't honestly think we *believe* in gods or goddesses, anymore than we believed in the old male God—that we can *accept* anything so ridiculously square as ancient immortals from *Olympus* taking *possession* of our clever, truly free modern minds? Oh, come *on*! Admit your guilt!"

There was a quick smattering of encouraged chatter, of frantic shifting of emotions to alliance with Di's assertions, confronted as the young women were by grotesque images quite beyond the boundaries of experience or imagination. Here and there, students angrily stared up at Carolyn Lord, hotly muttering among themselves that she *must pay* for this savagery, this betrayal, this unnatural and monstrous murder.

"*You* had the key, Dr. Lord," Diana continued, pressing her advantage eagerly, "and *you* were the only one who got into the chest and placed our poor friends—and these . . . *other* parts—into it. In an effort to *condemn* me, to throttle your opposition the way man always tries to do it, *to prevent Diana Stoker from taking charge of this group and turning it into a truly* modern, meaningful organization *with which we'll whip mortal man to his filthy knees at last!*"

"Arrest her!" someone shouted; "*Hold* her!" "Hell, *kill* the bitch!" someone else cried.

But Carolyn turned sweetly in the chaos to look Diana Stoker full in the face, speaking softly. Somehow, even above the tumult, she was heard as she uttered the single, challenging word: "*How?*"

"What do you mean '*how*'?" Diana demanded, instantly perspiring, her green eyes wild, her hair a dark tangle. "How do *we* know how you did it?"

"*Answer* the lady, honky bitch," Denny demanded from beneath the desk. "*How?*"

"Di, dear—" somehow Carolyn found calmness, a ring of sincerity—"you were the only one who *had* the chest with her. I was in the midst of more than *three hundred witnesses!* It was *you*, my poor demented child, who intercepted our search party—and it was no one but you who had the opportunity, the means, *or* the unnatural strength to murder them." She smiled out at the others. "I'm sure my ladies realize that."

Diana was rendered speechless. Confounded, she looked round her, questing for other words to use, with which to deceive—the kind of clever, deceptive words that Hell has always promoted and taught. But there *were* none, in the face of ultimate truth, and now three hundred angry young women were crowding toward her, moving *in* on her, their threat clear.

There would be no rulership of this organization or yet of the world, she saw that now. No one would follow her, with her true colors revealed. She'd lost, here at UCEV, she realized—but she could and *would* win elsewhere, for woman was the *spirit* of resilience—she would build glorious *new* triumphs, *new* groups of gullible women, *somewhere else.* . . .

The graceful body of Diana Stoker made its greatest athletic vault, incredibly soaring past the outreached, nail-bared hands of her former friends, over their heads, leaping toward the only exit from Greater Eleusinia and landing, Olympian-like, at the door, poised on the balls of her feet. Beyond the door was the ladder yet to jump, then the complex corridors which promised concealment, freedom, the *one* chance she required to start afresh elsewhere!

But then the vengeful idea filled her mingled mind, her twisted soul, in a manner befitting her immortally immoral role. *Once outside,* she thought with perverse passion, *I'll* barricade *this door and let them all* suffocate *in there! And I'll greet the truly bad ones, one day, in Hades*—personally!

But when she dashed through the door and spun almost in the same motion to slam the great door shut on Carolyn Lord and the others, *something* else *she had* not *counted on froze her in place:*

Dr. Lord was reciting the Lord's Prayer. "Our Father," she pleaded, eyes pressed shut, "Who art in Heaven. . . ."

A painful chill cut through Diana's body and yet she put back her beautiful head, laughing. Caught briefly by flickering shadow her face seemed to melt, to be briefly replaced by something so ancient, so sinful, that the onrushing students of ROTGOD also ceased in their movement toward her. "Praying to a *male God!*" she shrieked, mockingly. "You *hypocrite,* you'll dine on flaming coals with *me!*"

" . . . And lead us not into temptation, but *deliver us* from *evil!*" Carolyn Lord lifted the occult magic stone, her great-grandfather's famous *hekakontalithos,* high above her golden head, her own face transfigured, but by faith, by belief. The stone *gleamed* in her clutching hand, *tremored.* "Please, for the love of God, the Father, *destroy the evil that is Hecate!*"

Those who were present said, later, that they never doubted for an instant that prayer was answered—yet whether it was God, alone, who answered Carolyn's prayer, or that which God made for His own reasons as well, they could not be certain.

The sound, at first, was faint; but it increased rapidly in volume: An immense, crevassed *rumbling*, vastly deeper than any tunnel system, deeper than mere man has ever been able to penetrate Mother Earth. Beyond the door—behind the anguished, mingled faces and figures of Diana Stoker and her alter ego—gigantic fissures sprang in the concrete like arcane fingers aching for release from undreamt caverns, *eons* below. The sound was like thunder, as though interior earth mirrored the threatening sky above man. Portions of the sewer wall cracked. Chunks of cement dropped like behemoth snowfall, thunderingly colliding with the floor in the corridor beyond the door and the ladder. *Now* the rumbling was nearly intolerable, deafening; the women inside the room pressed hands to outraged ears, screamed piercingly yet heard not even the women beside them.

The *leys,* Carolyn thought, *the connected amplification and intensity of the leys!* Now *she knew what the megalith Omphalos was raised for thousand of years ago—and* whom *it honored!* Again she shut her eyes in prayer, not to goddesses of a past that can never be reborn but to a Presence that was only half-forgotten. Over her head, valiantly, she waved the metaphysical remnant, the magical *hekakontalithos*—

—And at that instant the ground in the tunnel behind Diana/Hecate seemed *torn apart,* ripped asunder by such potent, clearly purposive strength that Kay Chandler and many of the younger women fainted, fearful to the soul that they might see *THAT* which vaulted upward from the distant, doomed, and dismal chambers of Hell itself—*THAT* which, even now, dripping clots of steaming soil, grasped the rungs of the ladder to climb up, thunderingly, toward *them*.

Those who were made of sterner stuff or who were merely rooted to the spot could only stare, petrified with terror, with awe, when at last they *saw—HIM*.

Something related to immortality, I promised them, recalled the still-sane segments of Carolyn's mind, *some dark secrets of the Eternal, linked to life and death.* And, remembering her prayers to God alone. *Perhaps, ladies, you shall encounter in the Greater Eleusinia the fundamental truths about the universe in which you shall surely live, and die. . . .*

HE appeared to them in a reddish, hazy, indistinct cloud reeking with sulphur, with brimstone, with *other* stenches no mortal would care to identify. Extraordinarily tall, red-skinned, he was fiendishly handsome from angled and brutal curved horns to indescribably perfect, evil features, from masculine organs engorged to surrealistic proportions and filled with hellbound lust to feet that were massive and shaped as cruel, cloven hooves. In one massive, hirsute hand he carried a tri-pointed staff, *dripping* with scarlet gore and dank entrails. He ignored the praying teacher and the cowering women students with an air of ferocious grandeur, then spied Diana/Hecate. She swung at him in terror, three times, blows powerful enough to fell an ox. He watched them land, then laughed, boomingly, stooping swiftly to take her protesting body in a single powerful arm, holding her *close* to him in a hideous parody of reunited love.

"Come, wife." That was the beginning of all he would say on the fourth planet from the sun, that day, his voice a mastadonish bass that rocked the desks and streamers and typewriters in the room of Greater Eleusinia like the searing shriek of a cosmic sonic boom. *"Come. It is time you were* home, *with me."*

THE END, ALMOST. . . .

A Necessary Adieu from the Author

It's not generally considered good form for the author to inject himself into a work of fiction, ostensibly because his presence reduces the reader's acceptance of the tale but *actually* because (a) the publisher seldom allows it, and (b) the reader wants to get on with the story.

But Argument B is easily answered by virtue of doing an Afterword, which this happens to be; and Argument A will prove too persuasive even for the publisher to quibble with, this time. *Witnesseth:*

On April 30, 1978, John Dart of the Los Angeles *Times* reported that Santa Cruz, California, was the scene of a new phenomenon linked to the feminist movement. An extension course offered at the U.C. Santa Cruz campus, entitled "*The Great Goddess Reemerging,*" claimed Dart, was turning away "potential registrants after the maximum 450 spaces were filled." Cheering ancient goddesses, "spontaneous groups of circling women danced barebreasted in scenes suggestive of wood nymphs."

A comic might remark, with a waggle of the cigar, "You haven't lived till you've seen a suggestive wood nymph." If lessons in what was called "goddess consciousness" were sum and substance of this exceptional activity, the story might be taken as reporting another passing collegiate fad—nothing more than updated goldfish-gulping, perhaps a female version of panty raids—albeit a version that might be marvelously more intriguing to observe!

The fact is that a dead-earnest sense of purpose undergirded this extension course, if Dart was right. Argument is made that female students must divest themselves of belief in God—the *male* God, that is—in order to avoid psychological dependence upon masculine Authority Figures.

For some who've learned of this merriment and the

latest attack on the Almighty, strong hints of something akin to witchcraft may be disturbing enough. It also happens that your author is pretty well fed up with lowercase authority figures himself. But an educative insistence that belief in God should be supplanted by prayers to ancient goddesses, with nothing to suggest a tongue-in-cheek attitude, indicates an embryonic return to polytheistic or pagan worship which should be disturbing to *most* Christians and Jews. Of *whatever* sexual endorsement.

Revision history is practiced everywhere, these days, always hazardously; frequently one may yawn, safely enough. But attempting to replace the Almighty is an abomination even to such a casually religious fellow as your author. This book is my mild protest, my reply. It depicts an admittedly exaggerated, even satirical outcome of such careless revisionism and may serve as a hearkening trumpet as well as an entertainment. *Final thought:* The frightening characteristics and magical skills of Hecate, as herein portrayed, are consistent with those described for centuries in books of mythology. It's barely possible that all of us need to be more prudent and reflective about that in which we invest the motivational quality of our legitimate belief systems.

J. N. Williamson
Indianapolis, Indiana
December, 1980

HEAR THE CHILDREN CRY
By R.J. Hendrickson

PRICE: $2.50 LB968
CATEGORY: Novel

A NOVEL OF UNRELENTING TERROR!

One...two...three small children have died hideously. Only their five-year-old brother, Danny, is left.

The only possible suspects are the parents—and, of course, little Danny himself.

One person knows the truth, and that evil someone is preparing the final, unspeakable atrocity!

THE TULPA
By J.N. Williamson

PRICE: $1.95 LB799
CATEGORY: Occult

Charlie Kavanagh felt all of his 73 years. He was worried about his aging mind, and his "spells," his dreams — or visions? No one would listen. No one except his son-in-law, who saw things coming, building, promising unheard of horror. Then it came. It rose from within, slowly at first, shuffling through shadows, learning of violence, developing a special hunger. Then it struck—and again. It grew, not quite quenching its thirst on blood and fear. And only one thing could hope to destroy the terrorizing appetite of...THE TULPA!

SEND TO: **LEISURE BOOKS**
P.O. Box 511, Murry Hill Station
New York, N.Y.   10156

Please send me the following titles:

Quantity	Book Number	Price
_____	_____	_____
_____	_____	_____
_____	_____	_____
_____	_____	_____
_____	_____	_____

In the event we are out of stock on any of your selections, please list alternate titles below.

_____	_____	_____
_____	_____	_____
_____	_____	_____
_____	_____	_____

Postage/Handling _____

I enclose..... _____

FOR U.S. ORDERS, add 75¢ for the first book and 25¢ for each additional book to cover cost of postage and handling. Buy five or more copies and we will pay for shipping. Sorry, no C.O.D.'s.

FOR ORDERS SENT OUTSIDE THE U.S.A., add $1.00 for the first book and 50¢ for each additional book. PAY BY foreign draft or money order drawn on a U.S. bank, payable in U.S. ($) dollars.

☐ Please send me a free catalog.

NAME _____
(Please print)

ADDRESS _____

CITY _____ STATE _____ ZIP _____

Allow Four Weeks for Delivery